Breaking Hearts

MJ SUMMERS

HarperCollins*PublishersLtd*

Published by HarperCollins Publishers Ltd

First edition

HarperCollins books may be purchased for educational, business,
or sales promotional use through our Special Markets Department.

HarperCollins Publishers Ltd
2 Bloor Street East, 20th Floor
Toronto, Ontario, Canada
M4W 1A8

www.harpercollins.ca

Library and Archives Canada Cataloguing in Publication
information is available upon request.

ISBN 978-1-44343-912-1

Printed and bound in the United States
RRD 9 8 7 6 5 4 3 2 1

Dear Reader,

When *Break in Two* came out, I was asked over and over about what happens to Trey, Gabriela and their little boy. At that time, I didn't actually know what would come of them, but I knew I would have to figure it out. So after two years, here is their story.

It's about redemption and tragedy, falling in love and falling apart. It's about making mistakes and learning to forgive yourself, it's about learning what being a parent *really* means. It's about choosing between chasing your dreams and following your heart, when the two aren't taking you in the same direction.

The story is set in Brazil, for the most part. Brazil is a place I've always longed to go. The people I've met from this vast and beautiful country are full of kindness and fun. Preparing to write *Breaking Hearts,* I needed to research both Brazil and bull riding. I was incredibly fortunate to come across two lawyers (Adler Martins and Homer Carvalho), one former bull rider turned bulling riding agent (Shawn Weise), two journalists (Bill Hinchberger and Marcelo Teixeira) and one very special avid reader/English teacher (Cyssah Oliver), all of whom gave me hours of their time. Thank you to all of you from the bottom of my heart for your generosity and eagerness to assist me in ensuring that Trey and Gabriela's story is rich in detail.

For those of you who have read my other books, especially *Break in Two,* this one takes a little longer to get to the steamy stuff—but when you get there—yum. I hope you enjoy it!

All the best to you and yours,

MJ

For my big sister, who taught me to read
and who can make me laugh until my ribs hurt
and my dignity is a long-forgotten concept.
For my Aunt Kathy, who taught me
what compassion looks like
and what it can do.
Love you both.

ONE

San Diego, California

"Alright! Let 'er rip!" Trey Johnson called, letting a sexy grin peek out from under his black cowboy hat. He was perched on top of a large brown mechanical bull that sat just off the dance floor at Spurs 'n' Suds, the biggest country bar in San Diego. It was the go-to place for those who wanted to let down their hair and kick up their heels, where every night the music was loud, the beer was cold and the waitresses were hot. Short skirts and dangerously low-cut tops drew fat tips as the staff served their rowdy patrons greasy burgers with a side of wishful thinking.

"Save a Horse" burst out over the speakers as soon as the bull began turning, bucking forward and back in a pattern that Trey knew like the back of his hand. Pointing to a cute girl standing nearby, he gave her a wink and mouthed, "For you!" before getting down to business. He and the DJ, Clark, performed their usual routine. Clark started the bull slow, increasing its speed every few seconds as he got the crowd worked up.

Clark cut the music. "Trey bet me he's gonna stay on that bull for a full minute tonight! If he can't do it, there's a free round for everyone, on him!" The crowd roared as the possibility was dangled in front of them, drowning out the guitars as the music resumed. By the end of the minute, it was clear that the women were so impressed they had all but forgotten the free drink. Their cheers had turned to loud screams as Trey let go of the rope on the bull, leaping off with style and landing on an air mattress below. Jumping to his feet, he flipped off his hat and gave a quick bow before exiting the ring.

"There you have it, folks! One of the best mechanical bull riders ever to have lived in the great state of California! Trey Johnson!" Clark shouted into the microphone. "And if you thought he was good on that bull, you should see him mix drinks. He'll be over at the main bar for the rest of the night . . . And ladies, he's single!"

The whoops of the female patrons were deafening as Trey made his way across the crowded room. He hoisted his lean, muscular body up, then slid over the counter, landing behind the bar.

"Who's thirsty?" Trey yelled. He stood for a moment in his cocky glory, letting a line form before taking the first order. The tips would be sweet tonight. As a rule, the money was good on Fridays, but tonight the bar was more packed than usual, and he knew he'd put on one hell of a good show. He was the epitome of the carefree, fearless fun that the patrons had come to find.

* * *

An hour later, Trey sat in the staff room, as big a contrast to the bar itself as you could get. Other than the muffled sound of the music, the hum of the fluorescent lights above was the most noticeable noise. His laptop and economics textbook were on the table in front of him as he squeezed in fifteen minutes to study for his last-ever university exam. Taking off his cowboy hat, he tossed it on the chair to his left and raked his hands through his short, sandy-brown hair.

Music invaded the room for a moment as the door swung open, revealing Tiffany, a blond bombshell of a waitress who had transplanted herself from Texas a year ago. "Hey, sugar!"

Trey glanced up, giving her a quick smile. "Hey yourself."

Coins being deposited in the vending machine indicated that Tiffany was making her late-evening dinner choice.

"Good night out there. I think I've pulled in at least two hundred already, and it's only eleven."

"Yeah, I think spring fever has hit," Trey answered absentmindedly as he scanned a spreadsheet for the value he needed.

A bag of chips hit his keyboard, then slid onto his lap.

"For the starving student," Tiffany said, dropping onto the couch. She yanked off her red cowboy boots with a little groan and put her feet up on the ancient coffee table.

"Aw, thanks, Tiff. You didn't have to do that."

"Didn't do it to be nice. Now I can tell the other girls I had dinner with you. They'll all be *real* jealous." She opened her own bag, selecting a chip then biting into it as she studied Trey for a moment. "It's hard to know who you are, Trey Johnson. Out there, you've got that whole cocky cowboy thing going on, but in here, you're kind of a nerd."

"Can't I be both?" he asked with a grin, opening the snack she had given him.

"I guess so. I've just never seen anyone so determined. I'm dying to see what you're like when you let loose. Come out with us tonight after work. We're going to the beach to party and watch the sunrise."

"Wish I could." Trey dropped the chip that was halfway to his mouth back into the bag as his eyes finally found the number he'd been searching for on the chart. "There you are," he muttered.

"The girls and I have bets going about you. About why you never take anyone home, even though we're all shameless as far as you're concerned. Angie thinks you're gay, maybe, but I don't think that's it."

Trey looked up from his laptop with a little laugh. "Nope. Angie's wrong there. There's no real mystery, though. I'm what you call goal-oriented. I need to get my degree as soon as possible so I can get on with making some real money."

"Oh, there's a mystery to you and everybody knows it. Nobody spends three years busting their ass and never answering a booty call unless there's something behind it."

Trey considered her words for a moment then plucked his cellphone off the table. Opening the photo album, he tossed the phone to her. "He's what's behind it."

Tiffany caught the phone awkwardly with one hand after it bounced onto the couch beside her. Her mouth dropped open in surprise as she stared at the photo.

"My son, Tomas. He lives in Brazil. If he's not a big enough reason to stay on task, I don't know what would be."

"Yeah," Tiffany agreed, clearly shocked. "He's adorable."

"Yup. And he deserves a dad who can support him, not some deadbeat who's out looking to bang a new chick every weekend." Trey packed his things into his backpack, then stowed it in his locker. "Better get back at it. See you out there." He took the phone on his way out. "Thanks for the chips, Tiff. You're a good friend."

TWO

Rio de Janeiro, Brazil

"Mmm, just look at you. You're perfection."

The deep voice of Joel Salles interrupted Gabriela's sunbathing. She lifted her head and smiled over her shoulder in time to see him set his gaze on her body. He reminded her of a lion about to pounce on his prey. Gabriela was stretched out on her stomach, completely nude, on a poolside chaise at Joel's estate. The sun shone down on her silky olive skin as she soaked up its warmth along with his compliment.

"You're home early," she replied, basking in his appreciative look.

Joel dropped his cellphone on the table beside her and unbuttoned his dress shirt. He then picked up a bottle of suntan oil, squirting some into his palm before propping himself on her chair with one knee between her ankles. He spread the oil onto both hands before rubbing them along the backs of her calves, then up and down her legs. "How can I stay on the set knowing you are here at my home, exactly like this?"

"Oh no, I shouldn't have sent you that photo earlier." Her words were utterly insincere. "I guess I wasn't thinking."

"Of course you were thinking, Gabriela. You're always thinking. For another man, that would be very dangerous, but not for me," he said, pouring more oil into his hands. "I know how to handle a woman like you. Besides, you knew the crew would be fine without me for the rest of the day."

"This is true," she agreed, feeling his hands work their way up her thighs. "You do know how to handle me. I was also sure they could film without you there for a while. What do movie producers even do, anyway?" she teased, propping herself up on her elbows and turning her head to look back at him. She smiled into his deep brown eyes, fully loving the feeling of his hands rubbing her bottom.

"Let me show you," he replied, letting his thumbs wander down her crevice and into her warm sex. Gabriela shuddered in delight.

Joel was a man who knew what he was doing. He was the perfect catch for Gabriela—rich, sexy and exciting. She had been staying at his beach house just outside Rio for the past six weeks, hoping that this time away from her son, Tomas, would pay off. If she could secure her position as a permanent fixture in Joel's life, she would be able to give her son the father she wanted for him. Joel didn't mind that she had a child and, in fact, had been very good with Tomas during the brief times they had all spent together. She knew he wouldn't likely be all that involved in raising her child, but he would be able to provide them with every luxury, and Tomas with every opportunity.

This goal had allowed Gabriela to push aside any feelings of guilt that kept her from missing her little boy too much each time she left him. She knew it would all be worth it in the end. Besides, Tomas had just turned three. He was so little he would quickly forget these weeks in which he'd been left alone with the nanny.

Joel worked his thumbs in between her upper thighs, rubbing in slow circles until Gabriela let out a quiet moan. "Let's take this to the bedroom. The gardeners just got here."

"I'm all yours." Gabriela sighed happily as he moved his hands back down her legs and got to his feet. She stood and pulled her robe on, kissing Joel softly on the lips as she tied the sash around her waist. Joel gave the robe a little tug to bring her to him, kissing her neck and letting his hand travel into the opening of her robe. His fingers dragged over her nipple, finding it already pert.

"You *are* all mine. And I intend to keep you all to myself."

"Promise?"

"Yes, I think I do." Joel looked into her eyes, taking his hand out of her robe and straightening it for her. They laced their fingers together as they walked into the house. Cool air greeted them as Joel shut the patio door and they made their way across the expansive kitchen to the stairs.

"Will the filming still finish by Friday? I have everything set for the wrap party, but the caterer needs the hard date by tomorrow morning," Gabriela said as they ascended the staircase.

"Yes, we're still set for Friday. Thank you for taking care of that for me, by the way. You have the makings of the perfect producer's wife."

"I hope you're not just figuring that out now. I would hate to think you are little more than a handsome face."

Joel laughed. "You always keep me on my toes. It's one of the things I love about you. That, and how sexy you are."

"Go on." Gabriela pursed her lips into a smile.

"You're very beautiful, you know how to dress and how to host, you never get star-struck or say the wrong things. Plus, you're like an animal in bed," Joel replied, tugging his shirt off as they passed through the double doors to the master suite.

Gabriela tugged on the sash of her robe, opening it and letting it fall to the floor. She crossed the large room to the king bed and crawled onto it on all fours, turning her head to look back at him. "You mean like this?"

"That's exactly what I mean," Joel answered with a smirk.

São Paulo, Brazil

Alessandra Santos stood at the kitchen sink washing dishes. She had just gotten little Tomas, her charge, down for his afternoon nap. He had a bad cold, and his nose was so stuffed up that sleep had been extremely difficult for him the past few nights, leaving him cranky and Alessandra very tired. She thought of everything she still needed to do that day, but her soft pillow called to her relentlessly. She decided to finish the lunch dishes quickly so she could go lie down for a couple of hours.

Her thoughts were interrupted by the phone. Drying her hands, she answered the call.

"Alessa? It's Gabriela. I'm calling to check on my little darling."

"*Olá*, he's still got that cold, Gabriela. He's really not feeling well. His fever is down today but he is horribly overtired. I just got him down for a nap."

"My poor sweetie," Gabriela said into the phone. There was a pause, then she called, "*Não!* Don't put those over there. The drinks are all going to be served by the pool and I want a table set up with the glasses by the bar outside." Pause. "*Fora!* Outside, by the pool. Yes. All of them."

Gabriela sighed and then spoke into the phone again. "Listen, Alessa, I think this is it. Joel and I are hosting the wrap party for the movie and I think he is going to ask me to marry him tonight. He's been hinting at it all week. I wanted to see if you could move to Rio for a few months to take care of Tomas while I'm getting ready for the wedding. There is no way that I'll be able to manage him alone when I'm so busy."

Alessandra paused, her mouth hanging open, not sure what to say. "I don't think that will work, Gabriela. After I finish my degree, my family needs me to come home to Bebedouro. I'm sorry. Maybe Joel knows of someone?"

Gabriela made a clicking sound with her tongue, clearly annoyed by her nanny's answer. "*Parem!* I don't want those flowers in the house. Everything out by the pool! Take them out through the kitchen!" she shouted, causing Alessa to hold the phone away from her ear.

Gabriela took a deep breath. "I don't want to trouble him with this. Listen, you think it over. If things work out the way I hope, I'll make sure you get a nice big bonus once we are settled here."

"I don't know, I—"

"I don't have time for this right now. I have to go. We'll talk about this later," Gabriela replied in a rushed tone. "Give Tomas a big kiss from his mommy."

"Okay, I will," Alessa answered, her words cut off as Gabriela ended the call. Rolling her shoulders back a few times and letting her head tip from side to side, she tried to release the tension she was feeling. Working for Gabriela had become much more than she had bargained for.

She had been hired two years ago to work as a part-time nanny. The original arrangement allowed Alessandra to attend school on weekdays and watch Tomas at night and on weekends, giving Gabriela a chance to run errands and go out. Alessandra had been searching for a free place to live, somewhere quiet so she could study. For the first year, the job had worked out perfectly. Tomas's naps and early bedtime had given her enough time to complete her schoolwork.

That had all changed when Gabriela met Joel Salles, however. Alessa found herself working as a full-time caretaker for weeks at a time, missing more classes than any fourth-year law student could afford. Now, her once-strong grades were falling. Alessandra's mother had been urging her to quit for months now, to just drop Tomas off at his grandparents' house and get back to school.

"You are being used, Alessandra. Don't allow that woman to do this to you. You're exhausting yourself for someone who really doesn't care about you at all."

"*Mãe*, I'm fine, really. I'm handling everything. Besides, it's not like he has a father to take him in, and he doesn't even know his grandparents. I can't leave him like that."

They'd been having this conversation for months, but it was only now that Alessandra was able to admit that maybe her mother was right. She was already stretched to her limit, and she knew the next few weeks would be much more taxing. The thought of managing to complete her last few assignments, study for finals *and* look after Tomas was like staring up at a mountain, knowing it was thousands of steps to the peak.

Alessa pulled the plug in the sink and watched the water drain. She touched the tiny tornado created by the last of the water swirling down and out of sight. A wave of exhaustion swept over her. At twenty-two, Alessa was plain worn out. She slowly crossed the floor of the living room and walked down the hall, ignoring her textbooks in favour of the soft mattress waiting for her in her tiny bedroom.

Dropping onto the bed with a soft thud, she fell immediately asleep, waking up two hours later to the little coughing sound Tomas had been making when he woke since getting sick. She could hear him calling for her. "Lessa!"

It had been weeks since he had called for Gabriela. He seemed to have adjusted to the fact that she was gone again. Now that Alessa thought about it, she realized that even the last time Gabriela had been in town, he had never gone back to calling for his mother. Something about that broke Alessandra's heart. Quickly standing, she smoothed her hair out of her face as she stumbled down the hall, fuzzy-headed from her long sleep.

When she reached his room, he was sitting up in his bed, rubbing his eyes and sniffling. "Lessa, I'm firsty," he said in English.

"Well, let's get you a drink," Alessa replied, smiling at him as she walked over and picked him up in her arms. One of the job requirements was that she speak to him in English. Gabriela was very determined that her son be fluent in more than one language, and English was the language of choice for the rich parents of Brazil.

Giving him a little peck on the forehead, Alessa noticed that his fever had returned. It wasn't as bad as the day before, but they would be in for another rough night if this kept up.

Rio de Janeiro, Brazil
Twelve Hours Later

Gabriela blinked her eyes, trying to adjust to the light in the kitchen as she walked into the house. She stumbled a little as she crossed the room, having had several cocktails as the party wore on. Outside, the music was booming, causing the toaster to make its way across the counter from the vibrations. Giggling to herself, she caught the small chrome appliance just before it found the edge of the granite and dropped to its doom. The party was going amazingly well, and nothing could lower her sense of elation.

She danced across the cool tile floor in her bare feet, staring at her left hand, which now bore an enormous diamond surrounded by a band of equally stunning white gems. Joel had asked her to marry him while they were getting dressed for the party earlier. He had thrown the little black box onto the bed beside the dress she had laid out for herself.

"Here," he said, smiling at her. "This will go well with your dress."

Gabriela, in only her black lace bra and panties, snatched up the box, her smile as she opened it giving away her high expectations.

He stood across the room in only a towel, watching for her reaction.

Squealing, she took the ring from the box and slid it onto her finger. "YES!"

"Yes what?" he asked, striding over to her.

"Yes, this *will* go with my dress," she teased.

"I think it goes with what you're wearing right now even better."

Gabriela threw her arms around Joel's neck and kissed him wildly on the mouth. She had done it. She had managed to find the perfect man to take care of her and Tomas. She had finally found love and was going to be forever free from relying on her parents for money. Never again would she have to face their disapproving looks when she asked for more cash or when they took in the sight of their grandson. She was starting over in Rio, far from her family, with a sexy, rich, exciting, powerful man.

Tugging off his towel, Gabriela ran one hand down his abs and straight to his waiting cock. He was as ready for her as she had become for him as soon as she had cracked open the lid of that black box. Lowering herself to her knees, she held his length in her hand as she plunged her mouth over him. Joel's hands made their way to the back of her head so he could push his throbbing cock deeper. She had a way with her tongue and skilled hands that had him close to coming within mere moments. She knew the way she serviced him was purely addictive for Joel.

Now, as Gabriela crossed the living room, she spotted a mirror on the coffee table with four neatly arranged lines of white powder and a small straw sitting beside them. She had been on the way upstairs to wait for Joel, who had told her to meet him in bed in five minutes. She passed the table and then turned back, remembering how intense the sex was after they had done some coke a few months ago. Every sensation had been heightened incredibly. Picking up the straw, she held it to her nose, closing one nostril and taking a long whiff to inhale the powder. Her nose twitched at the tingling feeling, and she rubbed it for a second before sniffing the next line. The drug's effects were immediate. Putting down the straw, she tried to stand but her legs folded under her instead. The room started to spin viciously as the lights grew dim around her. Gabriela's head smacked against the white tile under the coffee table as she blacked out. The wooden leg of that table was the last thing she would ever see.

THREE

San Diego, California

Trey stepped out into the bright sunlight, relief and pride bringing a huge smile to his face. Punching the air with his fist, he jogged down the steps of the economics building. After three solid years of assignments, projects and studying, Trey was finally completely free. He figured he'd earned a couple of days of surfing and soaking up the sun. And sleep. Dear God, he'd be able to actually go to bed at a reasonable hour, instead of studying until two in the morning only to get up a few hours later to make it to class.

He'd give himself two days of surfing before his parents arrived in town for his commencement ceremony. After that, Trey would buckle down again and find himself a job—no, a career. Something that would allow him to finally make some real money so he could start a college fund for little Tomas as well as send child support payments to Gabriela. He'd save up so he could visit his son as often as possible. Since Gabriela had taken Tomas back to Brazil, Trey had felt an ever-present emptiness, knowing a part of himself was so far away. But he couldn't fix that today, so he hoped an afternoon of pure adrenalin would help fill that void, even just temporarily.

An hour later, he found himself paddling out against the waves on his roommate's surfboard. A broad smile crossed his face as his arms cut the water on either side of the board, propelling him farther from shore. Trey knew he was lucky to have hit a spring day with such perfect conditions. The surf was head-high, and the sun warmed the black fabric of his wetsuit while the cool, refreshing water lapped over him. He lay with his stomach flat against the board, alive and powerful as he fought the tide with ease. When he'd gone far enough out to sea, he turned the board to face the shoreline of Sunset Cliffs. This was freedom.

In one quick and graceful move, he gripped both sides of the board with his strong hands as he lifted his torso and flipped onto his feet. He stood balanced and completely in tune with the wave that now carried him to the shore. His heart pounded, in part from the work of paddling against the current and in part from the exhilaration that he always felt at this moment. Adrenalin rushed through his veins. He loved to push himself to the limit in everything he did and this was no exception. Surfing was one of the few pure pleasures he allowed himself, and it would be a difficult one to give up if he had to move away from the ocean to find work.

Several runs later, he dragged himself out of the water for a break. The sun was starting to lower itself in the sky, giving a lazy glow to the world. He dropped down onto his beach towel and caught his breath as he watched the water hurtling toward the shore. Lying back, he closed his eyes and took in the sounds of the crashing waves, the gulls in search of an early dinner and the exuberant groups of students now starting to wander down to the beach.

University was over and he was a free man. The comfort of this thought, along with the warmth of the sun on his skin, caused him to drift off into a peaceful nap. Moments later, a ping from his cellphone brought him out of his bliss. Wiping his hands on the towel, he dug around in his backpack for his phone. He saw that he had missed a call from Gabriela. He accessed his voice mail to hear the message.

"Trey, this is Joel Salles. I am . . . was . . . with Gabriela for the past several months. I have some horrible news, and I hate to leave this message, but you need to know immediately. Gabriela passed away suddenly last night. You will have to come and get Tomas. He will be with the nanny until you can get here. I'm so sorry, I know this is a terrible shock." There was a long pause before Joel's voice resumed, his words now rushed. "I will have Alessandra text you her information so you can reach her." *Click.*

Trey sat up and replayed the message several times. Between the sounds of the beach, Joel's thick accent and the way his voice cracked with emotion, Trey had trouble making it out. His heart dropped into his stomach with the gravity of what he had just heard. Gabriela was dead. How could this have happened? His son had just lost his mother.

Trey sucked in a huge breath of air as though he had completely forgotten to breathe for the past several minutes. His heart pounded as his chest expanded. He rubbed his hand through his wet hair and stared down at the phone in his palm. "Fuck," he whispered to himself. "I must have it wrong. There's no way she's dead."

Trey stood, flicking sand off his towel with a snap before shoving it into his backpack. He slung the pack over his shoulder and scooped up the surfboard, hurrying back to campus. *What the fuck will I do if she's really gone?*

FOUR

São Paulo, Brazil

Alessandra sat on a blanket in the shade of a large tree, watching Tomas as he and a girl about his age took turns on a small slide. He was finally feeling better, having made the type of remarkable recovery that only children can, going from being listless to having energy to burn overnight. Her heart ached, seeing him play so innocently, with no understanding that his mother had died. They had not gone to the funeral at the request of Gabriela's parents, who did not believe it would be good for Tomas. She thought of Gabriela, a mother he would barely remember, and sadness crashed over her again. Digging around in her purse, she found her cellphone and called her sister, Betina.

"*Olá*, Alessa!" Betina answered. "How's Tomas?"

"He's good—happy today. He doesn't really know what has happened. We're at the park this morning."

"Poor little guy."

"I know. It's all so sad." Alessandra sighed.

"Has the American shown up yet?"

"Not for a few more hours."

"You have to call me first chance you get. I can't wait to find out all about him." Betina's voice switched in an instant from sympathy to excitement. "I'm living through you right now until I can get off this stupid farm and finally have a life."

"Believe me, my life is far from thrilling. There's a lot you'll miss when you leave home."

"You keep saying that, but I really don't believe it." Betina was twenty-one and headstrong, full of that exuberance for life possessed only by those who have yet to leave home.

"You'll just have to see for yourself," Alessandra answered evenly.

"So, what are you going to wear today? Are you dressing up?"

"Why would I do that? There's been a tragic death, remember?" Alessandra started to feel annoyed with her sister.

"Yes, but sometimes great passion can start out as one person comforting another."

"Oh God. Not in this case. First of all, he's way too old for me. Second, he has a wife, I think. Or a girlfriend. The chef that he left Gabriela for, remember?"

"Well, maybe they broke up. And who cares if he's old? He's rich! I think it's worth some makeup and a push-up bra, just in case. Maybe he'll fall madly in love with you and whisk you away to his ranch." Betina's voice took on a dreamy quality as she spoke.

"I don't want to be whisked away anywhere. I'm finishing school and moving home. Besides, I don't know if he even has a ranch. When I spoke with him a couple of days ago, he mentioned something about wrapping things up in San Diego, not Colorado."

"But still, just in case, some lipstick maybe?" Betina was like a dog with a bone.

Alessandra shook her head in irritation, even though her sister couldn't see. "Betina, romance is the last thing on my mind when it comes to this man. The only thing I need to do is make sure I don't send Tomas off with someone who may not be fit to raise a chicken."

"Oh, you're no fun."

"There are more important things in life than fun."

"So *Mãe* keeps telling me," Betina complained.

"She's right. We're adults. We have responsibilities, and at the moment, my biggest one is Tomas."

"But, Alessa, even if he would be a horrible parent, what could you do about it? He's Tomas's father."

"I'll find a way to stop him if I have to. I know the law, and what I don't know, I know how to find out. I can't count on Tomas's grandparents to take care of this, so he needs me to make sure he'll end up in a good home."

"I suppose . . ."

"Exactly." Alessa's voice was all business. "Hopefully everything will be fine, but I'll only have a few days to figure out if he can be trusted. I should go. Tomas needs lunch and a nap. I just wanted to say hi."

"Okay. Call me tonight."

"If I can, I will. Hugs to *Mãe* and *Vô*."

* * *

Trey stared out the open window of a cab as it crawled along the congested roadway that led from the airport toward Gabriela's condo. In spite of his exhaustion, he forced himself to focus, to take in the sights, sounds and smells passing by as he travelled through the most impoverished streets he'd ever seen. A wave of nausea hit him, and he wasn't sure if it was from the long trip or the feeling of being suddenly very much alone and out of place. Reality was setting in.

His life would never be the same. He was on the opposite side of the world from home, with no one to help him.

Colourful buildings passed by, many of them held up by walls that had been shared over the years by generations of graffiti artists. Makeshift houses sat huddled together, fashioned from scrap metal and wood in such a haphazard way that Trey wondered how they hadn't just fallen over at the first big breeze. Children ran around with no shoes to protect their feet from the hot pavement. Still, they smiled and laughed, and it occurred to Trey that no matter what they had or didn't have, kids were incredibly adept at making the best of life.

The stench of sewage blended with the smell of cooking meat. Trey wrinkled up his nose in spite of himself, and he tried to subtly cover his nostrils with his hand, hoping the driver wouldn't notice. Although Trey had seen places like this on television, actually finding himself here was an entirely different experience. It was all too real and made him long for his safe, tiny dorm room in San Diego.

He knew he was heading to a much nicer neighbourhood, however. When he'd shown the driver the name and address of Gabriela's building, the driver had given an impressed nod and made a remark that sounded approving. Now, as they continued on, the man glanced back in his rear-view mirror at Trey.

"Very poor." The driver pointed out the window with one thumb. "*Favela* . . . um, guns, drugs, no safe. No stop car here at night. Even red light. Go." He gestured with one hand as he looked back at Trey.

"Yes, I see. Thank you for the tip," Trey answered, turning again to look out as they slowly passed a group of shirtless boys playing soccer in a small dirt patch.

Then suddenly, within only one block it seemed, he was surrounded by luxury apartments, gated homes, and stores displaying designer clothing in the windows. Tall, lush tropical trees flanked the road, providing shade to the upscale coffee shops and bistros tucked in behind them. Here the men were dressed in crisp shirts and tailored suits, and the women hurried along in heels and over-sized sunglasses. Some held the hands of equally well-dressed children who looked bored, as though they longed to be barefoot playing soccer somewhere. Trey felt as out of place here as he had in the poorer district.

He closed his eyes for a moment, realizing how good it felt to rest them with a long, slow blink. Including two delays, he had been en route for over twenty hours now. He was emotionally and physically drained, his long legs cramped up from going so many hours without stretching them out. Looking at his watch, he realized he should be at his commencement ceremony right now. He sighed, knowing he would never get that moment back, but it was nothing compared to the lost moments in Gabriela's life.

He had called his parents as soon as he got back from the beach to give them the sad news and to tell them not to come to San Diego because he'd be somewhere over South America come Saturday. They were in nearly as much shock as he was. His mom had wept at the thought of her grandson having no mother. His dad had been more pragmatic about the entire thing, peppering Trey with a host of questions he couldn't answer about how he intended to care for his child. When it had become clear that Trey had no plan yet, his father quickly switched over to making suggestions.

Trey had spent the next three days packing, booking flights and visiting the Brazilian consulate. He had to go there to have them file and stamp the DNA test and admission of paternity forms that had been completed when Tomas was a baby. That appointment alone had taken hours, but as the man at the consulate explained, this was nothing compared to the road ahead of Trey. He would first have to hope that Gabriela's parents wouldn't fight him for custody of his son.

If they did, it would likely take years to get Tomas to the US, if Trey even won in the end. The man couldn't estimate the length of time the legal proceedings would take if the Ferreiras *didn't* fight him, but he did warn Trey that the court system moves very slowly. Trey had no idea where he would get the money for any of it. For now, he would take things one step at a time. The first step was to find his little boy in a city of eleven million.

His thoughts turned to Gabriela, a lump forming in his throat for both her and Tomas. Tomas was so young that his mother would be little more than a vague memory for him. When Trey had spoken with Alessandra, she'd told him the details of Gabriela's tragic death. She explained that the owner of the heroin had left it on the table to go get a friend, only to return a few minutes later to find Gabriela sprawled lifeless on the floor. They'd called an ambulance but it was already too late.

Trey's gut churned with anger and fear of what was to come. Why the hell would someone leave their drugs out for anyone to find? And how could Gabriela have been so irresponsible? She was a mother, for God's sake. What was she doing taking drugs like that? Now she had left her son without a mom and Trey with the task of raising their child alone. A child he barely knew would be stuck with him, someone who was basically a stranger to Tomas, but worse than that, someone who didn't have the first clue about raising children. Someone with no means to do so.

Guilt crowded in as soon as Trey allowed his anger to reach the forefront of his mind. What kind of parent had *he* been? Tomas had seen him on Skype every few weeks but was too little to understand the connection between them. The word *dad* had been little more than an empty title up to this point. Trey had planned to visit and start sending money, but he had never imagined he would raise Tomas. The thought terrified him. Could he even be trusted to raise a human being properly? With good morals and values and manners and enough responsibility and confidence to make it in this world?

As the cab turned a corner, his stomach flipped over. He seriously doubted that he could do it. Trey's shoulders dropped. At age twenty-four, he was preparing to start a new chapter in his life, one that was going to test his limits in every way.

FIVE

Trey soon arrived at Gabriela's apartment, sweaty and bone tired. He rubbed his hand over his chin, feeling the two-day-old stubble that he wished he could have cleaned up before getting there. He would have liked to make a better impression than that of a sweaty, unkempt man. Taking a deep breath, he gently knocked on the door and waited.

A moment later, he heard the chain being unlatched and the door was opened. A young woman stood before him and smiled solemnly. His first thought was how serious she seemed. Then how naturally lovely she was, with impossibly huge grey eyes and full lips. His next thought was that there was no way he should be thinking that last thing.

"Hello, Trey. I'm Alessandra. Welcome." Her voice was quiet. "Tomas is napping right now." She moved aside to give him room to come in.

"Hi, Alessandra. I wondered if he might be asleep. How's he doing?" Cool air refreshed Trey as soon as he stepped into the large space. The luxury of quiet comfort was a sharp contrast to the congested heat he'd found himself in during the final leg of his long journey.

Alessandra turned to lock the door behind him. "He doesn't really understand what's happened. I have told him his mom is gone, but she's been gone for a few weeks now so he thinks she'll come back. I don't know how long it will take before he understands."

Trey scrunched his eyes shut, trying to block out his emotions. Instead of answering, he just nodded.

"You must be very tired." Alessandra walked to the kitchen and opened the fridge. She poured him some water from a jug and handed it to him. There was a wariness in her eyes as she stared at him, a look that made Trey a little uncomfortable.

He took the glass and gulped back the cold liquid, feeling it slide down his throat. "Thank you. I am a little tired; it was a long trip. I'm a total mess too. I could use a shower, if you don't mind. I don't want this to be his first impression of me."

"Of course. Right this way," she replied, leading him to a bathroom down the hall and switching on the light. Towels were laid out on the counter, already waiting for him.

"I won't wake Tomas, will I?" he asked.

"No. This is my bathroom. His room is at the end of the hall. I'll prepare something for you to eat when you get out." She gave him a little nod, then left.

* * *

Alessandra cut up some onion, potatoes and carrots and put them in a pan along with a bit of olive oil, then lit the burner underneath. She thought about Trey as she worked. He seemed polite enough and he'd been considerate in not wanting to wake Tomas, so those were good signs. He was much younger than she thought he'd be. Now that she had met him, it seemed impossible that he was the owner of a large guest ranch. It seemed much more likely that Gabriela had bent the truth somehow to suit herself.

Taking a skirt steak out of the fridge, she sliced it into quarters as she tried to make sense of what she'd been told. Whatever he did for a living, he was certainly handsome. Those hazel eyes that matched Tomas's were absolutely mesmerizing. And that smile. Something about it made her stomach flutter a little in spite of herself. She could see how he'd managed to gain Gabriela's attention. Alessa found herself wishing she'd taken her sister's advice and put on a little makeup and something pretty to wear before he arrived. She knew she looked plain with her dark brown hair tied back in a no-nonsense ponytail and a sundress that was a little too big.

Admonishing herself for these frivolous thoughts, she mashed a couple of cloves of garlic with the side of a knife, then sprinkled a pinch of salt onto the garlic. Betina's meaningless priorities had gotten into her own head. All that really mattered was that Trey intended to leave with Tomas, and the thought of it made her sick with worry. She'd grown so close to the little boy that a sense of protectiveness had come over her, and it had grown fiercely strong in the days since Gabriela's death.

Patting the steak dry, she rubbed it with pepper, salt and a little bit of fresh parsley. She added vegetable oil to a skillet and waited for it to sizzle before adding the meat. In a separate pan, she began heating garlic butter, which sent a delicious aroma through the air. Her work was interrupted by the sound of Trey clearing his throat behind her. Alessandra turned and looked up at him. He looked like a different person in the way that men do after a shave and a shower. He was wearing a clean white T-shirt that was a little rumpled from its long journey, and slightly baggy navy plaid shorts hung from his narrow hips.

"That might be the best smell this nose has ever had the luck of encountering." He took a deep, appreciative breath, closing his eyes for a second.

Alessandra waved off his compliment with one hand. "No, this is nothing."

"Well, Alessandra, it smells like something to me." He smiled at her. There was something so disarming about his smile. It had a genuine warmth to it that made her want to trust him. But she wasn't going to be fooled by a gorgeous face like she had been in the past. She owed it to Tomas to determine Trey's true character. She opened a cupboard door, then stood on her tiptoes to reach a glass jug on the top shelf.

"Here. Let me help," Trey offered, getting it down and handing it to her. Her fingers brushed against his as she took it from him, sending an unwanted thrill through her entire body.

Turning to hide the heat in her cheeks, she replied, "Thank you," as she tested the vegetables with a fork.

*   *   *

A few minutes later, Trey sat down at a table facing a large picture window, taking in the shimmer of the city in the late afternoon sun. Concrete and glass seemed to go on almost as far as the eye could see, stopping abruptly at the lush green mountains beyond. He longed to be somewhere in those mountains, somewhere quiet. He longed to be home, even though he didn't know what that meant at the moment. California wasn't home. Neither was Colorado, anymore. The thought made his chest feel heavy. He had no home to go to, no home to bring Tomas to, either.

Alessandra set down a heaping plate of food in front of him, temporarily distracting him from his sadness. She sat opposite Trey with her own modest portion, and the pair ate in awkward silence for a few minutes. Small talk seemed too trivial given the circumstances.

The sound of two little feet slapping against the tile floor caused them both to look across the kitchen. Tomas was rubbing his eyes and holding a silky blue blanket to his cheek as he made a beeline for his nanny. He crawled up onto her lap and snuggled himself against her chest for a moment before turning his eyes to Trey.

Trey put down his fork, suddenly feeling his heart jump into his throat. This was the first time he'd been in the same room as his son since Tomas was a baby. They were basically strangers and yet this moment was to be the first of a lifetime together. From now on, he was charged with fulfilling this little boy's every need. He smiled cautiously at Tomas, who was staring at Trey with his little eyebrows knit together.

"Hey, Tomas," Trey said softly, feeling emotions that were entirely new to him bubble to his throat. "It's me. Your dad."

Tomas lifted his head off Alessandra's chest and stared at him for a moment before looking up at her, as if for confirmation.

Smiling down at him, she said, "Yes, this is your father. Remember I told you he was coming today?"

Tomas nodded and then looked at Trey. "Dad from 'puter."

Trey chuckled and nodded back. "That's right, little man. Dad from the computer. Only now I'm here in real life." He wanted so badly for his son to run to him and climb up onto his lap for a huge hug, but he knew he would need to wait for that.

Tomas rested his head against Alessandra for a second and stared at Trey before scrambling off her lap and hurrying out of the room. Trey watched, his face full of concern. A moment later, Tomas returned with a grin on his face that very much matched his father's.

He stopped in front of Trey. In his little hands were two toy horses bearing cowboy figures on their backs. Trey had sent them for his birthday. "Pay towboys, Dad!"

Trey pushed his chair back from his partly eaten meal, holding his hand out for a toy. He followed Tomas to the living room coffee table, shooting a surprised smile to Alessandra over his shoulder. "That sounds great, Tomas. Let's play cowboys."

SIX

"There's no way he owns a ranch. If I had to guess, I'd say he was a ranch hand, if that's even where Gabriela met him. He looks very young—close to my age—but that's all I figured out. We didn't get a chance to talk much. Tomas seemed to take to him right away, so they played the entire evening, which was very sweet, actually." Alessandra was sitting on the balcony, talking on the phone with her sister. She could picture Betina lying on her stomach on her bed, phone in hand and feet waving in the air lazily.

"Sweet? So, does this mean you might be able to trust him to raise a chicken, or is he good looking?"

"*Maybe* to raising a chicken, *yes* to being good looking."

"Really? How handsome?"

"Too handsome. Impossible-not-to-notice-type handsome," Alessandra admitted reluctantly.

* * *

A few minutes later, Alessandra hung up the phone and stared out at the city for a moment. She longed to be at the farm with her family. It would be quiet there, with only the sound of the breeze rustling the leaves on the orange trees. The stars would be out in all their glory right now, not competing with the millions of lights that surrounded her. To Alessandra, there was no place on earth safer or more peaceful than the farm. Nothing ever changed there. It was always the same—steady, calm, full of beauty and an old-world charm that grounded her in the traditions and simple pleasures of a way of life that was disappearing from the world. There was never any reason to rush, only to experience life's little moments to the fullest. Not like here, where the world seemed to move at a pace that caused her head to spin. There was no one who ever made her feel as special as her grandfather, who looked at her and Betina as though they were the most precious humans to have ever lived. On the farm, she wasn't just another university student. She was cherished, important even.

She also missed her little sister badly. They were only a year apart and had shared everything until the day Alessandra had left for university. A sick feeling settled over her when she thought of school. She rested her elbows on the glass tabletop and pressed her face to her hands, groaning. Her family had been counting on her to finish law school and start earning a good living to help them out, but now the amount of work she had left to do in the next month seemed almost insurmountable.

Her worrying was halted by the sound of the patio door sliding open behind her. She turned quickly to see Trey standing there in a T-shirt and shorts. He stepped out onto the patio and slid the screen shut.

"Mind if I join you?" he asked.

Alessandra gave him a small smile and nodded. "Of course. Couldn't sleep?"

"I slept hard for a while there, but now that I'm up, I'm up. I should have taken your advice and tried to resist sleep until bedtime here."

"You'll get yourself straightened out soon enough. What time is it in San Diego?" Alessandra asked. She tugged her pink cardigan tighter around her and crossed her arms, feeling suddenly self-conscious around someone so handsome.

"Hmm, we're four hours behind you, so I guess it's suppertime there," Trey answered, plunking himself in the chair next to hers.

"Are you hungry? I can make you something."

Trey shook his head. "No. I'm fine. Thank you, though. You don't have to cook for me. I can always get myself something if you don't mind me poking around in your kitchen."

"It's not my kitchen, so go ahead," Alessandra said with a hint of a smile.

"And if it were your kitchen?"

Alessandra thought about the question before answering. "I actually still wouldn't mind." She laughed at her earlier attempt to be ominous. Trey joined in, surprising her with how pleasing the sound of his laughter was—it was deep and friendly.

When the moment passed, Alessandra studied Trey as he looked out over the city, his expression suddenly solemn. "This must all be quite a shock for you."

Trey nodded, keeping his gaze far away. "Yeah, it is. I've hardly slept since I found out. I keep thinking about her and what happened. It's just so awful, you know?" His voice was quiet and thick with emotion.

Alessandra nodded. "It really is," she replied softly. "I'm very sorry for all three of you. Especially for her and for Tomas, having no mother to love him. But also for you. You must have cared for her a great deal, even though you weren't together anymore."

Trey wore a strange expression for a moment, one that Alessa couldn't read.

"My heart is really only hurting for the two of them and everything they've both lost. I can't stop thinking about it. Now the poor kid is going to be stuck with me, and to tell you the truth, when it comes to raising a child, I don't know what the hell I'm doing." Trey let out a puff of air, glancing over at her, his face full of doubt.

Alessandra smiled reassuringly at him, her heart breaking a little at seeing him so worried. "You'll figure it out."

"God, I hope so."

"People a lot less intelligent than you manage to raise children. You can do it too. Just be patient with yourself. You might not always know what the right thing to do is, but if you learn from your mistakes, you'll get him where he needs to go in life. The important thing is to be there for Tomas, to guide him and care for him."

"Thanks, Alessandra. I appreciate you saying that."

They sat quietly for a moment, Alessandra fidgeting with her hands, before either of them spoke. Trey broke the silence. "Can I ask you something?"

"Yes, of course."

"How did you learn to speak English so well?"

"I did my first year of university in Chicago. The Brazilian government gives out scholarships so people can spend one year in the United States to learn English while they study."

"Wow. You took your first year in a foreign language? On a scholarship? So, you must be really friggin' smart, then."

Alessandra laughed. "I'm no dummy."

"I got to say, I'm feeling a little bit intimidated now," Trey replied with a twinkle in his eye.

"Good. You should. I'm very intimidating." She gave him one solid nod, her voice firm even as she felt her stomach drop. There was that word, *intimidating*. It was like the romance kiss of death for any smart girl. It had gone this way her entire life. She was always the smart one, and from her experience, boys didn't like smart. They lusted after beautiful, bubbly girls that made *them* feel intelligent.

Turning quickly to look out at the view, Alessandra hoped her disappointment didn't show on her face. She decided her time would be better spent studying than gawking at this gorgeous man who under normal circumstances wouldn't have given her a second glance.

"I need to go study. I still have four weeks of law school, and I'm afraid I've let myself get a little behind," she said, pushing her chair away from the table and getting to her feet.

"You're in law school? And you've been taking care of Tomas on your own this whole time? How have you managed that?"

"There is another nanny, Priscila, in the building, who I am friends with. She takes Tomas for me when I have to go to class."

"I can't even imagine trying to look after him while I was in school. Listen, now that I'm here, you don't need to worry about Tomas. It's a big enough help that we can stay here until I'm allowed to bring him home."

"Thank Gabriela's parents for that. If you don't mind, I will also be staying here. I am finishing my school year and I want to spend as much time with Tomas as I can before you leave." She tried to sound matter-of-fact but she knew that her sadness over losing Tomas was obvious on her face.

"You're going to miss him, then."

She nodded. "I was naive. I thought being a nanny would be just a convenient job while I was in school, but I didn't anticipate how hard it would be to say goodbye. I've been with him for two years now. Almost every day since he was only one. I know everything about him."

Trey stared up at her with a sympathetic expression. "And here I'm his father, and I don't know anything about him. I've missed every day of his life since he was a baby."

"Take it from me, it's nicer to be at the beginning of your time with him than at the end. He's the most special little boy."

"I already believe it. I know how lucky I am to have him. It's weird, but since I found out I had a son, I've felt like part of me was missing. Just this emptiness that was always there, and as soon as I saw him walk into the kitchen today, it was like that hole was filled up. That probably sounds crazy, right?"

"Not at all. I think that's exactly how a father should feel when he's apart from his children." Alessandra looked at him, a little in awe of his openness about his feelings and shocked by how sad they made her feel. She wondered if her own father had even once felt an emptiness where she should have been. She doubted it very much. "Well, I should get some sleep. I have a lot of studying to do tomorrow."

"Okay, I should call home and let my family know I made it here." He nodded. "Good night, Alessandra."

"Good night, Trey. I hope you can sleep."

SEVEN

"Hey, ugly, how was your trip?" Dustin grinned as he answered the Skype call.

"It was long, you little turd, but I'm here in one piece," Trey replied.

"Glad the plane didn't crash. How's the little guy doing?"

"He seems alright. He doesn't understand about Gabriela yet. I don't know how long it will take before he gets the idea that she isn't coming back. I guess she left for Rio six weeks ago to be with her boyfriend. It sounds like that was happening a lot in the last year."

"You serious, man? That's a little weird."

"Well, I don't get to judge. I haven't been around at all for his entire life. Alessandra, Tomas's nanny, said that Gabriela was hoping to get married. It sounded like she was trying to fast-track a proposal by staying there for long periods of time. It worked, too. He asked her to marry him the evening she died."

"You serious? That is unbelievably shitty."

"Sure is." A silence fell between them for a while before Trey spoke up again. "On a happier note, when Tomas saw me, he ran and got out the toys I sent him. He wanted to play with me right away, so that was a good start."

"Wow. I can't even imagine having a son right now," Dustin said, almost as though thinking out loud.

"Well, I've had years to get used to the idea. It actually feels a lot better to be with him than knowing he's thousands of miles away. You're going to love Tomas, by the way. He's such a smart little guy, and he's a bit mischievous too. You can see it in his eyes."

"So, he's got a little of his old man in him, hey?" Dustin laughed. "If that's the case, you're gonna be in trouble!"

"Don't I know it," Trey replied.

"How long do you have to stay there before you bring him home?"

"Wish I knew. I have to file with the court to prove I'm his father. It's probably not a bad thing to have some extra time here. I wouldn't want to take him away from Alessandra before he's used to me. He's so attached to her," Trey replied, his face serious.

Dustin nodded at his brother. "That makes sense. He's going to be confused enough, coming to a whole new country where everyone speaks a different language and everything looks different. We're all a bunch of strangers to him, really."

"Yeah, I'm going to have to take things slow. Whatever I can to make this easier for him. As far as moving back to the US, I don't think I'm bringing him back to Colorado, Dustin. I don't think I can handle all the tension right now."

"What are you talking about? Mom thinks you're coming home. She's been getting ready to have a little boy in the house again."

Trey sighed heavily at the news. "Shit. I don't want her to do that. Can you tell her to stop for now? I don't want her to spend any money."

"Um, no. I don't want to be the messenger on that one. I don't have a bulletproof vest."

Trey rolled his eyes. "Alright. I had to try."

"You doing okay?" Dustin asked. "You look beat."

"I'm a little tired. It's been a long few days and there's a lot to get used to."

"I bet. All the more reason to come home. Mom will dote on Tomas all day and you can get a job."

Trey sighed. "Yeah, that would make things a lot easier, for sure, but what kind of grown man moves back home and gets his mom to raise his son for him?"

"Just till you get back on your feet, Trey. You're in a tough situation. There's no shame in admitting when you're in over your head."

"Yes, there is." Trey yawned and rubbed his temple with his hand, suddenly feeling exhausted, both by the trip and the decisions he now faced.

"Listen, I better get going. It's late here and Tomas is up early."

"Alright, you take care, you ugly mutt."

"You too, turd."

Trey hung up and let his shoulders drop, as if that would allow the considerable weight on them to slide off. He stood and walked across the balcony, leaning his forearms on the railing. The thought of going home to Colorado was not a welcome one.

He had disappointed everyone who loved him the most in the world, and now the idea of facing them again was completely without appeal. As much as he missed them, he had yet to redeem himself. He didn't know if there would ever be a way to make things up to his cousin, Cole. He didn't know if he'd ever be able to look his Aunt Mary and Uncle Jake in the eye again. He had disrupted their entire family with his carelessness. His mom and her sister, Mary, had barely spoken in years, not since the truth came out about Trey—not Cole—being Tomas's father. The fellowship they had once shared had disappeared, and he hated like hell that he was the cause of it all.

But letting himself dwell on that wasn't going to help anything. He had enough to deal with here, and sitting around feeling guilty wasn't going to accomplish anything. He needed to find a lawyer who would work for next to nothing to help him out. Trey's mind wandered to Alessandra, and he wondered if she might be willing to help him find someone.

Her soothing voice swept through his mind like a gentle breeze. Next, her pretty grey eyes and her smooth skin, the colour of honey, somehow found their way into his thoughts. She was lovely, and there was something about her calm nature that gave him the comfort he had been needing since he found out how his life was going to change. He'd surprised himself with how honest he'd been with her. He'd never told anyone about how empty he felt when he was apart from Tomas, and he had no clue why he'd decided to tell her. It had just spilled out of him. He tried to tell himself it was because he was tired and full of uncertainty, but deep down, there was some other reason that he couldn't put his finger on.

EIGHT

The next day was Sunday. Trey spent it keeping Tomas busy so Alessandra could complete a final project for one of her classes. She sat at the kitchen table in front of her laptop, with a yellow notepad and several reference books scattered around. Trey caught himself staring at her more than once as she worked. Her wild hair was piled up on top of her head with dark curls tumbling down, and she wore black-framed glasses that Trey found adorable on her. How could a girl in glasses and an insanely bright yellow T-shirt be so attractive? There was nothing revealing about her clothes and she wore no makeup that Trey could see, but somehow he found himself wishing she would look up from her work just to smile in his direction.

Deciding it was better to go out than to sit gazing at her like an idiot, Trey took Tomas for a walk to the park. Tomas ran around for the better part of the morning before they returned to the apartment for lunch. In the afternoon, Trey found himself unable to stay awake and nodded off on the couch during Tomas's nap. He woke to the feeling of something pressing against his cheek. Opening one eye, he found his son peering at him, about three inches from his face. "Aah!" Trey yelped in surprise, jerking upright.

Tomas shrunk back and his bottom lip began to quiver.

"Oh, no . . . It's okay, Tomas! Don't cry, buddy. I just got startled, is all." Trey reached for Tomas, but Tomas backed away and went in search of Alessandra. He found her at the kitchen table and climbed up onto her lap. He buried his head into her chest and wept. "I want *Mãe*," he sobbed.

"Oh, I know you do, *rapazinho*. You miss your mom." Alessandra rubbed his back as he cried.

"You get her now!" He lifted his head and gave her a hard look. "Get my mommy!"

Alessandra's eyes filled with tears. "I wish I could. I would do anything to bring her to you right now."

"*Go*, Lessa! Get her!"

"I can't, baby. I'm so sorry. She's not coming back again."

Trey had followed him into the kitchen, feeling helpless. "This is all my fault. I scared him," he said quietly, rubbing a hand over his face.

"It's okay," Alessandra said. "It's not your fault. He needs to let this out. It's good for him."

"I wish I could do something." Trey's face screwed up with emotion.

Alessandra nodded, blinking back her own tears. She rocked Tomas back and forth a little and pressed her lips to his head. "Are you thirsty, Tomas? Maybe you would like some strawberry juice mixed with milk?"

He nodded, his small head rubbing against her shoulder.

"I'll get it." Trey walked to the fridge, glad to be of use. He mixed his son's favourite drink and returned a moment later, then placed his fingers lightly over Tomas's sandy brown hair as he held out the cup. "Here you go, little buddy."

Tomas sat up and took the drink from Trey. "Fank you."

"Anytime." Glancing at Alessandra, Trey sighed. She gave him a sad smile and Trey knew she felt as helpless as he did.

The rest of the day went surprisingly smoothly. When the heart-wrenching moment had passed, Tomas seemed to warm back up to Trey and wanted to play again. Trey kept him occupied kicking a soft ball back and forth in the kitchen while he fried up some eggs and made toast for supper.

When it came time for Tomas to say good night to Alessandra, he looked up at her with huge, sad eyes. "You sing me to seep?"

She smiled at him and nodded. "Of course, *rapazinho*."

Trey gave her an apologetic look. "He asked me to sing to him when he was in the tub. I think that tipped the scales in your favour."

"What do you mean? You sounded like a professional, especially on the high notes," she said with a teasing grin.

Trey gave her a nod, a wry look on his face. "Thanks."

"I need a break from my studies anyway. My eyes are going crossed." She scooped up Tomas in her arms and carried him down the hall, inhaling his freshly washed hair as he rested his head on her shoulder. It was all so natural, so familiar. "I missed you today. I've been so busy doing homework, but you seemed to be having so much fun with your dad."

Tomas lifted his head, his eyes lighting up. "We played lots and lots."

"I saw that. You know, he will be with you always from now on. Isn't that wonderful?"

He smiled, putting his little hands on her cheeks. "Me and Dad and Lessa!"

Alessandra gave him a quick kiss on the forehead, feeling a tug at her heart at the thought of losing him. "Time for bed, little one. What song for you tonight?"

* * *

Trey listened to their exchange from the kitchen, worry overtaking him yet again. He was going to take his son away from this woman who loved him so much, and who his son obviously adored. He wouldn't have had the first clue how to handle Tomas crying for his mom, but she had been so calm, saying exactly the right things. He dreaded the thought of trying to figure this out on his own. He let out a long, slow breath, then reminded himself of what a terrific day they'd had together. Making his way to the living room, he started the arduous task of cleaning up the mess of toys. By the time he had finished and was settling himself at the kitchen table with his laptop, Alessandra came out of Tomas's room. She had a sleepy look about her, having been in the calm dark.

She stopped in the kitchen to pour two glasses of water, then brought one to Trey and set one in front of her spot at the table. "He certainly is happy to be with you."

"Oh, well, the feeling is mutual. I'm just amazed by him. He's so damn smart, you know? It's amazing how he is so at ease in two languages. He must get that from his mother's side," Trey joked before he remembered that Tomas's mother was gone. His face fell a little.

Alessandra was quiet for a moment before speaking. "Well, no matter who he gets it from, he's a very special boy."

The two got to work, Alessandra on her assignment and Trey searching the Internet for his next move in trying to take his son home. Unfortunately, he had very little idea of where to start, and his was far too complicated a situation to get help online. Finally, Trey sat back and scratched his head.

"What's wrong?" Alessandra asked.

"Just trying to find out what the next steps are in getting Tomas home, but I'm afraid I'm coming up short."

"I can get some help for you. Tomorrow, I'll talk to one of my professors who I think would be willing to advise you on this."

"Nah, I couldn't ask you to do that. You've got enough to deal with right now. I'll figure it out."

Alessandra gave him a serious look. "Trey, I will make time to help you. I want the best for Tomas, and it seems that you are the right person to raise him. His grandparents disapproved of Gabriela and what happened and have kept their distance from Tomas. They don't know him at all."

"Really?"

"They are not interested in their grandchild. Don't you think it's strange that they haven't contacted you yet? It's been over a week since Gabriela died, and I've spoken to Mr. Ferreira only once in that time. They know their grandson is here with me and I told them you are coming, but they do nothing. Shouldn't they want to know if you are a decent man before letting a stranger near that little boy?"

"I guess I don't think of myself as a stranger, but when you put it that way, it seems pretty odd that they haven't at least checked on Tomas."

"It is wrong. They do not love him the way they should but I can see that you do, so I will find someone who can help you."

"Thank you, Alessandra. It means a lot that you would do that."

Alessandra smiled. "It's nothing."

"To me, it's everything."

NINE

The next afternoon, Trey carried Tomas up the steps to the lobby of the condo building. Tomas was soaked and covered in mud, having discovered a particularly slippery bank on a tiny stream that ran through the neighbourhood park. Trey had found twigs they could use as boats to float downstream, not knowing that a three-year-old, lacking in impulse control, would most certainly try to retrieve the boats at some point along their journey. Now, back at home, he held the front door open for a small, well-dressed man carrying a large briefcase. Wiping his dirty running shoes on the mat, Trey gingerly made his way to the elevators, hoping not to make a big mess. The man stood next to them, waiting for the elevator door to open. He glanced at the pair often enough that Trey started to feel uncomfortable.

They rode up to the tenth floor together, with Tomas suddenly announcing, "Dad, I haf to poop."

"I wondered about that. You've been tooting up a storm since we left the park."

A smile crossed the stranger's face, indicating his understanding of the exchange.

The three got off the elevator and walked down the hall in the same direction. When they reached the same suite, Trey turned to him. "Can I help you with something?"

"This boy is Tomas Ferreira?"

Trey shifted Tomas to the opposite side of his body, away from the man, and gave him a hard look. "May I ask who you are?"

"Of course. My apologies. I am Paulo Martins, the lawyer for Mr. and Mrs. Ferreira. May I come in?"

"Oh, sure. I'm Trey Johnson." He unlocked the door and held his hand out for Mr. Martins to enter ahead of him.

"Nice to meet you. We have much to talk about."

"Okay." Trey gave him a wary look "Let me get him to the bathroom first."

"Certainly."

Trey carefully took off their dirty shoes then carried Tomas down the hall to the washroom. Once inside, he helped him onto the toilet and washed his own hands. "Listen, I need to talk to that man out there. Do you take care of this yourself or do you need some help?"

Tomas gave him a confused look.

Scrunching up his nose for a second, Trey then tried to look like it was all cool. "Right, I guess I'll help you out until you can do it for yourself. You call me when you're ready, okay?"

Trey quickly changed into some clean clothes before finding Mr. Martins sitting on the couch with a number of papers set out on the coffee table. "Can I get you a coffee or water or anything, Mr. Martins?"

"Please call me Paulo, and water would be very nice."

"Sure. Sorry I'm a bit of a mess," Trey called to him as he made his way to the kitchen. "Somehow Tomas found the only mud in the entire city."

"Yes, I noticed." His tone gave no hint as to his personal opinion on the matter.

As Trey filled two glasses, he imagined that Mr. Martins would make an excellent poker player. On his return to the living room,

Trey's hands shook a little, causing the water to slosh dangerously close to the rim. The irony wasn't lost on Trey, a seasoned bartender who, at the moment, could barely manage to serve a glass of water. "So, how are Mr. and Mrs. Ferreira doing? I can't even imagine what they're going through."

"It is very hard for them, of course. I saw Mr. Ferreira after the funeral. His wife was not ready to see anyone. They are both very much in shock. It's a grief that I don't think goes away." He paused to sip his drink. "For now, Mr. and Mrs. Ferreira have decided that it would be too difficult, emotionally speaking, to be in close contact with Tomas. They are concerned that they would not be able to handle such meetings in a dignified fashion, which would very likely be confusing for Tomas. They have asked me to act on their behalf."

"Seems kind of odd, but I guess they have to do what's best for *them*, right?" Trey's tone bordered on sarcasm, which he immediately regretted. He knew he needed to play nice.

"They are careful in their decisions, even at such a time." Paulo answered evenly. "You must be also very . . . surprised by what is happening."

"I am. I'm still trying to wrap my head around all of this. Every day I spend with Tomas, I feel worse for Gabriela, for what she'll miss." The sound of Tomas singing softly to himself in the other room made Trey smile sadly.

Paulo nodded. "Yes, it is certainly a tragedy. So, are you intending to take guardianship of Tomas?"

Trey could feel his heart in his throat. "Definitely. I'm his father. He belongs with me."

"At the moment, my clients have no intention of trying to obtain custody of Tomas. At their current age and with the sudden loss of their daughter, they do not feel as though they would be able to give him all the attention that he'll need."

Relief crossed Trey's face. "Good. Okay. I mean, I've been worried about that, of course."

"However, they want what's best for Tomas and will do whatever they have to in order to protect him. They will fight you for custody if they think you won't be able to raise Tomas."

Trey stared at the man, waiting for him to continue.

"They have some concerns about you, which I'm sure you can understand. One of the tasks they have given me is to ensure you have the means and support to look after him. You have no real bond with him, you are young and fatherhood is not always easy or fun. They want to know that you won't decide, in a little while, that it isn't for you."

Trey set his jaw. "I would never do that. I know I haven't been here for him, but I have done what I could back home to be worthy of being his father. As soon as I found out that he even existed, I took a DNA test and had documents drawn up that prove I am his father. Gabriela's the one who wanted to bring him back here, so I went along with it. It's not like I could have supported them as a university student. We decided it would be best for me to finish school so I could provide more for him over time. I worked my butt off to get my degree a year early. And, as you know, I flew here as soon as I found out that Gabriela was gone. I'm serious about raising my son."

"While this is all good, I still need to ask you some questions. I'm not trying to insult you, only to decide what will be best for Tomas."

"I understand. You have a job to do, so go ahead."

"You have never been to Brazil until this trip."

"That's right."

"You have just completed your degree at the University of San Diego?"

"Yes."

Paulo glanced down at the pad of paper on his lap. "How much debt do you have?"

"None."

"None? Most American students are tens of thousands in debt by the time they complete their first degree."

"True, but I'm not. I kept my grades high, so I was able to get some scholarship money each year. Plus, I worked part-time and lived as cheaply as I could."

"Yes. You had a job as a bartender?"

Trey gave him a hard stare before answering. "It sounds like you already know the answers to all of your questions."

"I do. Like you, I make sure to do my homework," Paulo said.

"Why ask the questions, then?"

"To see how you would answer them."

"I see. So, did my answers meet your approval?" Trey asked.

"So far."

The sound of Tomas talking to himself in the bathroom took a little tension out of the moment, reminding Trey why keeping his patience was vital right now.

Paulo smiled at the sound. "Tell me about your job at the bar. Sometimes it's easy to end up with some . . . bad habits in a place like that."

"Well, I didn't. I worked, I collected my tips and I went home sober every night."

"Yes, that is what we have been told as well. My clients were glad to hear it."

"That's comforting," Trey said, an edge to his voice that opposed his words. "How about next time you have a question about me, ask me."

"I'm sure this is awkward for you, but my job is not to protect your feelings, it is to look out for Tomas."

"I can assure you I'll look out for him, so if you don't mind, please tell Mr. and Mrs. Ferreira to call off their dogs." Trey gave him a hard look. "Are we about done here? I should really get him into the bath." Trey stood and crossed his arms.

"Yes, of course," Paulo replied as he clicked his pen to close it. "Mr. Johnson, I am impressed with your determination, I want you to know that. I also want you to know that to properly represent my clients, I will speak with the prosecutor and request that he ask the judge to ensure you can provide for Tomas before you would be allowed to take him out of Brazil."

"How exactly do I do that?"

Paulo finished putting his things into his briefcase before standing. "The judge will decide. You will either need to demonstrate through affidavits that you have family and potential job connections, or you will have to go back to the United States *without* your son in order to find a job and set up a home."

"So, they might force me to leave my son here just to prove he won't grow up poor?"

"It is a possibility. The judge will make the determination."

Trey sighed out of frustration. "I'm sure you can understand how badly I don't want to leave him here alone. He only has one parent left. Don't you think he should be able to stay with me?"

"What I think is of no consequence. I'm sure it seems harsh, but it really is Mr. Ferreira's way of protecting Tomas. You need to know Mr. Ferreira is a very powerful man and he won't allow Tomas to end up destitute. But at the same time, he is trying to be reasonable. For now, he has said that you are allowed to live here in their condo while the court case proceeds. He also is going to set up a large trust fund for Tomas to access when he turns twenty-one. You will see he is being very fair when it comes to the child."

"I'm sorry if I seem rude. This is just a lot to take in." Trey raked a hand through his hair. "Can you please pass along my condolences to the Ferreiras. And thank them for allowing us to stay here."

Their conversation was interrupted by Tomas's voice calling for Trey.

Paulo opened the front door and gave him a sympathetic look. "Good luck. It was a pleasure to meet you."

Closing the door, Trey mumbled to himself, "I wish I could say the same."

* * *

That evening, Alessandra and Trey worked together to clean up the dishes while Trey told her about the visit from the Ferreira's lawyer. When he was finished, he gave Alessandra a concerned look. "So, I guess I have to be grateful that they aren't planning to fight me for custody of Tomas, but they're not exactly planning to make it easy on me either."

"Okay, well, at least we know where you are starting from now." Alessandra said while she wrung out the dish cloth. "I had a talk with that professor I was telling you about. She said she thinks I can handle most of the paperwork for you to petition the court for permission to take Tomas home."

"Really? You serious? That would save me a lot of money I don't have." Trey looked at her with a smile that soon faded. "Oh, but I don't want to put you out, Alessandra. You've got enough to take care of with your studies."

"It won't be that much work. I don't have class tomorrow morning, so we can go to the courthouse to hand in the forms. We'll also need to get any of your existing legal documents pertaining to Tomas translated into Portuguese. That may take a few weeks, but my professor gave me the name of a man at the university who does that sort of thing."

Trey shook his head. "Wow. Thank you so much. I don't know how I'll ever repay you."

"*De nada*. Can you show me the documents you have?"

Trey retrieved his file from his bedroom, then sat next to Alessandra at the table while she looked through the pages. Her brow furrowed. "Your name isn't listed on the birth certificate," she observed.

"I imagine that will make things more difficult?"

"My professor asked me about this. She said it would mean things will take longer. We can ask for an emergency hearing but it may not be granted. Because Gabriela isn't alive to add you to the birth certificate or otherwise verify that you are the father, it will mean the court needs to first validate the documents you've got. They may even ask for another paternity test to be performed here. Maybe not. It depends on the judge, and from what you've said, it will also depend on how much the Ferreiras' lawyer interferes. Even if he doesn't interfere, the entire process will take several months to even a year."

Trey's face wore a shocked expression. "A year? Wow." He blew out a puff of air. "I thought . . . Well, I guess I didn't know what to think."

"I know. The Brazilian government is very protective of any children born here. They do not let anyone remove them easily, even a biological parent."

Trey raked a hand through his hair. "I really had no idea it would be this hard. God, I hope they don't force me to leave him behind. I mean, who would I even leave him with?"

"I would be happy to take care of Tomas if you have to leave him here. But the judge might not even insist on this. Let's take it one step at a time, okay?"

Trey nodded in agreement. "Okay."

Alessandra put her hand over Trey's. "Tomorrow we will file the first set of papers to request that you be named as father and to request that you be allowed to leave the country with Tomas. Then

I will take the paperwork you brought to the translator. Don't worry about it, okay? You've got the right nanny on your side."

Trey chuckled at her joke, seeming relieved. "I sure do."

*   *   *

Trey lay in bed that night tossing and turning. Staring at the clock, he realized it was almost 3 a.m. Tomas would be up in less than four hours. He needed to get to sleep, but the thought of going to the courthouse the next day kept him wide awake. He scrubbed his hand over his face in frustration. He felt powerless here. His fate and that of his son were in the hands of strangers, one of whom had come here to put him on notice of the hoops he would have to jump through. He wished he'd pushed Gabriela to add his name to Tomas's birth certificate when he had the chance. And how the hell was he going to pay for all of this? How would he pay for food while he was here? He didn't want to live off the Ferreiras for months on end, but he didn't even have a work visa.

His thoughts turned to Alessandra and how she was going out of her way to help him. Then he could feel her hand over his, the warm look on her face as she smiled at him. The thought calmed him. She had that effect on him, as she did on his son. There was something so soothing about being around her, it was as though she could make everything alright. His heart swelled when he thought of her. He had so badly wanted to kiss her. He'd had to fight that urge, to swallow it down. This was not the time or the place for him to be thinking things like that. There was no way that would help anything, no matter how good it would feel. It would only complicate things in a way that he couldn't afford right now. And if he'd learned anything from his night with Gabriela, it was that giving in to the wrong moment could have a lifetime of consequences.

TEN

The next morning, Alessandra woke to the quiet sounds of Trey and Tomas having breakfast. Glancing at the time, she realized she'd slept in. She made her way to the kitchen and found French toast and fruit waiting for her. Tomas ran over and took her hand to show her the surprise. "We maked breakfast!"

"You did? Wow!" Alessandra sat at the table and gave him a big kiss on his forehead. "Thank you so much."

She smiled at Trey, who was standing in front of the sink. "Thank you, Trey. What a treat to sleep in and now have such a nice breakfast to eat."

"No problem. I figured you were probably up late studying," he said. "Coffee?"

"I can get it," she answered.

"I'm already here. How do you take it?"

"Just with a little milk. But you really don't have to."

"Let me anyway," he answered in a light tone. He carried the coffee over to her, along with his own, and sat across the table from her.

Tomas crawled up onto her lap as she ate, opening his mouth in case she wanted to share.

"Here, *rapazinho*," Alessa said, popping a piece of the soft bread into his mouth.

"You're having more? You must be growing, buddy." Trey smiled at his son, then looked at Alessandra. "What's the name you call him? *Rapazinho?*"

"It means young man, which I think suits someone as dignified as Tomas."

Tomas smiled at her, then opened his mouth for another bite of her breakfast.

Alessandra ate quickly and excused herself to get ready to go to the courthouse. Twenty minutes later, she walked out of her bedroom dressed in a black pencil skirt, a matching short jacket and an ivory camisole with just a bit of lace visible. Her hair was swept up in a twist with a few pieces framing her face. Trey, who was crouched down helping Tomas put his shoes on, glanced up at her, then did a very obvious double take. "Wow," he blurted out. "You look . . . very professional."

Alessa felt her face flaming. She looked down at her outfit. "Is it okay? I was worried the skirt might be a little short."

"No, not at all. You look perfect." He whispered something in Tomas's ear, causing the little boy to grin up at her.

"You look pretty, Lessa!" Tomas called.

"You boys look very handsome too." She looked at Trey, who was wearing a black golf shirt and khaki pants.

"I'm afraid I don't have any dress clothes," he said. "This is all I could come up with."

"You're just fine. I'm only dressed up in case I see anyone who might one day be my boss."

Two hours later, after a long bus ride followed by a much longer lineup, the three finally left the courthouse. Alessandra was surprised how easily Trey had managed to keep Tomas from getting bored. He always seemed to have some way to entertain him, whether with a magic trick or by pointing out something to look at or finding some way to tease him. Something about seeing them together tugged at her heart. She had never known her own father and she wondered if this is what it would have been like.

As they walked back to the bus stop, Trey picked up the now sleepy little boy and carried him while Tomas rested his head on Trey's broad shoulder. They looked very much like a young, happy family from the outside, and part of Alessandra couldn't help wishing they were one. If they were a real family, she wouldn't have to face the loneliness of saying goodbye to Tomas. The thought of that felt like too much and she brushed it aside.

* * *

Late that evening, Trey sat on the balcony and used his laptop to call his parents. After a twenty-minute conversation, he bid them a good night and sat for a moment, reflecting on the call. He had filled them in on what he knew about the hoops he would have to jump through for the court case as well as the expected timeline. They had been just as upset as he thought they'd be and had offered to send money, which Trey declined. Getting up to go back inside, he looked at Alessandra, who was on the couch studying. Her hair was up in a messy bun again and she had a pencil tucked behind her ear. The word *adorable* popped into his head.

* * *

Alessandra heard the patio door slide open but forced herself to keep her eyes on the page she was reading. Her stomach fluttered, as it did every time Trey came near her. She sensed he was watching her, and her cheeks warmed suddenly. Finally letting herself glance up at him, she gave him a shy smile and quickly took off her glasses. "How did the call with your parents go?"

"They're disappointed by how long it'll be before we're home."
He plunked himself onto the couch next to her.

"I'm sure it must be hard for them to be so far away."

"Yeah, they hate the idea that I'll be living off the Ferreiras for months, maybe even a year. To be honest, I do too. I can't stand the thought of freeloading like this. It makes my skin crawl."

"Well then, I have an idea that you might like. I've been thinking about how I'll be leaving to go home when I finish school. My family has an orange farm and we need a lot of help. My grandfather has been sick and isn't able to take care of things the way he used to. If you and Tomas came with me, you could work for him and I could have a few extra months with Tomas."

"Really? Would he really let us come live there?"

"Yes, he would actually be very grateful for the help. I spoke with him and my mother yesterday. There is a tiny house on the farm you could live in."

Trey's eyes lit up. "That sounds perfect! That way, I don't have to take Tomas away from you yet. I've been really worried about you leaving before he's really comfortable with me." His face fell a little. "But only if there's enough work for me. I won't go from freeloading off the Ferreiras to freeloading off your grandpa."

"Oh, trust me. There is more than enough work!"

* * *

Trey heard the shower running as he walked down the hall. He stood outside the bathroom door for a moment, his hand poised over the knob. Something told him he could go in and that it would be okay. More than okay. She wanted him to. But he shouldn't. Turning, he made his way to the kitchen and took a beer out of the fridge. He stood, back to the counter, sucking back the beer, trying to put out the fire. Why was he sweating? What had he been doing before this?

He listened as the shower was turned off, and almost instantly, she was standing in front of him in nothing but a towel. He stared as droplets of water trailed from her bare collarbone into the top of the towel. He was suddenly overcome by the urge to lick that water off. He had never been so thirsty, and he knew nothing was going to quench him like that would. Her eyes were silvery swirls of brilliance and lust as she stepped toward him.

"Yes, Trey." Her voice had a breathy quality that resonated through his body in the most delicious way. "I want you. Now." She ran a finger from his neck all the way down to his jeans with a naughty look. Alessandra lifted herself onto her tiptoes to bring her mouth to his. She was so close now, he could feel the heat off her body. She was perfectly feminine, from her curves to her thick mass of lashes to her full, pouty pink lips. She smelled of lightly scented flowers and shampoo. She was irresistible. But he needed to resist.

He watched in shock as she flicked open the button on his jeans, then tugged the zipper down. "Do you want me too?"

He nodded, unable to speak. He told his mouth to say something, to be smooth about it, but somehow his mouth refused to obey. He stood powerless, waiting, wanting. He could feel his cock straining against the fabric of his jeans and watched in awe as her delicate hand slid into his underwear. *Oh God. That feels amazing.* Her warm, soft hand against his skin. *Kiss her, you idiot. She's right here, naked under that towel. Just give it a little tug and it will come off.*

What the hell? Why was his body refusing to do what he told it to? Why was he just standing there? Alessa was practically naked, giving him that look. *Oh God, she just licked her lips. Fuck, that's hot. Do something! She wants you to.*

Trey woke with a start, sitting up. He was so hard it was almost painful. Grabbing his cell, he saw it was a little after 2 a.m. *Jesus. What was that about?*

He lay back, his mind and body gripped by his dream. Alessandra's face, her words, her touch. He shouldn't be thinking of her that way, but each day his desire for her grew more unyielding. He couldn't help but peek when she bent over to help Tomas with something, giving Trey a view of her full breasts down the top of her shirt.

He had to kill these thoughts. She was his son's nanny. She was his lawyer. He'd be leaving soon, so there was no way he could act on his longing for her. But he could think about it, couldn't he? That was okay. And it would be okay to work out some of the sexual tension that buzzed through the air when he was near her. Yes, working out the tension might even prevent him from letting his feelings get in the way. If anything, this was the responsible thing to do.

Sliding his hand down his abs and into his boxer briefs, he allowed himself that moment of pleasure, of temporary relief he'd been needing. He instantly conjured up an image of tugging at that towel and letting it fall to the floor, leaving her honey-coloured curves exposed to him. Now his hands were running over her supple, naked skin. Those breasts were in his hands. Her mouth was on his. It was warm and delicious. Her smooth body was pressed against his as she glided her hand up and down his cock. *Oh yes.* He could hear her moaning in his mind and the sound made him throb with excitement. Visions of his hand making its way down between her thighs and feeling the heat of her wet skin against his fingers coaxed Trey along as he quietly let go.

ELEVEN

The next weeks found Alessandra studying most hours that she was awake. Trey took care of the cooking and laundry in addition to looking after Tomas. Alessandra showed him where the grocery store was, and Trey would walk down with Tomas to pick up what they needed. They would stop at a *padaria* to pick up sweet buns to bring home, sometimes sitting side by side at the counter to enjoy a treat right there in the bakery. As her final exams drew nearer, Alessandra had nothing to do but study.

One unexpected side effect of this luxury was that it allowed her to spend far too much time thinking about Trey. He surprised her every day with his kindness and good humour. He would bring lunch and supper to her room if she was too busy to stop working. Later, he would quietly clear her dishes. Several nights, Alessandra fell asleep on the couch studying, only to find herself covered up with a blanket when she awoke the next morning. He was good to her and to Tomas, leaving no doubt in her mind about his ability to be a good father.

She knew she was falling for him in spite of herself. Every kind act, every smile drew her to him. At night when she lay in bed, she willed him to come to her. She ached to feel his lips on her skin, his mouth on hers. She was desperate to feel the weight of his powerful body over hers. But these thoughts were perilous for her heart. It was never going to happen, no matter how hard she wished for it.

Late one evening, she had woken on the couch and stood to walk through the darkened apartment. She started down the hall, only to be surprised by the bathroom door swinging open. There he stood in nothing but a towel, so near she could touch him. The memory of it was burned into her brain. His sculpted body, those powerful arms flexing, the surprised and slightly embarrassed look on his face as he apologized. Why was *that* look so sexy? Because it was on *his* face.

Her mouth had dropped open and she had gasped a little, which caused his embarrassed expression to instantly shift to one of amusement. He stood his ground, grinning down at her, watching as she turned into a puddle in front of him before she put her head down and all but scurried to her room. He knew. He must know how badly she wanted him. How could he not?

Closing the door, she had leaned against it for support. Everything he did made him irresistible to her. Even watching him play with Tomas was somehow insanely hot to her. She had never felt this way about a man before. Not like this. But she had to stop herself before she did something stupid like throw herself at him. That would end badly and she knew it.

She was sure her lack of experience with men would prove humiliating for her. He must have been with lots of women. She'd only been with two men before; really they were more like boys. Her first, Dimas, was a boy she'd gone to school with. Her friends had thrown her a going-away party before she left for school in the United States. They had both had a lot to drink at the party, and she'd decided that he was a good candidate to prevent her from arriving at college a virgin. Their affair lasted all of ten minutes, ending in the most anticlimactic fashion possible, and left Alessandra wearing a *that-was-it?* expression on her face.

Her second was Kyle, a fellow first-year student who lived in her dorm building in Chicago. She'd been immediately attracted to him. He was on a football scholarship and, as luck would have it, he ended up in her statistics class. Her heart would pound wildly on the days he actually made it to class. Midway through the first semester, he needed help and Alessandra was all too happy to give it to him. They spent several sexually charged study sessions together, until one night he ended up in her bed. This went on until final exams were over and Alessandra found out he had tutors for most of his classes. All of them were girls, each believing she was the only one, each sleeping with him. His real girlfriend was back home in Idaho, pining away for him.

Alessandra spent the rest of the year avoiding him, as well as anyone who knew him, and feeling like a complete idiot. She'd been duped and used, and had not slept with anyone since, focusing instead on getting her degree and starting her career. Sex could wait. Men could wait. She had goals to achieve and wouldn't be stopped by lust.

But now, with Trey living in the same apartment, knowing he was a mere room away all night was torture for her. And each day, her desire for him grew, becoming a little more unbearable than the day before, leaving her a hot mess by the time she dropped into bed.

She stared up at the ceiling, thinking of him at dinner that night. She had taken a break from studying to whip up a *churrasqueira* chicken and some rice.

Trey took a bite, an appreciative look crossing his gorgeous face. "Wow, you are some cook. A guy could put on a lot of weight living with you."

Alessandra blushed a little at his compliment. "Well then, I would have to help him work it off."

Trey's eyes popped open. "Oh, in that case, he'll be one very lucky man."

Alessandra covered her mouth as she laughed, feeling shocked at herself for her bold joke. Now that she thought of it, she wished she'd been forward enough to tell him he could be that lucky man if he wanted. But she couldn't. He was so good looking and confident that the contrast between them caused her own insecurities to bubble to her throat and made even swallowing her sip of juice difficult. He would never be interested in someone like her. Not when he could get a swimsuit model. Someone with angel-blond hair and legs that went on for miles. But even that sobering thought coouldn't stop her from wishing.

The day of her last exam finally arrived, and as she hurried across campus afterwards, it was not with thoughts of what she had just accomplished—it was with thoughts of going home to Trey. She couldn't wait to get back to him and Tomas. Tonight, she would cook a special dinner, and maybe they could go for a walk and let Tomas play at the park. Then she would spend the next three days preparing for his court case, and the thought of that challenge excited her almost as much as going home to Trey. Smiling to herself, she secured her backpack over both shoulders and swung her leg over her bicycle for the sunny ride home to them.

TWELVE

"We'll be ready for tomorrow," Alessa announced with a confident nod. She and Trey were seated on the couch together, going over all of his legal documents one last time. "At least, I'm pretty sure."

Trey leaned back and ran his hands through his hair. "Yeah, it really seems like you've got all the bases covered. I just can't thank you enough."

"Like I've already told you several times, there is no need." Alessandra put the papers into a folder and set it on the coffee table.

Trey watched her for a minute before speaking. "You know, it's funny. This is not how I thought I would start a family—waiting for permission from the court to be a father to my own son."

Alessandra gave him a speculative look. "Yes, it's not exactly the usual path, is it?"

He shifted his body to face her, propping the side of his leg on the couch. "Not exactly. Not that I've really spent a lot of time thinking about it, but I guess I figured I'd meet a nice girl, fall in love, get married, then have kids when we were ready."

Alessandra turned toward him. "I wonder how many people have that happen?"

"My parents."

"Not mine. Well, sort of. My parents were teenagers, both when they fell in love and when it ended. They found out they were going to have me very early in their relationship, so they left Bebedouro, the town they were from. They came here to São Paulo because they knew their families would be very angry with them. Two years later, they had two little girls, and my father decided it wasn't the life for him. I guess the fun wore off under all that responsibility. He told my mother he was going north to find work but he never came back."

"That's awful. I'm really sorry to hear that." Trey's voice was soft.

"Yes, my mother knew he wasn't coming back for us. She took us straight home to her parents' farm. He would have known where to find us if he'd ever wanted to, but he didn't. We never heard from him again."

"Wow, that must have been so hard for you all." Trey shook his head.

Alessandra nodded, her eyes falling on Trey's jaw. It was set tight, making it look even more chiselled than it normally did. As her gaze moved up, she could see he was visibly upset by her story, and it made her long to touch him. It was in this moment that she knew without a doubt that Tomas was lucky to have Trey as his father. He was a good man—young, yes, poor for now—but he was good to the core, and it made her want to wrap her arms around his neck and pull him in for a long, slow kiss. Finding herself unable to look away from his intense gaze, she bit her lip as thoughts of his mouth hovering over hers filled her brain. Alessa could feel her heart pounding in her chest as she waited for him to make a move, but the moment was interrupted by the sound of Tomas whimpering. They both turned to see him standing at the entrance to the hall, holding his blanket.

Alessa tilted her head. "*Rapinzho*, what is it?"

"I had a bad dream." His tear-stained face was pulled into a pout.

"Oh dear. Come on, let's get you back to bed." She stood and walked to him, holding out her hand.

"You stay with me?"

"Yes, sweetie, I'll stay with you." She scooped him up and carried him to his room, wondering what would have happened if Tomas hadn't woken up just then.

She returned a few minutes later to find Trey in the kitchen scooping out two bowls of ice cream. "Did he go back to sleep?"

"Yes, he'll be fine." She peered around him. "What's this?"

"I almost forgot, I picked up a little treat to thank you." He handed her a bowl and they made their way to the kitchen table.

"Is this pistachio?"

"Yup. I remembered you saying it was your favourite."

"It is. This is very thoughtful of you, Trey," Alessandra said, grinning over at him.

He watched as she picked up her spoon, dipped it into the ice cream, and then took it out again, as though considering whether she should have some.

"I noticed you don't treat yourself very often. Why is that?"

Alessandra blushed. "I'm not one of those girls who can eat whatever she wants without paying for it. I might as well just attach this ice cream to my hips, since that's where it will go."

Trey furrowed his brow at her joke. "You can't be serious. You have a great body."

"No, I don't."

"Trust me, you do. I'm a guy, we're much better at assessing women's bodies than women are."

Lifting one eyebrow, Alessandra gave him a skeptical look.

"Eat the ice cream."

She opened her mouth to say something, then stopped herself. Trey kept his eyes on her as she lifted a tiny bit of ice cream onto the end of her spoon. She closed her lips around it, then her eyelids lowered, accompanied by an appreciative little moan. It was a sound he wanted to hear again.

"See, that was worth it, wasn't it?" he asked in a low tone.

"It is. You'll have to turn away now while I inhale the rest in a most unladylike way."

Her words caused him to burst out laughing. "*That* I'd like to see."

They ate in blissful silence for a minute. Trey looked over at Alessandra and reached up to dab a bit of ice cream off her bottom lip. His eyes locked on her lips and he leaned in, coming dangerously close to kissing her. Stopping himself, he cleared his throat and straightened up. "Pistachio. I never would have guessed it was so delicious."

"Yeah, glad you like it," Alessandra replied in a slightly breathy voice. When Trey looked into her eyes, he was met with her desire.

Her lusty expression turned slightly suspicious. "You're a little scary. The way you talked me into this so easily. I can see how Gabriela fell for you."

"Oh. She didn't fall for me. It was more the other way around." His face grew serious.

The sensual moment had evaporated.

"How did you two end up together? I hate to ask, but I don't think Gabriela's version is adding up exactly, and I think it might be good for me to know the truth. For the court case, I mean."

"What did she tell you?"

"That Tomas's father owns a luxury ranch in Colorado and that he threw her over for a chef."

Trey's face fell. "Oh, well, she was *hoping* he was Tomas's father.

He would have been in a much better position to take care of them both." He blew out a puff of air, hating what he had to say next. "He is my cousin. I worked for him."

Alessandra's eyebrows flew up. "Oh."

Shame filled Trey as understanding crossed her face. "Yeah, not my finest moment. Pretty much tore my family apart when the truth came out."

"Why did you do it?" she asked quietly.

"That's a question I've asked myself about a thousand times. She made the offer one night and I took her up on it, like an idiot. We were really drunk at the time. She was very . . . attractive, and we'd spent a lot of time flirting during the year she lived at the ranch—which I now see wasn't harmless at all." He paused, hating the look of disappointment in her eyes. "I'm sure you'll think much less of me now that you know what happened."

Alessandra nodded her head. "It's a very bad thing to do, but I can imagine a woman like her would be hard to resist. She was gorgeous and very sexy."

"Ahh, it wasn't her fault. I knew better, no matter what she looked like."

"That's true."

"You know, the other question I've asked myself was why someone like her would want to sleep with me. I was only twenty at the time, just a ranch hand with a high school diploma. I think she might have been looking for a way out. She had been complaining about how bored and lonely she was. My cousin, Cole, was gone a lot, and she didn't have any friends there. I think she had grown to hate it and needed to do something to make it impossible for her to stay."

"So she used you?"

Trey tilted his head. "Maybe. But I don't want to make it sound like it was all her fault or anything. If she did use me, I was definitely a willing victim."

"I see." She stirred at what was left in her bowl. "But after, were you hurt?"

"I was. I thought I was in love with her. I tried to convince her that we should tell Cole and we could run off together. Dumb-ass." He stared down at the table.

"She didn't feel the same way?" Alessandra asked quietly.

Trey let out a little scoff. "Not at all. She told me I meant nothing to her. That it was a mistake. She went back home a couple of days later, before Cole even got back from the cattle drive he was on. She told everyone her father had had a heart attack and she needed to rush home. She broke up with Cole from here."

Alessandra shook her head. "That's terrible."

"Like I said, it was my own damn fault. I did my best to forget about how I'd betrayed Cole until one day she showed up with Tomas. Then it was time for me to face what I'd done."

"And you did. You took responsibility for what you did. That shows your true character."

"Don't give me too much credit, Alessandra. I'm not such a good person. I kept working for my cousin for over a year after, right up until I started school. I somehow managed to justify it in my mind, you know? I told myself that telling him what had happened would only hurt him. I told myself there was no point, since she'd left him. I even flirted with his new girlfriend, that chef you heard about from Gabriela."

"Why would you do that?" Alessandra gave him a hard look.

"I don't know. Part of me was just always used to flirting with girls. I liked it. But deep down, I think I was envious of Cole. He had everything I wanted. The ranch had been in his dad's family for a long time. My dad is an accountant. I grew up in the city but spent as much time as I could out at their place. But it's not the same, you know. It was in his bones. Cole's one of the best horse trainers in the state. He's ten years older than me, so he was always tougher, stronger, better at everything. Everyone who meets him loves him. And then he had Gabriela, and she seemed to want me, and I think maybe part of me felt like that made me as good as him for once."

Alessandra shifted in her chair uncomfortably. "Why are you telling me all of this?"

Trey suddenly realized that he himself was confused as to why he was unburdening himself to her. "I don't know, actually. I've never told anyone that before. Not even my brother. For some reason I feel like it's important for you to know the truth about me. I guess because you're investing so much time helping me, I feel like I owe you the truth, no matter how ugly it is. Maybe it'll make you hate me, but I'm not going to live a lie ever again. No excuses, no omissions. Just the truth of who I am."

She sat quietly for a minute before saying anything. "This is a lot to absorb. To be honest, I'm not sure what to think."

Trey looked over at her, feeling a bit sick about having just told her so much. "You're a really good person, Alessandra. It's clear in everything you do. I hope someday I'll be a man that someone like you can respect, a man that my son can look up to."

"You *are* a good person, Trey. I can see that in how you are with Tomas and in how you've even tried to take care of me these past weeks, even though you don't really know me. You already *are* someone Tomas can look up to. It would be different if you hadn't learned from what happened. But you have."

"You're being too easy on me."

"Not really. Some people use others, some get used. You got used. I know what that is like." When Alessandra met Trey's eyes, they weren't just seeing each other's faces, they were seeing each other's hearts. "My first real boyfriend turned out to have several other girlfriends. It turns out he was using sex to pay us all for helping him keep his grades up. He was at the University of Chicago on a football scholarship, and he conveniently found a girl who could help him with each subject. I was such a fool not to see the truth sooner. I even did some of his homework for him when he was away on team trips so he wouldn't get behind. Looking back, I can see that all the signs he didn't care about me were there. I just chose to ignore them in favour of what I wished was true."

"I'm sorry that happened to you."

"Don't be. It made me stronger. I won't be used by a man ever again."

"I'm assuming your next boyfriend was better."

Alessandra's face flushed as she glanced at the table. "That remains to be seen, actually. But I can say that now that I've had my eyes opened, I will never shut them again."

"Good for you." Trey stared at her, feeling completely unworthy of her. It was better that he hadn't kissed her. "You deserve a really great man, Alessa. Someone who will treat you right." Getting up, he cleared their bowls. "We should get some sleep. Tomorrow's going to be a big day."

"That it is. I'm very nervous. You are my first sort-of client."

"Don't be nervous. I have nothing but faith in your ability."

"I'm afraid we'll need more than that to win."

THIRTEEN

Trey sat at the back of the small courtroom, listening to the hum of the air conditioner. Alessandra sat next to him, nervously looking through the file on her lap for the tenth time since they had arrived. They'd been waiting for the judge for the past twenty minutes, each one feeling like an hour. Trey turned his attention back to the papers in Alessa's hands. They shook a little as she flipped from one to the next—the admission of paternity forms, the DNA test, his university transcripts and a character reference provided by one of his professors, all in English and translated into Portuguese.

Alessandra looked up at Trey, giving him her best attempt at a confident nod. She leaned in and whispered to him, "It will be okay."

Trey gave her a little nod back, then silently reviewed the advice Alessandra's professor had passed along. Give complete answers but don't ramble. Don't get overly emotional but speak from the heart. Most important, tell the truth.

When the judge arrived, Trey broke out in a cold sweat in spite of the comfortable temperature of the room. Trying not to fidget, he smiled at the woman who had been randomly assigned as ruler over his and Tomas's fate. Trey guessed she was in her late fifties, and she looked to be in a bad mood at the moment, unless that was just her general demeanour. She peered over the top of her glasses at him with a serious expression before looking back down to the forms in her hand.

"I am Judge D'Souza. I will handle your case. You are American. No Portuguese, yes?" she asked in a thick accent.

"Um, yes. I mean no, ma'am."

"No? You speak Portuguese?" Her face lit up a little.

"No. Sorry. No Portuguese." *Damn it, I blew the first answer already. Way to make a good impression, butthead.*

She pursed her lips together, then said something to the court reporter in her native language that caused the young woman to snicker. Turning back to Trey, she said, "No Portuguese? How can you raise a child if you can't speak to him?"

"I'd like to learn, ma'am. Also, my son speaks English."

Alessandra cleared her throat and addressed the judge in their native tongue, her voice shaking. The judge spoke back, her tone unmistakable.

"Is this woman your lawyer or your nanny?" Judge D'Souza asked Trey.

"Both, ma'am. She's very talented."

"You trust her?"

"Pardon me?"

She took off her glasses and used them to point at Alessandra. "She is a law student. You trust her to do this?"

"Yes, ma'am. I do."

"Did she tell you that by law the proceedings must be conducted in Portuguese?"

"Yes, ma'am, she told me."

"You can have a formal translator if you like, but we may have to reschedule if we can't find one. Or you can trust your nanny and have the transcripts translated afterwards. What would be your choice?"

"I'd like to go ahead, ma'am. I trust her, and the sooner I can get home with my boy, the sooner I can get him settled."

"Okay," she answered, flicking her hands in the air in disapproval. She addressed Alessandra and the prosecutor in Portuguese.

Trey watched, temporarily grateful that he wouldn't have to say anything for a while. He sat at the table for the next five minutes, a bundle of nerves as Alessandra handed the translations to the judge and the prosecutor and spoke on his behalf. Raking his sweaty palms over his lap, he wished he understood what was happening. He'd put his life and his son's in the hands of a law student, someone barely old enough to drink back in the US. Now, as he waited on pins and needles, he wondered if that had been a mistake. The judge looked very serious for the most part, but at one point she gave Alessandra a knowing smile and the two women laughed briefly at something she said.

Things grew quiet as the judge wrote something down. Alessandra gave Trey a little wink as they waited.

The judge looked at Trey for a moment. "Tell me about your son's mother."

Trey stood. "Her name was Gabriela Ferreira."

The judge nodded impatiently. "Yes, I know that. How did you have a child with her?"

"Oh, um, we met when she was in the US on vacation."

"How?"

"How did we meet?" Trey asked.

"Yes."

"She came to stay at a ranch I was working on."

"So, you were her boyfriend there?"

"Not exactly, ma'am."

The judge glared at him, clearly irritated. She said something to Alessandra in Portuguese. Alessandra turned to Trey and lowered her voice. "She thinks you are hiding something because you seem to be stalling and giving short answers. You need to give more detail."

Trey's entire face heated up with humiliation. He swallowed hard before speaking. "She had lived at the ranch for about a year. She was my cousin's girlfriend. One night, we went out and drank too much and ended up together." His eyes were glued to the floor as he finished speaking.

The judge shook her head in disgust. "Your own cousin?"

"Yes, ma'am. It's not something I'm proud of."

"You go with your cousin's girlfriend. For how long?"

Trey's face was full of confusion. "Oh, well, I don't really know. About fifteen minutes, maybe? Could have been ten. I was pretty intoxicated."

The judge suddenly burst into laughter, her entire body shaking for a long time as she tried to compose herself. "No, no, I mean . . ." She looked to Alessandra for help.

Alessandra filled in the blanks for her. "How long were you in a relationship with her?"

Trey blushed, feeling foolish. "That makes more sense. Just the one night, ma'am. Sorry."

The judge tried to hide a smile as she jotted on the pad again. She then gave Alessandra more instructions to pass along.

Once Trey was sure he understood what was expected of him, he continued. "I didn't know about Tomas until he was eight months old. Gabriela had returned to Brazil a couple of days after our . . . time together. She brought him back to the US about a year and a half later. We had the DNA test done, then I had the admission of paternity form drawn up. She returned to Brazil with him so her parents could help her out financially. She told me to finish school. I thought that would be the best way for me to really contribute to his life in the long run. I was a student and before that I worked as a ranch hand, so I couldn't help much."

Trey paused, waiting for the judge to finish making notes. He decided to go on. This was the only shot he would get to convince this woman that he wouldn't be a complete loser as a father. "Ma'am, I'm not proud of what I did. It was the worst mistake I've ever made. I hurt my cousin and the rest of my family and I'll always regret that. But I'd never take back what happened. I love my son more than I thought possible. I can't even believe how much, because I'm only just getting to know him. He's a really special little guy, so smart and just cute as anything. And he gives the best hugs . . . If you give me a chance, I'll make sure I give him the very best life I can. A great life, I hope."

The judge tapped her pen on the pad of paper as she stared at him for a moment before turning to the prosecutor. In an instant, the conversation became unintelligible for Trey again. The prosecutor spoke for a long time, pointing at Trey as he did, presenting papers of his own. Trey heard him say something about the Ferreiras. The judge seemed angry, her hand flying wildly as she spoke back to the man.

Judge D'Souza paused, asking Alessandra to translate. "He said that the Ferreiras have done a background check on you and that you have no assets, no home, no job, and they are concerned about letting you have custody without those things. He said their lawyer has requested that Judge D'Souza intervene on their behalf and put strict orders in place for you to get a house and a job before you can take Tomas. If not, they intend to fight for custody. She said that she doesn't like this type of coercion by the rich. And that there are many poor people in Brazil but the court doesn't take their children away. She also said she hates that they have made this ultimatum because it gives her no choice. To ignore their demands will only hurt you and ensure that you end up in a lengthy custody battle."

"You understand what the Ferreiras are asking?" the judge said.

"Yes, ma'am, I do."

"So, you will need to find someone to keep him while you go home. But you can't go yet. You need to stay in Brazil for a few more weeks until we verify that you are the father. I am ordering another DNA test, by request of the child's grandparents. I will need time to look over these other documents as well. Do you have a place to stay?"

Alessandra spoke up. "Your honour, he and his son can stay on my family's farm in Bebedouro. I have spoken with my grandfather, and he will allow them to live there as long as they are required to remain in Brazil. I'm moving back home. If Mr. Johnson chooses, he can leave Tomas with us when he goes home. I have been his primary caregiver for over two years now, and Tomas and I are very close. I believe this arrangement will be better than finding some stranger for him to live with on a temporary basis."

The judge turned to Trey. "You agree to this?"

"Yes, ma'am. As much as I don't want to leave him behind at all, if I have to, I believe having him stay with Alessandra would be the best option for my son. He's already been through more than any three-year-old should have to deal with."

The judge continued in Portuguese for a few minutes, then made some notes. Finally, she looked up at them again and said, "You can go for now, but first give my assistant the address of the farm. We need to know where to find you."

*   *   *

Walking out into the bright sunshine, he and Alessandra made their way down the courthouse steps before Alessandra burst into laughter. Trey looked down at her, his face full of confusion.

She laughed so hard she snorted, then grabbed Trey's forearm to steady herself. "Fifteen minutes! Maybe ten!"

Trey started to chuckle along with her, and before long, the two were standing in the middle of the sidewalk, laughing loudly enough to attract the attention of passersby.

"I'm sorry. I know I shouldn't laugh!" Alessandra managed.

"No, it's totally okay. I can't fucking believe I said that!" Trey shook his head and chuckled a little more. "Sorry for cussing. I was just so nervous I couldn't even think straight. Of course she didn't mean how long it took to have sex with Gabriela! I sounded like a total idiot!"

Alessandra waved off his self-deprecating remark. "Not at all. It was a confusing conversation. I think saying that helped, actually. She seemed to lighten up a lot afterwards. Plus, it showed you were willing to be honest."

"It showed I'm a dumb-ass, is what it did," Trey said as they started walking along the sidewalk again.

Alessandra opened her mouth to speak but Trey cut her off. "No, don't try to deny it. *Maybe ten.*"

He shook his head in disgust and they both started laughing again as they crossed the busy street. When the moment ended, they were quiet, both thinking about the courtroom and what lay ahead.

"Alessa, thank you for all you've done for Tomas and me," Trey said softly. "I'd be lost without you."

"It's nothing," she answered casually.

Trey stopped and put his hand on her arm, causing Alessandra to turn and face him.

"No, it's not nothing. What you've done for me, for Tomas—it's everything." His voice was thick with emotion, his handsome face all sincerity.

"*De nada*, Trey. You're welcome."

{77}

The connection between them was more than that between new friends, more than that between two people tied to each other by circumstances and by the desire to care for the same little boy. It was that of two people who longed for each other's touch.

A slight breeze blew a lock of Alessandra's hair across her cheek. Trey lifted his hand and tucked it behind her ear. "I want to take you out to dinner."

Alessandra paused for a second, considering. "I would love that. I'll call Priscila to see if Tomas can stay for a while longer."

FOURTEEN

The pair found themselves seated at a table in Ella, a trendy Italian restaurant. Alessandra sat on a cushioned red bench that ran the length of the wall, while Trey sat on a wooden chair across from her at the table for two. She crossed her legs under the table and shrugged off her suit jacket, revealing a fitted blue button-up shirt that brought out her eyes. "I've heard the food here is very good."

They opened their menus and Trey looked up at her with a slightly embarrassed expression. "I just realized I can't read any of this."

"Oh, right. Don't worry, I'll help you."

The server, a young man with light blond hair and a friendly grin, came by to take their drink orders. When he walked away, Trey took a moment to look around the restaurant before turning his gaze back to Alessandra. "So, is it me, or is it strange to be away from Tomas while we have dinner?"

"A little, yes. But he's having a wonderful time. Priscila said he woke up from his nap very happy and is playing with the other kids. He won't miss us."

"Good. If he's having fun, we should have fun too."

The waiter brought their wine and they ordered dinner.

Trey held up his glass to Alessandra. "Here's to you finishing school."

She touched her glass to his and took a long sip of the smooth liquid. "Thank you. It doesn't feel real yet, actually."

"I know what you mean. I still keep thinking I have to study every evening. I don't know how long that takes to go away."

"For some, I'm sure it's as soon as they finish their last exam, but you are not that type of guy. You are very driven."

"I could say the same about you. You're very impressive, Alessa. I hope you know that." Trey gave her a serious look.

"Oh, not really. I'm at most very, very normal. Easy to miss in a crowd."

"If anyone didn't notice you in a crowd, it would only be because you're so short."

Alessandra pretended to take offence at his comment. "Short? You know, that is not considered a compliment by most women."

"Why not? You're sort of like a sports car—compact and curvy, with a lot of power to you."

Alessa blushed at his description of her, tracing the rim of her wineglass seductively with her finger. "Well, when you explain it like that, it sounds better."

"I mean it in the best way. But it's not just how you look, it's also your mind that impresses me. You're really intelligent."

"Oh, no more than the average lawyer," she teased.

Trey smiled at her joke, then had another sip of wine. "What made you want to get into law, anyway?"

"Well, I believe it is important for a woman to be independent, and to do that she must have a good career. Also, I want to do something important with my life, to help people, of course. But mainly, I want to have a job that I'm passionate about. Something I love."

"I totally get that. I look at my dad and I can't even imagine doing what he does, day after day."

"He doesn't like his work?"

"Not really. He's an accountant. When I was in high school, I had to write a report on what my parents did for a living. One of the questions I had to ask them was if they enjoyed their work. I'll never forget my dad's answer. He told me that no one likes their job. They do what they have to so they can get by and, if they're really lucky, have enough for a few extras to give their families. It was the first time I realized that he wasn't necessarily happy with how his life had turned out, and I thought to myself, I'm *never* going to do that. I'm not going to waste most of my life doing work I hate. I figured I'd find my dream job and the money would start flowing in magically." He shook his head at himself.

"And now what do you think?"

"Now that I have a child depending on me, I'd definitely take some crappy desk job for the next twenty years if it meant he had what he needed. I don't even think I'd mind, really. Except that it would mean my old man was right all along."

The server brought out the salads, interrupting the moment. Alessandra picked up her fork and knife, then cut a sliver of mozzarella to taste along with the leafy greens. "So, how did you go from being a cowboy to being a business student?"

Trey gave her a sheepish grin. "To be honest, I originally went to university to meet girls. We had this team of college volleyball players come to the ranch and after they left, I realized what I had been missing out on."

Alessandra covered her mouth and laughed a little. "Some of your admissions are too honest for your own good."

"It's probably because I'm not smart enough to keep track of a bunch of lies," he said with a little wink.

"Oh please, this whole 'I'm just a dumb cowboy' routine won't work on me."

Giving her a crooked smile, Trey put on a thick southern drawl. "Well, shucks, little lady, it appears you're on to me."

Alessandra laughed for a moment. "I *am* on to you, and don't you forget it." She took a sip of her wine, her eyes smiling over the glass at him. "You know, if you only went to meet girls but instead you ignored them all and studied, it seems you failed to meet your goal."

"Uh-oh, are you going full lawyer on me?" Trey asked with a grin. "I shifted my focus, is all. Once I got there, I realized that studying might lead to a better future than tomcatting around." He got a mischievous look in his eye. "Besides, it's the rich guys who get the best women in the end."

Alessandra laughed. "Oh, so it's *still* about getting hot chicks!"

Trey chuckled along with her, then shook his head. "I didn't say *hot* chicks. I said the *best* women. I'm looking for the whole package—smart, funny, kind, strong."

"But I'm sure she'd need to have long legs and hair perfect all the time too."

Trey shook his head. "Nope. I prefer a girl who lets her hair look a little wild most of the time because she's too busy doing important things to care about what she looks like."

Warmth radiated through Alessandra's body at his words. She couldn't help but think he might be referring to her. Scared that he might say something to dash her hopes, she decided to change the subject. "So, if you got to pick your dream job when you got home, what would it be?"

"I'd definitely like to take what I've learned in school and have my own business. Something where I could be outside a lot of the time. Actually, I'd love to run my own ranch someday. But, like I said, at this point I'll take what I can get." Trey took a sip of wine. "And you said you want to move home to practise law?"

"Yes. I will try to join a small practice in my hometown,

Bebedouro. I miss it there, I miss my family. Life moves slower there than here. So, if I could have a good career surrounded by my family and friends, that would be my best dream."

"Did you ever think about starting a life somewhere totally new?"

"Not really. Bebedouro is my home. I've been away for long enough to know what I'm missing." She waited while Trey refilled her wineglass. "I have never fit in anywhere like I do there. Never found friends like my best friend, Cyssah. And my grandfather. There is no one who has ever believed in me like he does. I want to be near him so I can return all the care he has given me. At first I won't make much money, but after a while I will, so I can pay for someone to manage the farm for him. I'm afraid he's not a businessman, so a lot of money that he should be keeping slips through. We are not poor, but there is not much left for luxuries, either. And he works too hard. I want to see him slow down and enjoy the rest of his days."

"That's remarkably generous of you. And I'm assuming there's at least one guy back home waiting with bated breath for you to return."

"No. Of course not."

Trey raised an eyebrow. "I bet you're wrong on that one."

Alessandra rolled her eyes. "Trust me, I'm not. I have never left any place where men are longing for me to return."

Their main dishes were brought out. For Trey, Alessandra had ordered *milanesa*, breaded steak with a crunchy coating, and for herself, pink beet tortelli sprinkled with walnuts and wilted sage. They took a moment to taste their first bites before Trey picked up the conversation where it had left off.

"I find that hard to believe, that there aren't heartbroken guys everywhere you've been."

"I don't *think* you are mocking me, but I can't come up with another reason for you to say that."

"Mocking you? I would never do that. I'm serious. Alessa, you're a really beautiful person. Not just how pretty you are, but inside. Any guy would be very lucky to have a girl like you. How do you not know that?"

"Careful observation of men in the world." She popped a bite of pasta into her mouth.

"Those were boys. I think you're going to notice that as you start meeting men, you'll find you're exactly what they're looking for."

Alessandra stared at him for a moment, wishing with everything in her that he meant she was exactly what *he* was looking for. She took a sip of wine, turning to watch a couple lazily walking past the window, hand in hand. "Can we change the subject? I don't really like talking about myself in this way."

"Sure. Let's talk about how amazing you were in court today."

She laughed, then tried to level him with a mock glare. "You couldn't understand what I was saying. Maybe it was all nonsense."

"Oh no, I understood the entire thing."

"Really? How?"

"I've picked up Portuguese in the last month. I'm fluent now," he said with a teasing grin.

"Oh, have you? *Você bebeu?*"

"*Sim.*"

"Yes? What did I ask you?"

"You asked if I was good in bed, which, quite honestly, is a little bit forward of you . . ."

Alessandra laughed loudly, covering her mouth. "I asked if you were drunk."

"Right." Trey snapped his fingers as though he had just remembered something. "I keep getting those phrases mixed up. Other than that, totally fluent."

Tucking a curl behind her ear, she shook her head at him, feeling a little tipsy. "You're fun. You know, you're not what I expected. When you came, I was confused. I thought you would be much older and maybe very cold. And I needed to figure you out as soon as I could for Tomas's sake." She stared into his eyes for a moment. "Until you got here, I thought I was the only person left in the world who really loved Tomas. I hope it doesn't upset you to hear me say that."

"It doesn't. I'm glad Tomas has another person in the world who wants to protect him as fiercely as I do."

"I would do anything for that little boy. He has my heart."

Nodding, Trey answered, "Mine too. He's just so vulnerable and so little."

"He is. But he's strong too, and he'll be okay now that he has you. In these past weeks, I've realized that there is no one I'd be happier to see him with than you. You're wonderful with him."

"A lot of it I'm learning from watching you. I'm secretly glad I can't take him back to the US too soon. I still have a lot to learn."

"In that case, you should never go back. I am *so* full of wisdom, it would take a lifetime for me to pass it all along." Alessandra tried to make it sound like she was joking, but she knew the expression on her face was betraying her.

Trey's eyes locked on hers. "It's too bad that you've got your future all planned out already. Otherwise . . . well . . ."

Alessandra gave him a wistful look, begging her heart not to want more. "In another life, maybe . . ."

FIFTEEN

A few days later, Trey, Alessandra and Tomas loaded themselves onto a bus to make the long trip to Bebedouro. Alessandra, with Trey's help, had worked tirelessly to pack and prepare for the move. Since their dinner out, nothing more had happened between them. They both realized that they needed to keep things platonic, no matter how much they longed for each other.

They rode along for a few hours before stopping for a lunch at a small restaurant along the highway. Tomas ran around in large circles in the grass near the patio while Trey and Alessandra finished eating.

Once they were settled back in their seats on the bus, Trey let out a sigh. "I'm so glad to be out of the city finally."

"Me too. I can't wait to get home. I've missed everything about it."

"I can relate to that. It's been a few years since I've been home." Trey leaned his head back against the seat.

"I hope you will enjoy life on the farm. I think both of you will like it there. It's a small orange plantation but there are also four horses, a few cows, lots of chickens. It's very peaceful and beautiful. Like heaven on earth."

"Heaven?" Tomas sat up and looked excitedly at Trey. "We go find *Mãe* today?"

"What's that, Tomas?" Trey asked, feeling a stab to his heart.

"We go to my mom. Long bus ride to heaven to get *Mãe*?"

"Oh, Tomas, no. I shouldn't have said that. We're not going to heaven, we're going to my family's farm. I meant . . ." Alessandra's voice trailed off and she looked helplessly at Trey.

Trey's brow furrowed. "No, little man. We can't go to her. There's no bus to the heaven where your mom is. It's more like, she's gone way up into the sky and we can't ever get her back."

Tomas's bottom lip quivered and his eyes welled up with tears. "No *Mãe*?"

"No *Mãe*, Tomas. I'm sorry."

Tomas's face grew angry. "I want my mom! You take me!"

Alessandra's eyes filled with tears. "Tomas, we would go to your *mamãe* if there was a way. But your dad is telling the truth. There is no bus to heaven." She reached out to touch Tomas's face but he recoiled from her.

"You take me now! I want her now!" Tomas balled up his fists and slammed them into Trey's chest before dissolving into tears. He sat rigid on Trey's lap, his mouth hanging open and his entire face turning red, as though he had stopped breathing. Several tiny gasps escaped his lungs before he finally let out a long wail.

Trey pulled him in close to his chest and rubbed his back, not caring about the curious passengers turning to stare at them. His little boy was in pain and all that mattered was helping him through it. "I know, buddy. You go ahead and cry. It's sad that your mom isn't with you anymore."

Tomas sobbed until he finally dropped off for his nap, his breath still catching every few seconds even though he was asleep.

Alessandra turned to Trey and spoke quietly. "I'm so sorry. I never should have said that."

"You didn't mean anything by it. Besides, like you told me, he needs to get it out, right?"

"Yes, but it just breaks my heart to see him hurting." Alessandra's voice cracked as she ran a finger along the little boy's cheek.

"Mine too."

They sat in silence for a while, neither sure what else could be said on the topic. The steady motion of the bus, along with the sight of Tomas sleeping, had Alessandra's eyelids growing heavier by the minute even though she willed herself to stay awake. She didn't want to fall asleep in front of Trey, only to end up with her mouth hanging open and snoring sounds coming out. Or worse, drool. That would be horrifying. She fought sleep for as long as she could, her head bobbing down then jerking back up again several times before she finally gave in.

She woke to find her head on Trey's shoulder. Straightening up, she looked over at him, feeling embarrassed. "Sorry about that."

"Why? You needed some rest." He gave her an easy smile.

"But I was leaning on you when you already have Tomas sleeping on your lap. That must have been so uncomfortable."

"Not at all. I'm a big guy, I can handle two tiny people sleeping on me." He angled his head to look at her and lowered his voice, seeming a bit unsure of what he was about to say. "Besides, you smell really nice.'"

Blushing a little, Alessandra smiled. "Must be my shampoo."

* * *

Soon the city limits for Bebedouro came into view. Minutes later, they stepped off the bus, weary and a little sweaty. Tomas was still fast asleep on Trey's shoulder, his cheeks red, as Trey stepped down into the bright sunlight and fresh air.

They stood with the other tired passengers, waiting for the driver to unload the baggage. Trey carefully transferred Tomas to Alessandra so he could help an older gentleman with the heavy bags. Alessandra smiled to herself as she watched him, realizing how different he was from what she had originally expected. She had been so sure he would be a total jerk, or at least very irresponsible. But in the past few weeks she had discovered that he was the complete opposite. Each day, he surprised her with some thoughtful gesture or unexpected kindness.

A middle-aged woman standing beside her smiled at Alessandra. "You have a beautiful family. I was watching you on the ride, and your husband certainly dotes on you both. You are very lucky."

"Oh, um, thanks," she answered, glad that Trey couldn't understand what the woman had said.

Just then, she heard her sister's voice. "There she is! Alessandra!"

Alessandra turned to see her grandpa and Betina hurrying over, both sporting broad grins. *"Ali está minha garota!"* Carlos called.

Alessandra grinned back, waving enthusiastically with her free hand instead of running to them. *"Olá!"*

Her granddad gave her a long hug and a kiss on the cheek, careful not to disturb Tomas. *"Você está muito bonita."*

"Oh please, I'm a sweaty mess."

"Mesmo assim, você está incrível," he replied, smiling adoringly at her. He put his hand gently on Tomas's little back, leaning in to get a glimpse of his face.

Betina kissed Alessandra's cheek. "Welcome home," she said quietly. Lowering her voice to a whisper, she pointed in Trey's direction. "Oh my God. Is that him?"

He was unloading the last of the bags, the muscles in his arms rippling as he worked.

Alessandra nodded, watching her sister's reaction. Betina raised her eyebrows and muttered, "Oh, wow."

"Yeah, I know." The pair tried to hide their giggles as they watched Trey hand the other passengers their bags. The driver shook his hand, thanking him profusely for his help. Trey nodded and smiled at the man before slinging Alessandra's two bags over his shoulder and picking up their suitcases. He approached them, carrying the bags with ease before lowering them to shake hands with Alessandra's grandfather.

"Carlos Santos," he said. "Hello," he managed in English.

"Nice to meet you, sir," Trey replied, holding his hand out to Carlos. "I just can't thank you enough for offering to put up Tomas and me in your home. I'm honestly not sure what I would have done otherwise."

"Yes, yes," Carlos responded, shaking Trey's hand and then patting the back of Trey's hand with his other one. He said something to Alessandra in Portuguese and gave Trey an apologetic look.

"He said his English is very poor and he is sorry he can't say more to you. He hopes you won't feel left out when we speak in Portuguese."

"Please tell him that I'm going to consider it my job to learn as much Portuguese as I can while I'm here. And thank him for his generosity in opening his home to us."

Alessandra passed the message along, and Carlos reached up to pat Trey on the shoulder with a warm smile, his sun-baked face creasing with the effort.

Betina glanced over at Trey. "If you want to learn Portuguese, I'm afraid my mother and I won't let you practice very much. We are both working on our English. My mother has wanted to work in tourism for many years now and has finished the courses, but she thinks her English is too bad."

"Well, I'm happy to help if you like. Maybe I can sweet talk Alessa into teaching me Portuguese," Trey said.

Betina gave him a knowing grin. "I'm sure you could."

Bebedouro, Brazil

Trey stared out the window as they drove past field after field of orange trees in full bloom, reaching the farm fifteen minutes outside Bebedouro. Just as they turned up the driveway to the Santos family farm, Tomas woke. Trey watched as his son rubbed his eyes and blinked slowly. He smiled up at Trey before peering out the window. Trey's gaze followed that of his son to take in the first glimpse of their new home. The sun was just setting, giving the most peaceful glow to the world. Lining the long driveway were rows of old orange trees stretching over the lane as though trying to reach for each other. They were ripe with blossoms that gave off a wonderful, deliciously light scent as the truck rolled slowly toward the house.

Tomas smiled over at his dad and took a big whiff. "Mmm."

The house itself was perfectly suited to its environment, even though it had most certainly seen better days. It was a long ranch-style home that had been brilliant white at one point but had yellowed slightly with time and weather. The red, clay-tiled roof and dark wood window frames, rounded at the tops, gave the house an inviting appearance. Shrubs and plants at various stages of growth surrounded the house, and a slightly overgrown lawn stretched out from the shrubbery to the driveway. Everything about this place was tropical and lush. Two rows of wide steps led to the covered porch that wrapped around the house and undoubtedly served to protect the house from the heat of the midday sun. Arched double doors welcomed visitors at the front entrance.

As soon as the truck stopped in front of the house, Lorena Santos walked out the door. She stood on the porch, wiping her hands on a dishtowel. She had the same tiny frame as Betina, and the lovely features that both of her daughters shared. Her dark hair was pulled back in a loose bun and she wore a pale green housedress. She smiled broadly as her father parked.

Hugs were exchanged among introductions and handshakes.

A small grey cat meandered over, staring at the party curiously. Tomas lit up with excitement when he saw the small animal. "Cat! I pet cat?"

Alessandra nodded to him. "Yes. She's a nice cat, but you have to be gentle with her, okay?"

Tomas nodded and took off toward the animal, causing her to dart across the lawn and under the porch. Carlos watched, chuckling a little as Tomas, looking disappointed, returned to the grown-ups.

"*Onde está o gato?*" Carlos asked, putting his hands up in the air.

Tomas smiled at him and pointed under the house. "*Ali embaixo.*"

Carlos gave him a smile and held out his hand. "*Aham. Vem aqui comigo.*"

"He will help you get the cat, Tomas. He's going to put some milk on a plate for you to give to her," Alessandra told him. Turning to Trey, she said quietly, "It drives my mother nuts. You'll see."

Lorena turned to her father and said something Trey didn't understand. He watched as the old man waved her off without looking back and went into the house. Something about the scene made Trey feel right at home, and he could tell already that he was going to like Carlos.

"I think Tomas is going to be happy here," Trey remarked.

"And my father will enjoy having another little one to spoil. Lately he just has that skinny cat." Lorena said, shaking her head before announcing that it was time for everyone to wash up for dinner.

"I hope you're hungry, Trey," Betina said as they walked out the back door from the kitchen onto the tiled patio. "My mother has made enough food to feed the US army tonight."

Before he could answer, Lorena interjected, "He needs good food after only Alessandra's cooking."

"Oh, actually, ma'am, Alessandra is an excellent cook. Her meals have been a real treat for me." Trey smiled over at Alessandra reassuringly.

"Of course," Lorena replied. "I only joke with her."

"Right." Trey nodded in agreement but couldn't help but notice the tight smile on Alessa's face as they made their way to the table.

Trey took in the colours and incredible smells of the food laid out on a long wooden table under a pergola, understanding immediately that Betina hadn't been kidding. There were several salads, a bowl of roasted potatoes, a basket of small rolls, a cast iron pot filled with black bean stew, and a whole chicken on a platter as well as a plate of beef cut into strips. Two bottles of wine flanked the food on either end of the long table.

Alessa pointed to the various dishes, offering explanations of each one. The rolls were called *pão de queijo* and were baked with cheese in them. The stew was *feijoada* and was similar to chili, but with beef and sausage in it. She explained that these were all traditional Brazilian dishes and family favourites. They dished the food out, making sure Trey got a lot of everything before they began to eat.

Carlos held up the wine bottle to Trey.

"*Obrigado*," Trey said, smiling at Carlos.

"Please pass the rolls," Alessa said to Betina, who was nearest the basket. Tomas, who was seated in a wooden high chair next to her, was trying to wear his plate as a hat.

Lorena looked down the table at Trey. "The *pão de queijo* was Alessa's best food as a girl. She ate so many we called her our chubby little cheese roll."

Alessa's face turned a deep shade of red. "It is for Tomas. Please pass me the salad, *Mãe*."

Carlos patted his granddaughter's hand, seeming to have caught the conversation. Based on the sympathetic look he gave Alessandra, Trey guessed this was a scene that had played out more than once. He hadn't been raised to make fun of people and seeing Alessandra's mother make her so uncomfortable bothered him. "Alessandra's quite the impressive young woman. You must be very proud."

Lorena nodded. "Yes, of course I am."

Trey took a sip of wine. "Betina said you'd like to work in tourism. I've always thought that would be a very interesting job. Fun too, maybe."

Lorena waved a hand dismissively. "It's a silly idea. I'm needed here."

Alessandra sat up. "You know, *Mãe*, now that I'm back, you could go. I will stay here with *Vô* and help run the house."

Lorena shook her head. "No. You will only fall in love with some young man and leave my father alone. I need to stay."

"No I won't. I want to be here with *Vô*. I would never let him down like that."

"You can't know that," Lorena said. "Love does not come when you should have it. If it comes at all, it is always at the wrong time." She gestured to the table. "But now is the right time for food."

The rest of the meal passed pleasantly enough. After dinner, Lorena commandeered Betina to help with the cleanup while Alessandra took Tomas for his bath and Trey unloaded their things from the truck, bringing Tomas's and Alessa's bags to her room and his own things to a tiny house on the property. Alessa and Trey had decided it was best for Tomas to sleep with her in the big house for a little while, until they were settled in and he was more comfortable with Trey.

{94}

Lorena led him out to the small house that would be his temporary home. She explained that it had once been used for hired help, but in the past years it had been used for guests. Unlocking the door, Lorena stepped out of the way to let Trey through. Off to the left of the entrance was a tiny kitchen with a table for two, a few bright blue cupboards with colourful curtains in place of doors, the smallest stove Trey had ever seen and an equally diminutive refrigerator. To the right was a living room with an ancient television topped with rabbit ears, a loveseat and one armchair. Two doors at the back of the room led to the bedroom and a simple bathroom.

"I'm sure you will find it small," she said.

"This will be just fine. It's much bigger than the dorm I've been living in." Trey smiled warmly at her. "I really can't tell you how grateful I am that you're letting us stay here. It means the world to me."

Lorena gave an appreciative nod at his show of gratitude. "If it will keep your family together, that is an important cause. Nothing is more important than family."

"I agree."

"You know I have no husband so I must do some of the jobs of a father. Today, a father would tell you to keep your pants zipped up. You can live here but not if you are trying to sleep with one of my daughters. That day, I would have another job to do, and you would find it much more painful than this talk. Is this clear?"

Trey swallowed hard. "Yes, ma'am."

"Good." Lorena gave him a hard stare before walking out.

Trey stared at the door for a second after she closed it. "Okay, glad that's over."

SIXTEEN

Trey took a few minutes to put his bags into the bedroom and unpack his toiletries before making his way back to the main house to read a bedtime story to Tomas. He sat on the floor in Alessandra's room with his legs stretched out in front of him and his son on his lap. Alessandra busied herself putting away her clothes and preparing the small toddler-sized bed for Tomas while Trey read out loud.

A poster of Justin Timberlake caught Trey's eye, and he suddenly realized the room was still that of a schoolgirl, complete with stuffed animals on a pink bedspread. "JT fan?" Trey asked Alessandra, nodding to the poster.

Alessandra wore a sheepish grin. "Oh, I don't know why I haven't taken that down yet. Ignore him, please."

Trey pressed his lips together, trying not to laugh, which prompted a stern look from Alessandra. "Aren't you supposed to be reading?"

"I am, but I can't help wondering if maybe my lawyer is a little younger than I originally thought," he teased.

Alessandra laughed in spite of herself. "You're free to find yourself another lawyer." She pursed her lips together and shook her head. "I like things to stay the same. Is that so bad?"

"Not at all. There's comfort in that, isn't there?"

"Yes," Alessandra answered, seeming to relax a bit.

"Besides, he is bringing sexy back," Trey said, referring to the poster again.

Alessandra gave him an exasperated look. "You better be careful or I'll fire you, Mr. Johnson. Lawyers can do that, you know."

"Ah, you wouldn't fire me, I'm your best client."

"Yes, but you're also my worst client. Now read." She pointed to the book.

Trey did as he was told, continuing the story for Tomas but making sure to glance up at Alessandra with a smirk every chance he got. When the story was finished, he carried his son over to his new bed. It had a beautiful wooden frame that looked like it had been carved by hand.

"This is a very nice bed," Trey remarked.

"Thank you. My grandfather made it for me."

"He's obviously quite talented," Trey said. "What do you think, Tomas? A cozy bed, just the right size for you. I'd say you're pretty lucky to get to sleep here."

Tomas nodded eagerly, then snuggled into the pillow, clearly tired. Alessandra handed him his blanket and his favourite stuffed animal, a well-worn blue puppy, before she tucked him in. "Here you go. You've been a very good boy all day on the long bus ride. I'm proud of you," she told Tomas.

"I'll let you get him to sleep," Trey said quietly, bending down to give Tomas a kiss.

"Dad, stay for song time," Tomas said. It was the first time he'd asked for Trey to stay at bedtime.

"Yeah? Okay, buddy." Trey grinned as he flopped down onto the floor beside his son's bed and held his little hand. Seeing the embarrassed look on Alessandra's face, Trey gave her a smile. "You've heard me sing. There's no way you're worse."

Alessandra winced as she sat on the edge of the bed and started to sing. The first notes came out so quietly they were almost inaudible, but she soon found her confidence. Trey watched and listened, entranced by her voice. Even though he didn't understand the words, their tenderness and love came through. Trey watched as she traced little patterns on Tomas's face with her fingertip. His eyes soon travelled to her full lips. He found himself wishing he could kiss those lips. Deciding it was safer to look away, he fixed his stare on Tomas, whose eyelids were now closed. Rubbing his thumb over his son's palm, Trey felt a sense of contentment that was entirely new to him. They were together here in this tranquil place, and he knew instinctively that this would be a good home for his son, even if they only stayed a short time.

* * *

When they left the room, Trey quietly closed the door behind them and touched Alessandra's arm with his hand. "That was a lovely song. I can see why Tomas insists on having you finish his bedtime every night. You have a beautiful voice."

"Oh, not really." Alessandra rolled her eyes.

"What's the song about?"

She suddenly looked very embarrassed. "It's maybe not such a good lullaby, but I know all the words so I sing it. It's actually a song by an old rock band, *Legião Urbana*. It's about a boy missing the girl he loves. Translated, the name is something like, 'Wind at the Seashore.'"

His eyes locked on hers. "Why aren't they together?"

"The song doesn't tell you. But the singer goes to the sea to try to get over her. He hopes the wind and the waves will wash her out of his heart. He knows she is gone but he still feels she is with him. It's very sad."

"Yes, but maybe having someone to miss is better than never letting anyone close." Trey stared down into her eyes, sexual tension surging between them.

Alessa swallowed hard. "Letting someone close, that sounds pretty risky."

He took a step forward, erasing the distance between them. "But so worth it."

Her eyes flicked down to his lips and then back up. The sound of someone clearing their throat down the hall broke the spell and sent them both moving in different directions, Trey accidentally heading toward the other bedrooms when he should have been on his way outside.

They laughed silently for a second before both going to the kitchen, where Lorena sat flipping through a magazine. She took a sip of coffee, giving Trey a hard look over the rim of her mug.

"I should go get settled in for the night," he said, trying to wipe the guilty look off his face.

"Me as well. I'm quite tired from our trip." Alessandra tried to sound businesslike.

"Same here. Have a good sleep."

"You too. See you in the morning."

He hurried out, shutting the door behind him without looking back.

* * *

After three hours of lying on Betina's bed with her, engaging in full-on girl talk, Alessandra made her way to the bathroom. She brushed her teeth, letting the day's events float through her brain like a dream. She thought of waking up on Trey's shoulder and what he'd said about how she smelled, and how he had teased her about her room, and then that moment when she was singing and Trey was holding Tomas's hand in his. When her mind wandered to what had happened in the hall, she sighed happily. She thought of the look on his handsome face and let herself dream for a few minutes, imagining that Tomas was their son and that Trey always looked at her that way.

She pictured him standing up and the two of them sneaking out of the room, as they had done earlier, but this time, instead of going their separate ways, they would go to the bedroom they shared and he would undress her and move the hair off her neck so he could kiss her. There was nothing on earth that sounded more perfect to her. She could feel his lips on her skin and imagined running her hands over his hard body, knowing he was hers. That slice of heaven would be worth any price. Staring at herself in the mirror for a long moment, she was surprised that she found herself looking quite lovely tonight.

* * *

Trey lay in bed in his small room, staring at a crack that ran the length of the plaster ceiling. Somehow, being in a separate house from Tomas and Alessandra made him feel very alone. He hadn't realized just how used to being with them he'd become. Tomas wouldn't be able to pad into his room to wake him up as he had done every morning for the past month. The knowledge of this didn't sit well with Trey and made him want to get Tomas moved into this house as soon as possible.

How had he suddenly found himself here? In a stranger's guest house in the middle of rural Brazil? Only the month before, he had been in his dorm room in San Diego, where it had never occurred to him how alone he was. In a very short period of time, he had grown so attached to both Tomas and Alessandra that he found himself wanting to be near them all the time.

Thinking of his son's tiny hand in his own earlier that evening made him smile. Their connection was so strong that Trey's concerns about being a father were quickly starting to fade. He knew he would love Tomas and protect him with everything he had to give. And what he didn't have now, he would get for Tomas.

What seemed strange to him was how fiercely he wanted to protect Alessandra too. He had come to Alessandra's defence twice against her own mother, and his reaction had surprised him both times. It had come so easily to him. How the hell had that happened? He thought of Alessa—how lovely she was, how soothing her voice was as she sang to Tomas. He loved the sound of the soft, beautiful song and her rich accent. She was enchanting. She was warmth personified. She drew him to her with her generosity and her laugh as much as she did with that curvy body of hers. There was no denying it, he wanted her, and after tonight in the hall it had become clear that she wanted him right back. He thought of everything she'd done for him since he had gotten to Brazil. She had somehow managed to find a solution to each of his problems—all of which would have been insurmountable were he on his own. It was as though he'd been sent an angel at the exact moment he needed one, but he had no idea what he'd done to deserve her.

He didn't know how much longer he'd be able to stop himself from acting on the need coursing through his veins day and night. He fluffed his pillow and tried to find a comfortable position, but his restlessness was now reaching a fever pitch. If only she would knock on that door right now.

SEVENTEEN

The next morning, in spite of his trouble falling asleep, Trey woke just as the sun was starting to rise. Blinking for a moment, he rolled over to check the time on his cellphone. It was a little after 6 a.m., and his restlessness from the night before hadn't gone away. He decided to get up and spend the day burning off that energy, in hopes of reducing his lust to a dull roar. Getting up, he made his way to the bathroom to brush his teeth and splash some cold water on his face. As he dried his hands on a towel, he glanced out the window to see Carlos walking out to the field, pushing a wheelbarrow in the low light of dawn.

Trey caught up with the old man just as he reached a crooked fence post on the edge of the property. He watched as Carlos let go of the handles of the wheelbarrow and took a rag out of his back pocket to wipe his face.

"Good morning, sir," Trey called. "Can I give you a hand?"

Carlos turned with a surprised smile and a nod in Trey's direction. "*Olá*."

"This fence has seen better days," Trey said as he straightened the loose fence post with one hand. Plucking a shovel out of the wheelbarrow, he began to dig around the post to loosen the dirt. Trey made quick work of digging a hole around the post. He continued to dig until he unearthed the cause of the problem. A large rock had made its way up from below, causing the post to shift. Trey dug it out and put it into the wheelbarrow before continuing to dig. "There's always at least one more waiting," he said, referring to the rock.

Carlos peered over his shoulder as Trey found the next culprit. He gave Trey a nod of approval as the second rock was deposited into the wheelbarrow. Carlos opened a bag of cement mix and poured some of the powder into a plastic bucket, then added water from an old jug and began to mix it with a wooden spatula.

"How did you do that?" Trey asked as he watched the cement form to just the right consistency. "You didn't even measure!"

Carlos seemed to get the gist of what Trey was saying from his tone and gestures. He nodded, saying simply, "Okay."

"That's impressive, sir. That's not something you can learn on Google. Well, I mean you could Google it, but I imagine it takes years to be able to just do that by feel." He cleared the dirt from around the hole as Carlos continued to stir the contents of the bucket.

"This is sure a beautiful place you've got here, sir. It makes me realize how much I miss life on a ranch," he said as he evened out the hole for the cement.

Trey looked up at his host, receiving another smile and nod from him. "You don't understand a word I'm saying, do you?" He paused, then continued to dig and talk. "In that case, I might as well get something off my chest that's been stuck there for about a month now. I have very strong feelings for your granddaughter. I've never met a girl quite like her before. She's pretty as a peach and obviously very smart and so kind. She's been a real lifesaver for me since I got here. And she's amazing with Tomas. He loves her to bits, which makes sense, really. She's so warm and fun too. As far as I can tell, she's basically perfect." Trey stopped digging for a moment and leaned on the shovel. "Your daughter told me to keep it in my pants last night. I guess maybe I'm not hiding my feelings as well as I thought I was."

Getting back to work, Trey continued talking. "Your daughter's a little hard on Alessandra, don't you think? To be honest, some of the things she said last night at supper bothered me a lot. I don't think parents should make fun of their kids, do you? I mean, the world's cruel enough. Shouldn't parents help build their kids up whenever they can? I don't mean to be disrespectful or anything. I just felt bad for Alessa, is all."

"Okay," Carlos answered again.

Soon the hole had been filled and the two were making their way back to the house, this time with Trey pushing the wheelbarrow and feeling a deep sense of satisfaction at having completed the first in what he hoped would be many much-needed improvements to the farm.

The morning dew on the grass glittered as the sun's rays hit it. Trey looked ahead to the house; it had a magical quality in this light, and it made him realize that he needed to make his life's work on a farm or ranch somewhere so he could enjoy moments like this every day. Glancing over at Carlos, Trey cleared his throat. "I want to help out in any way that I can while I'm here. Please give me lots of jobs every day, alright?"

The back door to the main house slammed shut and Tomas came running toward them with Alessandra in tow. "Dad!" he called as he ran straight to Trey with his little arms swinging from side to side.

"Good morning, Tomas!" Trey called with a broad smile. He crouched down for a hug as Tomas reached him. "Did you have a good sleep, buddy?"

Tomas nodded. "Pancake time," he said enthusiastically.

"Do we get pancakes this morning?" Trey put him down and picked up the handles of the wheelbarrow again. "That sounds terrific. I need to put these tools away and then get washed up. You wanna come with me?"

"Yup." Tomas nodded and walked beside his dad, his little hand on the wheelbarrow next to Trey's.

"I bet you're going to make a great helper, aren't you?"

EIGHTEEN

Over the next few days, they fell into an easy rhythm. Trey would get up and feed the animals before Tomas woke. The family would eat breakfast together, and Tomas would follow Trey and Carlos around as they did chores on the farm. In the afternoons, Tomas napped and Carlos rested in his hammock in the shade while Trey worked on putting up a new tool shed next to the barn. He worked hard, managing to get the yard tidied up and looking much better. After supper, he would bathe Tomas and read to him, then sit as Alessandra sang. Each night, their feelings for each other grew stronger.

When they'd reluctantly leave the intimacy of that space, they would join the family to play dominoes in the kitchen before bed. Trey was picking up Portuguese one phrase at a time, and Lorena seemed to be easing up on him, which Alessa attributed to his hard work and efforts to remain friendly with her.

Trey managed to sneak in time to search the Internet for jobs back in the US, trying to figure out a solid plan to prove to the court that he could provide for his son. Alessandra had filed the necessary paperwork to transfer Trey's case to the local courts and had left her resumé at all of the local law firms as well as the courthouse. She watched as Trey grew closer to Tomas, enjoying those little moments when the two walked to the barn together hand in hand, Trey looking down at his little boy as Tomas chatted and jumped around. The more relaxed Trey became with her family and Tomas, the more his true personality came through. He was playful and had a wonderful sense of humour, effortlessly making everyone in the family laugh—even her mother, who was not quick to enjoy a joke.

On Saturday afternoon, Alessandra sang along quietly to the radio as she cooked. Trey had taken Tomas to her room for his nap. The entire Santos family would be arriving soon for a dinner to celebrate Alessandra finishing her law degree and coming home. It was a day she was very much looking forward to. Their parties were so full of joy and laughter, with all the ladies working together in the kitchen, sharing little wisdoms and teasing each other while the men stood around the barbecue until they finally all came together to eat and drink late into the evening at long tables set out on the patio.

Betina and her mother had gone out to the market to get some last-minute items. Carlos was dozing in his hammock under the shade of two trees on the other side of the yard. Alessa could see him from the window and she smiled, grateful to be home to see her *avô* in the familiar ritual of his afternoon rest. She had worried about him since his heart attack, often feeling a nagging sense of doom, as though she were running out of time to be with him. But now that she was here, that feeling had become little more than an occasional whisper.

It was a hot day and the oven was heating up the kitchen, making her sweat a little in spite of the tank top and light summer skirt she wore. Her white apron tugged at her neck as she worked. She was making *pão de queijo* and had her hands in the doughy mixture. She'd just added the egg and cheese, the final step before forming little balls. Wiping the hair away from her face with her arm, she wished she had remembered to tie it back before getting started. Trying to ignore her hair, she started scooping portions of dough onto a spoon and rolling them into balls in her hands. She hummed to herself, feeling blissfully content. At the sound of Trey's voice, she turned and saw him watching her.

"What are you building?" he asked, stepping toward her and peering over her shoulder at the bowl.

"Those little cheese buns," she answered, trying in vain to get her hair out of her eyes again with her upper arm.

"Mmm. *Pão de* . . ." His voice trailed off. "Don't tell me. I think I can remember . . ."

Smiling over her shoulder, she waited expectantly for a moment.

"Nope. You'll have to tell me." He shook his head and grinned at her. "There's no way it's coming back. I got kicked in the head by a horse when I was a kid and now my memory's shot."

"Really?" Alessa's face fell.

"No. Not really. I'm just a dumb-ass."

Alessa laughed. The sound was genuine and full and brought a little twinkle to Trey's eyes.

"It's a hard name. *Pão de queijo*," she replied as her hair fell forward into her face again. "I'm the dumb-ass, as you say. I forgot to tie my hair back. My mom will kill me if I get any in the buns."

Glancing at her messy hands, he gave her a thoughtful look. "Maybe I could help you out. Do you have something to tie it back?"

"Yes." She hesitated, her voice soft. "There should be a band in the front pocket of my apron. If you don't mind digging around in there." She turned her body to him, carefully holding up her hands so as not to get dough on him.

She sucked in her tummy as Trey reached in and found a hair elastic, holding it up triumphantly. Turning to face the counter again, Alessa stood completely still as he lifted his hands to her hair.

"I have to warn you, this won't exactly be a pro job," he said as he carefully gathered her hair off the nape of her neck. "It's my first ponytail."

"That's okay, I'm not going to a formal event. As long as it holds, it's fine."

"It should hold." His words came out slowly as he slipped the elastic over her hair and then tucked the hair through. He stood close behind her as he worked, inhaling her scent. It reminded him of his dream. She smelled delicious, like peaches, and her hair felt like silk. Letting his feet inch forward, he could feel the warmth of her body close to his. A strong desire to run his hands over her curves came over him. Being around her was like walking into the deepest, warmest hug. He loved everything about her, from her bright smile to the way she tilted her head a little when she talked with Tomas, as though she were really listening.

The light blue tank top she wore showed off her tanned skin. Swallowing hard, he fought the urge to ball up her skirt in his fists and lift it. He noticed that she had stopped working and had leaned her body back ever so slightly, turning her head to the side as if anticipating something more.

"Can you also loosen the tie on my apron? It's a bit too tight." Her voice was almost inaudible.

"Sure," he answered, grateful for another chance to touch her. Moving the ponytail to the side, his fingers brushed along her neck as he untied the strings, an act that was unexpectedly intimate. Retying the bow, he then let his fingers glide slowly along her collarbones. He knew he shouldn't but he couldn't help himself. The heat between them was building to something almost tangible. "There. How's that?" he asked, his voice thick with desire.

"Much better," she answered, turning her face over her shoulder.

Trey lowered his face to hers, his lips now touching her cheek.

Alessa closed her eyes as Trey let his lips skim over her smooth skin. She felt hot to the touch and soft, like satin. He traced her bare shoulders and arms with his fingertips so gently, he wasn't sure if she could even feel it. He watched as she licked her lips. Those full, beautiful lips he'd been longing to kiss for weeks now. Searching for her mouth with his, he finally allowed himself that first touch. His lips barely brushed against hers. Closing his eyes, he willed himself to back away from her, but he couldn't. He needed to do this. Her lips parted a little as if to say she needed this too. The temptation of being so near her without touching had grown utterly impossible for him to deny. His tongue slid carefully in between her lips and he finally got that first taste of her.

Lifting his hand to her face, he angled her head back. Her body turned to face his now, and he closed the space between them, feeling her breasts pressed up against him and her arms wrapping around his neck. Their tongues danced together, igniting the fire that had been a slow burn for so many weeks. Trey was so hard now, his cock straining against his jeans, begging to be released. He had to fight with everything in him not to reach under her skirt and yank off her panties. There was something so innocent about her, something vulnerable, that made him want to protect her, even if it was from his own lust. The urge to go too far scared Trey, causing him to pull back suddenly.

He rested his forehead against hers, frustration overtaking him. "I'm sorry. I shouldn't have . . ."

Suddenly her hands were on his face, sticky with dough as she stared at him, her eyes wild with passion. "Yes, you absolutely should have." She kissed him hard on the mouth, pulling him back to her. Pressing hard against her, he let himself fall back into the beauty that was Alessandra. Thoughts of lifting her onto the counter and tugging off his jeans flew through his head. His hands were on her large breasts now and oh God, they felt amazing. He kneaded them with his palms, feeling her hard nipples through the layers of fabric in his way. He wanted to feel those nipples in his mouth. And the way she had just moaned, that soft sound of yearning begging him to take her, had Trey reaching down with both hands to lift her skirt.

The sound of a truck rumbling down the driveway came through the open window and snapped them out of their rapture, making him pull back as he suddenly remembered Lorena's warning.

"Shit," Alessandra whispered in frustrated agony as they both tried to slow their breath. Her eyes grew wide as she stared at him. "I got dough all over your face." She laughed a little as she plucked a towel off the counter and tried to wipe it off. "There's some in your hair as well."

He grinned nervously as she worked, and then unable to help himself, took hold of her hand and kissed the inside of her wrist. The sound of the door opening at the front of the house sent them scrambling. "I better go get cleaned up," he whispered, heading down the hall to the bathroom.

* * *

Lorena's and Betina's voices filled the room as they carried in bags of groceries. Alessa quickly got back to her dough. "How was the market?" she asked, trying to sound casual.

They chatted for a few minutes until Trey emerged from the bathroom with damp hair. He avoided eye contact with the women as he excused himself to get some work done. When he'd gone, Lorena lifted an eyebrow at her elder daughter. "Exactly why does he have dough on the back of his collar?"

"I have no idea. He helped retie my apron. Maybe he got some on his fingers." Alessandra refused to look at her mother.

"Be careful, Alessandra. A man like that will use you to get what he wants and then leave. He's already got you taking care of his son and doing his legal work for nothing. You'd be a fool to warm his bed too."

"Mother! I am not a child. And I am not stupid, either! I am helping him because I love Tomas. That is all."

"Make sure it stays that way."

NINETEEN

Trey stood in the barn for a moment, feeling completely alive. Exhilaration surged through him as he relived what had just happened. Soon, his sense of decency kicked in. How could he have done that? It was wrong. There was no way he should be leading her on like that when he was planning to leave as soon as possible. He would need to apologize and make it clear that they could never do that again. But shit, that would hurt. Every fibre of his body ached to feel those lips, those curves, again. To feel her warm, supple flesh beneath his fingers and against his body.

Shaking his head, he picked up a comb and began brushing the nearest horse. After a few minutes, he heard a rustling sound behind him. He held his breath, expecting Lorena coming to give him hell, but when he turned, he saw the kind eyes of Carlos.

"Oh, hi, sir. Did you have a good rest?"

"Okay," Carlos said, nodding as he turned the hose on to fill the horses' water pails.

"I'm glad it's you, actually. I was worried it was your daughter. I'm afraid I've gone and kissed your granddaughter. Like, *really* kissed her. I'm sorry about that. I just couldn't help myself." Trey paused in brushing the horse to look over at Carlos. Carlos showed no sign of being upset or of understanding him, so he went on. "I think if I wasn't going back to the US, I'd be tempted to see if maybe we could try to make a life together. But I'm not going to be able to stay, and she won't ever leave, so don't worry. I won't let that happen again."

"Okay."

* * *

Late that afternoon, Trey was treated to the sights, sounds, and flavours of a Santos family celebration. The party included Carlos's two brothers, their wives, children and grandchildren, as well as Carlos's other two daughters and their families, all bearing food to add to the table. Tomas played excitedly with the other kids, most of them older than him, much to his delight. Trey was made to feel welcome, even by the older relatives who didn't speak English. Warm smiles passed between them, and messages were conveyed through younger family members acting as interpreters. The whole scene made him long for the family meals at the ranch: always noisy affairs, often outside in the warmer months, always something he had looked forward to.

Even some of Alessandra's cousins were cowboys, complete with hats and belt buckles, which made Trey feel even more at home. Two of them came over to meet Trey soon after they arrived.

"I'm Bruno and this is Miguel. If you get us confused, remember Miguel is the ugly brother."

Trey laughed, thinking that he would introduce Dustin in much the same way. "Nice to meet you both."

"So, what do you think of Brazil?"

"I like it a lot. It reminds me of home, actually."

"Yes, Alessa said you grew up on a ranch."

"Kind of, yeah."

"You must be getting bored here, though. No women, no booze, no fighting. You should come with us to the rodeo next weekend in Adamantina. It will be a good time. We can get into lots of trouble. We're both going there to compete."

"Really? What do you compete in?"

"Bull riding," Miguel answered, hitching up his championship belt buckle so Trey could see it.

"Bull riding? Wow. I see you must be good at it," he said, glancing at the buckle.

"I do okay. You ride bulls?"

"No. Just horses."

"Come to our ranch. We raise bucking bulls. We'll let you try to ride one."

"Seriously?" Trey grinned. "I'd like to come watch you, but I don't think I'd try it."

"What? Come on, man. Here in Brazil, we say '*ou vai ou racha.*' It means do or die. Being a man. You come tomorrow, we'll show you how to be really macho."

"I already know how to be a man, thanks. But bull riding might be quite the rush . . ." Trey looked up at the sky, considering.

Bruno slapped him on the back. "It will be fun. Get Alessandra to bring you tomorrow. She's coming by to help our mother with some paperwork. Don't worry about anything. Nothing could be easier. We'll help you get on, and the bull will help you get back down."

* * *

After dinner, the children dragged Trey out into the grass to play soccer while the others lingered at the table, picking at the desserts that had been laid out.

"You like him," Alessandra's oldest aunt, Daniela, said to her with a bump to her shoulder. Alessa had been watching Trey for a long time without noticing that she was also being observed.

"What? Who?" she asked distractedly.

"Who? Your American cowboy," Daniela teased. "He's easy on the eyes, that one. If I wasn't madly in love with your uncle, I think I'd be out there on the soccer field trying to see if he might like a slightly older woman."

"*Tia* Daniela!"

"I can look, can't I?" she responded. "So, what's happening between you two, anyway?"

Lorena, who had been listening to the exchange, cut in. "If she knows what's good for her, nothing. There is no future there, so I don't want anyone encouraging it."

Daniela narrowed her eyes at Lorena but kept her playful tone. "What, Lorena? The girl can have a little fun, can't she? She's twenty-two."

"She should be focusing on her career, not boys. She got a call yesterday for an interview at the courthouse. It would be a very good job. I don't want her distracted now, especially not by that one." She pointed to Trey. "That one will break her heart if she lets him."

Alessandra rolled her eyes and stared down at her unfinished dessert, trying to let her mother's words roll off her.

"He seems nice, to me. Look at him out there with the kids. There's more to life than just school, Lorena. You of all people should remember the joys of being young and in love. I remember how you and Otavio used to carry on when you thought no one was looking."

"And look where that got me. Broke, with two babies to raise on my own by the time I was nineteen," Lorena answered firmly, standing to clear the dishes. "No! Don't fill her head with ideas that will only get her hurt, or worse, distract her from her goals."

Daniela waited to speak until Lorena had gone into the house. "I say you see where things go with him. When you're my age, the memories of the romances of your youth can keep you surprisingly warm on a cold night. Your goals will still be there in a few weeks." She gave Alessandra a little wink.

The conversation was interrupted by the sound of Tomas crying. He had been running a little too fast to keep up with the big kids and had tripped, falling on the gravel path. Alessa quickly got up and rushed over to him, getting to him just before Trey. She picked him up and held him to her shoulder, shushing him as Trey walked over and stood behind her to examine Tomas's palms.

"There's one way to know for sure if you're okay, Tomas," Trey told him. "I'm going to smell your feet and if they're still stinky, you're going to be fine."

Tomas stopped crying and gave him a confused look while Trey lifted one of the boy's sandal-clad foot to his nose and gave it a whiff. He recoiled, pretending that he was horrified. "Man! That is stinky! Whew!" Tomas giggled as Trey picked up his other foot, saying he needed to check that one to be sure. This time, he clutched at his nose and chest, pretending he was going to faint from the smell. Tomas gave a deep belly laugh as he wiggled out of Alessandra's arms and rushed over to his dad. Alessa laughed as she watched Tomas try to pick up his dad, who was now lying on his back in the grass.

"Smell dem more!"

Trey gave Alessa a little wink as he lifted his head to Tomas's outstretched foot.

* * *

Later, as their guests slowly made their way to their vehicles, Alessandra brought a freshly bathed Tomas out in his jammies to bid everyone good night. She and her aunt shared a long, knowing look, having an entire conversation with their eyes. Daniela gave her a firm nod before she got into her car. Trey stood beside Alessandra, waving goodbye before gently lifting Tomas from her arms.

"You go relax. I'll get him to bed. He's so tired, I don't think he'll even last through story time," he said, looking into her eyes.

She smiled at him, stroking her neck with her fingers absent-mindedly. "That would be nice."

Soon after, Trey found her sitting in the yard under the stars on a large porch swing.

"Can I join you?"

"Of course." She slowed the swing by gripping the grass with her toes. The air was finally cooling down as the evening wore on and now the world felt calm again. "That was fast."

"Yeah. He was worn right out from all that excitement," he said, settling himself next to her on the swing. "You have a wonderful family, Alessa. I'm grateful to be a part of it all, even just for the day. You've all made us feel so welcome here."

"I'm glad," she said, looking up at him. Her mind wandered to what had happened in the kitchen that afternoon, and her entire body ached for him to touch her again. Thoughts of throwing caution to the wind, of reaching for him, of kissing him, swept over her, but she shouldn't. Her mother might see. Besides, she had never been one to make the first move. She had never been bold like that, but being with him right now made her want to take her aunt's advice. Being so

{118}

near him had her pulse racing even though she was doing her best to appear calm.

Trying to think of something intelligent to say, Alessandra blurted out, "I have a job interview on Monday. With a judge at the courthouse in town."

"Really? That's terrific. I bet you'll get the job."

"I hope so." Alessandra's train of thought vanished as she stared into his hazel eyes.

Trey glanced at her lips for a moment before clearing his throat. "Your cousins said you're going over to help your aunt out for a while tomorrow. They invited me to come along to watch them practise for the rodeo."

"Oh yes. They mentioned that to me. You can come if you like, but be careful with those two. They like to make trouble."

"I'll make sure to keep that in mind, especially since my lawyer is the one advising me on the matter."

Alessandra raised one eyebrow. "Why do I have a feeling you're going to forget?"

"I have no idea," Trey answered, looking innocent.

They sat in silence. Trey leaned his head back, gazing at the stars for a minute. "You've been really amazing to me. And to Tomas. I don't know how we're going to be able to leave you. He loves you so much." He turned to her, his face close to hers, and stared into Alessandra's eyes as though he couldn't look away.

Alessandra nodded, feeling herself disappear into his gaze. "I love him too, with all my heart. It will be hard if . . . when you go." *Maybe you don't have to . . .*

"Well, it's likely going to be a long time before we leave. We haven't heard anything yet about the custody case. Who knows how long it will take?"

"It could take another year, even," she answered, finding herself inching a little closer to him. Suddenly, the sound of Lorena's voice cut the moment short.

"Alessandra! I could use your help in the house!" Her tone was sharp.

"Be right there," she called. "I should go in."

"Yup, it's probably for the best."

TWENTY

Trey woke early to the memory of kissing Alessandra and he realized he must have been dreaming about her. He yawned and stretched his body, giving himself a minute before getting up. His mind started to race from what *had* happened with Alessandra to what he *wanted* to happen with her to what *might* happen if he actually went through with what he wanted. Things would get messy. There was no doubt about it. Lorena had warned him that she'd run him off if he tried anything with either of her daughters, and he had no doubt she meant every word, especially now that Alessa had a line on a great job. He got up and splashed some cold water on his face, trying to think of a way to tell Alessandra they should leave things well enough alone.

He dressed and walked out to the barn, his mind full of his feelings for Alessandra and how she'd responded to him in the kitchen the day before. She wanted him as much as he wanted her. And the urge to feel her lips on his again and to hold her in his arms and to strip off her clothes and feel her body against his was almost too much for him to take. By the time he had finished feeding the animals, he'd decided he didn't care what Lorena would do; he needed to act on his feelings. For both their sakes. He would really be putting them both out of their misery, wouldn't he?

He made his way back to his house to wash up before breakfast, excited by the possibilities that lay before him. His cellphone was sitting on the kitchen table buzzing when he walked in the door. Picking it up, he saw that his mom, Fern, was calling via Skype. He swiped the screen and waited a minute until her face became visible. He could see she was sitting in the kitchen and that it was still dark out, and he quickly figured out it was about four in the morning in Colorado. His heart started to pound with worry.

"Hi, Mom. Is everything okay?"

"Yes. Fine, Trey. I just couldn't sleep so I thought I'd call you."

"I guess that's one advantage of being in different time zones. But how come you couldn't sleep? You look worried."

"I did something that I know you're going to be a little angry about."

Trey narrowed his eyes, knowing he was about to hear something very bad. She was one to downplay things, and if even she was admitting he would be a little angry, he knew he'd be furious. "What'd you do?"

"I went to see Cole and Ben yesterday to ask them to help you out. I explained your situation, and they both agreed that you and Tomas can live in one of the guest cabins at the ranch and that you can have your job back."

"You did what?" Trey's head snapped back.

"Just hear me out before you get mad. You don't have to actually go *live* at the ranch. You can just *tell* the judge you have everything set up on this end so you'll be allowed to bring Tomas home already. As soon as I came up with it, I knew it was the perfect plan. I asked them to write a letter as proof for the court that you worked there for years and that you'll have both a home and a steady job waiting for you."

Trey raked his hand through his hair, frustration bubbling to his throat. "How could you do that? Do you know what an *ass* that makes me look like? I haven't spoken to them in years, and now I'm coming to them with hat in hand to beg for a job and a place to live? In fact, it's even worse because it looks like I asked my mom to do my begging for me!"

"Nobody's judging you, Trey, I promise. You're in a tough situation and they understand that. They're family, and it's time to mend fences. I thought you'd be happy to know that Cole's over what happened. In fact, he said you and Tomas will always be welcome."

Shaking his head, Trey raised his voice. "You didn't think you should maybe run that by me first?"

"I knew you'd say no."

"You're damn right I would have. Call them back and tell them that you acted on your own and that I said thank you but no thank you."

"I will not. They're writing up the letter, and I'm going out there on Tuesday to pick it up and mail it to you."

"Tell them not to."

"It's already done, Trey. Accept it. Now, you need to get over this whole notion that you can do everything for yourself. You have a son to think about, and it truly *does* take a village to raise a child. You're not going to be able to do this without help, no matter what you think."

"Listen, I don't—you know what? Just stay out of it. Tomas is fine. I'm fine. We're together and safe, on a nice farm with good people who need me right now a lot more than Cole and Ben ever will. And I'm not about to lie to the court just to rush things along. Tomas needs a father who will teach him about integrity. I can hardly do that if I'm going to be dishonest and take shortcuts whenever it suits me."

"Well, if you don't want to lie to the court, you could go live on the ranch for a while and work for them. Then it won't be a lie," Fern said in a clipped tone.

Trey sighed. "Moving to the ranch is *not* an option. Neither is asking for their help. I'm really disappointed that you would do that."

"I'm just trying to do what's right for my grandson."

"I'll decide what's right for my son, not you. You don't even know him."

"And how am I supposed to get to know him if you refuse to bring him home?"

"Jesus, Mom. Don't you think I have enough to deal with right now without you making me feel guilty? You want to see your grandson, get on a plane and come see him. You could have done that anytime in the last three years but you didn't."

"Oh, so are you saying I'm a horrible grandmother?"

"No, I didn't mean it like that. I'm just really angry that you did what you did."

"I know I should have made a better effort to get to know Tomas. That's part of why I went to see Cole. To try to help get him home where he belongs."

"This isn't about you, no matter how much you want it to be."

Fern gasped indignantly. "So I'm self-centred now? For trying to help *you*?"

"Wow. You're unbelievable. You're just twisting everything I say when *you're* the one who stepped way over the line."

"There should be no lines with family, Trey. No lines!" Fern's voice was bordering on shrill now.

Trey matched her anger. "You know what? There *are* lines. Very clear ones, and I'll be drawing more if you do anything like this again. I'm done with this conversation."

"Well! Maybe *I'm* done with it. You're completely ungrateful, so I don't know why I'd want to talk to you when I should be sleeping anyway."

"You called me, remember?"

"I'm getting that letter from your cousins whether you like it or not. You send me the address to the farm when you're ready to do the right thing and let go of your stubborn pride."

"I won't. Goodbye, Mom."

Fern stared at him for a long moment. "Goodbye, Trey."

TWENTY-ONE

The clang of metal was almost deafening as the two-thousand-pound animal slammed his side against the pen to protest his new rider. Trey sat atop the bull and rubbed his gloved hand up and down the bull rope to warm up the sticky rosin before he secured his hand, palm up.

"Hold your pinkie finger here, right beside his backbone," Miguel instructed. "Lean forward, remember? Almost on top of your hand." Miguel helped him test the slack on the rope and pulled it for him until it was properly snug, just behind the animal's shoulders.

"He'll be fine, you old hen," Bruno scoffed.

The bull snorted and knocked himself against the other side of the chute, coming close to pinning Trey's leg between the gate and his own side. "He seems a little angry," Trey muttered. "I thought you were putting me on one of your more docile bulls?"

"This is!" Bruno answered. The brothers laughed as he jumped off the gate and got ready to open it.

"You ready?"

"As ready as I'll ever be," Trey answered, wanting to change his mind.

"*Ou vai ou racha!*" Bruno hollered, tugging the gate open.

The huge black beast bucked hard, kicking his hind legs high into the air at the same time as he twisted his body to the left. Trey was shocked at the violent force under him, but even more shocked by the fact that he hadn't fallen off yet. "Holy shit!" he called as the bull's back feet hit the ground hard and he used the momentum to push his front legs into the air. Trey rocked his body forward, staying on for another brief second before a sharp twist of the animal's body sent him flying through the air, landing on his butt in the dirt. He paused for a second before scrambling out of the way of the hooves that were aiming to pummel him. The two brothers distracted the bull until the animal slowed to a jog and circled the pen before finally standing opposite the chute, looking bored.

Bruno turned to Miguel. "You owe me ten dollars. He stayed on for more than one second."

"Alright, alright," Miguel said. He asked Trey, "You wanna go again? I need to earn my money back."

Trey's breathing was recovering as he stood bent over with his hands on his knees. Adrenalin flowed through him and a slow smile spread across his face. This was fun. Easily as much of a thrill as surfing. "Hell yeah, but I want in on the action. Ten bucks says I can stay on for five seconds next time."

He caught a glimpse of Alessandra out of the corner of his eye and realized she must have finished helping her aunt and uncle. She stood with Tomas on her hip, shaking her head at Trey before yelling at her cousins in Portuguese. They answered back, body language defensive, but they were laughing a little.

Trey walked over to her, dusting off the chaps they'd lent him. "Are you worried? You look worried."

"Yes, of course I'm worried. *Você bebeu?* I *knew* they would do this. They live to make trouble wherever they go. You are not a bull rider. You're going to get hurt."

"I'll be fine. We're just having fun. Besides, I did pretty well on my first try."

"We put him on the easy bull. It's totally safe. Even *Vovô* could stay on this one," Miguel said.

"If he gets hurt, I'm blaming you both!" She made a motion like she was slitting her throat as she glared from one to the other. "*Vocês vão estar muito ferrados!*"

"He won't."

"You better hope not, because what those stupid bulls can do is nothing compared to me when I'm pissed off!" Her accent was suddenly much stronger as she spat out her words, leaving Trey torn between being amused and being turned on by seeing her like this.

"I'll be fine. Just one more time. Then we can go," Trey offered.

"I'm not going to watch this. I'm taking Tomas inside." The little boy wriggled to get out of her arms, but she held him firmly and turned back to the house.

"I stay with Dad! I ride bull too!" Tomas whined.

She glared at her cousins. "You see?" she yelled, before taking Tomas into the house.

An hour later, Trey's entire body ached after another dozen attempts. On his last go, he'd managed to stay on for a full eight seconds, leaving Bruno and Miguel shaking their heads in wonder at his abilities. They both kept insisting he'd ridden bulls before.

"Nope. I swear, today was my first try. I grew up riding horses, and I love to surf, so I guess maybe that's given me good balance. I don't know. I've also ridden a mechanical bull every weekend for the past two years. But that wouldn't really help, would it?" Trey asked them.

"Well, probably the horseback riding and surfing were more helpful. Whatever it was, you're pretty good. You should come with us to the rodeo next month. It is open to anyone. You could win a little money, maybe."

"How much?" he asked just as Alessandra appeared again with Tomas in tow.

Miguel glanced at her, then answered Trey's question. "You come in first, you might get about a thousand. A few hundred for second or third."

"Forget it," Alessandra said firmly. "He's busy next weekend."

"Doing what?" Bruno asked.

"The same thing he'll be doing for the next sixteen years! Raising his son, who *doesn't* need to be turned into an orphan by you two idiots."

* * *

The ride home was quiet. Alessandra sat in the passenger seat, staring out the window, lost in an internal struggle. Her logical side told her she had to convince Trey to never get on another bull again, but there was another part of her that had felt a pull as she watched him from the kitchen window. There was something undeniably sexy about seeing him wrap the rope around his hand and try to tame that huge beast. Something about the danger, the over-the-top masculinity of it, stirred a very primal part of her, a part of her that Alessandra had always denied. Surely, she should be smarter than this. She should want a sensible man who would play it safe. But she didn't. She wanted Trey. And after seeing him ride that damn bull today, she wanted him in a way that made her hate herself.

Trey glanced back at Tomas. "He fell asleep as soon as the truck started moving."

"Hmm. Yes. He was tired." Alessandra looked out the window, her tone curt.

"I'm guessing you're upset that I'm going to the rodeo next month."

"Of course I'm upset. It's very dangerous," she snapped, feeling angry and confused about who, exactly, she was angry with at the moment.

"Ah, it's not so bad. Besides, what's a few broken bones if you win?"

"A lot worse can happen than broken bones," she scoffed. "And that little boy sleeping in the back seat right now has no mother anymore. You may want to think about that."

"I know," he answered evenly. "I also have to find a way to make some money for him, remember? I don't have a work visa, so I can't work here, but I can compete. This could actually be the answer to a lot of my problems right now."

"It won't be. And if you decide to do it, you're much stupider than I thought. It's just a dangerous waste of time!" Her tone was angry but she kept it quiet enough not to wake Tomas.

"Maybe, but what if it isn't?" Trey glanced over at her from the driver's seat.

TWENTY-TWO

Trey checked over his body in the mirror as he waited for the shower to heat up. He had bruises on his arms, butt and legs from his afternoon spent riding the bull. He also had the thrill of opportunity resonating through his bones. This could be it. The answer to his money problems. There were rodeos nearly every weekend in the area. If he could earn enough, he'd be able to put a down payment on a place back home. That would give him a huge head start and he wouldn't have to leave Tomas behind in Brazil for months.

He stood under the spray of the water, feeling it relieve some of his pain, thinking of Alessandra. She was far from impressed at his get-not-very-rich-quick scheme, and he knew she would fight him on it. She wasn't wrong. It was risky. Seeing her all fired up like that deepened his desire for her. He'd only seen her very calm until now, but he could see she'd give him a run for his money if they ever argued. Something about that thought made his body awaken with lust. He liked a feisty woman who wouldn't back down.

Stepping out of the shower, he patted himself dry with a towel, then wrapped it around his waist, wishing he had an Advil. Or a few beers. That would dull the pain nicely. A soft knock on the door of his house surprised him. "Just a minute!" he called, pulling on his jeans.

"It's Alessa." Her voice was muffled.

He quickly crossed the room and swung the door open.

* * *

There he stood in nothing but his jeans, rubbing his wet hair with a towel. The sight of him like that almost made her forget why she'd come. Alessandra stared at him for far too long before saying anything. "I asked Betina to listen for Tomas in case he wakes up. I wanted to apologize."

He moved aside to let her in. "No need. It's alright, really."

She forced herself to look at the loveseat so she could think straight. "No, it's your life. I have no right to tell you what to do. Also, I want you to know I don't think you're at all stupid." She walked in and turned to face him. Her gaze fell on his sculpted body and her mind went completely blank. When she finally realized she was gawking like an idiot, her cheeks heated up and she shook her head a little as her eyes met his. He wore a look of amusement at her reaction to him.

"I . . . I came here to apologize," she said distractedly.

Trey gave her a sexy smirk. "You said that already." Tossing the towel onto the couch, he took a few steps toward her and tilted her chin up with his thumb. "You're forgiven."

He stared at her, and she saw that his pupils had grown large, crowding out those swirls of hazel she had come to love. Unable to stop herself any longer, Alessa reached for his waistband. He lowered his mouth over hers, crushing it with a deep, long, hard kiss. She slid her hands around his back, gliding them up and down his muscular torso as she felt his hands on her ass, squeezing her and pulling her to him until their bodies were pressed together. She could feel his erection through his jeans as she kissed him wildly now. His fingers traced her from her bottom to her waist, and he tugged her tank top over her head, leaving her in a bra and skirt. His large hands were covering her breasts now, squeezing them in a way that made her moan with anticipation. She felt him slide the straps of her bra off, and her breasts spilled over the top, giving him access to her firm nipples. He lowered his mouth over her right breast, suddenly taking Alessandra to a world of ecstasy she'd never known before. She wanted to undo his jeans, to free him, but her hands were temporarily out of order. She was weak in the knees from what he was doing to her with his tongue. He raked his teeth over her nipple as he moved on to her left breast. Sucking and flicking and bringing her close to the edge although he'd yet to touch her throbbing core. She hardly noticed her bra being unclasped or exactly when it left her body. Her panting was so loud that she doubted she'd hear a gunshot if it went off right next to her.

Finally managing to get a grip on his jeans, she fumbled with them until the button popped open, then tore the zipper down. With a little tug, his jeans were off and he stood completely nude in front of her. She glanced down, feeling a little intimidated by what she saw. He was much bigger than she'd expected, and the sight of his huge erection reminded her of how long it had been since she'd had sex.

His lips were on her neck now, doing something that made her forget her worry in favour of wanting to do very naughty things. "Oh, Trey," she whispered. "Yes."

She could feel that her panties were soaked and felt a twinge of embarrassment at how wet she was as he yanked down her skirt and reached his hand between her thighs. A growl erupted from his throat as he covered the fabric of her panties with his palm. She knew from that sound that she had nothing to feel shy about. He rubbed his hand over her, pushing his fingers, along with her panties, in just a tiny bit. He pulled back and looked her up and down for a second, his expression full of lust.

"God, you're just so completely beautiful."

His words made her feel powerful in her femininity, in the effect she was having on him, as she reached up on her tiptoes to kiss him again. This gorgeous man, chiselled to perfection, wanted her. She reached for his hard length, gripping it in both hands. Her hands seemed small in comparison as she glided them over the smooth shaft, feeling it twitch with excitement.

He pushed the fabric of her panties aside and she could finally feel his rough fingers exploring her. Alessandra's hips bucked forward, begging him to enter her. He moved his head back from her. "We shouldn't do this."

"Yes we should. I need you, Trey. Please."

"We can't have sex. I don't have a condom," he said.

"You don't need one. I'm on the pill," she whispered, feeling slightly embarrassed again.

He kissed her again as though he couldn't stop himself. "But this might—"

"It won't. Please, Trey. I want you so bad I can hardly breathe."

Picking her up by her ass, he rubbed her over his cock as she wrapped her legs around his waist. She could feel him through the wet cotton and she was filled with an urgency she couldn't deny. Reaching behind her, she tugged her panties out of the way and was finally rewarded by the feeling of his smooth, hard length touching her sex. He dragged her over himself in long, slow movements, making her so wild she didn't care if she had even a shred of dignity left. She needed to feel him inside her. She would do anything, even beg if she had to.

Walking them through the bedroom door, Trey sat on the bed, holding her on his lap as he manoeuvred her panties down her legs. Alessandra wriggled her hips until the head of his erection was just inside her. She winced a little at the size of him as she carefully pushed herself over him, each inch stretching her.

The look on her face must have been shock. Trey's hands gripped her face. "Are you okay?"

"Yes. I haven't done this for a long time and you're . . . sizeable."

Trey grinned at the description before his expression changed to concern again. "I don't want to hurt you, so let's take it slow. You do what feels good."

Alessandra nodded, then lowered her lips back to his before grinding her hips into his from side to side. She loved how careful he was being and she knew he was holding back. It was the first time she'd been with a man who was at all concerned if she was okay, and it made her want him so much more. She dragged her body over his lap, filling herself with him, feeling her sex rub against him as she shifted herself forward, then back again. She moved slowly and cautiously for a long time, until she grew so ready she couldn't stop. Her movements became more quick, more sure, more fierce now. It was all so perfect as he lowered his mouth over her breasts again, sucking and flicking her nipples with his tongue. Waves of toe-curling pleasure crashed through her body as she let go, arching her back and pressing herself onto him with everything in her.

Trey ran his hand from her neck down between her breasts to the place where their bodies joined. He watched as she came for him. He had never seen anything so sexy in his life, never felt anything better than her tight muscles squeezing him, drenching him. Her large breasts bounced with each thrust of her hips in a way that made him crazy. His own orgasm tore through him, an unstoppable force as he erupted.

He felt her arms wrap around his neck as she sat on his lap and nipped his bottom lip between her teeth. Her beautiful face was flushed with desire and exertion, and her entire being wore nothing but utter satisfaction. Trey was completely caught up with the perfection of being with her. Here in this moment, he knew that this couldn't be just a one-time thing—this needed to last. This was what forever was supposed to feel like. For the first time in his life, Trey felt true love moving him, and it was by far the best thing he'd ever known. It was all-consuming, fantasy and reality blending in the most delicious way. And now that they had finally acted on it, there would be no turning back. They clung to each other for a long time, slowly recovering, him still buried inside her.

"I've been wanting to do that since I first saw you," he said in a low tone. "All these weeks of being so near you without touching you have been absolute torture."

"For me too." Alessa's voice was barely a whisper.

"Good," he murmured happily, angling his head so he could plant kisses on the nape of her neck. "Let's get married."

"Sure, why not?" She laughed, her voice as dreamy as his own.

He stopped and lifted his head to face her, his expression very serious yet a little bit shocked. "No, I mean it. I want to marry you. More than anything I've ever wanted to do in my entire life. You're perfect. I've tried to deny my feelings for weeks now, but I can't. I want to be with you. I know it seems crazy. This may be happening insanely fast—hell, we're from two different continents—but when I look at you, none of that matters to me. I've never felt this way about anyone, and I know I'll never want another woman after you. I'm completely in love with you, Alessandra, and if I'm not mistaken, you feel the same way."

"I do. I am, Trey. I am so completely in love with you. The thought of you leaving is unbearable to me."

"Then I'll never leave you."

TWENTY-THREE

The next morning, Trey was up with the sun. Filled with excitement, he'd been unable to sleep for more than a few hours. Alessandra had stayed late into the night and they'd made love for what seemed like hours before he walked her back to the main house, kissing her until he forced himself to let her go. She wanted to be nearby in case Tomas woke up, and she needed some sleep before her job interview the next day. Trey had stood outside the house and watched her disappear into the kitchen before he managed to tear himself away and stroll back to his house under the stars.

Now that he was up and dressed, he stood next to the window for a moment, staring out at the rows of orange trees. He should be exhausted but he wasn't. He was bursting with energy—the energy of being in love for the first time. Thoughts of the night before flooded his mind. The smell of her, the taste of her skin. He'd never spent such a long time exploring a woman's body before and had revelled in every second with her. He wanted to know every inch of her, what she wanted, what she needed, what he could do to make her addicted to him forever.

He started for the tool shed, where he'd left the painting supplies yesterday. The day before, he'd finished scraping the loose old paint off the outside of the barn, and now he was going to start the first coat.

His stomach twisted into knots at the thought of Alessandra's mother finding out what they'd done the night before. That would get ugly. But maybe Lorena would forgive him once she found out they were getting married.

The proposal had come as a shock to both of them, to him maybe even more than to her. It had just come out without him thinking about it, but as soon as the words left his mouth, he knew he meant it. *Really* meant it, like nothing he'd ever said to anyone before. He knew everyone else would think they were insane. They'd only known each other for a few weeks. But in that time, they'd lived with each other, and cared for a child together, and gone through the stress of her exams and his custody case together. Surely that was more telling of how perfect they were for each other than even a year of going on dinner dates.

He knew asking her to marry him like that was impulsive. He knew he had done things backwards. He'd asked her to spend her life with him before the *I love you*'s had even come out. He could picture her face, flushed with passion then wide-eyed with shock for a brief second before she answered him. She hadn't even needed convincing, which just proved to him that he had been right to ask. She understood him like no one else ever had. She was the one person that he'd bared his soul to, that he'd let into his heart. She'd seen him for who he was and she loved him anyway. He had hidden nothing from her and it hadn't scared her off. Instead, she had accepted him the way he was. And that made him the luckiest guy on earth.

So what if they were from different countries? So what if they hadn't known each other long? They would find a way to make it work. They were in love with each other and could make a life together. He'd find a good career back home and the three of them would live happily ever after. They would be a family.

Smiling as the first rays of sun hit his face on the way to the barn, he felt better than he had in years. More sure of himself and of the world. He had Alessandra, and with her by his side, he felt like he could do anything. He could jump through the hoops required to get his son, he could find a good job and he could ride any bull he'd mount in order to achieve his goals.

Pouring some paint into a tray, he then put the lid on the can, grinning as he got started. He would paint until Alessandra was awake and ready to go to town. They would file the papers showing their intent to marry at the courthouse when she went for her interview. And he couldn't wait. He wondered if she was still sleeping. Maybe she would be able to sneak out here before anyone else woke up so they could have a little time to themselves again.

The sound of the back door to the main house opening interrupted his thoughts, and he waved as Carlos approached. The old man's mouth was set in an unfamiliar grimace this morning, and it made Trey's heart pound. The last thing he wanted to do was upset this man who'd been so good to him and his son. Carlos walked up and gave him a nod. "*Olá*."

"*Olá*, sir. I hope you slept well."

The look on the old man's face made him wonder for a minute if maybe he *did* understand English. He swallowed hard as he watched Carlos open the paint can and dip a brush in. Holding the can in one hand, Carlos began working on the trim in long, even strokes.

Trey got back to work without saying anything for a long time. Finally, he decided to get it off his chest. "What would you think if I asked Alessandra to marry me? I know I told you I wouldn't let things go past that kiss the other day, but the truth is that I'm really in love with her and I can't imagine my life without her. I hope you and your daughter will give us your blessing. I know Alessandra and I haven't known each other that long, but we've been through a lot already, and we're really perfect together. I want to marry her.

I actually asked her last night and she said yes. She wants to keep it a secret for now, but I thought I should tell you. In fact, I'd like to shout it from the rooftops, because I've never been so excited about anything in my life."

Carlos stopped his brush mid-stroke and then continued without saying anything, leaving Trey to wonder exactly how much English he really knew.

*   *   *

When they parked in front of the courthouse, Trey put his hand on Alessandra's knee. "Can you believe we're doing this?"

"Not really. Can you?"

"It doesn't seem quite real yet, but it sure feels right." He pulled her in for a kiss before opening the door to the truck. "Stay there a minute."

A moment later, he opened the door for her and held his hand out to help her down.

"Thank you."

"Say, if I ever forget, remind me how much the little things matter, okay?" he asked.

"I have a feeling you'll need to remind me." She lifted her hand to his cheek and guided his face down to hers again. Their kiss lasted longer than what would be considered appropriate for a courthouse parking lot, but they could hardly help themselves. The sound of a car pulling in reminded them of where they were.

"Let's do this," Trey said, taking her hand and starting for the front door.

A couple of hours later, Alessandra hurried to meet Trey, who'd been waiting in the park next to the courthouse watching a soccer match since they had filed their papers and she had gone to her interview.

"I did it! I got the job!" She rushed into his arms and he picked her up, swooping her around in a big, celebratory circle. "Wow! That's so great, Alessa! Congratulations."

"I can't believe it. I start on Monday!" She spoke quickly with big, enthusiastic gestures as they walked to the truck. "I'm going to have to buy some work clothes. And a briefcase. I'll need a briefcase. I should get my hair cut, maybe. Oh, and some nice shoes. Can you believe I just got a job?"

"I can."

"I'm going to be an assistant to the judge. The pay is horrible, but it's a good start. I'll always have work, and I'll get so much experience," she continued.

"Sounds perfect, really." Trey smiled at her. "I'm really excited for you."

"Me too! I did it! I'm working as a lawyer now! And we're getting married!"

"We sure are," he said, giving her a firm kiss on the lips.

Alessandra beamed at him. "It feels like my entire life is starting and it's going to be perfect. I have you and Tomas and now a job."

* * *

That evening as Trey stood in the shower, he couldn't help but feel a pang of envy. As happy as he was for Alessa, he wished he was starting a career as well. As it was, he would have to wait indefinitely for the custody case to be decided. He could hardly stand having his fate rest in the hands of a stranger. He rinsed shampoo out of his hair, feeling worry set in again. He needed to find a way to provide for his little guy. Even though his wife-to-be had found a job, that didn't remove the pressure he felt. He needed to make his own way as soon as possible, and he knew that once he had his chance, he'd do well. He just had to be patient, which wasn't necessarily his strong suit. For now, he would continue working hard on the farm to earn his keep and that of his son. Inside, he ached to be free to finally step up and take care of his son the way he knew he could. At least there was a rodeo coming. If he did well, he could bring home some money for the three of them. It would be a start.

*   *   *

It was after eleven when Alessandra finally appeared. "My mother was up watching one of those practical-joke shows," she said as she kicked off her flip-flops and crossed the room to him. Trey had been reading on the loveseat when she came in and Alessandra was excited that she could finally act on the impulse to straddle his lap.

Trey gave her a long kiss before pulling back a little. "Doesn't it seem a little weird to you that you're a lawyer and yet you're sneaking around so your *mom* won't know you're sleeping with your fiancé?"

"I know it's strange, yes. But can we just keep this our secret for now? Trust me, as soon as she finds out, you'll wish she didn't know. I want us just to enjoy this time together. Just you and me. Okay?" She trailed kisses down his neck then tugged at his T-shirt, pulling it over his head and tossing it behind her.

"Alright, if that's what you want. But I can handle the fallout, whatever it is." Trey lifted her tank top off and tossed it over her shoulder. He took a moment to look her over, then let out an appreciative puff of air. "You're so sexy." He traced the outline of her bra, letting his fingers glide over her skin until she shivered a little.

Alessandra lowered her face to his, kissing him wildly as he reached around behind her and unclasped her bra. Soon his mouth was on her full breasts and she was arching her back to keep him there. "Ahh, yes, Trey," she moaned.

He continued working his magic for a deliciously long moment before flipping them so that she was on her back on the loveseat and he was kneeling before her. She laughed a little in surprise. "Whoa, how did you do that, even?"

"Talent." He raised and lowered his eyebrows playfully before gripping her hips and pulling her closer to the edge of the seat. "I have another talent I'd like to share with you." He unzipped her jeans and pulled them off along with her panties.

He started to lower his mouth over her but she covered her body with her arms.

"What's wrong?"

"Nothing. I feel silly."

"Why?" He gave her a concerned look, resting his hands on her thighs.

"No one's ever done this to me before and I feel a little . . . exposed."

"Really?" he asked, clearly surprised. "So, I'm the first one to . . ." His voice trailed off and a look of satisfaction replaced his surprise.

"Yes." She closed her eyes. "I know I shouldn't be embarrassed. It's just so bright in here and you're going to be able to see everything."

"I *want* to see everything," he said, giving her a kiss on her hands, which were covering her tummy. "And I want to *taste* everything."

She shifted uncomfortably. "What if, after, you aren't attracted to me the same way?"

Trey had an incredulous look on his face. "You know that's not possible, right?"

"No."

"You remember a few minutes ago when I told you how sexy you are? I wasn't lying. You're gorgeous. Seriously. Any guy would kill to be exactly where I am right now. How do you not know that?"

"Because you're making it up."

"I am not," he said, shaking his head. "Not at all. You're beautiful. You've got the softest, smoothest skin I've ever seen. You're like butter—creamy and delicious, and I just want to lick you all over." He moved her hands aside and trailed slow kisses over her tummy and hips. "Trust me, I wouldn't do this if I didn't want to. There's nothing I'd rather be doing. I'm hard just thinking about it."

He tugged at the button fly on his jeans, letting them fall open. Reaching into his boxer briefs, he freed himself. "That's better. It was getting a little uncomfortable in there."

Alessandra looked down to see his erection aimed up at her. He wasn't lying. He was turned on by this. She started to let her body relax, trying to shut out all of her self-hating thoughts and just let his words sink in to her heart. He had said she was beautiful and sexy. *Why would he say it if he didn't mean it?* She shut her eyes, pretending the lights were out, soon finding that she didn't have to try to fool herself. She was completely lost in what he was doing as his tongue skimmed along the front of her sex. It was an entirely new sensation for her, one she'd wondered about many times but had never experienced. He gently parted her legs with his hands, then used his thumbs to tease her as he let his lips drift along the insides of her thighs. *Okay, that feels sooo good.* She gasped when he put his mouth over her and sucked, then slid his tongue inside. How did he know what she wanted when she didn't even know herself?

His movements were slow, careful, thoughtful, and she knew he meant to bring her the most exquisite pleasure as he worked. The pressure he applied was just perfect, firm but not overzealous. He groaned and she could feel the groan vibrating through her, causing her hips to buck of their own accord. She was greedy for more now. She wanted him to thrust deeper, and the way she moved left him with no doubt. He obliged, pushing his tongue in farther, then pulling back with long, slow drags before plunging in again. Deeper, harder, over and over until she came undone, grabbing his hair and pressing herself against his tongue as she felt the waves of her climax roll through her entire body. "Oh yes! Trey! Yes!" She cried out.

When it was over and she had finally started to recover, she laughed in surprise at how loud she had been. Trey grinned at her. "I take it you won't mind if I do that again?"

"Not a bit. That was . . . Wow." She smiled down at him, completely satisfied.

"Good," he murmured, kissing her breasts. "Because I'll never get tired of doing that to you." He sucked on her nipple, causing it to tighten again. "Mmm, you are just like butter. You melt in my mouth."

TWENTY-FOUR

The next three weeks flew by as Trey looked after Tomas and continued his work on the farm. Alessandra started her job as planned. Each morning, she left for work early and returned close to suppertime. Each evening, she arrived home to some type of improvement that Trey had made, returning the farm to its former glory. The exterior of both houses had been scrubbed down and given a fresh coat of paint, the overgrown shrubs had been trimmed and shaped, and the fences stood at attention again. His hard work made her love Trey even more. The way he was helping out her *avô* showed how he would take care of them all. Trey was as good as he was sexy, and she wanted to pinch herself, knowing that a man like that wanted to marry her.

Trey managed to make it over to Daniela and Ricardo's ranch to practise bull riding with Miguel and Bruno several times. Each ride, his knowledge and confidence in his ability grew. Bruno gave him a protective vest, lent him a pair of chaps and helped him enter his name in the next competition.

With Betina's help, Trey and Alessandra were still keeping their relationship a secret, but this would end soon. For now, they stole private moments to kiss and drive each other wild whenever they could. At night, Alessandra would sneak to Trey's to make love until the sun was almost up, then sneak back into her room. Each day, she checked the notice boards at the registry office at the courthouse for notice of their intent to marry. All impending marriages were posted there and in the newspapers before approval was given for the licence. The Santos didn't have the newspaper delivered to the farm, but her mother usually picked it up when she went to town for groceries. This led Alessandra to offer to stop in at the grocery store on her way home from work every day. She knew that once the notice was in the newspaper, someone would read it and call her mother, but she wanted to give her and Trey's fledgling relationship a little more time to grow before her mother interfered.

On Friday afternoon, Alessandra got home from work early, her boss having sent everyone home as a thank-you for the long hours they'd been putting in. Trey met her in the kitchen of the main house. He grabbed her hips and pulled her in for a long hello kiss, but Alessandra cut it off and backed away. "Someone might see. We have to be more careful."

"No one's in the house. But honestly, Alessa, let's just tell them. I don't like all this sneaking around. It just feels wrong." He wrapped his arms around her.

"Trey, can we just please do it my way? I know it's immature, but I don't want any fighting in the family right now. I just want to enjoy this time in my life." She gave him a lingering kiss to help make her point. "Okay?"

The sound of the back door opening had her scrambling to move away from him, and her reaction had Trey temporarily giving up on the idea of coming clean. Lorena came around the corner just as Trey headed for the door, giving her a little nod on his way out. With no need to wait until he was out of earshot, Lorena turned to Alessandra, speaking in Portuguese. "You think I don't know what's going on, but I'm not a fool, young lady. I know everything!"

Alessandra stared at her defiantly. "What do you know, Mother?"

Lorena raised her voice now. "I know you've been sneaking to his bed every night. You think I can't hear the squeaking door?"

Carlos came down the hall and into the kitchen, a worried look on his face.

"This is a mistake, Alessandra! I raised you to be smarter than this! You're going to throw your life away for a good-looking man who's no better than your father! He's *using* you and he will leave you with nothing!"

"No, he isn't! He loves me," Alessandra growled through her teeth.

Lorena laughed, oozing frustration. "He's certainly got you fooled, hasn't he? With that nice smile and some pretty words? You'll do anything for him if he'll just love you, right? First, he got you to take care of his legal problems! Then you bring him here to give him a roof over his head! Then you give him your body! You're so stupid! A man like that will take what he wants and leave you. He's going to go home and leave you broken-hearted, but you're too blind to see it!"

"It's not like that. He's a good man! Look at everything he's done for this family since he's been here! And when I was finishing school, he made all the meals and took care of everything so I could study. You don't know anything about him, so just stay out of it!"

"I'm *not* going to let you make the same mistake I did! Never!" Lorena screamed. Taking a huge breath, she lowered her voice to an icy tone. "He has to leave here. He is no longer welcome."

"What? You can't do that! Where will he and Tomas live?" Alessa cried. Tears of anger sprang from her eyes.

"I don't care. Tomas is not my problem. And he's not your problem either. But *you* are my problem and I'll *die* before I see you waste your life on that *galinha*!"

"He is not a *galinha*!"

"Of course he is! If he isn't a womanizer, then how did he end up with a son and no wife!"

"Enough!" Carlos barked, slamming his hand on the counter. Both women turned, shocked. "That's enough, Lorena. He's a good boy. He loves her. Every time we're out in the barn together he goes on and on about her. He thinks I don't understand anything, so he talks. And all he says the whole time is how much he cares about Alessandra, and how beautiful she is, and how kind she is, and how her hair smells like peaches, for heaven's sake. He loves her enough that he asked her to marry him. And she said yes."

Lorena's head snapped back as she rounded on Alessandra. "What? No, you are *not marrying him!*"

"I am and there's nothing you can do to stop me!"

Just then Trey walked in and stood, filling the entrance to the kitchen with his tall frame. His jaw was set tight as he gave Lorena a long, cold stare. Turning to Alessandra, he spoke, his voice quiet. "Everything okay in here?"

Alessandra's heart surged at the sight of him, a wave of relief rushing over her. She gave him a little nod, then looked back at her mother. This time she spoke in English. "You see? He cares about me."

The sound of whimpering in the hall stopped the fight. Tomas appeared at the entrance to the kitchen, having been woken from his nap by the yelling. His bottom lip was trembling and his eyes were wide with fear. Trey strode over to him and scooped him up in his arms. "It's okay. Everything's fine, little man." He gave him a kiss on the forehead and started for the back door. Turning to Lorena again, he said, "I know you don't trust me and I understand why. We shouldn't have been sneaking around. We should have been upfront with you. But I promise you I'll never hurt Alessa. I love her and nothing's going to change that. I'm not using her, I'm starting a life with her."

Lorena waved her hand at him as though swatting a fly. "He is nothing but a *galinha*!" she snapped, glaring at Alessandra.

Trey looked calmly over to his bride-to-be. "Come on outside, Alessandra. You look like you could use some fresh air."

He held the door for her before carrying his son out into the tranquility of the bright sunshine. Alessandra wiped her tears as she followed him.

Carlos stared at his daughter for a long minute. "He's not Otavio. He's a good young man and Alessandra is a smart girl. They will take care of each other and little Tomas. Now is the time to trust that you did a good job of raising her and to let her go. I know it's hard, but you'll only lose her if you try to stop her."

* * *

The three sat on the swing in the shade with Tomas on Trey's lap. He snuggled his head against Trey's chest and closed his eyes. Alessandra rubbed his little back. "You're still tired. I'm sorry we woke you with that yelling, *rapazinho*. Everything is okay, though." Tears filled her eyes at the memory of the ugly scene, and from the guilt of scaring Tomas.

"You alright?" Trey asked softly, putting his arm around her and pulling her close to him.

Alessa nodded. "I'm fine. I guess we weren't fooling them."

"Guess not. I could hear you all from the barn. I hope it's okay that I came in. I couldn't just leave you to deal with what I was pretty sure was my mess."

"The mess belongs to both of us, but of course it's fine that you came in." She nodded her head. "I'm sorry we scared Tomas."

"He'll be alright." Trey gave her a curious smile. "I have to ask. What's that word she called me?"

Alessandra scrunched up her nose. "Oh, *galinha* is the word for hen. A womanizer is called a *galinha*."

"Well, I guess there are worse things she could have called me, right?" he asked. "On the bright side, maybe now we can have your family at the wedding. Make it a real celebration."

Alessandra gave him a skeptical look. "We'll see if she comes around or not. She can be very stubborn."

* * *

That night, they moved Tomas's bed into the guest house and set it up in the small living room. Tomas had trouble settling down because he was so excited to sleep in the "widdle house," as he called it. Alessandra brought a few of her things with her, having decided the three of them should stay together. She and her mother had artfully avoided each other for the rest of the evening. Lorena left at supper-time and hadn't returned by the time they'd moved everything. When they finally got into bed, Trey could see that Alessandra was still a little shaken from the day's events. He lay next to her and gave her a kiss on the lips that was so gentle, it was almost chaste.

"I'm alright," she said in response.

"It's okay if you're not," he answered quietly. "We don't have to do anything. I'm happy enough to have you in my bed so we can wake up with each other every morning."

She parted her lips, pressing them to his as she ran her hand over his bicep. "I want to be with you. Like this." She lowered her hand down the front of his body, hearing him suck in a deep breath when her fingers reached his underwear. He returned her kiss the way she had hoped he would and rested his hand on the small of her back. Pulling her close, his kisses became more urgent. Moments later, what little clothing they had on was strewn on the floor and he was hovering over her, his lips grazing her bare flesh. Moving down her body, he lingered at her breasts, working her nipples with his tongue until he felt them tighten and she moaned with pleasure. "We're going to have to get used to being very quiet. Do you think you can do that while I'm doing this?"

Alessa smiled down at him. "Yes, I'll try."

Lowering his mouth again, he paused, then looked back up at her. "You'll try?" Shaking his head, he gave her a mock-apologetic look. "I'm sorry, then. We can't do this. I need a guarantee."

Giggling softly, Alessandra nodded. "I promise."

And then his mouth was on her again, teasing her, coaxing her toward the pleasure only he could give. He slowly worked his way back up to her mouth, grinning at her as he flipped onto his back and pulled her on top of him. She sat facing him on his lap. It was her turn to tease him now. Lowering her mouth close to his, she came close to kissing him but then pulled back. Again and again she let him chase her before sneaking out of range. Then she sat up, straightening her back and running her hands up and down his chest. She ground her hips into his lap. Her ears took in a moan but it wasn't hers this time—it was his. She wanted to remind him to be quiet but that sound did something to her that made her feel a little wild. Reaching behind herself, she took his cock in her hand and guided it along her wet sex slowly, back and forth until she couldn't stop herself. She positioned herself over him and lowered her hips, taking in his smooth length like a diver plunging into water. Trey's hands travelled up her sides to her breasts and he gave them a squeeze and ran his thumbs over her nipples. Alessandra's legs parted even more and her hips moved in long drags, drawing him in even deeper with each thrust. She could feel him pulsing inside her with desire, and the look he wore was the strongest aphrodisiac. In his eyes, she saw pure lust and it made her feel powerful. And it made her want to give him everything she had to give. She lowered her face over his, her hair falling around him as she kissed him, and felt his tongue working inside her parted lips the same way his cock was working between her parted legs. Her pace sped up—she rode him hard now, faster, longer, deeper. And then it happened. She could feel herself coming, her entire body tensing and releasing as she let the effects wash over her. Trey slid his thumb into her mouth and she bit down on it so she wouldn't cry out.

When she was finished, Trey pulled her down on top of him, letting her head rest on his chest. "I love you, Alessa. We're going to make this work."

She lifted her head off him so she could kiss him on the lips. He rolled them over so that now she was on her back and he was on top of her. She gazed up at him, overcome by love for him. He wanted to marry her. He wanted to make a life with her. He was every fantasy she'd ever had, only better because he was real. Their tongues danced together, perfectly matched, as their bodies moved. This was real. He was real. He was hers. He moved over her easily, his hips rocking them both, slowly edging them toward that point of pure connection. There was no hurry for either of them. No fear of getting caught. The pleasure of the build-up was as complete as that of what was to come. She could feel herself growing ready again. And then the moment arrived, both of them together, so close it was as though they were now one perfect being in this most intimate of acts. Their mouths never parted as they felt the pleasure flowing from one to the other and back. When it was over, Trey lay on top of her, their bodies glistening with sweat and gratification. He rolled them both onto their sides, their bodies still tangled, him still buried inside her as they recovered, naked and warm.

"I love you, Trey," she whispered, too overcome by emotion to say more. It was as though this were their wedding night, though no ceremony had happened yet.

They dozed together like this for a long while before their bodies started moving together again, and they found themselves back in that place that belonged only to them.

TWENTY-FIVE

August began, bringing Alessandra a sense of exhilaration with an undercurrent of tension. Lorena was still furious but chose to pretend that neither Trey nor Alessandra existed. When their intent to marry was posted in the newspaper, dozens of well-wishers, along with the curious, phoned. Lorena chose to stop answering the phone altogether. Her resistance only strengthened the resolve of the young couple, pulling them together in the way adversity alone can do.

They were granted a marriage licence ten days before Betina was set to leave for the US to start university. As soon as they received the court's approval, they set to work in hopes of creating a lovely wedding Betina could attend before she left. Carlos had given his blessing for the ceremony and reception to take place in the yard, and immediately the family was called to help with the hurried preparations. Excitement swept through the farm as traditional foods were prepared and the property was readied for the big day.

Trey had wrestled with whether or not to tell his parents. Since the big argument with his mother, they had avoided calling each other, both wanting to wait until the other gave in. He knew he needed to tell his mom and dad about his relationship with Alessandra and about their wedding plans, but he wasn't sure how to tell them he was about to marry someone they'd never met. They would try to talk him out of it, and that would lead to another fight and more weeks or possibly months of silence between them. He knew how hurt they would feel, and in the end, he decided it would be easier for them to hear that it had already happened than to be at home knowing the event was taking place without them. Besides, he planned to tell them they could hold a reception in Colorado when he and Alessa returned.

The morning before the wedding, Carlos found Trey and Tomas feeding the animals in the barn. "Come," Carlos called to them, walking out into the sunny yard. Alessandra, who was wiping down the long wooden table on the patio, stopped to watch as they approached.

"Alessandra," Carlos called. "Come."

She put down the rag and joined them. *"Sim, Vô?"*

"Para você," he said quietly as he opened his hand. Two rings sat in the palm of his hand, both made from dark Brazilian rosewood. They were smooth and had been polished carefully to display the delicate grain of the wood. The inside of the rings was silver.

Alessandra gasped. "You made these, *Vô?*"

"Sim," he answered with a proud smile. *"Da mesma árvore que o anel de sua avó e o meu foram feitos."*

"Obrigada." Alessandra gave him a huge hug, then, her eyes glistening, she explained what he'd said to Trey. "He made these rings using wood from the same tree he used to make the wedding rings he and my grandmother wore."

She picked up the smaller of the two and held it up. "You see, he has carved your name inside my ring. And mine inside yours. This is the custom."

Trey picked up his ring and turned it in his hand. *"Obrigado,* sir. I don't know what to say. They're really beautiful. But how did you get the silver on there?"

Carlos said a few words to Alessandra, who translated with a grin. "He said he's old, so he knows how to do everything."

Tomas tugged on Trey's leg, trying to reach up on his tiptoes to see the rings. "Oh, here, Tomas, come see," Trey said, picking him up.

Carlos took a small bracelet that matched the rings out of his pocket. Inside were engraved the date and all three of their names, along with the word *família*. Tomas took it, his eyes wide with excitement. "I get a big one!"

"For wedding," Carlos told him with a kind smile.

Tomas gave him a big hug around the neck and said, *"Obrigado, Avô!"*

* * *

Soon Alessandra's aunts and female cousins arrived, bearing gifts and the ingredients to make the wedding favours.

"What is all this?" Alessandra asked as they filed into the house, loading her arms with presents and pausing to kiss her cheeks.

Her Aunt Bertha grinned at her. "You've given us no time to arrange a kitchen shower for you, so we will do it now while we cook!"

Tears filled Alessandra's eyes. "Thank you, everyone! You are too good to me."

Bertha gave her an inquisitive look. "Why does this make you cry? You are *pregnant*! Betina said you weren't, but I knew there must be some reason for this fast wedding."

"No, *Tia*, I'm not pregnant. I just didn't want to get married without Betina here."

Her aunt raised an eyebrow at her. "You can only pretend for so long, Alessandra. Eventually, we're all going to see the proof."

A knock at the door saved Alessandra from the uncomfortable conversation. It was Daniela, bringing in a large rectangular box. "What are you wearing tomorrow, my dear?"

"I've rented a dress. I need to go pick it up later."

"No you don't. This is the dress your grandmother wore when she and *Vô* got married. I've been saving it for you since I found out Bruno wasn't a Bruna. I think it will be perfect for you."

Tears flooded Alessandra's eyes again as she took the box from her aunt. Unable to speak, she just nodded, her face screwed up with emotion.

"Go try it on!" Bertha ordered, ushering her down the hall.

"She should wait until Lorena is here," commented one of Alessa's other aunts.

"No. She should try it now. We need to know if it fits." Betina's normally quiet voice was strong and firm. "Besides, our mother isn't here."

Daniela gave Betina a worried look, then smiled at Alessandra. "Never mind that. Come, I'll help you."

Once they reached her bedroom, Alessandra placed the box onto her bed, then flopped down next to it, dissolving into sobs. "She won't come. She's so angry with me."

"Nonsense, she'll be here to see her eldest daughter get married."

"No, she said she won't watch me ruin my life with some foreign cowboy." Alessa shook her head, staring at her aunt, her cheeks stained with tears.

Daniela placed her hands on Alessandra's cheeks and used her thumbs to wipe away the tears. "You've always been my favourite niece. You're smart as a whip and you've always made your family proud. There's nothing I wouldn't do for you, including dragging your mother outside in her nightgown for the wedding tomorrow. But it won't come to that. *Vô* will make her come. You'll see, it will all be fine."

"Really?"

"Really. Now, go blow your nose and wash your face. I don't want any snot getting on the dress."

A few minutes later, Alessandra caught the first sight of herself in the mirror. The dress was made of ivory lace, with a scalloped, off-the-shoulder neckline. Long lace sleeves cascaded down her arms and ended in a delicate point on the backs of her hands. The fitted bodice came to a *V* just below her waist and led to a full, floor-length skirt. Alessandra beamed as she looked at herself. "I look like a real bride," she whispered.

A knock at the door interrupted her just as she was about to start crying again. "It's Betina. Can I see?"

"Yes, of course," Alessa called back.

Daniela opened the door a crack. "Nobody else, though. They can all wait for tomorrow."

Betina squeezed through the opening, then gasped. "Oh, Alessa, you look so beautiful!" She lifted a hand over her mouth and stared at her big sister for a moment before rushing to her for a hug.

When the moment was over, Alessa turned to her aunt. "What do you think of the fit?"

"Very good," Daniela commented, tugging a little here and there along the bodice. "We'll need to let it out in the chest. Your grandmother wasn't as blessed as you are in that department. But otherwise, I think it's perfect."

"Can it be done so fast?"

Daniela winked. "It's nothing. You get changed and I'll get to work right away."

Betina held up the veil that was in the dress box. "Wait, she should try this on."

Daniela shook her head. "No. Your mother will put that on her tomorrow. No matter how she is acting today, it is her honour."

* * *

Soon the house was filled with delectable aromas as the *feijoada* was started on the stovetop and the first batch of cookies was popped into the oven. The kitchen was a crowded space for so many cooks, but they managed to work well enough and they shared many laughs. The whir of the sewing machine in the corner of the kitchen added to the chaos as the women told stories of weddings past and gave Alessandra advice on marriage.

"The cookies have cooled. Let's start putting them together," Bertha called.

They heard a light knock at the door and turned to see Trey and Tomas in the back entrance. "We heard there might be cookies in here," Trey said sheepishly.

"Come, come! We can spare a cookie for the groom and our new nephew!" Daniela called. "These are *casadinhos*; they are called a 'well-married' cookie. We are wrapping them to give to the guests." She pointed to a basket holding several packages. "We pair two cookies together, like a bride and groom, see? Then they are glued together with something as sweet as true love. We are using marmalades and jams because they are Alessandra's favourites. When they are put together we call them *bem casados*, which means a wish for a sweet life together."

"That's a very nice tradition. Thank you all so much for doing this for us." Trey flashed a grin at the ladies before he and Tomas helped themselves. "We should go eat these outside. We don't want to interrupt."

"Wait a minute, Mr. Groom," Bertha said. "Has she told you what will happen tomorrow?"

Trey wore a confused look. "We're going to get married?" he asked slowly, glancing at Alessandra.

"Yes, but did she tell you about the *bumba meu boi*?"

"The bumba what now?" Trey asked, a suspicious look crossing his face as the women broke into laughter.

Alessandra rolled her eyes. "No! We are not doing that."

"Yes, we are! The donkey will be here an hour before the ceremony. The *bumba meu boi* is normally done before the engagement but it will be last minute, like everything else with this wedding!"

"Donkey?" Trey asked, his eyebrows knitting together.

"There won't be a donkey. Don't worry about it." Alessandra glared at her aunt.

"Worry about it. And don't put on your suit until after everyone arrives. You'll have a messy job to do." Daniela waved him out the door. "Now, out you go! We have work to do"

A few hours later, the house was still again. Everyone had gone home for the night. Daniela had taken the dress to press it. They'd worked so hard that Alessandra hadn't stopped long enough to open the presents from the kitchen shower. She plunked herself onto the couch next to Betina, feet aching.

"You should open your gifts." Betina said.

"After the wedding. Let's just sit. My head is swirling."

They sat silently for a few minutes before Betina rested her hand on top of her sister's. "I can't believe you're getting married tomorrow. It seems so grown-up."

Alessandra felt a lump in her throat again. "I know. I can't believe you're going to America in two days."

Betina's eyes welled up. "I know. I'm going to miss you. It's been so nice to be together in the same place again."

"It has, hasn't it?" Alessandra whispered, leaning her head against Betina's.

"Why do things have to change?" Betina wondered out loud.

"I don't know. Sometimes I wish I could freeze time in a perfect moment and stay there."

"Me too. Would this be your moment? I mean, this day?"

"Almost. If Mother was talking to me maybe. I feel sick when I think about how upset she is."

Betina nodded and stared at her sister. "She'll come around. Tomorrow will be the perfect day."

"If it is, let's freeze time."

Betina sighed. "What's it like? Being loved like that, I mean."

Alessandra's eyes lit up. "It's like . . . we share a wonderful secret that no one else would understand. It's like no one has ever loved this much in the history of the world and never will again. It feels like I can see my future, finally, because it will be spent with him, and I'm sure about it like I've never been sure of anything in my life."

"Oh, that makes me want to fall in love right this very minute," Betina replied wistfully. "Do you think I will ever find a man like Trey?"

Nodding, Alessandra gave her a bright smile. "Yes, of course you will. When the time is right."

The moment was interrupted by the sound of the front door. Lorena walked in, locking the door behind her before looking up to see her daughters on the couch. She froze for a second, then put her nose in the air and made her way out of the room and down the hall. Alessandra felt the sting of her mother's anger in the pit of her stomach, which flipped and flopped as she watched Lorena walk away.

Much to Alessandra's surprise, her mother came back to the living room and cleared her throat. "Betina, I would like to speak with Alessandra alone."

Betina glanced over at Alessandra. "Do you want me to stay?"

"No, thank you, honey." Alessandra gave her a small smile.

"Okay. I'll go get ready for bed." She walked past her mom and said, "Be nice."

Lorena gave her an irritated nod, then sat with a sigh in an armchair opposite the couch. "I was seventeen when I got pregnant with you."

Alessandra rolled her eyes. "I know all this. You had to give up your dream of being the first person in your family to go to university. By the time you were nineteen, you had two babies and no husband and no money. I am nothing like you. I've been to school. I have a good job."

"True, Alessandra. In some ways you are nothing like me, but you are also exactly the same. You are headstrong like me and you can't see the writing on the wall. And I know that nothing I say will change your mind. You think you have the greatest love of all time and that no one in the world could possibly understand, certainly not your horrible mother."

Alessandra tried to hide any proof that her mother was right. "You *don't* understand. You don't think a man like him could ever love someone like me, do you? But he does. He loves me and he wants to make a life with me. And we're going to start that tomorrow. And it kills me that you can't just be happy for me." Alessandra sniffed and dabbed at the stream of tears gliding down her cheeks.

Lorena shook her head. "Those are the words I used on my mother when she found out I was pregnant. You're so smart in some ways, child. And in others, so naive. What if he is only marrying you so his son will have a mother? Have you thought of that? And where will you live? Are you going to pack up your things and start over in the United States? Can you even be a lawyer there or just his servant?"

"Enough! Enough, *Mamãe*. Just please stop. You don't know what it's like when we're alone together. His feelings for me have *nothing* to do with Tomas!" Alessandra put up both hands. "No, forget it. It's the night before my wedding and I don't want to hear this. I'm not going to change my mind. We're in love and we're smart and we'll figure out how to make a life together."

{163}

"*You're* smart, but he thinks he's going to get rich riding bulls for a living! For God's sake, Alessandra! He's *exactly* like your father. Right down to the crazy dreams, and it scares me to see you tying yourself to someone with foolish notions like that."

"Enough. He's not like that. The bull riding is only temporary. Things will change once he's part of this family and he won't need to do it any more."

Lorena scoffed. "Don't be so sure. Once they get a taste of the excitement and make some quick money, they don't give up so easily. You're going to end up alone and raising a son who isn't even yours."

Alessandra's words escaped clenched teeth. "That is not going to happen. But if it did, I would be happy to raise Tomas. I have loved him like a son for two years now. He's as much my little boy as he is Trey's!"

"And exactly how can you be sure that *you* aren't confusing your love for Tomas with your love for his father? Maybe you only *think* you're in love with him because you don't want to lose that little boy!"

Alessandra sighed and shook her head. "Because I'm not confused, Mother. I'm in love with Trey. Now either wake up tomorrow ready to be happy for me or stay in your room all day and miss the entire thing. *Vô* can give me away if you refuse."

With that, Alessandra got up and stalked down the hall to her room. She shut the door and growled in frustration. This was the last thing she needed the night before her wedding. Her mother filling her head with doubts about the man she loved, when she was nervous enough. Why couldn't Lorena just be happy for her? All her life, Alessandra had done everything her mother wanted. She'd learned English, gone to law school and done well, working a job the entire time to pay for her room and board so she wouldn't burden her family with those costs. Now she had returned to Bebedouro to help out. She'd quickly found a job and was also here every day helping them. In fact, she'd managed to find a *good* man, who had made huge improvements to the farm in just a matter of weeks. Trey couldn't be more perfect for her family, really. He would take over running the farm so her grandfather could slow down. But all her mother could do was accuse him of using Alessandra or, now, even go as far as to suggest that *Alessandra* was using *Trey* so she could keep Tomas. Ridiculous.

She stripped down, tossing her clothes into the corner of her room, and grabbed a nightie out of her drawer. This wasn't how she should be spending her last night as a single woman. She should be having a heart-to-heart talk with her mother over tea at the kitchen table. Not another huge blow-up. But her mother was bitter and scared and always would be. And at the moment, Alessandra hated her for it.

*   *   *

Hours later, Alessandra lay in bed, no longer angry but now very nervous about the next day. She heard a tapping sound on the window. She quickly got up and opened her curtain to see Trey standing on the grass. Sliding the window open, she smiled at him. "You can't sleep either?"

"I doubt I'll sleep for five minutes, even. I needed to see you."

"I'll come outside. One second."

Alessandra crept down the hall on her tiptoes. When she got outside, her groom was waiting for her. She stepped into his warm embrace. The air had grown unexpectedly cool and she wished she had taken the time to put on a robe over her nightie. He stepped back and took her hands in his.

"I just wanted to double-check that you still want to marry me."

He said it as though he was joking, but Alessandra could tell there was some truth to it.

Her heart pounded in her rib cage. "Of course I do. Why? Have you changed your mind?"

"No, of course not. But tonight, I was lying in bed and I just got to thinking that maybe I rushed you too much with this. If you aren't ready, we can always postpone."

"You didn't rush me, Trey. I know how fast this is, but I want to be your wife and I want to start our life together right away. This feels more right than anything I've ever done before. I can feel it in my bones."

He broke out into a relieved smile. "Thank God, because I think we're absolutely perfect for each other. I actually don't know what I would have done if you said you didn't want to marry me. It would have damn near killed me, I think." Pulling her in for a long hug, he sighed happily. "Mmm, it feels good to hold you. I've gotten so used to falling asleep with you that now it's hard to sleep apart." Trey lowered his mouth over hers and gave her a lingering kiss.

"Me too. Whose dumb idea was it to sleep apart tonight?"

"Yours."

"Right. I forgot. You should never have agreed to that." She grinned up at him for a moment, then her face grew serious. "Are you nervous about tomorrow?"

"No. Well, I'm not at all worried about marrying you. That, I'm completely sure about. But I am kind of nervous about messing things up in the ceremony. I don't exactly know all the customs, like that donkey thing. What the hell is up with that?"

Alessandra laughed. "Don't worry, you're fully equipped to handle it. You'll go into the corral, where a donkey will be waiting. You have to catch him and tame him to prove you will be a worthy husband."

"So, a man catches one donkey once and he's got what it takes to be a good husband? Seems logical," Trey teased.

Alessandra laughed. "Oh yes, very."

"I'm assuming I'll be making an ass of myself in front of everyone you know?"

"Yes. There will likely be quite a big crowd."

"Perfect. Have I told you I've never been very good with donkeys?"

Alessandra covered her mouth with her hand to hide her laughter. "Oh dear. I'm sorry about this."

"I'm sure you'll make it up to me."

"Oh I will, I promise," she answered in a sultry voice.

"Can't wait. Any chance they'll bring a very agreeable donkey? Maybe one that's about ten minutes from dying of old age?"

Alessandra shook her head. "None. My aunt said she and my uncle are going to their neighbour to see if they can get his. Her words were, 'That animal's a real mean son of a bitch.'"

"Perfect."

The pair laughed quietly before Trey got back to the business at hand. "What else do I need to know?"

Alessandra screwed up her face in thought. "Well, whatever you do, don't drop the rings. It's considered a very bad omen and means our marriage won't last long."

"No pressure though, right?" he asked.

"Yes, some pressure." She gave him a serious look.

"Even if I do drop the rings, it won't change anything, Alessandra. We're going to be married for the rest of our lives, and we're going to be in love just like we are now."

"Oh no, it will mean a horrible fate for sure. If the rings are dropped, the marriage is doomed." She shook her head solemnly.

"You're not serious, are you?" He narrowed his eyes at Alessandra until a hint of a smile escaped her lips. "Are you trying to mess with me?" he asked indignantly.

"A little bit," she answered, finally letting herself laugh. "But seriously, don't drop the rings."

"Oh, I'm in for quite the life, aren't I?" He took her in his arms again and kissed her. "God, I miss you. I can't wait for tomorrow night."

"Me too." Alessandra sighed. "I only hope my mother will come around. We had another argument about you tonight."

"She doesn't think I'm a good bet."

"I think she's just scared that you're making me give up her dreams for me."

"You mean *your* dreams."

"No, I mean her dreams. Of me being a rich lawyer. You are my dream now."

"Can't you have both?"

"Yes. But if I had to choose, you'd win. And I think that's what scares her." She reached up and gave him a long kiss.

"I'll never make you give up your dreams, Alessandra. We'll find a way for us both to live the life we want. We'll build it together, and eventually she'll come around. I hope it'll be tomorrow but if it's not, someday she's going to see I'm not a complete bastard."

"You're right. She will." A breeze flipped her nightie up, causing goosebumps to form on her skin.

"I should let you get back inside. You're getting cold."

"I don't want to. I want to stay like this in your arms all night."

They kissed and held each other until the next breeze came up and Trey stepped back, running his hands down her arms until he found her fingers with his. "I better go. If Tomas wakes up, I won't hear him."

"Right. Give him a kiss from me."

"I will."

Trey let go of her hands and watched as she turned to the house. "Hey," he called. "I forgot to ask if I can see you tomorrow before the wedding."

"Yes, but not after I'm in my dress."

"Okay, good. Because I don't know if I could wait until late afternoon to look at your beautiful face. Guess I'll go back to bed now so I can stare at the ceiling and miss you."

"Same here."

TWENTY-SIX

A crack of thunder woke Trey with a start. Snapping himself upright, he looked over to the window. Through the curtains, he could see it was light out and yet strangely dark in a way he hadn't seen since he'd been in Brazil. A second clap brought him to his feet to check on Tomas. He carefully opened the door to the living room and saw Tomas sleeping peacefully, his mouth hanging open. Trey sneaked over to him and tucked the quilt over his little body, then gently ran his hand over his soft hair. Looking at the time, he saw it was after 6 a.m now. He had finally drifted off around three in the morning and now felt an unshakable grogginess as he stumbled back to his bedroom. Pulling back the curtain, he looked out as rivers of water poured down the glass, making the world outside a blur of dim colours. Lightning flashed, then another boom shook the house.

"Shit," he said to himself. "So much for a backyard wedding."

* * *

Twenty minutes later, he ran across the field with Tomas in his arms. He hunched over his son to shelter him from the pelting rain. Stepping into the bright warmth of the kitchen, Trey put him down.

Alessa got up from the table and quickly started unbuttoning Tomas's coat and sliding his boots off. "Good morning, *rapazinho*."

"Morning, Lessa." He touched her cheeks with his chubby little fingers. "It's raining hard!"

"I saw that." She glanced up at Trey with a worried expression.

Betina reached her hand out to Tomas. "Come, *rapazinho*, have some pancakes with *Tia*."

Alessa stood and watched as Trey finished hanging his coat, which was drenched from his dash to the house. He gave her a confident smile. "You look worried. Don't be worried. I have a plan."

"Don't be worried? This is the first huge storm in over a year! And it happens on our wedding day. What if it's a sign?"

"A sign? When did you get so superstitious? It's just rain. I don't figure the earth chooses weather based on our plans. Do you?" He gave her a kiss on the forehead.

"But—"

"It's just a little water. Besides, back home, rain on your wedding day means good luck. Or that you'll have lots of kids. Something like that. Anyway, it's good. Now, I'm gonna need some coffee, and Carlos. Is he around?"

"He just finished breakfast. *Avô*!" Betina called as Trey helped himself to a mug.

Carlos appeared a moment later. "*Olá*!" he said with a smile.

"*Olá*, Carlos," Trey said. "Betina, can you help me explain my plan to Carlos? Alessandra, you and Tomas relax and have some pancakes. Then I want you to spend the day doing exactly what you would have if it were sunny out. Take it easy, drink some champagne, get a manicure or whatever it is brides do before a wedding."

She put her hand on her hip. "How am I supposed to do that?"

"Use your imagination." He gave her a little wink. "And trust me."

An hour later, the first of several trucks started pulling into the yard. Alessandra's uncles and cousins got out, dressed in rain gear. Lorena sat by the window in her bedroom, watching as Trey led them over to the barn, pointing and gesturing as though giving detailed instructions. He had started erecting a lean-to using a couple of huge tarps and some long poles and was now soaked, water pouring off the rim of his cowboy hat. "What the hell does he think he's doing?" she asked herself.

The men hurried over to help pull the tarps taut and prop them up using the poles. Large sheets of plywood were brought from the tool shed and set down under the lean-to.

Lorena scowled. "If he thinks my daughter is getting married under a tarp, he's dumber than dirt."

Two tractors were driven out and parked under the tarps a few minutes later. "The barn? No, no, no. This is undignified."

Trey glanced at the house and saw Lorena sitting in the window, her eyes narrowed at him in an unmistakable display of disgust. He tipped his hat to her and gave her a tight smile.

*   *   *

Miguel backed his truck up to the barn. He had attached a long horse trailer to the truck and the men were now loading the animals into it. When they finished, Miguel gave a little wave and drove off. Soon, clouds of dust billowed out of the barn's main door. Betina stood at the kitchen window, holding Tomas in her arms.

"I go out," he told her.

"No, honey. You play with *Tia*. Your dad said it's going to be very messy out there while he works."

"Me like messes."

"More than cookies?" she asked. "*Tia* has cookies for boys who stay inside."

Tomas nodded. "Okay."

Alessandra's voice came from down the hall. "What's going on out there?"

"Nothing!" Betina called to her. "You're supposed to be in the bath relaxing, remember?"

"I can't relax. It's my wedding day!"

"Too bad. I've been given my orders: keep you away from the windows and try to make you relax! Now shut up and read a book or something."

* * *

"Okay, guys, let's bring the lights in next!" Trey called as he strode over to the wall to take a ladder down. The men unloaded boxes of candles and white Christmas lights they had all been instructed to bring. For the next hour they worked quickly, stringing the lights and setting out the candles. Trey worked with Bruno on setting up a large awning of beige canvas. They attached it over the main doors to the barn, then set down sheets of plywood to make an entrance for the guests. Taking out his measuring tape, Carlos measured the plywood at the front door and made some notes, then got into his truck and disappeared without a word to anyone. An hour later he returned, his truck filled with large black mats. Finding help from a few of his nephews, he began to position the mats on the wood. A long black carpet was the next thing to come out of his truck. They rolled it down the centre of the barn floor to make an aisle.

"Wow! That looks great, sir!" Trey called. He was perched on top of a ladder, stapling a string of lights along the wall. "*Obrigado!*"

Carlos gave him a thumbs-up and a nod of approval on the work

Trey had done. The floor of the barn had never been cleaner and had dried nicely by the time the carpet was rolled out.

"That's it for the lights. Did anyone manage to find that white cloth I asked for?"

Miguel raised a hand. "My mother sent me to the fabric store to get it. It's called tulle, and you owe me because I looked like a big sissy walking out with three rolls of it."

Trey laughed. "Thank you very much! When you get married, I'll be glad to look like a sissy for you."

* * *

Alessandra sat on her bed in a bathrobe, staring at herself in the mirror. The sight of Tomas's little tuxedo hanging in her closet caught her eye. She was about to become his stepmom, and the thought made her heart swell. After today, she would never have to worry about him being taken from her again. She would go from being his nanny to being his mother, giving her the chance to watch him grow up and guide him through all of life's trials. Raising a child, promising to be there for him for the rest of his life, no matter what, was the biggest of responsibilities. Her heart pounded with the enormity of it, but she wasn't overwhelmed or scared. Rather, she felt the purest joy. She had glimpsed the sadness of losing him and knew without a doubt that she was ready for this commitment.

Alessandra stood and opened the door.

"Tomas? Where are you?"

He poked his head around the corner of the hallway. "Watching cartoons."

"Come with me for a minute. It's time to put on your tuxedo."

He glanced back at the TV, then, with a shrug of one shoulder, he walked down the hall to her.

When he entered the room, Alessandra knelt in front of him and planted a wet kiss on his forehead. "Tomas, you know that your dad and I are getting married today. But do you know what that means?"

"We get cookies?"

Chuckling a little, she smiled down at him as she lifted his T-shirt over his head. "Yes, but also it means that after today, I will be your stepmom and you will always be my son. We will be a family. You and your dad and me. We will never have to go away from each other."

Tomas beamed at her as she pulled a white shirt onto him and buttoned it. When she was finished dressing him she shook her head in wonder. "You look so handsome, like a true gentleman. I love you so, so much, *rapazinho*. You will always be my little boy, no matter how big you get."

"I love you too, Lessa. I go watch cartoons now."

"Okay, no more snacks, though. I don't want you to get your clothes dirty." She watched as he turned and made his way out of the room, her heart bursting with joy. She couldn't wait for the day when he would call her *Mãe*, but she knew she needed to be patient. It would happen when the time was right for him.

*   *   *

By the time the guests started arriving, the barn was ready. Trey, however, was not. He was covered in both mud and dust. The rain continued to beat down on the yard as Daniela and Ricardo arrived with a small trailer attached to the back of their truck. Trey swore under his breath as he realized it was a carrying a donkey. The other men started laughing, and Trey gave them a wry smile in exchange. "Alright boys, thirty minutes till the ceremony. Let's get this done."

Putting on his hat and coat, he stood under the awning, watching as the donkey was set loose in the muddy pen next to the barn.

He stood with his hands on his hips, watching the burro for a moment before heading to the house instead of the pen. The guests who had decided to brave the rain heckled him as he walked away.

"Be right back!" he called.

Knocking on the kitchen door, he waited until Betina answered. "Is it safe to come in?"

"Yes. She's in her room getting dressed."

"Good. We're almost all set. Only three things left on my list. I just need to catch a burro, get your mother to come out of her bedroom, and go have a shower." He toed his cowboy boots off and hung up his coat and hat before starting down the hall to Lorena's room.

"Alessandra," he called as he neared her room. "Don't come out. It's me, but I'll be out of the house again in a minute."

"Alright. Is everything okay?" she called back, sounding worried.

"Never better, honey. We're going to have ourselves a terrific wedding."

He tapped gently on Lorena's door, then spoke into the wood. "Lorena. It's Trey . . . Listen, I understand that I'm not a good bet as far as your daughter goes. We only met a couple of months ago, I'm broke, I have no job and I'm a foreigner with a three-year-old. But except for my son, I love your daughter more than anything or anyone I've ever met. And I'm going to set my mind to taking care of her for the rest of her life. Once I set my mind to something, I do it. I'm lucky enough that she's agreed to share her life with me, and I promise you that I'll never take her for granted and I'll never ask her to give up her dreams, either. In fact, I'll fight like hell if she ever wants to give up her dreams. I promise you that."

He paused, waiting for Lorena to say something. When no response came, he continued. "In about thirty minutes, a moment in Alessandra's life is going to happen that you can never get back. She has no father. Only you. And if you're not there, you're going to spend the rest of your life wishing you had been. Even if I turn out to be a total bum, she's always going to be your little girl. And she needs you today."

He stood for a moment, waiting, and then let out a sigh and turned on his heel. Passing through the kitchen, he opened the sugar bowl and scooped up a handful of cubes. Once outside, he walked directly to the pen, where the donkey stood in the far corner, looking wet and miserable. Plucking a rope off the gate, he draped it over his shoulder, then opened the latch and entered the pen. Gently tossing a sugar cube beside the donkey, Trey stood perfectly still, waiting. The donkey stared him down for a moment before deciding to go for the treat. As soon as he ate it, Trey tossed another one a little closer, then another and another, until the burro was close enough. He stood sideways beside the animal with his hand outstretched. When the donkey finally started to nibble the sugar from his hand, Trey let his shoulder drop a little and, with his other hand, pulled the rope off his arm and onto the burro's neck. Giving the rope a small tug, he turned and led the animal out of the pen and into the back of the waiting trailer.

"Hmph, that was maybe the most boring *bumba meu boi* I've ever seen," Alessandra's uncle remarked as he put his video camera away. "I thought for sure he would end up sliding around in the mud for a long time, but there was nothing funny at all."

Trey gave the guests a smile and a nod as he started toward his house. He turned back and held up his hands. "Thank you, everyone! That was fun but I need to get cleaned up. I'm getting married in a few minutes!"

* * *

Daniela banged on the door to Lorena's bedroom. "Lorena, you're being a child! Open the door now!"

Pulling a hairpin out of her mess of naturally curly tresses, Daniela began to pick the lock but the door swung open, revealing Lorena in a beautiful red dress, her hair swept up off her neck.

She gave Daniela a little nod. "I'm here. No need to be rude about it."

Alessandra opened the door to her own room, and the two burst into tears, hugging each other. Lorena whispered, "I can't believe I almost missed this. I'm so sorry." She reached up and held Alessandra's cheeks in both hands. "You are my daughter and I love you. I want the best in life for you, which includes the best husband. I've been watching your man today and I think I may have been wrong about him. You should see what he's been doing all day. He must really love you to make such a wedding for you from nothing."

Alessandra nodded. "He does. I know he does. And we're going to be just fine."

"I hope so. Either way, I'll be there for you. Always, I will."

"I know." She squeezed her mother before letting go. "Now, I need to fix my makeup again. And so do you."

"And you need your veil."

"We better hurry."

"Not really, the bride is always late. It's good luck," Lorena said. Turning to her sister, she said, "Daniela, has anyone made the *caipirinha*? I think my daughter could use a drink to calm her nerves."

Daniela nodded. "Of course. I'll get us all one."

TWENTY-SEVEN

Alessandra stood under the makeshift awning with her *avô* and her mother on either side of her. The rain had slowed to a steady, soothing rhythm and the air felt refreshing against her skin. Her heart beat wildly as she looked down and saw her bouquet of lavender hydrangeas and roses shaking. "Breathe, darling, breathe," Lorena said.

Carlos turned to her and smiled. "You are so beautiful, my little one. You are like the sun. Every day your heart shines straight out into the world, bringing warmth wherever you go. I'm so lucky to have lived long enough to see you get married to such a nice young man. I know you will take care of each other the way your grandmother and I did."

"Oh, *Papai*," Lorena interrupted. "You'll make her cry and ruin her makeup."

"She'll still be beautiful," he said proudly.

Betina slid open the barn door a crack, then asked the bride if she was ready. Alessandra nodded, her nose wrinkling up with emotion.

"Okay, here we go!" Betina said, sliding the door open to reveal the transformation of the barn to her sister, and that of her sister to everyone who was waiting for her.

Alessandra gasped when she saw the huge space, now somehow so elegant, with tiny white lights strung everywhere and tulle streaming from the walls to a point in the centre of the ceiling to make it look like they were inside a large tent. Simple white folding chairs lined both sides of an aisle, and her family and friends stood facing her. Candles glowed from all sides, and a trail of white rose petals led down a black carpet to the other side of the room, where a wooden arbour covered in tulle had been set up. Trey stood in front of the arbour, looking devastatingly handsome in a black tuxedo, his face full of emotion as he gazed at her. Tomas stood at his side, looking like a miniature clone of his father and grinning from ear to ear. Alessandra was so overcome, her feet forgot how to move. Her entire body shook now as her hand covered her mouth. She tried, with everything in her, to blink back tears but they refused to be denied. Carlos and Lorena linked arms with her and gently nudged her forward. This was it.

Hundreds of eyes were on her but only one set mattered to Alessandra, and his were shining with love. When she finally reached him, Carlos offered her hand to Trey, who took it carefully in his own. "You look so beautiful," he whispered in her ear. "I love you so much."

"I love you too," she answered back. "I can't believe you did all this for me. You're amazing."

"Oh, this?" he asked nonchalantly. "This is nothing. I'm just getting started."

Alessandra's boss, Judge Bathory, stood in front of them, ready to oversee the ceremony. He smiled at her and spoke quietly. "You look very lovely, Alessandra. And you've got quite the groom here. I saw how he managed to catch the donkey with sugar cubes. It was inventive, and it made me curious about how he captured you."

Alessandra glanced at Trey. "It was much the same way, except he used pistachio ice cream."

The judge laughed. "Are you ready, my dear?"

"I am."

"Let's go!"

Trey squeezed her hand as Judge Bathory started his address to the crowd, speaking in both English and Portuguese. He spoke of the importance of marriage, his admiration for Alessandra and his wishes for their future together with little Tomas. When it was time to exchange vows, the couple faced each other. Trey was asked to go first. He took a small paper out of his pocket and unfolded it. "Betina helped me with this, so now we'll see if she really likes me or not." The guests who could understand English chuckled at his joke.

Trey looked at the audience. "Um, please excuse my poor pronunciation, everyone. I'm new to Portuguese."

Then he turned to her and started to read from the paper slowly, glancing up at her often as he made his vows. "Alessandra, sometimes life takes us places we never knew we'd go and takes us completely by surprise. If someone had told me a few months ago that I would be living on a farm in rural Brazil and that I would be madly in love, I wouldn't have believed them. But here I am and here you are. Life brought you to Tomas and then me to you. And that makes me the luckiest guy alive, because you are without a doubt the most beautiful person, both inside and out, that I've ever met. You seem to have enough patience and kindness for the entire world. And it didn't take me long to figure out that you were it for me. You have the most wonderful laugh I've ever heard, and I want to spend the rest of my life making you laugh and seeing your smile and knowing your heart. You make me want to be a better man, and with you by my side, I know I can do that. I believe in you, Alessandra, and I believe in us. I'll stay faithful to you, honour you, love you and support you for better or worse, in sickness and in health, for richer or for poorer, for the rest of our lives." Trey's voice broke a little as he gazed into the glowing face of his bride. "How was that?" he asked in English.

"Good, except for the part where you said you would turn her into a goat if she didn't cook for you," the judge said.

Trey's eyes grew wide until he saw Alessandra laugh. "No, you were perfect. Don't listen to him."

Judge Bathory prompted Alessandra to take her turn. She dabbed at her eyes with a tissue before speaking in English. "Trey, you are the most wonderful man I've ever known. You are smart and fun and kind. You are so determined to do the right thing, and I know in my heart that you will always be there for me. I've watched you with your son as you've learned how to love him and take care of him. The love I have for you is like nothing I've known before and I know without a doubt it will never end. I'm proud to become your wife today, and I'm honoured to be able to make a life with you starting now. Trey, I will love you and honour you, stay faithful to you and support you for better or for worse, in sickness and in health, for richer or for poorer, for the rest of our lives."

The judge motioned to Tomas to present the rings. Tomas grinned up at his father and Alessandra, plucking the rings off the satin pillow to hand to his dad. His little fingers didn't have a good grip on them and they both fell, rolling out of sight under a row of chairs. Gasps sounded from all around and Tomas's bottom lip quivered as he stared up at his dad. "It's okay, buddy, we'll find them," Trey said with a little wink as he crouched down to look for them. The guests in that row all scoured the floorboards underneath them, finally retrieving the rings.

"Here we go!" Trey held them up triumphantly. He gave Alessandra a reassuring smile and whispered, "It's going to be fine. Trust me."

Alessandra nodded but looked less certain than he'd hoped. The couple exchanged rings before finally reaching the moment Trey had been waiting for since the ceremony began: the kiss. He tipped her back and kissed her long and hard, feeling her happiness in the curve of her mouth. When he lifted her back up to standing, the incident with the rings was all but forgotten and thunderous applause echoed through the rafters of the old barn.

Trey and Alessandra started their walk down the aisle with their clasped hands held above their heads and their little boy running ahead of them. When they reached the barn doors, they walked out to the makeshift entrance, feeling the fresh air.

"We did it!" Trey exclaimed. "I can't believe we really did it!"

"Are you glad?"

"Quit asking me that. Of course I'm glad. I'm the happiest man on earth." He picked her up and spun around as they hugged and kissed in that moment of quiet before the guests started to join them.

*　*　*

The rest of the evening was noisy and fun and filled with delicious food and flowing drinks and laughter and dancing. One of Alessandra's cousins removed Trey's tie and cut it into small pieces, which were then sold to the guests to raise money for the newlyweds.

Even Lorena dragged Trey onto the dance floor. "He needs to learn to samba properly if he's going to be part of this family." She grinned at him as his eyebrows knit together in concentration.

"Keep your knees bent. No, that's too much! Like this!" she shouted over the music.

As the last notes of the song played out, she patted him on the cheek. "Okay, I'll give you a chance. You seem like a hard worker, and you made a lovely wedding for Alessandra in an old barn. Let's consider this a new start. But you need to know that if you mess this up, I'll make you wish you were dead."

The last pat on the cheek was much harder than Trey expected it to be. "Point taken," he said as she walked away and left him rubbing his cheek.

As the evening drew to a close, the guests rushed through the rain to their cars, full and happy. Betina took an almost-asleep Tomas to the main house to put him to bed, and Trey found an umbrella for Alessandra to use on their trip back to their house. He swept her up in his arms and made his way across the field.

"Your Aunt Bertha said I have to carry you into the house, entering with my right foot first. You're going to have to remind me when we get the door open. I'm a little drunk and I'm likely to forget."

"Okay, I'm more than a little drunk, but I'll force myself to remember. We can use the luck."

"Ah, who needs luck when you've got love?"

* * *

Alessandra reached down to open the door and Trey carried her inside, setting her down on the floor. "Don't move. I'll be right back for you," he said as he kicked off his shoes. She toed off her heels and stretched her arms out to the sides, spinning in circles with happiness.

They had done it. She was married to the sweetest, sexiest man she'd ever met, and he loved her. Only her. He had promised he always would. And she knew in her heart that he meant it. Finishing a slow spin, she stopped and saw him leaning against the bedroom door, smiling as he watched her. He shook his head. "You're unbelievably cute."

His feet were bare, his jacket was gone, and the top two buttons of his shirt were undone. As she gazed at him, he looked like the hottest man who had ever lived. He walked to her and held out a hand. "Come with me."

Alessandra took his hand and followed him to the bedroom. Candles flickered, bringing a soft warmth to the room. Tulle billowed from the ceiling, down to both sides of the bed. "Trey, when did you have time to do all this?"

"I managed to sneak back here during the reception. It only took a minute."

"It's wonderful. I love it." Alessandra ran her fingers along his cheek, then reached up and gave him a lingering kiss. "Thank you."

"Thank *you*."

"For what? You did everything today. I just got dressed and put my hair up."

"You married me. You could've said no."

"Well, I probably would have but you asked at just the right moment."

Trey laughed. "So, I'll know to wait until right after sex to ask you for anything I really want."

"If you do that, I'm in a lot of trouble. I'll be saying yes to everything."

Trey let his lips hover over hers. "That should work out well for me." His voice was thick with desire. Resting his hands on her hips, he pulled her to him. And finally his mouth was on hers again. His kiss was urgent, his tongue finding its way between her parted lips. He explored her mouth carefully, intently, while his hands travelled the length of her back. Alessandra felt his fingers on the top button of her dress. She smiled up at him adoringly. "You may want me to turn around. There are a lot of buttons."

Trey spun her. "Wow! That's going to take half the night. There must be, like, fifty buttons on this thing."

"Then you better get to work, Mr. Johnson," she said in a sultry tone.

She looked over her shoulder as he struggled with each button, stopping often to kiss the nape of her neck or suck on her earlobe. "Mmm, I think I'll get you to take off my clothes every night if this is how you do it."

"Good." He let his fingers glide down her naked spine to his next tiny opponent. When he finally reached the last button, he slid his hands inside and pushed the dress off her shoulders, letting it fall to the floor. She stood before him in a white corset clipped to nude stockings with satin garters. Lacy white barely-there panties peeked out the bottom of the corset. Trey let out an impressed sigh. "Wow." His hands gripped her waist, then made their way up her body to her breasts. Alessandra let herself lean against him as his thumbs traced the top of the corset, his rough skin running along her soft flesh. She let out a little moan, then lifted her hands to her hair to take the pins out.

Trey's hands covered her forearms. "No. Let me."

"Really? Are you sure? There are more pins than buttons."

"I'm sure," he murmured in her ear, letting his lips graze over her neck.

Alessandra lowered her arms and closed her eyes, listening to the sound of rain pattering on the roof and feeling the touch of her husband as he gently removed hairpins until her curls fell down her shoulders. He ran his fingers through her hair, making sure he'd found every pin before spinning her back around to face him. "You're so sexy."

Ignited by a new passion, Alessandra quickly started to unbutton his shirt. Their kissing became frantic as she tugged his shirt off and it got caught around his wrists. They'd forgotten to undo his cufflinks. He held up his hands to do it, but Alessa stopped him and did it for him, kissing the palms of his hands as she took care of each sleeve. Her fingertips ran over the sculpted perfection that was his chest and abs. Trey closed the distance between them and backed her up against the bed. Holding her hands, he lowered her onto the bed and stood before her, running his hands over her body from her legs to her chest and back down. He knelt in front of her and opened the clasps on her garters before pulling her stockings slowly off each leg. She closed her eyes again, feeling his fingers wrap themselves around her panties, and soon those were gone too and his lips were on the inside of her thighs, teasing her with their warmth and softness. "Oh God, that feels so good," she whispered. His tongue travelled the length of her wet heat, stoking the fire in just the way that would have her burning soon.

He let his tongue dip inside her and she heard a deep moan from his throat. Lifting her hips, she felt her legs distance themselves from each other without her telling them to. It was like this with him. Her body knew the pleasure of being with him and would move any way needed to get more. She was greedy and hungry when it came to his tongue and his lips and his body. She swivelled her hips and felt his tongue urging her to an explosive climax. Fleeting thoughts of waiting until he could come with her passed through Alessandra's mind but were soon abandoned as she heard herself cry out with ecstasy. Her body tensed in long waves over his tongue. When it was over, she opened her eyes and saw him smiling up at her. He kissed the insides of her thighs as he ran his hands over her front. Trey then stood before her, gazing at her with lust as he undid his pants and pulled them off, along with his underwear. Alessandra's breath caught at the sight of him like this, completely nude, bathed in the soft light of the candles, with his desire for her on obvious display.

He rested one knee on the bed next to her. "Now, how do I get this corset off? It looks a little complicated for a country boy like me."

Alessandra smiled. "It is. There are more clasps on the back than there were pins in my hair."

"You're making me work for it tonight," he said, gently turning her over on to her stomach. Instead of feeling his fingers on the back of the corset, she felt them running along the curve of her bottom. "You have the best ass I've ever seen." He gave it a squeeze. "Mmm, it's just so luscious."

Now his hands took on the task of removing her last article of clothing. He made short work of it before turning her over again so she faced him. "There you are." He took a moment to just look her up and down adoringly. Alessandra reached her hands out to his and pulled him down on top of her. Her legs wrapped around his waist and their mouths joined together again at last. She felt him move over her. His weight on top of her was perfection, his hard body pressing against her curves. His mouth was on her right nipple, sucking and licking, making it so tight with desire it almost hurt. Then he moved to her left breast, giving it the same rough, delectable treatment. Although it had been only two nights since they'd been together, he feasted on her body as though he'd been starving for years.

His hips rocked forward and she felt his hard length pushing its way inside. His mouth crushed against hers now as he thrust himself in to the hilt. A small gasp escaped her lips at the feel of him and her entire body tensed in response. He rocked them both back and forth in long, slow thrusts, each one a little harder than the last, each one touching her a little deeper. His body was more urgent in its need now; she could feel it as he moved. Her ankles clasped together over his back and her hands held his face as their tongues danced. He pulled his mouth back for a second, resting his forehead on hers. "I love you so much, Alessandra."

And then his lips were on hers again. And nothing else existed other than the two of them. She let him urge her to her next climax, feeling beautiful and loved and adored. She felt him tense and release everything he had to give in waves so strong she nearly blacked out for a moment. Their voices broke the silence in the air as they both cried out with pleasure.

He collapsed onto her when it was over, then rolled onto his side so they remained intertwined, him still inside her as he kissed her tenderly. Thunder rolled gently above them, soothingly, as the rain picked up, lulling them to a deep sleep in each other's arms. Just as he was about to drop off, Trey murmured, "This is forever, Alessa. You're my forever."

TWENTY-EIGHT

"We should get up," Alessandra remarked, looking over at the clock on the night table. The sun, already high in the sky, streamed in through the window.

"A little longer," Trey urged, pulling her to him.

"Tomas is probably missing us."

"I doubt it. Your family is probably filling him full of pancakes and cookies. I bet he's forgotten who we are by now."

Alessandra smiled as his hand traced the inside of her thigh. Trey let his teeth graze over her earlobe.

She moaned. "Okay. We compromise by showering together."

"Practical and sexy. That's such a turn-on," he teased.

They laughed together for a moment. Alessandra spoke up again, in a mock-sultry voice. "Plus, we'll save water, so it's good for the earth."

"Oh yeah, baby. Keep talking."

Alessandra laughed before flipping the covers off them both and getting up. Any protesting he was about to do died in his throat as he watched her reach her arms up and stretch her naked body. She gestured for him to join her and disappeared out the door.

"You make a compelling case, counsellor," he admitted when he reached the bathroom. He stared shamelessly as she added toothpaste to her toothbrush and began scrubbing her teeth. "I had no idea breasts did that when ladies brush their teeth. Wow. I could watch that all day." His eyes remained locked on her chest. "I think I'm going to love being married."

He stood behind her and pressed himself against her back, letting his hands wander for a minute before picking up his toothbrush. Alessandra finished brushing and took a big gulp of water. "This is the perfect way to start the day. Let's do this every morning."

"Agreed."

She stepped away from the sink and turned on the water in the shower to let it warm up. "I can't believe I'm just walking around naked in front of you. I've always been too shy to do this with anyone else."

"You've seriously got no reason to be shy. Actually, by law, you have to walk around naked from now on. It was in the marriage contract."

"No it wasn't." She narrowed her eyes at him, pretending to be annoyed.

"Oh, it was. I had your boss add it."

"No you didn't."

"But I should have."

A moment later they both stood together in the small shower, lathering each other with soap and lingering over wet kisses under the warm spray of the water. Their hands explored and teased each other's slippery bodies until Alessandra made her way to her knees, swirling her tongue over the head of Trey's hard length. His breath caught as she plunged her mouth over him, taking him in as far as she could before pulling back to the end again. Four quick plunges had him gripping the wall and feeling off balance until she slowed her mouth again. He stared down at her from under heavy eyelids, the sight of her full lips over his cock making him even harder than he already was. Her hands groped his lower abs and upper thighs while she worked her magic on him, sucking gently and licking him over and over. He knew he would have to stop her before it was too late, and that the time was closing in on him. Holding her hair, he gently pushed her away from him. "Wait. I don't want to come without you."

Alessandra gave him a naughty look as she plunged her mouth over him again. He leaned against the shower wall, mesmerized by what she was doing. She had him under her spell and he let out a deep moan as he gazed down at her again.

"Stop. Come here," he said, taking her wrists and pulling her up to stand before him. His hand slid between her legs and massaged her core as he kissed her and teased her with his mouth. Alessandra turned to face the wall and Trey leaned over her, pressing his chest to her back and bending his knees so he could enter her wet, waiting body. Careful not to hurt her, he pushed himself into her inch by inch until he filled her tight sex. The sound she made was his undoing. There was no stopping him now as he thrust his hips into her over and over, feeling her squeeze him every time he pulled back.

"Yes, Trey, yes," she breathed, the side of her face touching the wall. "Just like that."

Reaching around, he held her breasts, feeling their warmth in his palms, the back of his hands pressed against the cool tile. Working faster now, he slammed himself into her, feeling the head of his cock reach the end of her. She screamed another "Yes!" as he felt her body tense and release, tense and release. She was coming, drenching him, and the feeling of it pushed him over the edge. He stood over her, gripping her breasts as he gave in, and held her there for a long, perfect moment.

"So far, being married is very fun," she said finally.

He chuckled, his face buried in her neck. "So fun."

After breakfast in the main house with the family, Trey took Tomas out to get some fresh air while he started disassembling the wedding decor. Miguel would be returning the animals that afternoon, and the barn had to be ready to house them by then. The day was bright and warm under the sunshine but the earth was still soaked through, making it all kinds of muddy fun for Tomas to explore.

An hour later, Lorena found Trey in the barn still taking down the lights. "It's a shame to take it all down. It was so beautiful," she said.

"It was nice, wasn't it?" he remarked.

She started folding the lengths of tulle that Trey had dropped onto the floor. "And look, today the sun is shining. It's too bad the wedding wasn't today."

Trey stopped what he was doing and looked down from the top of the ladder. "I'm glad it was yesterday. That storm gave us a great story to tell. Plus, I don't have to spend the entire day being really nervous."

The sounds of Tomas and Carlos laughing together made their way into the barn, bringing a smile to Lorena's face.

"What are Betina and Alessa up to?" Trey asked.

"Your wife is helping her sister pack for her trip. I think she is the best one for the job. I don't know what Betina should bring and I would only cry."

"It must be hard to let her go so far."

Lorena's face screwed up and she nodded quickly, blinking back tears.

"She'll be okay. She's got a good head on her shoulders." Trey nodded reassuringly.

* * *

By suppertime, the barn had been returned to its normal state, the animals were home and everyone was hungry. Betina's luggage sat ready at the front door. A quiet fell over the family as they shared one last meal together on the patio. They were all tired from the day before, but a bittersweet sadness had also settled in. Tomas became the centre of attention as the adults all tried to distract themselves from the emptiness of parting so soon. Carlos had been especially silent throughout the day, tears coming to his eyes whenever he looked at his younger granddaughter.

Lorena tried to make a going-away speech, but the words got caught in her throat and she ended up just telling Betina she loved her. After the meal, it was time for Betina to go to the bus station in town.

Betina looked at her mother with a tentative expression. "Can Alessandra take me? I think if you all come, I'll be a wreck by the time I get there."

Lorena nodded. "Very sensible of you."

Trey carried her bags out to the truck, stopping after he loaded them in. They were alone, and he suddenly felt the worry he would feel for his own child in this situation. "Listen, Betina, I hope you don't mind me giving you some brotherly advice. It's not the same there. Some places are not so safe for girls. Be sure to make some good friends when you get there. Girls, *not* boys. And when you go to parties, bring your own drinks. Something bottled or canned. Never leave your drink unattended. Never. If you do, don't finish it. Just dump the rest out. Never go anywhere alone at night. Always go with a friend you trust and never let each other out of sight—"

Betina held up her hand. "It's okay. I know all this. Alessandra has been telling me the same thing for days now."

Trey smiled and scratched his head. "Sorry, it's just that we want you to be safe."

"I know." She gave him a big hug. "Thank you. You're a wonderful brother-in-law. You be good to my sister, okay?"

"I promise I will."

The sound of footsteps on the gravel interrupted the moment. The rest of the family joined them, Lorena already in tears as she hugged her daughter. "I love you. Do your best. You'll be great."

"I love you too. I'm going to miss you, *Mãe*."

"I'll miss you so much. I can hardly believe I have to let you go already. It's too soon."

Betina laughed a little through her tears. "I'm twenty-one. It's time."

Carlos was next and he wasn't much better than Lorena. Tears rolled down his face, getting caught in the creases on his cheeks. He held Betina's face in his hands and told her how beautiful she was and what a joy she had been in his life. He told her that one of his greatest privileges had been to watch her grow up into the smart, strong woman she was, and that he would always be proud of her. He told her goodbye.

"No, *Vô*, not goodbye—see you soon," she said through her tears.

Carlos hugged her for a long time, then said, "Goodbye, my little one."

Trey picked up Tomas and walked over to one of the orange trees, blinking back his own tears at the heart-wrenching scene. Holding his son in his arms made him feel the pain of a parent letting their children go out into the world. He kissed the top of Tomas's little head, not knowing if he'd ever be ready for such a moment.

Alessandra got into the driver's seat of the truck and started up the engine. She rolled down the windows. "We'd better go if we're going to make it in time."

Betina climbed in and waved as they drove out of sight, leaving a deep void behind.

Trey sat on the swing, waiting for Alessandra to return. Tomas had gone to sleep without a fuss, still exhausted from the wedding. Trey closed his eyes and listened to the wind rustling in the trees. The world still smelled fresh from the rain, and he was calm and happy. When he heard the truck rumble down the driveway, he stood to meet Alessandra, pulling her in for a long hug as she dissolved into tears. "I'm going to miss her so much."

"I know."

They walked hand in hand over to the swing and sat together. Alessandra rested her head on his strong shoulder and let the tears come. He put his arm around her shoulder and rocked the swing back and forth under the early night sky.

"You okay?"

"Yes. I feel silly. She's only going for a year. We've been away from each other for longer already."

"Maybe it's harder to be left than to be the one doing the leaving."

Alessandra looked at him. "I think you're right. You're pretty wise for a not-so-old man."

"I know. That's probably why you married me."

"Don't be ridiculous. I married you for your body."

They laughed, then sat in comfortable silence for a few minutes before Trey spoke up. "You know, I was thinking that we aren't going to have a proper honeymoon. I wish I could give you one."

"No, our wedding night was perfect. All I need is for us to be together."

"Well, someday I'd like to whisk you away somewhere, just the two of us." Trey reached for her left hand and rubbed his thumb over her ring. "Where would you want to go, if we could go anywhere?"

"Bora Bora."

"Really? That's oddly specific for someone who just said she doesn't need a honeymoon."

"Hey, you asked. I saw it on a show once. They have resorts with private huts over the water. The floors are glass so you can watch the fish swim from bed. The water is the most beautiful blue and there are white sand beaches that are supposed to feel like icing sugar."

"In that case, I'll have to take you there."

"Yes, you will." Alessandra let out a happy sigh. She was starting a wonderful new life, and even though today had been hard, she had someone to share her pain with, which made all the difference in the world.

TWENTY-NINE

"What do you mean you're still going?"

"Why does that surprise you? I never said I *wasn't* going," Trey answered as he tossed some socks into his duffel bag.

Alessandra put her hand on her hip. "I just thought maybe you'd change your mind because—"

"Because we're married? If anything, that means I have *more* reason to go. I need to make some money. We can't be living off your grandfather forever. I wouldn't be much of a husband if I couldn't support you and Tomas."

"You won't be much of a husband if you're dead, either." Her voice rose a little, and Trey motioned for her to lower it.

"Let's not wake Tomas, okay?" He added a couple of T-shirts to the bag before turning to her. "Why don't you and Tomas come with me? It could be like a really weird honeymoon with absolutely no privacy."

"I don't think so. I can't watch you do this, Trey. I'm sorry," she said, tearing up.

He stopped packing and crossed the tiny room to her. "Hey, don't cry, okay?" Wrapping her in his arms, he kissed her forehead. "You don't have to worry about me. I'll go for two days, and in less than thirty seconds, I'll have my job done and we'll have some good cash in the bank."

"You don't know that. You could get hurt." Her body was stiff.

"I won't. I know it in my bones, just like I knew about you. And look how that worked out." He kissed her forehead. "But I really need my wife to believe in me." His lips grazed along her cheek, finding her mouth. She felt her body relax into him as he kissed her. She was his wife. He needed her to believe in him.

His words resonated in her heart until she decided he was right. Her fear wasn't going to solve anything anyway. "Okay, I'll try."

* * *

The evening was hot as Trey sat on a long wooden bench with a couple of other bull riders. He was to ride tenth, and after seeing the first three riders get thrown, his stomach was churning. The smell of bull shit filled his nose. It wasn't a smell that normally bothered him, but tonight it was noticeable. As soon as the bulls were loaded into the chutes, Trey felt as though someone had released a herd of butterflies in his stomach, and they had yet to flutter away.

One of the riders was pacing back and forth behind the chutes, looking as though he were preparing to enter a boxing ring. Trey watched as the man tipped his head from side to side and tensed his entire upper body, fists clenched. The look in his eyes was pure aggression, and it made Trey wonder if he should adopt a similar routine to talk himself up right now. He hadn't really considered having a pre-ride routine but now that he sat there, he realized it might be a good idea.

A retching sound drew Trey's attention to the area behind the bleachers. He glanced over in time to see another rider, in a black vest, dry heaving. Trey shuddered, wishing he hadn't seen that. Or heard it. *That* certainly wasn't going to be the way he prepared.

Leaning his head against the wall behind him, Trey balanced his cowboy hat over his face and closed his eyes, trying to convince his heart to slow down. A couple of moments later, he felt his hat being knocked off his face. Miguel stood in front of him with a beer in each hand. He offered one to Trey, who took it and lifted the can to his lips for a long pull.

"Liquid backbone," he said to Miguel as he moved aside to make room on the bench for him. "Thank you."

"You look nervous," Miguel said.

"I am."

"Then don't ride. You need to be fearless to ride. You must be calm to be able to read the bull. To feel him. If you are nervous, you will only feel your heart pounding and you won't know what the bull is going to do next. Knowing what he'll do next will save you."

Trey gave him an incredulous look. "You're telling me you're not nervous?"

"I don't get scared. Being scared is for little girls with braids in their hair." He sucked back the rest of his beer, crushed the can, and then slapped Trey's leg with his glove. "I'm up. I'll see you in eight seconds."

Trey watched Miguel walk over to the chute to get prepared for his turn. He took another sip of his beer, trying to convince himself he wasn't scared.

A moment later, Bruno walked up, toting two cans of beer. He held one out to Trey but Trey shook his head. "I've got one, thanks."

"Better have two, just to be sure. You ready?"

"Not even a bit."

Trey stood and the two walked over to the fence to watch as

Miguel mounted a large white bull. They waited with bated breath as the gate opened and Miguel managed to make his eight-second time with seemingly little trouble. When he got bucked off, he rolled out of the way just in time to avoid being stomped on. "Miguel said he never gets nervous."

Bruno burst into laughter. "He's more full of shit than those pens back there. If you aren't nervous, it's because the bull has already killed you," he answered with a slap on Trey's back.

* * *

Twenty minutes later, the gate opened. Trey felt his body being violently lifted into the air by an enormous brown animal called the Widow-Maker's Meaner Son. The entire world seemed to be moving in slow motion, and he could hear nothing over the sounds of his own breath and his heart pounding in his ears. His right hand gripped the rope, every fibre of his arm squeezing as if his life depended on it. And in an all-too-real way, his life *did* depend on that grip. The rope cut into his circulation as he held on with everything he had in him. His left arm was flailing in the air as he took the next kick. Instead of being thrown, as he had expected, Trey stayed on.

Suddenly it was as though he had been transported to the ocean, and it was just him and a wave under his surfboard. A strange calm came over him in spite of the adrenalin pumping through his veins. He felt powerful in a way he hadn't before. His body knew how to stay on the bull even if his brain couldn't explain how he knew. His mind's eye saw the bull lowering his head and raising his back end a fraction of a second before it happened. Trey rocked his body back just in time, keeping his spine straight. He knew the bull would lift off his front legs next in an attempt to throw Trey off behind him, and again, Trey was ahead of the animal by just enough time to stay on. The buzzer sounded and Trey's hearing came back. He had made it! He jumped off, landed on his feet, and then took his hat off for the crowd. A violent kick to his hamstring gave Trey a reminder of why you don't celebrate too early. He swore under his breath and scrambled out of the way, knowing the pain would be intense once the adrenalin wore off.

* * *

That night, Trey lay on his stomach in bed in the motel room, a large bag of ice strapped to the back of his thigh. He called Alessandra.

"You're alive?" she asked immediately, managing to sound both relieved and angry at the same time.

"Of course I'm alive. Even better than that, I made the quarter-finals." He smiled to himself, feeling very proud of what he'd managed to do.

"Wow! Congratulations. Are you hurt?"

"Nah, I'm fine. I didn't even get bucked off. I jumped when my ride was over."

"Really? That's impressive."

"It was. You should have seen it. How's Tomas?"

"He's good. He had trouble falling asleep, though. He's gotten used to holding your hand at bedtime."

Trey's heart tugged at the thought. "Well, only one more night, then I'll be back to hold his hand again."

"Yeah," she said, her voice quiet. "I miss you."

Trey sighed. "I miss you too, so much. Good thing it's only a few days or I don't think I could handle it."

"What are you doing right now?"

"Just lying in the motel room, thinking about you."

"That's nice. My idiot cousins aren't with you?"

"No, they went out drinking." He yawned, the long drive and the excitement of the evening finally getting to him.

"You didn't want to go?"

"I'm a married man now. The bar's no place for a married man."

"I'm glad you think that because if you started going out partying, it wouldn't be a bull that would get you. It would be me." Alessandra's voice was firm.

"You don't scare me, Mrs. Johnson. You're a tiny little thing." He knew that would make her smile.

"I may be smaller than you but I'm meaner," she answered, finally sounding more like herself.

"If you say so. So, what do you have planned for tomorrow?"

"Some of the family is coming over for dinner, so I'll be cooking most of the day."

"Aww, I'm going to miss a big dinner? In that case, I better damn well win the whole thing."

"You better," Alessandra teased. "I should let you go. You sound tired."

"I am. You still mad at me?"

"I'm scared, Trey. Not angry."

"Hmph. I'd prefer you were angry, actually."

"Why?"

"I don't ever want to scare you."

"But you want to make me angry?"

Trey laughed. "No. That's not what I meant."

"But it's what you said."

"God, I never should have married a lawyer. I'm in big trouble."

"Likely, yes," Alessandra answered.

"Well, I'll just have to get used to being wrong."

"In this way, you are no different than any other man," Alessandra said, laughing a little at her own joke.

"Objection!"

"On what grounds?"

"Sexism," Trey said, grasping at straws.

"Overruled. Now make sure you come back in one piece."

"I promise to."

"Love you."

"Love you too, Alessandra. Good night."

*   *   *

"How's my favourite newlywed?" Daniela asked.

"I'm doing well. How's my favourite aunt?"

"Getting so old that I can flash my breasts with one roll of the bottom of my shirt now." Daniela lifted the bottom of her shirt, causing Alessandra to bark out a loud laugh.

Her aunt waited until she recovered before linking arms with her and walking around the porch toward the back of the house. "So, are you doing okay? I hear that your husband is off with my boys making trouble at the rodeo."

Alessandra rolled her eyes. "I don't like it, but Trey's not out making trouble. He was in his room early to go to sleep."

"Well, I suppose he would be, with what happened to his leg."

Alessandra cocked her head to the side. Her face dropped. "What happened to his leg?"

"He got kicked in the back of his thigh. He didn't tell you?" Daniela gave her a concerned look but almost immediately appeared nonchalant. "He must have forgotten."

Alessandra plastered a fake smile to her face, fully aware that her mother was standing off to the side, listening. Breaking away from her aunt, she started setting out the cutlery on the table. "Yes, I'm sure he forgot. It must have been nothing or he definitely would have told me."

"Bruno said he was lucky the kick wasn't to his crotch!" her uncle added, chuckling as he popped an olive into his mouth. "Could have been the end of any chance for more kids!"

"Ricardo!" Daniela swatted his arm. "You'll make her worry."

"No, no, it's fine," Alessandra said, refusing to look up from the table. "If it was something bad, he would have told me. If you'll excuse me for a moment, I need to check on Tomas."

* * *

Trey winced as he carefully lowered himself onto the bull. *Fuck, that hurts. Okay, eight seconds. Any amount of pain can be tolerated for eight seconds. Get the money and go home.*

In spite of his better judgement, he nodded his head, indicating he was ready to go. The gate swung open and Trey got to work, tightening his legs around the bull in the hopes of not being lifted then slammed back down. He managed to get through the first three seconds without his leg taking another beating, but it still hurt like hell. It occurred to him that those last three seconds had been more like three hours, and the thought had him dreading the next five.

Slam! *Fuck.* Slam! *Shit.* Slam! *Son of a bitch!*

The buzzer sounded a millisecond before he was thrown off. He limped back to the gate as quickly as he could, keeping his eye on the bull the entire time. His face went pale with the intensity of the pain. *Well, that wasn't exactly like riding a wave.*

Miguel reached an arm over the gate to help him up. "You okay, Trey?"

Trey gave him a terse nod. "Fucking hurts, but I guess that's part of the deal."

"Yes, it is," he said with a grin. "Good ride. You think you can do it again today? You just made the finals."

Trey gulped, not sure whether to be happy or full of dread.

* * *

"Look who's home, Tomas!" Alessandra exclaimed as her cousin's truck came into view. She and Tomas had been in the shade of a mango tree, reading a book. Enthusiastic waves were exchanged as Miguel parked the truck in front of the house. Trey got out, looking a little worse for wear as he held his arms open for Tomas, who was running to him at full speed. A look of pain crossed Trey's face as he crouched down, but he was quick to hide it under the brim of his straw hat.

Miguel unrolled his window to holler a quick goodbye to everyone. "We can't stay. Bruno wants to get over to his girlfriend's place." He smiled at them. "Alessa, why didn't you tell us your husband was playing us? He pretended to be a novice and then, after we went to the trouble of bringing him along, he beat us both. He's a con artist, and we think you knew."

"Did not. Losing to him is your punishment for getting him involved with this insanity in the first place!" Alessandra waved her hand at him in irritation.

"We won't be fooled by you again, con man!" Miguel called to Trey before he turned his truck around and drove off.

Trey laughed a little and shook his head as the truck pulled away, then he turned his attention to his son and wife. "It's so good to see you!" Trey scooped Tomas up in a big hug and stood, waiting for

Alessandra to make her way over to them. He pulled her in for a long kiss. "Missed you both so much."

"We missed you too," Alessandra said. "I can't believe you came in second place."

"Not bad for my first time out there, right?" Trey beamed. "I've never made eight hundred dollars for only a minute's worth of work before."

"Congratulations. I'm very happy for you."

"Be happy for *us*, Alessa." He gave her a kiss on the lips. "What's mine is yours, and I intend to make sure there's plenty."

Alessandra gave him a grateful smile. "Did you get hurt?"

"Nope. Told you I'd be fine," he said as he set Tomas back on the grass.

The two watched as the little boy chased a butterfly in a zigzag across the lawn.

Alessandra gave him a skeptical look. "You're sure you're fine?"

"Of course. Do I look hurt?"

She took a couple of steps forward, tracing her finger down his chest. "Good, because later I'm going to climb onto your lap and ride you until the sun comes up."

Trey swallowed hard. "That'll be real nice," he managed, although Alessa saw him wince a tiny bit at her words.

"Oh yes. All night. *Hard.*"

"Can't wait."

* * *

That night, after Tomas was in bed, Trey started for the bathroom to have a shower. Alessandra stopped him as he was closing the door. "Why don't I join you?"

"Um, you know, as nice as that sounds, I'm pretty yucky right now. Can I meet you in bed in a bit, though?"

"Sure." Her eyes dared him to keep up the charade.

"Be out in a few minutes," he said with a quick kiss.

Alessandra got into bed and waited, torn between finding the situation amusing and antagonizing. *How could he refuse to admit he was hurt?* When Trey finally came into the room, he was wearing only his boxer briefs. He quickly flicked off the light, then climbed into bed, carefully lying on his side. Giving her a light kiss, he said, "I'm beat. That was a rough weekend."

Alessandra turned onto her side and let her lips hover over his. "Too tired for me? I'll make it worth your effort."

"I could never be too tired for you," he said as his mouth found hers. Alessandra parted her lips as he slid his tongue in search of hers. Trey's hand found its way to her breasts, brushing against the fabric of her nightie. He moaned as she ran her hand down the front of his underwear. Alessandra smiled as she tried to push him onto his back and he resisted, trying to position himself on top of her instead. *Still won't admit it? Okay, let's try this . . .*

She tugged at his underwear, pulling them down roughly. She heard his breath cut short as the fabric passed his thighs, and still he refused to tell her the truth. Reaching around behind him, she ran her hand down toward the back of his leg until he grabbed her wrist.

"Stop. Not there," he said quickly.

"Why not?" she asked curtly. "Did you get kicked by a bull or something?"

She watched in the dim light of the moon as he shut his eyes in defeat. "Who told you?"

Smacking him on the arm, she glared at him. "My aunt. And it should have been *you*, you *idiota*!"

"I'm not going to tell you every time I get a little bruise," he answered defensively.

Throwing back the covers, Alessa crossed the room in two steps and turned the light back on. "Let me see it."

"No."

"Let me see it. I'm your wife. This won't work if you're keeping things from me." Alessandra put her hand on her hips.

"Shit," he muttered under his breath, rolling over onto his stomach. "It's noth—"

He finally gave up when Alessandra gasped. "*Ai meu Deus! Isso está horrível!* Your leg is completely swollen. And purple and black. It's your entire thigh!"

"Seriously, it's not a big deal."

"Not a big deal? Looking at it makes me want to vomit!"

"Thanks. Nice to know you find me disgusting." He rolled back onto his side and tugged the sheet up over himself.

"Of course I don't find *you* disgusting. It's just so bad. It makes my knees weak to see you like that."

"Let's just forget it. Get back in bed, okay?"

"No. I'm going to get you some ice and something for the pain."

"You don't have to take care of me, I'm fine."

"Clearly, *somebody* has to take care of you because you're not going to do it yourself." Giving him a dirty look, she opened the door and walked out, returning a few minutes later. "Here."

"Thank you," Trey said, taking the glass of water and the pill she offered him. "And I'm sorry for not telling you."

"You're welcome. And you should be sorry. Keeping things from me is no different than lying."

"In this case, I didn't think it was worth telling you about. But if it makes you happy, I'll give you an inventory of every little scrape from now on." He put the glass on the night table and took a towel packed with ice from her.

"Good." Alessandra flicked off the light and got back into bed, sitting up with her back against the headboard.

"I just realized I don't know how long you stay mad about things," Trey said after a minute.

"Not too long. I'll get over this a lot quicker if you say you're done with bull riding."

"Hmm. In that case, you may be angry for a while."

"Trey—"

"Alessandra, you're not going to talk me out of this. I'm sorry that you don't like it, but it turns out I'm pretty good at it, and you're just going to have to accept that I'm doing this."

"Fine." She shrugged.

"Fine, like everything's actually okay or fine, like you're going to stop talking to me?"

"The second one," she said as though just deciding.

"Fine," he said firmly.

Alessandra lay down and fluffed her pillow furiously before turning away from him and curling up as close to the edge of the bed as possible.

THIRTY

The next morning, the three sat around the tiny table having break-fast. Trey and Alessa both doted on Tomas, hoping he wouldn't notice the awkward tension still evident between them.

"Play outside now," Tomas said to his dad as Trey stood to clear his dishes.

"Sure thing, buddy. Should we go do our chores?"

"Yup!"

Tomas tugged his rubber boots on and tried unlocking the door without much luck. Alessandra got up to help him. "Stay close to the house for a minute. I need to talk to your dad, okay, *rapazinho*?"

"'Kay."

Leaning against the door jamb, Alessandra watched as Tomas toddled over to an old tricycle that had become his favourite. He climbed on and grinned at her as he made motorcycle sounds. Alessa watched as Trey pulled on his cowboy boots. She cleared her throat. "I don't want to fight with you."

Trey straightened up and stared down at her for a moment. "Me neither."

Sighing heavily, Alessandra said, "When you share a life with someone, there may be times when one person does something the other doesn't like. Right now, you're going to do what you want and

I'm not going to like it. I'll try to be supportive of you but I can't stop myself from worrying."

Trey crossed to her and took her hands in his. "I'm not going to get hurt. I promise."

"That's a promise you can't make."

"I know it sounds hard to believe, but I just know it. I don't know how I know it, but I just do."

"That is very arrogant. I don't know if I can live with someone who allows arrogance to be his guide in life."

Trey let go of her hands. "Arrogance? It's not arrogant to know you're good at something and to know you can be a success at it. It's not arrogance to try to make a good life for your family." Walking out the door, he turned back. "For someone who says she doesn't want to fight, you're doing a good job of keeping this one going."

* * *

The rest of the week passed in an uncomfortable standoff, neither Trey nor Alessandra willing to move from their positions. They both ached to touch each other and make love, but neither knew how to come back together without giving in. They got into bed at night facing away from each other. Every time Alessa sighed in the darkness, Trey felt an urgent need to reach out and touch her, but he thought she might pull away.

Friday morning found Trey in the barn, grooming the horses. His cellphone rang and he took a break, seeing it was his mother calling on Skype. He had been avoiding her for over a month now and his stomach flipped over when he thought of how upset she'd be that he had gotten married without telling his family. Deciding he couldn't avoid her forever, he answered the call. They got off to a very tense start on the call, both trying to suss out what the other was feeling.

Once they'd gotten through enough small talk, Fern approached the tenuous topic.

"So, have you heard from the court yet?"

"Nothing yet," Trey answered.

"This is getting ridiculous. How can they keep you there so long?"

"It takes time, Mom, but there's no sense in worrying about it since there's nothing I can do anyway."

"Hmph." His mom gave him a skeptical look. "You still haven't sent me the mailing address for where you're living. That letter from Cole has been collecting dust on the kitchen counter here for weeks."

Shaking his head, Trey stared at her. "I already told you. I'm not accepting their help, so please stop trying to convince me."

"I can't believe that you won't accept help from your own family but you'll take a handout from some strangers."

"It's not a handout. Alessandra's family needs a lot of help and I've been working very hard for them since I got here."

"Well, how much money have you saved up so far to buy a house?"

Trey's shoulders dropped. "You'll be surprised to hear I actually figured out a way to make a decent living fast."

"How?"

"Don't worry about it. I've got it covered." Trey avoided his mother's glare, which was unmistakable in spite of the tiny screen.

"What is that supposed to mean? Why won't you tell me?" she asked before gasping. "You're not selling drugs, are you?"

"Jesus. No, Mom. I'm not a drug dealer. How could you even think that?"

"I don't know what to think anymore! You won't tell me anything."

"Alright. I've actually been doing some bull riding," he mumbled.

"What?" her face screwed up in confusion. "Did you say you've been *bullfighting*?"

"No!" Trey stifled a laugh. "Bull *riding*. I said bull riding."

"Trey! I can't believe you! Do you know how dangerous that is?"

"I've heard. I've been taking shit all week from Alessandra about it."

"Alessandra? The nanny? Why does she care?" His mother looked very confused.

"I . . . I don't know. I guess she's worried about Tomas."

"What aren't you telling me, Trey?"

"Nothing. There's nothing to tell." Glancing toward the barn door, he saw Alessandra, her eyes welling up with tears. *Shit.* He knew by the look on her face that she'd heard what he'd just said. She turned and hurried out the door.

Trey looked back at his phone. "Mom, I've got to go. I'll talk to you later."

"Trey, we need to—"

"No we don't. I gotta go. Something just happened here that I need to take care of immediately. Love you." Trey hung up and jogged out the door to find Alessandra.

* * *

Alessandra rushed behind the barn, where she hoped no one would find her. Tears streamed down her face. Sliding down, she sat with her back against the old building, shedding the emotions she'd been bottling up all week. The sight of his boots in front of her made Alessandra turn away from Trey to hide her tears.

Sitting down next to her, he gently tried to turn her face to him with his fingers on her chin, but she brushed his hand away. "I'm sorry, Alessa. I haven't told my family about us yet. I haven't spoken to my mom since we had that big argument in July, and now I'm not sure how to approach the subject. They're going to be really hurt that we got married without them. Without even telling them."

Alessandra stood, needing to get away from Trey. "You haven't even told her we're together! She still thinks I'm just the *nanny*!"

Trey stood and followed her as she hurried back around the barn. "Wait. Alessandra, wait a minute. Please let me apologize."

"Why should I do that? She even *asked* you what was going on and you told her there was *nothing to tell*. Nothing to tell! Is that what I am?" Her voice rose and her accent became thicker in the way it did when she was angry.

"No, God no! Of course not. I haven't talked to her in weeks and we were back in the middle of the same fight when you walked in. It just wasn't the time for me to bring up the fact that I'm married. I'm going to tell them, of course I am. That just wasn't the right moment. I'm sorry that I hurt you but it honestly has *nothing* to do with how I feel about you. You have to trust me on that."

"How can I trust a man who is keeping me a secret from his own family?"

Trey sighed, lowering his voice. "You're right. I'm sorry, Alessa. I know I should have told them. In fact, I'll call right now and tell them, if you like."

Their argument was interrupted by the sound of Miguel's truck pulling up near the barn.

"Shit," Trey muttered under his breath as they watched Miguel unroll the window.

"Hello, cousin! And new cousin! You ready to go?" he called to Trey.

Trey rubbed his face with his hand. "Yeah, can you just give me a minute?"

Miguel looked from Alessandra to Trey, then nodded, a look of understanding crossing his face. "Sure, but we're running a little late already."

"I'll be right there." Turning to his wife, Trey spoke quietly. "I fucked up. I know I did, but I can fix it. I'll be back late tonight and I'll call them then, okay? It will still be early there."

Alessandra rolled her tongue over her teeth, her lips closed tight. She shook her head at Trey. "I don't really care when you tell them. The damage is done."

She hurried into the house before he could say another word.

THIRTY-ONE

Alessandra lay on the bed, feeling dead inside. She'd just gotten Tomas to sleep for the night and now was faced with a long evening of stewing in her anger and heartache. Her cellphone chimed and her heart quickened at the thought that maybe it was Trey. But it wasn't. It was her best friend, Cyssah.

Hello, Alessa. I got back from Portugal late last night. We're all going out tonight. Rodeo, then dancing! You HAVE to come with us! I missed you way TOO much!

She stared at the text for a moment before deciding. *Why the hell not?* Her husband was going to do whatever the hell he wanted to, so she might as well start to do the same.

So glad you're home, Cyssah! I wouldn't miss your first night out for anything. What time?

Going into the main house, she asked her mother to watch Tomas for her. "I need a night out."

"Sure. I was just going to read anyway. You okay?" Lorena

narrowed her eyes, and Alessandra knew the tension between her and Trey had not gone unnoticed.

Alessa gave her what she hoped looked like a confident smile. "Yes, of course, everything is fine. I'm just going out with Cyssah. She got back from her trip last night and we want to get caught up."

The look on her mother's face made it clear Alessandra wasn't fooling anyone, but she agreed anyway. "Okay. I'm here if you need to talk."

"I know."

*   *   *

Alessandra waited until her mother had left to be with Tomas before mixing herself a pitcher of very strong *caipirinha*. She dug through what was left in Betina's closet and found a flirty little black number. On Alessandra, the dress allowed so much cleavage to pop out the top, she looked almost indecent. But she didn't care. Why should she, when Trey certainly didn't seem to?

She took her wedding ring off and left it on Betina's dresser before starting on her hair and makeup. She sang along to the radio as she let her hair down and ran a curling iron through it to tame her wild curls into big, sexy waves that trailed over her shoulders and down her back. Bright red lipstick made her full lips impossible to miss. As she surveyed the results in the mirror, she smiled at her slightly hazy reflection. She looked hot. Maybe for the first time in her entire life. The sound of Cyssah's car prompted her to gulp back the last of her drink before she rushed out, giggling to herself as she fumbled with the front door.

Twenty minutes later, Cyssah locked up her car and the two started for the small stadium grounds. "I'm so excited you came out! And I still can't believe that dress you're wearing. It's so . . . daring."

"I wanted to see what it would be like to go over to the wild side for a change. But is it too much?" She wrinkled up her nose, suddenly unsure of her choice.

"No. Not at all. I'm just not used to seeing you like this. You're definitely going to attract some attention tonight."

"Good. That's my goal," Alessandra said, waving a finger in the air.

Cyssah told Alessa about her trip as they paid their admission and stepped into the loud stadium. Alessandra realized her friend didn't yet know that she was married, but she had no desire to tell her. There was really no need, was there? Trey hadn't even told his own parents about her.

Cyssah's voice interrupted her stewing. "Oh, good! We didn't miss the bull riding!"

Alessandra's stomach flipped at the thought of watching Trey ride a bull. She was going to need more booze. "Come on. Let's go get some drinks first."

A few minutes later, Alessandra had one drink in each hand and one new cowboy on each side of her. She and Cyssah were chatting with the men when the announcer's voice boomed over the tinny speakers. "And now, we've got a special treat! We have Trey Johnson from the USA! Let's give him a big Brazilian welcome!"

Alessandra's back stiffened as the crowd cheered and applauded him. She turned, searching for Trey. Her eyes fell on him as he sat on top of a bull in the chute. Her heart lurched as she watched the enormous white animal try to slam Trey's leg against the gate. He continued to wrap the rope around his gloved hand, looking as calm as if he were sitting on a kitchen chair. Her entire body responded to the sight of him like that, looking so cool in spite of the fact that he was sitting on top of a dangerous two-thousand pound animal. How was that possible?

Just as the gate swung open, Trey glanced up and their eyes met. A look of confusion crossed his face as the bull's back legs reared up with violent force. She watched as Trey lost his balance for a split second. He slid to one side of the bull but somehow managed to recover and stay on. Alessandra felt completely helpless seeing the man she loved fighting to stay on top of a fierce beast who wanted nothing more than to be free of his rider. Trey got tossed into the air, landing hard on his shoulder in the dirt. She watched as the bull bore down on him and Trey turned to look back instead of getting out of the way.

"Run!" she screamed.

Trey scrambled to his feet and took off for the fence as one of the bullfighters slapped the bull on his hindquarters to get his attention. The bull spun away from Trey, giving him a chance to escape the ring.

Alessandra's knees went weak as she thought of what she'd just seen. He was kidding himself if he thought this wasn't going to end with him getting horribly hurt. But she wasn't going to sit at home worrying about him. Screw him if he wanted to ride bulls and pretend he wasn't married. She could pretend too. She watched as he climbed the fence, knowing he was going to come find her now. *Good. Let him see what it is like to be married to someone who likes to walk on the wild side.*

* * *

Trey scaled the fence and flew over it, his heart pounding in his ears. Humiliated at getting bucked off on such an easy ride, he slapped the dust off his chaps and started around to the other side of the stadium to find Alessandra. He'd completely lost his concentration when he saw her there. *What the hell is she wearing? That dress is smaller than most of her nighties. And who the fuck are those guys with her?*

He stormed around the ring, flexing his muscles and gearing up for a fight. His eyes finally settled on her back and legs, both of which were displaying far too much of her honey-coloured skin for his liking. Cracking his knuckles, he glanced at the men with her, seeing that they were bull riders who had already finished up for the night. He watched as she had a sip of whatever drink was in her hand, then laughed at something one of the guys said. Rage and possessiveness coursed through his veins. Reaching the group, he grabbed her arm and kept moving without slowing down.

Alessandra jerked her wrist away from him, spilling her drink. She stopped, causing him to turn back to her.

He glared at her and spoke in a low, even tone. "What are you doing here? And what the hell are you wearing?"

"Oh, this? It's my night-on-the-town dress. You don't like it? Guess what? I don't care, because it's really none of your business what the *nanny* wears when she's off duty!" she spat out.

Trey tugged off his vest, then quickly unbuttoned his shirt and yanked it off, leaving himself in only a T-shirt. "Put this on," he ordered.

"No! I look fine. In fact, these nice gentleman have assured me I look quite hot." She pushed the shirt away.

Trey spoke through his teeth, fighting to keep his patience. "Put this on, Alessa. Now. I don't like these types of games."

"And I don't like being kept a secret from your family or all this bull riding shit. But you don't care what I like, do you?" She had a nasty look on her face and her cheeks were flushed from too much booze. Her accent grew heavy as she spoke. "And now that I've seen you ride, I *know* I am right about this. You are fooling yourself if you think you're good at it."

"The only reason I fell was because you distracted me."

"Oh no, I'm not the one who's going to get you killed." She shook her head. "What will get you killed is pausing so long to look for the bull after you get thrown."

"That's bullshit. I don't do that."

One of the other bull riders spoke up. "Yes you do. You can't stop like that, man. You have to get out of the way or you're going to get really hurt."

Trey gave him a hard look, his nostrils flaring, before he turned back to Alessandra and put his fingers around her wrist. "Let's go. You're drunk and it's time for you to go home."

The girl standing next to her tried to brush his hand off Alessandra's arm. "She can do what she wants, asshole. What's it to you, anyway?"

He turned to her. "She's. My. Wife."

The girl's head snapped back and she turned to Alessandra. "You got married? Why didn't you tell me?"

"Because apparently it's not worth talking about." She shrugged Trey's hand off her arm and stared at him defiantly. Looking back at the other men, she smiled. "Now, weren't we all making plans to go dancing?"

Trey shook his head. "Jesus Christ, Alessa, don't make me go all alpha male here."

"I'm not *making* you do anything. I'm going out dancing with my new friends. But you should go home now that you've lost." She turned to leave, teetering in her heels. No one followed her, so she spun back to them. "What? Let's go, Cyssah!"

The other men stared at their boots and Cyssah gave her an uncomfortable look. "If you're really married, this isn't the way to solve anything. Besides, this isn't you, Alessandra. I'll give you a ride home if you like."

Alessandra looked shocked. "*Muito obrigada, que grande amiga você é!*" Her words were unmistakably sarcastic in any language. She turned again, crossing her arms in front of herself and hurrying away.

Trey reached down and grabbed his vest off the ground before following her. Part of him was tempted to let her go, but he couldn't very well let her walk around late at night on her own. Certainly not dressed like that. He caught up with her as she passed through the stadium gates to the parking lot and walked silently beside her for a minute. He was furious and hurt.

"Leave me alone," she said defiantly.

"Nope. Can't do that, sorry. Even if you were a total bitch to me just now."

She stopped walking and stared up at him. "That's a horrible thing to say to your wife."

"Yeah, well, you just said some pretty awful shit to me back there in front of a bunch of people."

"You deserved it!" She poked him in the chest as she yelled.

"Maybe, but your friend back there is right. This isn't you. You're better than this."

"Maybe I don't want to be! Maybe I want to be irresponsible tonight instead of doing what everyone expects! What the hell does it matter to you anyway? I'm just the nanny." She dropped her head and angled herself away from him as she started moving again. Pressing her hands to her neck, she shielded her chest with her arms to prevent anyone else from getting a glimpse.

"Oh, come on. I told you I'm sorry several times already. How long are you going to hold that over my head?"

She stopped and turned back to him. "Oh, so I'm not supposed to feel hurt anymore because you said sorry to me? You decide not to tell your own parents that we are together, *that we are married*, and then in a matter of hours I should feel better about everything?

Here's some news for you! That is not how women work when men betray us!" Alessa burst into tears in spite of herself. She had been trying to hold them in, but the booze, mixed with her anger and hurt, weakened her resolve.

Sighing, Trey covered her shoulders with his shirt, then took her in his arms, letting her sob into his chest. "I'm sorry. I know I hurt you today. And I should have told them. I can call them right now if it helps."

"It's too late, Trey. You should have told them because you were *proud* to be marrying me. But you didn't. You've been keeping our marriage a secret, which must mean you're ashamed of me." She backed away from him.

"That's not what it means at all. It's got absolutely nothing to do with being ashamed of you. Have you thought of how hurt my parents will be when they find out I got married without inviting them or even *mentioning* it to them? They're going to be really disappointed, and it kills me that I'm going to hurt them again."

She stared at him, teetering a bit. "That makes it worse! If you *knew* it would hurt them but you *still* didn't tell them, it must mean you never really wanted to tell them. Which means you must not want to be my husband." Her voice was too loud, and people in the parking lot were staring at them.

Trey shifted uncomfortably. "You're drunk and you're causing a scene. Let's just go home. We can talk about this in the morning when you sober up."

Miguel appeared out of nowhere at that moment. "There you are, man! I've been wondering where you—" He stopped, clearly understanding that for the second time today, he was interrupting what should have been a private moment.

Trey looked over at him, his face an admission that things were bad.

Alessandra sniffled and then turned to Miguel. "I need a ride home, Miguel. Can you drive me, please?"

Miguel glanced at Trey, his expression asking if that's what Trey wanted.

Trey gave him a little nod.

"Okay, why don't I drive you both home?" Miguel asked.

Trey left it up to Alessandra to answer for both of them, not wanting to spark another fight.

"Fine," she said in a clipped tone.

Fine. There was that word again. He was starting to realize it might never mean what it was supposed to.

THIRTY-TWO

Late the next morning, Alessandra woke in her old bed in the main house. Justin Timberlake smiled down at her from the wall. Her stomach was raw and her throat burned. Then the humiliation of the night before settled in. Pulling the covers over her head, she lay very still, wishing for death. Or a time machine. Or death. That would be good right now. Then she wouldn't have to feel so sick or face her husband ever again. Or her cousin. Or Cyssah. *Shit.*

A little knock at the door made her wince. "Lessa! Come play with me!"

"Okay, Tomas," she croaked. "Give me a minute."

Getting up, she realized how weak she felt as she pulled on her bathrobe. Her balance was off and her head was pounding. Opening the door, she gave Tomas a feeble smile. "I need to shower first. Can you go play with *Vô* for a bit? Or watch a cartoon?"

"Cartoon!" he said happily, waddling down the hall.

Twenty minutes later, Alessandra made her way to the kitchen, feeling slightly more human having showered and taken something for her headache. Lorena and Carlos were sitting at the table with Tomas, eating lunch.

"Good afternoon," her mother said in a disapproving tone.

"Is there any coffee left?" she asked, ignoring her mother's reproachful look.

"No. We drank it all."

Alessa silently set to work filling the kettle. "Anyone else want tea?"

"No, thank you," Carlos answered.

Alessa looked over at him and saw a look of pity on his face. At least he didn't seem disappointed in her.

"Where's Trey?" she asked finally.

"Back at the rodeo," her mother answered. "They were doing another round of rides today. I guess Bruno talked them into letting him fill an empty spot."

Alessa shut her eyes for a second. As much as she dreaded seeing him, she ached to apologize and try to fix everything. "Did he say when he'd be back?"

"He said after supper. Depends on how he does."

"Okay." She sat at the table and picked up a bun, ripping off small pieces and slowly popping them into her mouth one at a time.

Lorena reached into her pocket and then slapped Alessandra's ring on the table. "You forgot this last night."

Alessandra's face turned red as she slid the ring off the table and onto her finger. "Thanks," she said quietly.

"Maybe we should go watch him?" Carlos suggested.

"No. I don't think it's a good idea, Vô," Alessa answered. "It's distracting for him."

Late that evening, after Alessandra had gotten Tomas to bed, she sat just outside the small house in an old wicker chair with her feet on its mate. She tried reading over a brief for work but the words just passed through her brain without sinking in. Turning off the outside light she had been using, she settled onto the chair again, staring up at the stars and feeling sick with worry until she heard the sound of a truck, and then a door slamming. She watched as Trey walked across the yard toward her. He was moving slowly but he looked to be in one piece. In one hand he carried a large bag that held his riding gear. Her heart tugged at the sight of him. She wanted so badly to rush into his arms and apologize for how she'd acted, but then she remembered how angry and hurt she was.

He stilled for a moment, clearly noticing her sitting in the dark, then continued on.

"How'd you do?" she asked quietly.

"Not bad. Came in third." He dropped the bag near the front door and looked at her. "So, you're just sitting here in the dark?"

"I tried to work but I couldn't concentrate, so I thought I'd stare at the stars and wait for you." Alessandra moved her feet off the chair and slid it toward him.

Trey sat down, which she took to be a hopeful sign.

"I called my parents today," he said.

Alessandra felt her stomach sink with guilt at what she'd put him through the night before. Her voice was tiny as she spoke. "How did it go?"

"They were pretty upset."

Somehow, knowing this hurt Alessandra, even though she knew it shouldn't. "I can imagine. What did they say?"

"My mom didn't say much, mostly cried. My dad had all the same questions your mom had. Then he gave me shit for making my mom cry." Trey's voice was full of resignation.

"I'm sorry, Trey."

He shook his head. "After I got off the phone I realized that I might be hurting them for no reason. The way you were acting last night made me think maybe you want out of this whole thing."

"No, I don't," she whispered. "I'm so sorry about how I acted, Trey. I'm so embarrassed."

"Sounds about right."

"I humiliated us both and I said some horrible things to you." She wiped the tears off her cheeks.

"Yup, you definitely did both of those things in a most spectacular way."

"I know I did. And I'm really sorry. All day, I've been so scared that maybe you won't want to stay with me."

He sighed, leaving a short pause before answering. "Well, I'll admit I was briefly considering my options last night."

Alessandra nodded, pulling her knees up and hugging them to her chest.

Trey continued. "I guess this is where the 'for worse' part of the vows comes in, maybe. And I'm talking about both of us. I know I hurt you first and I'm sorry."

"It's okay."

"No, it's not. I can do better than that."

"So can I. I acted like a complete brat last night. It made me think I'm too immature to even be married," Alessandra said.

"Well, we've both been acting pretty immature, so we'll just have to finish growing up together. It's really the only way we can make this work."

"Really? I thought maybe . . ."

Trey shook his head and put his hand on her knee. "Never, Alessandra. I'm never going to want this to end."

Alessandra all but jumped into his arms, kissing him hard on the mouth. "Thank God. I was so scared this might be over."

He kissed her back with every bit of the remorse and longing that she felt. His strong arms folded around her and he held her tight. "We're going to disagree sometimes, and sometimes we might even fight like a couple of idiots, but we'll always end up right back together like this."

"Okay," Alessandra whispered as she pressed her forehead to his.

Trey lifted his head so he could look at her. "One thing that you're going to have to do is accept the fact that you married a man. Where I come from, a man needs to earn a living and provide for his family."

Alessandra nodded. "Yes, I know. It is no different here."

"Good. Well, in my case, it means that for now I'm gonna ride bulls. You're just going to have to accept that. You need to let me be a man."

"I can do that."

Trey kissed her softly on the lips, lingering as though he would never stop. Alessandra felt the warmth from his mouth as she let her tongue slide between his lips. She felt his fingertips holding her jaw gently and then his hand gliding down her neck as he tilted her head. His kiss was full of the love and passion she knew, deep down, he had for her. She was his and always would be. His hand moved down her shoulder, then along her arm until his fingers found hers. He slipped his fingers between hers and held tight.

Alessandra could feel a lump in her throat where the words were stuck. She wanted to tell him that he was the only man she'd ever love but her feelings were so intense that she couldn't find her voice. So she let her kiss say it for her. The yearning and need she felt after days of living with such fear and anguish spilled out of her as she reached up with her other hand and touched his face. He knew. She could tell he knew what this moment meant to her. It was everything.

"Let's take this inside," he murmured in her ear. She hummed her agreement, but soon they were both distracted by his lips on her neck, trailing kisses down to her collarbone. He sucked gently on her skin and she could feel herself coming to life. Desire sparked and she ached to feel him inside her once again. As if he understood, he picked her up and carried her into the house, closing the door behind them with his foot, then taking her to the bedroom. Leaning his body against the door, he closed it, giving them the privacy that they needed from the world so they could make up. Laying her on top of the bed, he lowered himself over her as she hooked her feet behind his back.

"I should go shower," he whispered, pulling back a little.

"No," she whispered. "I need this. We need this." She struggled with the buckle of his belt, finally managing to open it, then unzipped his jeans. Tugging them down roughly, along with his underwear, she pulled him back on top of her. He lifted her skirt and moved her panties out of the way before relieving them both of the longing they'd had for each other for so many days. Alessandra closed her eyes and took in the feeling of him entering her ever so slowly and carefully until he'd filled her completely. He lowered his mouth over hers, letting only his lips and tongue move, stilling his body for a long, torturous moment. Her hips started to move in circles against him as she shifted her knees up along his back.

"Yes, Trey, like this," she whispered, kissing his neck and tasting the salt on his skin as he started to move over her in passionate thrusts. She buried her face against his chest as he made love to her urgently, tenderly. Relief flooded through her veins as she felt his skin on hers.

"You're mine," he told her as he rocked himself into her again and again until they both let go and were one once more.

Trey showered, then they sat in the kitchen by the light of a candle while he ate some supper. Alessandra watched him while he ate, and they held hands and spoke in hushed tones so as not to wake Tomas. When they made their way back to bed, they stripped each other's clothes off and started making up all over again. It was late when they were finally ready to drift off to sleep, entwined in each other's arms.

Alessandra had one last question nagging at her. "Trey, how did I end up in my old bedroom last night?"

"I tossed you in there to sleep it off."

"Because you were so angry with me?"

"Of course not." His voice had a hint of indignation. "It was because I didn't want you to wake Tomas. You kept going on about being a lawyer and how smart you are. And you'll have to trust me that you had no control over the volume of your voice."

Alessa winced and buried her face in his neck. "Oh God, that is so embarrassing."

"To be honest, it was kind of hilarious."

THIRTY-THREE

"Okay, are we on? Can you see us?" Fern's face was screwed up in concentration as she peered into her computer screen.

"Yes, Mom. We can see you just fine," Trey answered patiently.

"Oh! There she is! Doug, I see her. Do you see her?" Fern turned to her husband and tugged on his arm. "She's so pretty! Just look at those beautiful curls!"

Doug wore an exasperated look. "Yes, I see her. I'm staring at the same screen as you."

Alessandra smiled nervously. "Hello!"

"*Olá*, Alessandra!" Fern said in a slow, loud voice. "How are you?"

Trey covered his mouth with his hand and murmured an apology to Alessandra. She squeezed his knee under the table in response, trying not to laugh.

"I'm very well, thank you. It is lovely to meet you both."

Fern looked slightly embarrassed after hearing her new daughter-in-law's perfect English. "We're very excited to meet you, dear."

"I feel the same way. I know you must both be very good people to have raised such a remarkable son."

"Thank you. Trey's told us wonderful things about you. I'm not going to lie to you, we would have loved to have been at the wedding.

Or at the very least to have met you before you became our daughter-in-law." Fern's face was petulant as she spoke.

Alessandra angled her head and gave Fern a sympathetic look. "Yes, I am so very sorry for that."

"Well, it's not your fault, dear. It was Trey's responsibility," Fern said, clearly irked.

"Still, I wish I had done more to encourage him to tell you," Alessandra offered. "I was too caught up in the wedding, but now I can only think of how I would feel if my child got married and I wasn't there to see it."

Fern's eyes filled with tears. "It's really been so hard. As a mother, you dream of it from the moment your child is born. And we missed it."

Alessandra pressed her hand to her mouth, blinking quickly. "Oh, I'm so sorry." Her voice cracked as tears sprang to her eyes.

Trey and his father stared at each other with matching bewildered looks over how quickly the two women were bonding.

After another moment of apologies and reassurances that it was all Trey's doing, Doug cleared his throat. "We'd like to throw you a reception when you get back home."

Alessandra nodded. "Yes, of course. That is so kind of you. Why don't we renew our vows when we get there?"

Fern's face lit up. "Why not another wedding? We could do the whole thing again!"

Alessandra grinned. "Why not? I already have a dress!"

Trey's mouth fell open as he looked from his wife to his mother, who was now dabbing her eyes and crying because she was suddenly so happy.

"Any word yet on when you can move back?" Fern asked. "I'd like to start planning things as soon as possible."

"We're still waiting for the court to grant Trey legal guardianship of Tomas and permission to take him out of the country. My boss, who is a judge, has been trying to pull some strings, so hopefully it won't be long now."

"Oh, now I'm excited!" Fern cried.

"Me too! I can't wait to meet you in person. I promise we'll come visit as soon as we're allowed."

"Visit? What do you mean, visit?" Fern asked, her face falling.

Alessandra opened her mouth to speak but Trey interjected. "She meant we'll be moving back as soon as we can."

Alessa turned her head to Trey but decided it was not the right time to discuss this.

"Good. Good." Doug nodded. "Trey, I was over at McFarlane's today and Ted said there might be a job opening up there in a few months. Sort of a marketing/sales-type position. I think it would be perfect for you."

"Really? That sounds great."

"Yes, it would be an excellent place to work. Good benefits, lots of opportunity to advance," Doug said.

"Well, let's hope we'll be back in time," Trey said, putting his arm around Alessandra's shoulder.

She gave a tight smile and said, "Yes," but her voice was very quiet.

Tomas climbed up on Alessa's lap, bringing a change of subject as well as more tears to Fern's eyes. The two grandparents became quite animated, trying to hold his three-year-old interest but soon losing it as a toy truck on the floor caught his eye. The call continued for another ten minutes, and Fern filled Trey in on everything he'd missed since they'd last spoken. Alessandra found it impossible to concentrate on the call given the fact that her husband had just made it clear he still intended to move them to the US. Her heart pounded in her chest, worry turning to anger and then back to worry.

When they finally hung up, Alessandra sat feeling numb.

Trey gave her a big grin. "I thought that went pretty well overall. Other than my mom thinking you don't speak English. Sorry about that, hon. She must have forgotten that I told her how excellent your English is." He gave her a quick peck on her cheek before standing up to stretch.

"No, that's fine," Alessandra said quietly.

"Uh-oh, there's that word again. What's wrong?" Trey teased.

"I was just surprised that your parents think we're moving to Colorado."

"Really? Why?"

"Because . . ." Alessandra's voice was tentative, knowing she was starting something. "I thought we were going to live here."

"But I can't work here. I don't have a work visa or citizenship."

"And *I* can't work *there*. I don't have a work visa or citizenship. And I need to stay here to look after *Avô*. My mother told me today that she wants to take a job for a tour company on the east coast. The contract is for six months, but who knows? She might decide to stay permanently. It sounds like a good job."

"You serious? Good for her. She should go."

"Yes, she absolutely should, which means we have to stay. If we leave, she won't go, and she really deserves to try something new with her life, don't you think?"

"Of course she should, but it doesn't mean we can't go. Carlos is very capable, and we can always find someone to help run the farm. I don't know why you and your mom think he can't take of himself."

"Because he's had three heart attacks. He can't be here alone to run the farm. Don't you remember the state of things when we got here?" Her voice had a distinct edge to it.

"Well, I'm sure we can find someone to manage things for him." Trey matched her tone.

"But I don't *want* to find some stranger to work for him. His whole life, he's taken care of his family. We can't abandon him now."

Trey blew out a breath. "So, what was your plan? That we stay here and I work as a farmhand for the rest of my life?"

Tomas ran up to Trey and sat on his foot. "Ride, Dad!"

Alessandra stood and started tidying up some of the toys strewn around the room. "Not a farmhand. I thought you would *manage* the farm. Eventually we can take it over. It's a good life and I thought you loved it here."

Trey, who was now walking around dragging a giggling Tomas, looked back at her. "I do, but I need to earn my own way, Alessandra. I can't just live off your family like that."

"They're your family too now. This is what families do. They take care of each other. They work together and fill in where the others aren't able to."

"What about my family?"

Alessandra sighed. "I don't want to fight with you about this. We'll find a way to figure this out."

"Yeah, I'm sure we will. I just . . . I guess I can't believe we didn't talk about this."

"Me too."

Trey's face brightened. "But you know what? For now, it doesn't matter anyway. We can't leave and we don't know how long it will be before we can, so there's no sense in worrying about it yet."

"True." Alessandra smiled, relieved that the difficult decision could be put off indefinitely. She walked over and gave Trey a big hug. "Anyway, your parents seem very sweet. I'm glad to have met them."

THIRTY-FOUR

Catalão, Brazil

"That was one hell of a good ride, kid!"

Trey felt a hard slap on his back and turned to stare into a shiny silver belt buckle with a bull on it. Looking up from where he sat, Trey's eyes travelled over a large beer belly that threatened to pop the buttons of the plaid shirt covering it. His gaze stopped when it reached the toothy smile of an older gentleman wearing a white cowboy hat.

"Thank you, sir," he answered politely. "He was a real spinner."

"Sure was. In fact, I'd say, pound for pound, he may be one of the rankest bulls I've ever seen. And yet, there you were making 'em look like he was having a bad trip." He held his hand out to Trey. "Hank Murphy."

Trey took him up on his offer of a handshake, soon feeling his hand being squeezed by one strong pump. "Trey Johnson."

"I know who you are. I've been hearing a lot about you since I got to Brazil. I'm a bull riding agent out of Colorado." Hank hoisted up his pants under his belly, but they didn't move as high as he probably would have liked.

"Really? I didn't even know there *was* such a thing. What are you doing all the way out here?"

"I was about to ask you the same thing. How come I've never seen you compete back home? I know just about everybody worth their salt in the business."

"Then I must not be worth my salt," Trey replied with a little grin.

"I see you're a quick-witted son of a bitch too. I like that." Hank settled himself next to Trey on the bench, the effort involved causing him to grunt. "So, I'm guessing you don't have an agent since you didn't know we existed."

"That would be correct. I only just started competing in the last couple of months, actually. Since I've been here."

"You keep riding like that and you'll have quite a career ahead of you. You need to get yourself a decent agent, though, so you can turn each ride into real money."

"I don't know about that. I'm just trying to earn a little money while I'm in Brazil. I hadn't planned on turning this into a career."

"So, you *do* need me then." Hank gave him a firm nod. "Listen, how about we go grab ourselves a beer and talk a little business?"

"I'd say I'm thirsty."

* * *

"So, who was he again? I'm confused." Alessandra used her shoulder to hold her cellphone as she finished drying Tomas with a towel.

"He represents bull riders on the pro tour. He's from Colorado, where the US national association is located. He's got some of the biggest names in the business working for him," Trey said, sounding excited in a way that made Alessandra nervous.

"Okaaayyy." Alessandra's voice was hesitant as she tugged Tomas's pyjama shirt over his head. Tomas ran out of the bathroom before she could put his pyjama pants on him. He squealed with laughter as he ran away from her, his little naked bum poking out from under his shirt. Alessandra grimaced to herself as she realized she hadn't heard what Trey had just said.

". . . a real shot at making the tour, and I could get some pretty sweet sponsorship deals if I do well. Apparently, I have the right look."

"You mean because you're gorgeous?"

"Well, I still have all my teeth, so I imagine that helps."

"So, what do you want to do, then?"

"I think I should check out his background, see if he's legit or not. Then spend some time with him while he's here so we can figure out if working together would be a good idea."

Alessandra hung up the wet towel and took the cellphone in her hand, straightening her sore neck. "I don't understand. I thought you were only doing this for a little while?"

"Yes, but that was *before* I found out how much money I could make. If things go the way he thinks they will, we could be sitting pretty within the next two years. We could have our own place, fully paid for, plus some cash in the bank."

"Trey, I—"

"I know what you're going to say. It's too dangerous. But it really isn't that bad. And think of the payoff. We could really get ahead, Alessa. We could give our children everything. And we could live without worrying about money. Can you even imagine that?"

She set Tomas's pants on a kitchen chair and poured a bowl of cereal. "*Rapinzho*, your bedtime snack is ready. Come and eat."

"Just think it over, okay babe? It could be the opportunity of a lifetime."

"Alright, I'll think about it for sure." She caught Tomas just as he reached the table, giving him a stern look as she held his pants close to the floor for him to step into. "I'm going to put Tomas on the phone. He wants to say good night to you."

* * *

"So, this is the standard agreement. You'll find all the agents pretty much use the same one." Hank handed Trey a thin set of papers held together at the top by a paper clip. "And this is a spreadsheet I've made up showing the competitions you've been to and how much you made versus how much you would have made if you'd had a good sponsor."

Trey took a minute to glance over the spreadsheet. "That's quite the difference."

Hank gave him a confident smile. "I know. If you're going to be riding anyway, you might as well make it worth as much as you can. Plus, if you're with me, I'd like to bring you back home so you can train with some of my other clients. You've got raw talent, but if you refined your skills a little more, I think there'd be a place for you at the top. Now, you said you didn't want to come home until you're allowed to bring your son home, is that right?"

Trey looked across the table at Hank. "Yes, sir. I don't want to leave him for a big chunk of time if I can help it."

"I told you, my name is Hank, not *sir*. Any idea how long that might take?"

"Well, I'm hoping it will be in the next couple of months, but it's really hard to say."

"Okay, well, we'll do what we can under the circumstances. I know a few of the top riders in Brazil. I'll see if you can train with one of them until you come home."

"Thank you, Hank." Trey looked back down at the papers in front of him and started to scan them.

Hank waited patiently, sipping coffee. "So, which way are you leaning?"

"Well, it's all a lot to think about, Hank. I mean, it's pretty exciting, but I need to talk to my wife first."

"Sure, it's a big decision. You might want to show it to a lawyer as well."

"She is a lawyer."

"Really? Well, I can't wait to meet her."

* * *

"So, what do you think?" Trey asked as soon as Alessandra looked up from the contract.

She took her glasses off and gave him a little shrug. "It all looks fine as far as I can tell."

"I should sign it then?" he asked, trying to contain his excitement.

"Yes, if this is what you want to do, then signing with Hank is probably a good idea."

Trey jumped up from his chair and leaned over to give Alessandra a big kiss on her lips.

"Yes! I'm so glad you agree. I really thought it was the way to go." He clapped his hands together. "Are you excited? I'm excited!"

"Trey, there are no circumstances in which I'm going to be happy about you riding bulls."

"Fair enough. I'll be excited enough for the both of us, then." Lifting his hands to her cheeks, he gave her another kiss. "This is the right move, babe. I know it is. A year from now, we're going to have so much money, we won't know what to do with it all."

THIRTY-FIVE

"This came today." Alessandra handed Trey a large envelope. It was from the federal court, addressed to him.

"Is this what I think it is?" Trey leaned his shovel against the stall gate and looked at his wife. She was still in her work suit and her face was devoid of emotion. Opening the package, he took out the papers, gave them a quick look and then handed them back to her. "Do you mind telling me what they say?"

"Of course." She stood for a moment, reading the letter. "This says you have been added to Tomas's birth certificate, which is enclosed, and that you have been granted guardianship. The court is satisfied that you will provide for him properly, and you are free to go back to the US with him." Her voice was quiet as she gave him the news. She flipped through the attachments and they looked at them together.

Trey let out a long breath. "So that's it, then?"

"Yes, that's it." She gave him a big smile that didn't quite meet her eyes. "Congratulations!"

"Thanks! It's such a relief. I feel like now the Ferreiras can't come back and fight for custody."

"You're right. They won't be able to."

Trey gave her a big hug. "Thank you so much for making this happen. I couldn't have done it without you."

"Sure you could have. It would have just cost you a lot of money."

"Which I don't have. Plus, your boss really managed to expedite everything for us. It could have been another year! I need to get him a gift. Maybe a bottle of his favourite wine or something? And we should celebrate—maybe we could go out for a nice dinner. But first, I'm going to finish this up and call my parents to give them the news."

"Of course. I'm going to get changed out of my suit and go say hello to *Vô* and Tomas."

Alessandra waited until she was out of the barn to let her face fall. She propelled herself forward although her feet felt like lead weights. She felt sick about what she knew was going to happen now. Trey would take Tomas back home so he could compete in the bull riding circuit. Lorena had left two weeks earlier, which meant there was no way Alessandra could join them in the US. She was needed here.

She stewed over the problem as she slowly changed into jeans and put her hair up in a ponytail. By the time she left the bedroom, Trey was sitting at the table in front of his laptop, speaking with his very excited mother. Alessandra sneaked out so as not to be noticed by Trey's mom. She didn't have the heart to pretend to share their enthusiasm at the moment. During the walk from the bedroom to the front door, she heard Fern say, "Well, of course you can use our place as a home base! We want to get as much time with our grandson as possible!"

Stepping outside, Alessandra could feel her heart shattering. Her eyes filled with tears as she watched Tomas and her grandfather sitting in chairs on the patio, sharing an orange.

* * *

"Come with us," Trey said as he took the plate Alessandra had just rinsed and started rubbing it with a dishtowel.

"I can't. You know I need to stay here. I have my job and I can't leave *Avô*." Alessandra concentrated on the glass she was washing so she could avoid looking at him.

"How long is your mom's contract again?"

"Six months, but I'm pretty sure they'll offer her an extension and I know she won't want to come back. She's really happy."

"Okay, what if we find someone to come here every day and look after the farm and Carlos? Maybe one of your cousins?"

"If we do that, my mother will quit her job and move back home. It's not just the chores around the farm. He needs someone to cook for him and make sure he takes his medicine. Soon, it will be time to harvest the oranges, and things get very hectic. We'll have a large team of migrant workers that will need to be managed for several weeks. And what if something happens to him? We can't just let him be alone."

"Alessa, I really admire that you want to take care of him, but do you even think Carlos would *want* you to stay? I mean, honestly, it's not like we'd be gone forever. For now, it would just be for two months. He would want you to go and meet my family, wouldn't he?"

"I'm sure he would, but that doesn't make it right. If I leave, I will be doing exactly what my mother predicted I would—falling in love and leaving my grandfather alone. She will come rushing back and I'll never hear the end of it. Besides, I don't want to do that to her, just when she's finally getting a chance to do what she loves. I wish it could work, but there's no way. I can't just leave my job, either. I have too many responsibilities here. I need you to understand that."

Trey sighed heavily. "I guess I do, but I really have to go *now*. Hank's got a big sponsor who sounds very interested in me. I could make more money by next year at this time than we ever thought possible."

Alessandra closed her eyes for a moment. "We don't need more money than we thought possible. We need to be a family. I still can't see why you refuse to consider staying here. The farm needs a good manager, you've been amazing at running it and it's good work. It's safe and we can all stay together."

"But it's not mine, Alessandra. It belongs to your grandfather. I need to make my own way in life, just like you're doing. Remember when we sat at the restaurant in São Paulo, talking about our dreams? We both agreed that life is just so much better if you can live your dreams. You're living your dream. Can't I do the same?"

"So, bull riding is your *dream* now?"

Trey sighed. "No, my dream is to give my family a wonderful life. Bull riding is the best way for me to do that. I've made a lot of mistakes in my life, Alessa, but this isn't one of them. I've found the one thing that I'm really talented at—not just as good as other guys, but really talented. And if I have a chance to do it, I just feel like somehow it's going to let me fix everything. I can go back home a champion, someone my parents can brag about, you know? I won't just be their son who had a baby with his cousin's girlfriend anymore. I'll be somebody. And my son won't just be the boy everyone thought was Cole Mitchell's son, he'll be the son of a champion bull rider. I know this whole thing sounds stupid to you, but to me it's a chance to wipe the slate clean."

"I didn't realize what this meant to you. I thought bull riding was all about the money."

"It started out that way, but it's so much more now."

Alessa stared at Trey for a long moment before answering. He was completely sincere. "Well then, I guess you have to do it. And I have to let you go, even if it means we will be apart for so long." Her voice broke.

Trey put down the dishtowel and tried to give her a hug but Alessandra shook her head. "I'll get you all wet."

"I don't care about that. Come here." He took her wet hands and placed them behind his back before folding his arms around her. "You know I'll come back for you, right? I'm not going to stay gone."

"How can you know that? What if you do really well with the bull riding and you decide to stay in it for years?"

"I won't. I'll just see if I can make the finals and if I can't, I forget the whole thing. I promise. You have nothing to worry about."

Alessandra pulled back and gave him a serious look. "But what about Tomas? You can't just take him there and leave him with your mother. He doesn't even know her. If you insist on going, can you please leave him with me? This is his home."

Trey shook his head. "I need to be with him, Alessa. My family needs the chance to get to know him. And he needs to get to know them."

Alessandra didn't answer but turned and started washing a pot.

"Let's think on it a bit. It's a tough decision, and it's one we don't have to make today. Worst-case scenario, we'll go to Colorado for a couple months and I won't win, but I'll still come back with some sponsorship money. Best case, I make it to the world finals and I bring home a million dollars. Just think what that money could do for our family. We'd never have to worry about money again. Hell, we could buy a place there and here and go back and forth."

Alessandra nodded her head. "I can see you need to do this, Trey, and I won't try to stop you. I just want you to consider leaving Tomas here."

Trey nodded. "I'll think about it."

* * *

The next five days passed in a quiet sadness. Trey had decided to bring Tomas with him, knowing how hard it would be for Alessandra.

She hadn't argued about it, but he could tell it scared her. On Trey's part, he felt as though time was charging forward at breakneck speed and then suddenly halting, until it seemed to stretch out endlessly as he prepared to start his thrilling new life. He took in everything with keen awareness, especially when it came to Alessandra. Each little sigh, every wistful look, those moments where she stared off into space—each one tugged at his heart. He knew she was trying to hide her sadness from him, and he knew it was harder to be the one left behind than the one doing the leaving. He would make this time apart worthwhile. He would return to her a champion and she would know it had all been for a good reason.

* * *

Alessandra sat at her desk in her office, staring out the window at the park. There was a tall stack of work in front of her that required her immediate attention and yet somehow she just couldn't make herself concentrate, no matter how hard she tried. She had barely slept for days. Late-night talks with Trey, along with her fears, kept her awake at night. She watched as a woman outside walked slowly along, holding hands with a little boy as he hopped along the path. The woman was in no hurry. She had all the time in the world to let him explore and watch him grow, and Alessandra suddenly felt a pang of envy.

Her time with Tomas was winding down and she couldn't be sure if she'd ever see him again. What if Trey decided to stay in the US? What if he decided he didn't want her anymore? It was entirely believable to her that the spell he was under might dissolve once he'd been home for a while. What if her mother was right? He might realize that what they had was nothing more than gratitude, nothing more than the need to cling to a warm, comforting body at a time in his life when he had been so alone. Everything was all so complicated because of Tomas. Maybe even her own feelings for Trey had developed in part because she didn't want to have to say goodbye to his son. The thought that Tomas might grow up and not even remember her was almost too much for her to think about. But it was possible.

She felt helpless to do anything but wait. She couldn't stop him. She wouldn't. She needed to let him go and hope he loved her enough to return to her. So she wouldn't beg, she wouldn't plead or get angry and push him away. She would just hope and pray. Hope he wouldn't forget how perfect they were together and pray that he would come home safe.

But maybe there was one thing she could do. Something that would really show her once and for all if his love for her would last a lifetime. She could offer him his freedom. She could make it very easy for him if he changed his mind about her. And if he came back to her in the end, she would know without a doubt that he was hers forever.

She knew it was a risk but it was one she was willing to take. He might choose his freedom, but wouldn't it be better to know now than to have him return out of a sense of obligation to live out a life he didn't want? Her hands shook as she opened a folder called Divorce Templates on her computer and got to work.

THIRTY-SIX

The night before Trey and Tomas were set to leave, Alessandra stood in the living room of their tiny house among the suitcases and boxes they would take. Tomas slept in his bed, looking so peaceful. He knew he was going on a plane ride but he was too little to understand what any of it meant. She crouched down next to him and cradled his cheek in her hand, praying she would be with him again soon. She loved him so much. She couldn't imagine loving him more if she'd given birth to him herself. He was three and a half now, and she'd been with him every day since he was one. He and Trey were supposed to come back in November, but somehow she couldn't see them being back together by then. She might miss Tomas's next Christmas. And his next birthday. And maybe the rest of his life. The thought shredded her.

A hand on her shoulder interrupted her thoughts. "Come here," Trey whispered, holding his hands out to help her up. He pulled her in for a long, deep hug. "You okay?" he whispered.

Alessandra shook her head into his chest, unable to voice her pain.

"Look at me." He held his hands to her face. "We're going to be together very soon. What's a few weeks when you're going to spend a lifetime together?"

She tried to smile. "Right. I know."

"You know I'm coming back. You believe me, don't you?"

She nodded. "I want to, but I'm scared."

"I read somewhere that the most dangerous part about bull riding is the flight to and from the competition. You're not scared of me going on a plane, are you?"

Alessandra raised a skeptical eyebrow. "That's not true. You never read that."

"Well, someone should write that down. I'm sure it would make you feel better. I'm completely safe on those bulls. If anything, *they're* in danger around *me*. So you see, there's nothing to worry about." He gave her a lingering kiss. "Nothing is going to keep us apart. I promise."

* * *

Later, after they got into bed, Trey rolled onto his side and gave Alessandra a long, slow kiss. Her hand was tucked in between their bodies and rested gently on his chest. She shut her eyes tight as she kissed him back. He knew from the feel of it that it was a kiss of grief and loss as much as it was a kiss of yearning. They stayed like that for what seemed like hours, drinking in their last tastes of each other. He lifted her nightie over her head, tossed it to the end of the bed and ran his large hands over her naked body. Burying his face into her neck, he breathed in the scent of her, a mix of cream and flower blossoms. He took his time kissing her from the nape of her neck to her earlobe. "I wish I could stop time right here," he whispered to her. "I don't want to leave without you."

She nodded her agreement and he saw her swallow her sorrow before she kissed him again. Their tongues melded together in their seductive, familiar dance, their need for each other building.

Alessandra pulled his boxer briefs down, pushing them the rest of the way off with her toes before wrapping one leg over his hip. There were no barriers now, only the small space between them. He ran his hand down her side, letting his mouth follow his fingertips. He wanted to kiss every inch of her, to make this last, to leave her with a beautiful memory that would get her through their weeks apart.

Letting his tongue glide over her breasts, he kissed and sucked on them, holding their fullness in his hands, hearing her moan softly. The next morning he would leave, and right now it felt like it would be forever before he could do this again. To breathe her in, kiss her, touch her, feel her body wrapped around his, have her curves pressed against him. But tonight he could do all of it, and he wouldn't stop until they'd both had their fill. Moving his mouth down her tummy, he lifted her leg, leaving her open so he could share with her the most intimate of acts. His mouth lowered over her sex slowly, his sweet kisses meeting her wet warmth. The taste of her would be seared into his memory and nothing would please his tongue like this until they were together again. Parting her with his thumbs, he entered her with his tongue, knowing what that would do to her. Circles and swirls of pleasure, over and over, his own satisfaction nearing hers as he moved one hand up to her chest, feeling her heart beat under her ribs. The rhythm of it matched his own. She was his only love, and regret filled him as he prepared to leave. He felt her pulse quicken and her sex tighten around his tongue. She lifted her head off the pillow and her breath caught as she silently came undone. He stayed there, tasting her and feeling her for a long time, not ready to stop until she pulled his face toward hers. "Come here," she whispered with a sad smile.

Their lips met and their bodies started to move together again, her legs coiling around his waist as he found his way inside ever so gently. He stilled his body, allowing himself to just take in the feeling of how tight and ready for him she was. She was still throbbing from what he'd just done to her, and now his mind was entirely captivated by the moment. They would stop time. They would stop the future from tearing them apart. If only he could show her with his body what was inside his soul. It was her and it always would be. Moving over her now in long, slow drags, his mouth never leaving hers, he made love to her until neither of them could hold off any longer. Their flesh took over, enveloping them in waves of undeniable pleasure that seemed endless. He felt her arms and legs tighten around him when it was over, and he heard a sob escape her throat.

"Don't cry," he whispered. "It'll be okay."

"I know, I'm just going to miss you so much," she whispered back.

"I'm going to miss you too, every day and every night." He kissed her gently, then pressed his forehead against hers. "I knew it was going to be hard to leave you, but right now I don't have the first clue how I'm going to tear myself away tomorrow."

He buried his face in her neck, breathing her in before lifting his head again so he could look at her. Holding her cheek with one hand, he gazed into her eyes. "Remember this moment, Alessandra. If you start to have doubts about us, remember this moment. Remember my face right now. You can feel how I feel about you right now, can't you?"

She nodded. "Yes. It's exactly how I feel about you."

"You're burned into my soul, Alessandra. Only you. I'm never going to want another woman and I'm never going to want a life without you in it. Promise me you won't start to doubt that."

"I promise."

* * *

They woke a few hours later, forcing themselves to get out of bed and do what had to be done. Alessandra dressed quickly and took a moment to wash her face and put her hair up, seeing the grief in her eyes as she stared into the mirror. "Stop being a baby," she told herself.

Taking a deep breath, she opened the door and attempted a smile. Tomas grinned excitedly and tried to lift the heavy luggage so he could help out. "We go on plane today!" he announced.

"Tomorrow, *rapazinho*. You go on a bus today. Tonight you stay in a hotel and tomorrow you go on the plane."

Trey, who had been adding his shaving kit to his suitcase, paused, pulling out a large envelope. "What's this?" he asked, turning to Alessandra.

"Oh, that's nothing. I meant to take that out." Her heart pounded with fear as she crossed the room to take it from him.

"What is it, Alessandra?" He furrowed his brow in confusion, holding on to the envelope.

"It's just another legal document, but I realized you won't need that one so I'll get rid of it." She refused to look at him and she knew she wore a guilty look on her face.

"Alessandra, what is this? It says, 'Open if you should change your mind.' About what? Bull riding?"

She shook her head, her heart sinking. She'd meant to get that out of his suitcase before he saw it.

Realization crossed his face. "About you."

He stared at her for a long moment before opening the door. "Hey, Tomas, why don't you ride your tricycle for a bit?"

Tomas zipped out the door, pretending to be an airplane with his arms out to the side as he ran. Trey turned to her. "Are these divorce papers?"

"I prepared them in case you changed your mind when you got home, but after last night I realized . . ." She kept her eyes trained on her bare toes, feeling completely exposed now.

"Jesus Christ, Alessandra! How am I supposed to feel about this? I'm about to leave for two months and you give me *divorce* papers? Do you want a divorce?"

"No! Of course not! I don't even want you to go for one night! It's just that when you met me, I was Tomas's nanny, you know? Maybe part of the draw to be with me was because of him. I've been thinking about it, and I've been wondering if maybe you were lonely and you needed to be part of a family. Maybe it wasn't me you loved as much as you loved having a family. You came here alone and worried about being a father and I somehow made that all better for you. And maybe you won't feel the same way once you've been gone for a while and are back home."

Trey's jaw was set tightly, an angry look sharpening his chiselled features. "Did you sign these?" he asked, his voice thick with emotion.

She nodded, tears filling her eyes. "I'm sorry. I never should have—"

"No, you shouldn't have. You're my wife, Alessandra, and that means something to me. It means for life. This wasn't just some fling for me. After everything . . . after everything we said and did? And you even *signed* them? I don't know what to say." Trey choked out the words, looking completely wounded.

Alessandra reached for him, but he backed away. "I'm sorry. I thought maybe it would be what you wanted. I wanted to make it easy for you."

"If you wanted to make things easy for me, you should have started trusting me. Having to keep reassuring you is just exhausting."

"It's hard for me to believe. But after last night, I finally know that you want to spend the rest of your life with me."

"Why was it so hard? Have I done anything to make you question me?"

"No. Maybe it's the way I grew up. No father, always hearing my mother warn me about men. And then you come along, and you're this handsome American cowboy. You could have any girl you want and I couldn't understand why you wanted *me*. It didn't make sense. I'm not beautiful like you are. I'm not exciting or sexy, and I don't want to do daring things. So I'm always asking myself why you would choose me, and I keep coming back to the fact that Tomas loves me, and that with me, you get an instant family. It was easy with me, but maybe your reasons for wanting to be married to me are more than just being in love with me. And now you're going because you *want* to go away, even though I can't go with you. And I got scared, you know?"

"I don't even know what to say." Trey shook his head. "If I wanted to be with someone else, I would be. But I'm in love with you, so I'm with you. I just am. And it's got nothing to do with my son. And you know what else? I'm not your father. He fucked up and abandoned you, I'm not going to do that. I'm leaving, yes, but I'm doing this for *us*, so *we* can have a better future together. You and me. And I've begged you to come with us. Doesn't that matter even a little bit?"

"It does. Of course it does. I'm sorry." She tried again to touch his arm but he moved away. "I couldn't understand why you would want me but now I do."

"If you couldn't understand before, you haven't heard a word I've been saying all these months. None of it got through to you, did it?"

"It did. I heard you. I just—"

"Didn't trust me." He shook his head, looking disgusted and hurt.

"I'm sorry. I'll try, Trey, I promise. I'll try."

He tossed the envelope onto the table and zipped up his suitcase. Pointing to the envelope, he gave her a cold, hard stare. "That hurts. That really fucking hurts."

He loaded himself with the bags and suitcases and strode out the door, leaving her with her regret and shame. Alessandra took several deep breaths, preparing herself to face everyone. She followed him out of the house for the long walk to the truck.

Carlos had a wary expression as he looked over at his grand-daughter. "*Olá*, Alessandra."

"*Olá, Vô.*" She knew her eyes must be swollen and her face blotchy.

Trey loaded Tomas into his car seat and turned to shake Carlos's hand, speaking in Portuguese. "Goodbye, sir. Thank you so much for everything."

Carlos nodded. "*Tchau, Trey. Fico feliz em ver que Alessandra tem alguém como você para tomar conta dela.*"

Trey looked confused for a minute and turned to Alessandra for help.

"He says you are a good person and that he's happy I have you to care for me."

"Please tell him I'm glad I've earned *his* trust and that I'll see him again very soon."

Alessandra passed along the message, and Carlos shook Trey's hand, using his other to pat it warmly as he had done when they'd first met. Next, he leaned into the truck to kiss Tomas goodbye. Alessandra waited patiently before climbing into the back seat to sit with Tomas for the short trip into town. Trey got in and started the engine, looking back at her in the rear-view mirror without a word. She looked down at Tomas, taking his little hand in hers and tracing circles around his knuckles. "Are you excited, Tomas?"

He nodded, his eyes wide. "You come too, Lessa."

"I can't today, but I will see you soon, okay?"

"I come back here to play with *Avô* on Monday."

She chuckled a little through her tears. "No, but soon."

Alessandra couldn't take her eyes off Tomas as he watched the fields rushing by and then the city limits coming into view. Her heart ached at the thought of being apart from him and from Trey. She was gripped by the fear that she may have just undone all the good Trey had done since they met. Glancing into the rear-view mirror, she saw that his eyes were set on the road and swirling with anger. Or was that hurt?

When they arrived at the bus station, she unbuckled Tomas and pulled him onto her lap for a long hug. "I love you, *rapazinho*. You must always remember how much you are loved."

She listened with her eyes closed as Trey opened the door and climbed out. This was ending. In a few moments, they would be gone. Tomas slid off her lap. "Open da door, please!"

"Okay, Tomas." She gave in to his request, then climbed down before lifting him out. She watched him stomp on the cracks in the sidewalk in front of the bus station while Trey purchased tickets at the counter and unloaded their bags. It all felt like a nightmare, one which she couldn't end by waking up. If only she'd had another day with them, she could have made sure she and Trey were on good terms when he left. She could have made sure he would want to return to her more than he had ever wanted anything in his life.

When he finally came back toward them, he gave her a serious look, one she hadn't seen before. She didn't know what it meant.

She stepped toward him, hoping to erase the distance between their souls as much as the distance between their bodies. "I'm so sorry, Trey. Please forget that I did that, okay?"

He nodded. "I'll try."

"I would give anything if I could take it back," she whispered, wiping the tears from her eyes.

"I know." He put his hand on her waist and Alessandra stepped into his arms, clinging to him, sobbing into his hard chest. She felt his lips on top of her head and the warm air of his sigh.

"I love you," she whispered. "I love you so much. If you want me to move to the United States, I will. I'll find a way to make it work."

"We don't need to think about that now. Let's just get through the next few weeks, okay?"

Nodding, she smiled up at him, her eyes sad. The bus parked next to them and the other passengers lined up with their bags. Alessandra could feel an awful tightening in her chest, as though she would suffocate in her sorrow. "I should let you go."

"Yes, we should get going. I love you." He gave her a kiss on the lips, but it wasn't the one she had hoped for. It was somehow hollow. She'd broken what they had and months would pass before she could try to repair it. He pulled away from her before picking up the bags and getting in line. Alessandra crouched down and gave Tomas a big, squeezy hug. "I love you. I want you to always remember, every day, how much I love you and how special you are. You be good for your dad, okay, *rapazinho*?"

"I be good." He pressed the tip of her nose with his chubby index finger. "See you Monday."

"See you Monday," she answered through her tears.

THIRTY-SEVEN

Colorado Springs, Colorado

"There they are! It's them, Doug! They're really here!" Fern exploded into ecstatic sobs at the first sight of Trey and Tomas walking from the arrivals gate.

"I know, Fern, I'm looking right at them," he replied as she grabbed his arm with one hand and waved wildly with the other.

As soon as the weary travellers made it through the doors she rushed toward them, holding out her arms. "Tomas, it's Grandma Fern!"

Trey smiled as he watched his mother, who didn't seem to know whether to laugh or cry so was doing both. She'd never looked as happy to him as she did at that moment. He glanced down at Tomas, who was staring at her with wide eyes. Trey's father stepped up beside her, holding out an enormous stuffed dog that caught Tomas's attention.

Trey lowered himself down next to Tomas and put his arm around him. "This is my mom, your grandma," he said pointing to Fern. "And that's my dad, your grandpa."

Tomas tucked his body closer to Trey's and stared shyly at the pair of adults beaming at him.

Doug crouched down and held the stuffed animal out. "This is for you, Tomas. Your grandma picked it up for you because we're so excited to have you home with us."

Fern joined her husband, nodding and gesturing. "Take it, honey. It's for you!"

"Go on, buddy. It's okay," Trey coaxed.

Tomas reached one hand out, keeping the other on Trey's knee as he gave the dog's ear a small tug.

A few minutes later, they walked out into the fresh air and Colorado sunshine. Trey's parents were full of questions about the trip and how they were doing. Trey yawned when he'd finished buckling Tomas into his car seat. It had been a long couple of days on the road with his little boy, and he just wanted to get him to the quiet of his parents' house so they could start getting settled in. His own exhaustion was from so much more than just the travelling. It was also from being on an emotional roller coaster with his wife. The sight of those divorce papers haunted him, filling him with a sense of betrayal. He tried to remind himself that Alessandra had only done it because she was scared, but he wondered if deep down she actually *wanted* him to stay gone.

"Almost there," he said quietly to Tomas, running his index finger down the length of the boy's nose. He sat next to him in the back seat of his parents' car as they left the airport parking lot.

"We hope you won't mind, Trey, but the family wanted to have a dinner to celebrate you and Tomas getting home," Doug informed him.

"What? Right now? Honestly, we're both exhausted, Dad."

"But honey, it's been years since any of us have seen Tomas. Or you, for that matter. We'll just pop out to the ranch. We don't have to stay long." His mom pleaded with her eyes.

"The ranch? Jesus. I really don't want to go there at all," Trey groaned.

"Nonsense. It's high time you and Cole buried the hatchet. Now, he's forgiven you for what happened. You need to see him face to face to get this whole thing over with once and for all. Besides, it'll be so nice for Tomas to play with Jake Junior and little Vivian."

"I suppose there's no sense in me protesting. We're going no matter what I say, aren't we?"

"Well, Trey, it would be pretty rude if we didn't go. Claire's been cooking up a storm and Dustin's out there working today and he can't wait to see you guys either."

*　*　*

Trey's heart pounded in his chest as the sign for Black Canyon Ranch came into view. He hadn't been here since Tomas was a baby. Now he was about to come face to face with his cousin. The man he'd hurt more than he'd ever hurt anyone in his life. He gazed out the window as the barn and lodge came into view.

"You'll notice they've expanded the guest quarters quite a bit. The ranch has been so busy that they've added about half a dozen new cabins," Fern said.

"Good for them," Trey replied, his voice quiet.

When they parked, Trey sat for a moment, mustering up the courage to get out of the car. He wished he'd had some warning that this would be happening today. Or at least the chance to shower and change into clean clothes. He looked over at his tired little boy, hoping that he'd manage to make it through what was about to be an overwhelming experience for him at the end of a very long journey.

Tomas smiled up happily at his dad. "Dey have lots of horses!"

"Yup, they do. You're going to like it here, little man." Trey unbuckled his son and opened the door.

Once out of the car, they were greeted first by Otis, the ranch's large sheepdog, who gave two short barks and ran over to them.

"Hey, Otis, long time no see," Trey said, giving the dog a pat on the head.

"Up!" Tomas demanded, shrinking back from the large animal.

Trey reached down and plucked him off the ground, away from the licks that Otis was giving Tomas on his cheeks.

"He's a nice dog, Tomas. Big, though, right?"

Tomas nodded.

Soon the family descended, welcoming them and smiling. Ben and Alicia were the first to reach them, along with their little boy, Jake Junior. Trey's Aunt Mary was the least enthusiastic, wearing a tight smile and staring at the boy she had once believed was her grandson. "Hello, Tomas. I haven't seen you since you were a baby. You're such a big boy now."

Fern ran a hand over Tomas's back. "Isn't he, though? He looks exactly like Trey at that age too." She beamed. "Tomas, would you like to meet the other kids?" She reached her hands out to take him but he shook his head.

"I stay with dad."

"Okay, honey."

"There you are, you ugly mutt!" Dustin's voice sounded from the door to the barn. He strode toward them with a grin.

"Hey, you little turd," Trey said with a laugh, feeling relief at seeing his brother.

The two hugged quickly, and Trey introduced Tomas to his uncle Dustin.

A few minutes later, the party moved to the patio of the lodge restaurant and Trey was greeted by Claire, head chef and Cole's wife.

She gave him a warm smile and a hug. "How are you, Trey? You must be tuckered out after all that travelling."

"I am. It's been a long few days," Trey remarked, feeling more than a little awkward as Cole walked up behind her. Trey froze in place, watching for his cousin's reaction to him.

Cole gave him a sad smile and a little nod of his head. "Trey, welcome home." He reached his hand out to shake Trey's.

Trey accepted, an unexpected wave of relief washing over him. "Cole, it's good to see you." Trey felt a lump in his throat and the two men seemed to communicate an entire conversation without saying a word. Cole was telling him that he was forgiven and Trey was conveying how very sorry he was and how grateful he was to be welcomed home.

"You too. I was sorry to hear about Gabriela. She was far too young. Must have been such a shock for you."

"It was one of those moments I'll never forget."

"I bet. How's Tomas doing with all of it?" Cole looked over at the little boy.

"He's doing surprisingly well, actually. He asks for her once in a while, which is heartbreaking, but for the most part he's okay. I don't think he really understands."

"I'm sure it will take quite a while before that happens."

"Yeah, I think it will. Is that your little one there?"

"Yes, that's Vivian." Claire smiled proudly at her daughter, who was sitting on her grandpa's lap, laughing as he pretended his leg was a horse.

"She's adorable. She's a perfect mixture of you two."

"Yup, she's a little spitfire too," Cole answered, putting his arm around Claire's waist. "Fearless little thing, just like her mom."

Claire laughed and swatted Cole's arm. "Oh yeah, just like me." Her tone was sarcastic.

"You guys look really happy. It's nice to see."

"We are," Claire said. "Speaking of happy, I heard congratulations are in order. When are we going to meet the new Mrs. Johnson?"

Trey's brows knit together. "Well, I'm not too sure. She's pretty busy with work right now. She just finished law school. She's also taking care of her grandfather."

"A lawyer? I never figured you'd get married to a lawyer," Cole said, shaking his head in wonder.

"I never figured he'd get married at all," Dustin interjected, handing Trey and Cole each a beer.

The evening passed pleasantly enough, with Tomas starting to warm up to and play with his new cousins. After supper, the group moved to the pool area. Mary, Jake and Alicia took the three little ones for a swim while the others got caught up. Trey watched, surprised by how relaxed he felt already. It was as though everyone had moved on from that horrible night when the truth came out. He watched Cole as he and Doug chatted as though nothing had happened. Being here felt so natural and yet it was so hard for him to believe. When he'd left here over three years ago, everything was wrong. Everyone was angry and hurt and he thought nothing would ever be the same again, and yet here they were, gathered for a noisy meal together. The only thing that could have made the evening better was having Alessandra with them. He wondered if he would get used to being away from her or if he would have this empty feeling until they were together again.

Fern sat down next to Trey and put her hand on his shoulder. "So, you still mad we brought you?"

"Nah. I'm glad you did."

"I wasn't sure if I should but then I thought about how when you were a kid, you always needed me to rip off your Band-Aids for you.

No matter what, you could never bring yourself to do it, but I knew you'd feel better having it over with."

Trey chuckled. "Mothers always know best, right?"

"Don't you forget that."

Their conversation was interrupted by Ben. "Say, Trey, I heard you've been bullfighting!"

Everyone laughed, obviously having heard the story.

"Yes, I've got my cape in the car if you want a demo," Trey answered with a grin.

Ben's face changed to a more serious expression. "I heard you made the pro tour."

"Yeah, can you believe it? It hasn't even been six months since the first time I got on a bull. It's crazy."

"Crazy is right. Trey's going to get himself killed!" Dustin chimed in.

Tomas stared at his uncle with wide eyes. He had been standing at the edge of the pool in a life jacket, about to jump back in. He turned to his dad instead and made a beeline for him, his lip quivering.

"Oh, no, Tomas," Trey said soothingly. "Uncle Dustin was just joking around." He shot Dustin a dirty look, receiving a sheepish expression in return.

Trey gave Tomas a reassuring smile. "Don't you worry about that. He was just teasing your dad. I'd like to see you jump in again and make a *big* splash this time. See if you can soak Uncle Dustin's ball cap."

Tomas looked over at his uncle with a determined look before hurrying back to the pool and jumping in.

Ben went on, "Well, anyway, good for you, Trey. That's big news."

Fern spoke up. "Don't encourage him. I don't like it one bit.

What he should be doing is finding a job in his field. He didn't graduate with honours from economics just to go to the rodeo!"

"Looks like he did!" Dustin laughed.

"It's temporary. I'm just going to do this until I can get myself established, then I'm aiming to get a real job," Trey said.

* * *

Trey crawled into bed late that night with a huge sigh. It was after 2 a.m. in Bebedouro, and he couldn't remember a time when he'd been more tired. Tomas had fallen asleep on the way home and Trey had carried him upstairs at his parents' house and tucked him into a little toddler bed that had been squeezed in next to Trey's old double bed. Trey looked around the room, realizing that everything was exactly the way he'd left it years ago when he'd gone back to college after the last Christmas he'd spent at home. He took a minute to send Alessandra a text to apologize for not calling her and then set his phone down on the night table and immediately dropped off to sleep.

THIRTY-EIGHT

Bebedouro, Brazil

Alessandra lay in bed wide awake, even thought it was the middle of the night. Her cellphone had woken her with a buzzing sound and she'd reached for it, hoping it was Trey. She had been expecting to hear from him many hours earlier and had worried until she finally drifted off, wondering why she hadn't gotten a call to let her know they had arrived safely.

> Hi, Alessa. Sorry for not getting a hold of you sooner. We went straight from the airport to my cousin's ranch for a big family dinner. Just got to my parents' now. I hope you're doing well. Tomas handled the trip well and is one tired little boy. We both miss you lots.

She texted him back immediately.

> Glad to know you're safe. I miss you both more than words can say. Xoxo

Her relief was quickly washed away by hurt that he hadn't bothered to contact her sooner. There must have been a minute or two in which he could have sent her a quick text, and the fact that he hadn't made her think he might already be pulling away from her. After the horrible way they'd left things, she knew she wasn't going to relax until they were together again. Getting up, she walked over to the window and watched as a cloud drifted lazily past the moon. She ached for Trey and Tomas to come home again. At the moment, a few months might as well be years. "Go back to bed," she told herself as she climbed back under the covers and checked her phone again. He hadn't answered her yet and she wondered if he was asleep, wherever he was. Staying up all night wasn't going to do anything other than make her useless at work later.

* * *

Five days later, Alessandra sat at the kitchen table waiting for Trey to call. Sighing, she looked at the clock. It was after eleven at night and she was tired from a long day at work. Trey was going to call her on Skype after he'd gotten Tomas to bed for the night, and she guessed he must still be having trouble falling asleep. When they'd spoken a few days earlier, Trey had said the time difference and new environment weren't easy for Tomas to adjust to. He had become surprisingly clingy, not wanting to let Trey out of his sight for a minute.

Her cellphone chimed, indicating that Trey was calling. She sat up straight and smiled as she answered. Finally his handsome face was in view and the sight of him filled her with longing.

"Hi. Did you get him to sleep?"

"Yeah, finally. Sorry that took so long. He's really off schedule. It must be late there."

"Not so bad. It's so nice to see you. How did it go today?"

"Really well. Hank introduced me to a rep from a new energy drink company here called HD Ice. She said they want to sign me!"

"Wow, that's amazing!" She forced the words out, hoping they sounded sincere. "What does that mean?"

"We'd sign a one-year deal. I get paid a hundred grand if I make it to more than seventy-five percent of the events in the pro tour."

"One hundred thousand dollars?"

"I know, right? It's a hell of a lot of money!"

"It is . . . And you'd have to stay there for one year?"

"No, I could come back to Brazil from November to early January. Then back here until the end of May, when that part of the season wraps up. Then back to the US again at the beginning of August, until November. It's not exactly what we thought was going to happen, is it?"

"No, it's not." Alessandra's face fell. She wasn't going to pretend to be happy. "What are you going to do?"

"I think I should take it. It would set us up real nicely." He looked worried as he said it.

"What about Tomas?"

"I'd want him to come with me. He's too young for school, so I think the best place for him would be with me, right? My mom said she'd come along and look after him when I'm busy."

Alessandra wrinkled up her nose. "You're going to drag him around from city to city for month after month? What kind of life is that for a child?"

"I think it'll be fun for him. There will always be something new to see and do. He'll be with me, which is the important thing, isn't it?"

"Stability is also important."

"Any routine can become familiar. We'll be home during the

week and I'll have all kinds of time to spend with him. Then on the weekends, we'll have a little adventure. Besides, it's not forever, it's just for a year."

Alessandra listened to Trey and watched him closely, knowing he'd made up his mind already. He was acting as though he wouldn't do it if she didn't want him to, but she knew in her heart that the decision was already made. "What about bringing him back here? Maybe he would be better off here with me?"

Trey narrowed his eyes at her. "I don't want to leave him for that long again, Alessa. I've already missed so much of his life. I can't stand the idea of missing another year."

"I can't either."

"Well, maybe you should come here, then. You could put your career on hold while I do this. That way we'd all be together. You can still be a lawyer a year from now, can't you?"

Alessandra sighed. "Maybe when my mom comes home, I could ask for a leave from work. But for Judge Bathory to lose me, with our heavy caseload, would be a big burden for him. Leaving might be really bad for my career."

Trey scrubbed his hand over his hair, looking frustrated. "It's a bit of a no-win situation, isn't it? I don't want to cost you your dreams in exchange for mine."

"I know you don't. I feel the same way."

"Well, you know, it's really all about how we look at it, isn't it? We're young and we have some amazing opportunities in front of us. Now's the time to take chances and get ourselves set up for life. We can make this work, can't we?"

Alessandra tried to smile but she knew there was nothing convincing about the look on her face. "Yes. We'll find a way. It's good news. You've been offered a huge sponsorship deal. We should be celebrating. I want to hear more about it."

"It *is* a huge deal, actually. It's almost unheard of to get as far as I have so quickly. Hank said he's only seen a handful of guys come out of nowhere like this and do what I've done. He also said the sponsorship money isn't even close to what I could earn. The event I'm going to this weekend in Montana has a forty-thousand-dollar prize for the guy who comes in first. Think of that. Forty grand in one weekend."

"It would be amazing."

"It *will* be amazing, Alessandra. I'm going to get in there, make what I can, and get us set up for life."

"Okay, then."

"It's going to be hard, I know that. But nothing in life worth having comes for free, does it?"

"No, you're right. Nothing comes free. Everything has its price."

Trey stared at her. "We'll be alright, Alessandra, as long as you don't give up on us."

She nodded. "I won't," she whispered, unable to find her voice. Tears sprang to her eyes.

Trey's shoulders dropped. "I'm sorry. I know this isn't the way either of us wanted to start our life together. But we can't think of it as a full year, okay? Tomas and I will be back in early November for two months. Maybe your mom will be home by then and things will look up as far as you coming here for a while. In that case, we might just be apart for another seven weeks."

"Let's hope so."

"I love you, Alessa."

"I love you, too. Please give my *rapazinho* a big hug from me."

"I will."

"Good. I should get some sleep. Good night, Trey. Congratulations."

"Thanks, honey. Good night."

Alessandra dragged herself to her bedroom. Closing the door behind her, she waited until her face was buried in her pillow before she let the sobbing begin. A year. And now he wanted her to give up her career to follow him around. And poor Tomas, living out of a suitcase. She didn't know who she'd married, didn't know he had these reckless dreams inside him. He was no different than her own father. She had managed to make the same mistake as her mother. History was repeating itself, only she wouldn't be left with two small children to look after. Only herself, very much alone.

She cried herself to sleep that night and woke the next morning feeling hungover even though she'd had nothing to drink. Getting up, she quickly got ready for work, wishing she could crawl back under the covers instead.

THIRTY-NINE

Tucson, Arizona
One Month Later

Trey sat with his right arm in a bucket of ice water in a dressing room at the back of the stadium. He sucked back a cold beer, hoping that when he took his arm out of the water in a few minutes, it wouldn't have that shooting pain anymore.

"You've had a hell of a good night, Trey!" Hank remarked from the doorway. "How's that arm?"

"Cold," Trey answered with a smile.

"You going to be okay for tomorrow?"

"Nothing could stop me."

"That's what I thought." Hank walked over and sat down next to Trey. "I've got some good news that'll take the pain away. I was just sitting with Nadine from HD Ice. They're moving into Australia and New Zealand, and they want you to lead the charge."

"What? Seriously?"

"Yeah. You've blown up here and they'd like you to go down there and do the same." He beamed at his client.

"Wow, Hank! That's huge!"

"It is, Trey. You won't believe what they're offering. They want to send you there to compete as soon as the Worlds are finished here. They'll give you thirty grand plus all expenses paid to hit one event each weekend in November and December. You'll even get a spot in the New Zealand Cup. You'd be back in time to start the season here in January."

Trey took his arm out of the ice and patted it with a towel. "Geez, that sounds amazing and all, but I'm supposed to go back to Brazil to spend Christmas with Alessandra. Tomas is really missing her something fierce and, to be honest, so am I."

"Bring her. Bring them both. They'll love it there."

"Yeah, maybe. I don't know if she'd be able to get away, though. Can I think on it?"

"Not too long, I'm afraid. Because it's all so last minute, I need to give Nadine an answer by tomorrow morning. If you don't want it, they're going to ask Hunter Rockwell."

Trey nodded. "Okay."

"Hey, try not to look so upset when you get great news. If your wife can't meet you there, I'm sure she'll understand. It's a hell of a lot of money to turn down. You'll have Christmases together for the rest of your life." Hank patted Trey on the leg then stood up, hitching his belt up under his belly.

"Thanks, Hank. I really am grateful for everything you've done. I'm not upset. I'm just not looking forward to that conversation."

"Women, right?"

"Yeah, well, I haven't exactly made things easy for her," Trey answered, stress written all over his face.

Hank left him alone to make his decision. Trey leaned his head against the wall, feeling the pain return to his arm. He'd been looking forward to having a break to let his body heal, but now it looked like that might not happen. And how was he going to tell Alessandra he'd been asked to go to Australia instead of coming back to her? She wasn't going to take this lightly, and in his heart he already knew she wouldn't come with him. Things had been very tense. Their last conversation had been quiet and awkward, neither of them wanting to start a fight but neither one happy. At this point, he wasn't even sure if he wanted to go back to Brazil to spend two months with her, only to have to deal with these same problems when he'd leave again after Christmas. The thought of escaping to Australia and New Zealand sounded a lot more appealing. And when he really thought about it, he felt like he was hitting his stride as a bull rider. The amount he'd learned about the mechanics of the sport had him feeling much more at ease when the gate opened every night. His last ride had been like floating on a cloud. He had stayed in the sweet spot the entire eight seconds and his score had shown as much. Even though his body was the worse for wear, it seemed like a shame to take a break just when he was getting so much more powerful with each ride.

Beyond that, he'd be putting a lot of money in the bank, and it wasn't like he could afford *not* to take the money. He needed to stay on track, make his cash as fast as he could, then figure the rest out once he was set up.

Trey could feel his stomach churning as he wrote the text.

*   *   *

Alessandra sat on her bed with her laptop, listening to music and scrolling through Pinterest. Glancing at the time, she realized she should have been asleep a couple of hours ago, but she was restless. A thought popped into her head. She wanted to check whether the publicity shots of Trey were up on his agent's website yet. They should have been posted by now. She wanted to look at his handsome face. Maybe then she could finally sleep.

She typed in the address of Hank's site, then clicked through to the list of bull riders. She found Trey's name and a thumbnail photo of him. She clicked on his name and was taken to the page featuring him. There was a photo of him on a bull that brought out that cavewoman in her. *Wow*. Scrolling down, she read his bio. It was very brief, mainly talking about how he got his start very recently in Brazil. Hmm. It didn't mention that he was married. That was odd. Her mouth went dry as she continued to scroll down the page and saw a few pictures from his HD Ice photo shoot.

He was dressed in a fitted black T-shirt sporting the HD Ice logo, along with jeans and his black cowboy hat and boots. His hands were on his hips, muscles rippling out from the short sleeves of the T-shirt, forearms looking huge. It was what was attached to each arm that gutted Alessandra: the delicate hands of two extremely hot girls, one on either side of him. They both wore black leather halter tops bearing the HD Ice logo, their ample breasts billowing out the top. Their flat, toned abs led to leather miniskirts that flared out to make their legs look even thinner. Both girls had long, loose curls of blond hair trailing down their sides and wicked grins on their faces, as if they were eye-fucking the camera and were about to do the same to Trey. At least that's how Alessandra interpreted their expressions.

She stared at their hands, one on Trey's forearm and the other on his upper arm. They were touching him. The very sight of it made her sick to her stomach. She glanced at the framed photo of their wedding, seeing that same face, except that in this photo, it was her own hand on his arm, and Tomas was smiling up from between them. Trey looked like a completely different person than the one she knew. How could he be the same man? How could he have agreed to pose for such photos? How could he have tried to keep it a secret from her?

She closed her laptop and put it on her night table before shutting off the light.

Her cellphone buzzed as she lay in the dark fuming. It was a text from Trey.

You still up? I have some big news I need to talk with you about.

When she didn't answer him in a few minutes, he sent another one.

I won tonight. And I've been given a pretty big opportunity, but I don't want to make a decision until I speak with you. Call me when you wake up. I don't care what time it is for me.

Alessandra stared at the screen, a wave of nausea slapping her. She couldn't talk to him right now. Not when she was so angry. Not when she knew without a doubt that he was about to give her more bad news. This was the end. But she couldn't bring herself to face it. Whatever big decision he had to make right now, he would have to do it alone.

* * *

"You're not coming home, are you?" Alessandra said when she picked up the phone. She sat at her desk in her office, glad she had shut the door.

Trey's voice was quiet. "No, I'm not. Not when we planned. I'm sorry. I tried to reach you last night and this morning before I accepted, but I guess I missed you."

"I had to rush out this morning, so I didn't have time to call you back. Where are you?"

"I'm in an airport in Tucson."

"Oh right, I'm having trouble keeping track. So, what's the big opportunity?" Alessandra's voice was cool.

"HD Ice is starting to sell in the South Pacific. They want to send me there when the world championships are over. They'll pay all my expenses plus a twenty-thousand-dollar bonus for me to spend two months over there."

"So, you won't come back at all, then? Just straight back to the US for the start of next season?" Alessandra fought with herself to remain calm.

"Yes, but I was thinking you could come with me, even just for part of the time. Or maybe we could meet in Bora Bora for our honey-moon. There's a ten day break at the end of November."

"Hmm, I don't know. What about Tomas?"

"If you were coming for the entire time, I'd bring him, but other-wise, I'm thinking I'll leave him with my parents while I'm gone. He's gotten settled in here. They take him to the ranch to play with my cousins' kids most days, so he'll be having a great time here."

Trey waited for Alessandra to say something but when she didn't, he continued. "I know I've thrown a lot at you in one phone call. I'm sure you need some time to think about it."

"Mm-hmm, it's a lot to consider."

"You okay?"

"Not really," she whispered.

There was a long silence as she sat trying to regain her compo-sure.

Trey's voice was thick with emotion. "I know this is hard for you. It's hard for me too. I miss you so much every day it hurts. But maybe meeting for a romantic getaway is just what we need, you know? You and me alone together, for the first time. We could stay in one of those over-the-water cabins you told me about."

"It sounds like paradise." She swiped her hand under her eyes to dry her tears.

"It does, doesn't it?"

The pictures of him with those models popped into her head, dissolving any fantasies she was starting to entertain about the two of them together. "Trey, I can't meet you. You're telling me you'll be gone from now until basically next June. That means nine months apart after only three months of being together. I think we should accept the fact that this is really over."

"Don't say that. All of this is just temporary, I promise you."

"No, it's not. The marriage was the temporary part. Let's stop pretending. It's just killing us both slowly." Her voice broke.

"I know this is hard, but we'll be okay, Alessandra. There's nothing I want more than to make our marriage work."

"I wish that were true, but I've recently seen proof that you're more interested in the single life." As soon as she had said it, she hated herself for it.

"What's that supposed to mean?"

"I looked at Hank's website last night. According to your profile, you're not married."

"What?" Trey asked. "I haven't even looked at it. Does it say I'm single?"

"No, it doesn't say at all. There's no mention of me. Only that you got your start in Brazil."

"Okay, well, I'm sure it's just a mistake. I'll call Hank and straighten that out."

"I'm pretty sure it's by design. They obviously want you to portray a certain image. I also saw the pictures of you with those models from HD Ice, and they certainly don't make you look like a family man."

Trey sighed audibly. "Oh shit. I was hoping you wouldn't see those stupid pictures. I didn't want to tell you because I knew you'd be upset. And frankly, I'm totally embarrassed about the whole thing."

"The fact that you didn't tell me about it makes me wonder what else you are keeping from me."

"Nothing, I swear. There's nothing else. And I'm really sorry about the entire thing. I should have told you. Honestly, I didn't know those girls were going to be there until we got started. I also didn't feel like I could say no. HD had just cut me a cheque for twenty-five grand the day before and it's not like I'm at a point in my career where I get to call the shots. I hate the pictures. But they are fake, Alessa. They're lighting and makeup and illusion. The whole thing was just really awkward . . ." Trey trailed off, sounding defeated.

"Well, that may be, but it would have hurt much less if you'd told me about them right away or . . . at all, I guess. Finding out on my own and knowing you lied to me makes it all so much worse." Alessandra's voice cracked. "You know, Trey, one of the reasons I fell in love with you in the first place was because of your honesty—even about things that would make you look bad. You told me everything. But now you've started hiding the truth from me, and I can't be with someone who won't be completely honest with me. I also can't be with someone who doesn't have any interest in being married to me. You want to travel the world and ride bulls and spend your time with hot women who wear clothes that would fit a toddler. So fine. Do it. I'm done. I'm done waiting."

"What are you saying? Are you breaking up with me?"

"I can't just sit here waiting and hoping you'll come back. It hurts too much. I deserve better than this. I deserve to be with some-one who is so in love with me that he can't stand the thought of being apart for more than a few days."

"Jesus, me being away has got nothing to do with how I feel about you. I wish you understood what I'm trying to do here. I'm doing all of this for *us*. I'm trying to make a better life for our family."

"We already had the better life. You gave it up."

A voice over a loudspeaker interrupted their conversation.

"Shit. That's the final boarding call for the flight to Vegas. Can we talk later tonight?"

"No. We can't, Trey. Good luck in Vegas. I hope you win it all."

She hung up, trying to keep it together. She had made the right decision. It made sense and she knew that in her heart. He was doing what he wanted to do and his new life didn't include her. She needed to let him go, just as she had thought when he first left Brazil. He loved her because she had been there when he was alone, because she had offered him hope and comfort. But he didn't need her anymore. Maybe someday she'd find someone who loved her more than he needed her, but that man wasn't going to be Trey.

FORTY

One Week Later

Trey boarded the flight to Auckland and sank into his seat. He closed his eyes, regret settling over him like a thick fog. He hadn't made it past the first round in Vegas, which gave him an extra two days in Colorado with Tomas. Unfortunately, that wasn't enough time between trips for his son to forget what it was like when Trey left.

Since he had left the house, his mind had been torturing him with the memory of how hard Tomas had sobbed when Trey left. He'd clung to Trey's neck, tears pouring out of his eyes. Trey's heart snapped in two pieces when Tomas had asked him, "Will you be all gone like my mom?"

"No, little man, I'm going to be back before you know it. It'll be a little longer than these last trips, but then I promise I'll be back. Nothing will keep me away."

In the end Fern had had to pry Tomas's hands off Trey's neck and hold him while Trey walked out the door. She'd let go of him and Trey had made the mistake of turning back when he reached the end of the sidewalk, only to see his son trying to open the front door and his mom struggling to stop him. His last look at him when the cab pulled away was of Tomas's beet-red face, his mouth hanging open like it did when he was in pain. It was a scene as ugly and raw as anything Trey'd ever witnessed, and he felt like total shit to have abandoned his little boy.

Now, as he waited for the plane to take off, he was almost certain he had made the wrong choice. He should have said no to this. Or, at the very least, maybe he should have brought Tomas with him. He was doing exactly what he had promised himself he wouldn't do— leaving his son over and over again, just as Gabriela had done. Tomas deserved better than this.

The night before, when he'd gone over his winnings and the earnings from his sponsorship deal, this had felt like the right choice. He was close to one hundred thousand in his account. But he could only fool himself for so long. Eventually he'd get smacked in the face by the knowledge that chasing this insane dream had likely already cost him his marriage. Most days he refused to think about that, though, and he still hadn't told anyone about how bad things were with Alessandra. Even though they hadn't spoken since he was in Tucson, his heart wouldn't let him believe it was over. She was angry and hurt but she was also his. A love like theirs couldn't simply dissolve because of a little time away from each other. He was sure that once he was released from his contract, he could win her back. He was giving her some space, but he planned to stop in Brazil to see her on his way back to the US.

But now that plan didn't seem like such a sure thing. He had to face it—he'd left his little family scattered all over the globe in pieces, hurting. The two people he loved the most were feeling the sting of being abandoned by him. As he sat listening to the distant sound of the safety instructions being read out, he told himself that once this trip was over, he would tell Hank that he was hanging up his chaps for good. Another year like this wasn't worth any amount of money.

FORTY-ONE

Christchurch, New Zealand

Trey stood in the dark, listening to the roar of the crowd, watching as fireworks lit up the stadium and music began to blare out of the speakers. He felt strangely calm but he didn't know why. "He's one of the newest members of the International Bull Riders Association, and he's been tearing it up all over the world this year! He's the points leader so far at the New Zealand Cup. All the way from Colorado, USA, Trey Johnson!"

Adrenalin coursed through his veins as he heard his name announced and stepped forward into the spotlight. He took off his hat and waved it in the air, squinting under the bright lights, unable to see into the crowd. The thrill of this moment woke him up to the possibility of another chance to float on a cloud. His draw that night was called Yolo, and he was rumoured to be the rankest bull in all of the South Pacific Rim, which was both terrifying and affirming. Yolo was smart, changing up his kicks and spins to make himself unpredictable. No rider had ever gone the full eight on him but some-how Trey knew that tonight, he would be the first. He was there to win, and if he could stay on that bull he would take the New Zealand Cup. It wasn't a lot of money, but he needed to scrape every dollar out of this trip, and he'd sure love to end his short career with a national championship under his belt. The sound of the crowd faded as he walked back to the dressing room to wait his turn. He had given up watching the other riders weeks ago, electing to sit in the quiet to prepare himself.

An hour later, a knock at the door signalled his turn. He got up, put his black hat on and made his way to the ring. The deafening sounds along with the lights burning down on him were a shock to the system, but one he needed to get himself fully pumped up. This was it. His moment to shine. Making his way to the chute, he climbed up and found his perch on top of the huge white beast. As he secured the rope around his riding hand, he realized how very strange it was that this seemed normal to him now. It was as though he'd always done it and it was the most common thing in the world. He eased himself forward so he was sitting as close to his hand as possible and took a deep breath, determined not to let anything, certainly not this bull, throw him. Yolo huffed, then tried a little kick in the chute, giving Trey a warning of what was to come. Music poured over the stadium but that, along with the cheers, faded as the sounds of his own breath and heartbeat filled his ears.

He nodded his head to start the ride. The gate opened and Yolo exploded out of the chute with a violent twist coupled with a powerful kick of his back legs. Trey knew immediately that he would not be riding an ocean wave tonight. Instead, he would have to fight like hell to stay on. Eight seconds on this bull would be an eternity in themselves. Rocking himself back, he managed to counter the bull's next impulse to spill him over his horns. One second. *Pivot forward.* Two seconds. *Lean left. Get back to the sweet spot.* Three seconds. *Hold tight. Use that entire arm.* Four seconds. *Back again and again.* Five seconds. *Stay on your feet.* Six seconds. *Grip with your spurs. Tug your legs down hard.* Seven seconds. *Shit! He's going up again! Got it!* Eight seconds.

The sound of the buzzer brought Trey's mind back to the arena as he let go and let himself slide off the bull, landing on his feet and hands.

Yes! He pumped his arm in the air and lifted his hat, grinning. That ought to bring him the championship. Turning his head, he saw a white blur with black horns coming straight at him. *Oh fuck!*

FORTY-TWO

Bebedouro, Brazil

Alessandra stood at the kitchen counter, mixing the dough for the *pão de queijo*. It was Saturday afternoon and she had decided to make a special meal for herself and Carlos. Even though it was just for the two of them, she had cooked enough to feed the entire Santos family today. Beans and rice, shredded beef and chicken, along with a salad with fresh tomatoes. For dessert, she was making tapioca pudding. Cooking gave her something to do, a way to give value to an otherwise empty day, even if it was just a distraction from her pain and loneliness. After supper, she was going into town to take in a movie with Cyssah. There was a new horror movie out and they wanted to scare themselves so they could laugh later about how foolish they were.

Her hair was in her face. Again, she had forgotten put it up. Her mind wandered to the first time she had felt Trey's hands on her skin, when he had tied her hair back for her. The thought tortured her, causing that horrible ache to return to her chest, the one she woke up with every morning. She would give anything to feel his hands on her skin again. To feel his kiss. It had been weeks since their last angry exchange, and she was becoming certain that her last words had been the final nail in the coffin of their marriage. She looked at her ring, which was sitting on the windowsill where she had placed it before she started the dough. Was he still wearing his ring? How could they have grown so distant that she would have to wonder that?

Over the past few days, an unsettling realization had crept over her. She finally understood that Trey wasn't the only one who'd let them drift apart. She had as well. She could have gone with him, or agreed to meet him, even if only for a few days. Judge Bathory would have understood and given her some time off. *Avô* would have understood too. He would have wanted her to go to her husband to save their marriage. But she hadn't. She had chosen not to. She had stayed where she felt safe to protect herself. She could trust what was here in a way she hadn't learned to trust her husband. Her decision wasn't only about her obligations or opportunities, it was about the fact that she didn't trust him. And that mistrust had made her unwilling to bend, even a little, in order to make their marriage work. If only she had trusted their relationship, maybe it would have lasted. But she hadn't. And now, she was certain it was over.

She sighed, wishing Tomas was here running around the kitchen. She could hear his squeal of laughter and picture Trey chasing him around the table to tickle him. The thought crushed her, and she shook her head and lifted her chin to deny her sadness. Wiping her hands on a towel, she decided to put on some happy music to lift her spirits. She smiled as her eyes fell on *Avô* napping in his hammock in the shade. He had worked too hard this morning picking oranges, and Alessandra had had to go out and practically drag him inside to have lunch and rest.

"It can wait, *Vô*. The work crew will be here on Monday to take care of it."

Carlos had waved his hand at her. "I'm a farmer, my girl. Let me farm."

She thought of how they'd sat together on the swing after lunch, her grandfather holding her hand as he spoke. "You take such good care of me. How did I get so lucky to have such a wonderful family?"

"It wasn't luck at all, *Vô*. We learned it from you." She smiled at him and placed her other hand overtop of his, feeling his delicate, crinkled skin against her fingertips.

"You are a good person, Alessandra. You deserve to have the best in life. Promise me that if your cowboy doesn't come back, you will find someone who will make you happy, okay?"

"Oh, *Vô*, I can't even think about that right now." She sighed, saying nothing for a long moment. "Do you think he'll come back?"

Carlos nodded. "I do. You're far too special to leave behind." He lifted her hand to his lips and gave it a light kiss. "I believe he will find his way back to you. But if for some reason he doesn't, don't spend your life missing him. Find a way to move on. You're a beautiful, strong young woman. If only you could remember that."

Alessandra nodded, unable to speak.

"I'm going to have a sleep now. My hammock is calling me." He stood and smiled at her. "What a perfect day for a lucky old farmer like me."

After she put the tray of cheese buns into the oven, she danced a little to the song on the radio. The music and the meal to come had lifted her spirits. She smiled to herself, knowing that her *avô* would be surprised she had made his favourite chicken. Glancing at the clock, she realized it was getting late. He was usually awake by now. Walking to the window, she saw he was still in the hammock. He looked so peaceful with the soft light of the late-day sun. He had tired himself out that morning, but if she didn't wake him soon he'd have trouble falling asleep tonight.

Stepping outside in her bare feet, she crossed the yard to him, her blood running cold when she saw how pale he was. "*Avô?*" she called quietly, holding on to a trace of hope. "*Vô*, it's time to wake up. It's almost supper."

But she knew from the look of him that he was gone. No matter how much her brain screamed at her that this wasn't happening.

A sob shook her body as she stood next to him. "Please wake up, *Vô*," she choked out, taking his hand. It was cold to the touch, just as she feared it would be. "I can't lose you too. Please. Come back."

Her body gave out and she crumpled onto the grass and wept until there were no tears left in her body.

For the first time in her life, she was completely alone.

* * *

Late that night, she lay in bed, completely numb. She picked up her cellphone and dialed Trey's number. She needed to hear his voice, needed him to comfort her, even if he no longer loved her. He would come to her. If there was anything left between them, if there ever had been, he would come to her now. He wouldn't let her go through this alone. She willed him to answer, but he didn't.

When he didn't pick up, she heard herself sob into the phone before any words managed to come out. "It's me. *Avô* died today. Please call me, okay? I . . . I need you."

FORTY-THREE

Christchurch, New Zealand

Trey lay on a bed, coming in and out of consciousness. Pain shot out from his jaw whenever he tried to open his mouth. *What the hell had happened?* He was so thirsty. Why couldn't he move? His back hurt and his chest did too. He wanted to roll onto his side but there was something digging into his ribs. He wanted to move it but he couldn't, for some reason. Turning his head a tiny bit, he saw daylight through the window. Where was he, even? He closed his eyes and drifted off again.

The next time he woke, it was completely dark. He tried to speak but again he couldn't move his mouth. Only a grunting noise came out. He wanted to call for someone. He needed to know where he was and what had happened. Then he heard it. A beeping sound next to him. Followed by another. He started to come to and piece it all together. He must be in a hospital. A flash of the bull coming at him jarred him awake. He could feel the horn piercing his side and tossing him into the air, the metal bar of the gate smashing his face as he landed on it. And then everything had gone black.

He lay there for a long time, waiting for someone to come. Long enough to see the moon pass by the window. He wished with everything in him that he could just get up out of this bed and go get Tomas, then go back to Alessandra. Nothing would feel right until they were all together again. He knew that now. The second thoughts he'd been having about riding were telling him he needed to stop, but he'd ignored them, thinking he could stop later. Now he realized that later is not a guarantee, it's just something you hope you'll get. He'd spent months assuming life would wait—that she would wait for him—while he raked in as much cash as he could. But while he'd been off doing that, his son and wife were hurting. He needed to get out of this bed and get to her before it was too late.

Finally the sound of footsteps brought relief to his loneliness. Someone was here. A clicking sound was accompanied by a bright light that made him blink hard. When his vision adjusted, he stared into the pretty blue eyes of a nurse. She smiled at him. "There you are. Awake, I see. That bull got the better of you last night." Her accent had a pleasant sound. It was friendly but also made understanding her a little hard for him.

His eyes followed her as she turned and replaced the IV bag hanging next to his bed.

"You broke your jaw and we've had to wire it shut for the time being. And you've had quite the injury to your side. The horn pierced your ribs but somehow there wasn't major damage to any of your organs, so you got lucky there. Four of your ribs are cracked, your right arm is broken in three places and you also have one hell of a concussion. I hope you like drinking your meals because it's going to be some time before you're eating them. But I suppose you're more concerned about how quickly you can get back on a bull than you are about food. I'll let the doctor know you're awake." With that she turned and walked out, leaving the light on.

* * *

"Trey? Trey?"

Trey blinked his eyes open. The sun was up now, and he stared into the faces of Flint and Warren, two of the other riders on the tour. Their expressions gave Trey an indication of just how bad he looked.

"How you doing?" Flint asked before realizing that Trey wasn't able to answer him. "Shit, sorry. I can see how you are. That was a rough one, man. The good news is you won!"

Trey's eyes lit up.

"Yeah, you scored forty-eight, Yolo scored forty-seven. Nicely done, man! You're the champion of New Zealand!"

Trey made a noise he hoped would sound enthusiastic, but it came out sounding more like a nondescript grunt.

"We called Hank. He got a hold of your parents for you."

Trey realized then that his parents had no way of calling Alessandra. And he needed to see her. He lifted his arm in spite of the pain it caused and gestured as though he were writing.

"He needs to tell us something. Go get him a pen and paper," Flint said.

Warren nodded and left the room. He was gone for a while before returning with a clipboard of paper and a pen. "Sorry about the delay. There's a blond nurse out there who is, well, let's say very distracting. I hope she'll be looking after you." He put the pen into Trey's left hand, then held the clipboard at an angle so Trey could see while he wrote.

Cellphone.

"What's that say? Cellophane?"

"Nah, that can't be it. Why would he need Cellophane?"

"I don't know. Maybe he wants us to wrap something."

Trey glared and wrote, "My phone."

"Hmm. Can you write it again, Trey?"

Cellphone.

"Oh, your cellphone. Sure, Trey. I'll go ask at the nurses station."

Warren returned a few minutes later. "They said they don't have it with your stuff. They just have the clothes you were wearing when you came in, so your bag must have been left at the stadium. We'll head over there and see if we can track it all down."

*　*　*

Two hours later, Trey woke to his friend's faces staring at him again. "Bad news, Trey. We found your bag but no cellphone. Someone must have swiped it. We went over to the motel and collected your things, but the phone wasn't there either."

Trey closed his eyes, a sense of doom coming over him.

"Shit, man. We'll call Hank on our way to the airport. We have to fly to Melbourne in a couple of hours."

"I hate to leave you like this. But those nurses are going to take real good care of you," Flint said.

Warren nodded. "Yup, they're nice. It's the best reason to become a bull rider, isn't it? To meet a nurse."

Bebedouro, Brazil

Alessandra stood next to her mother, the two of them dressed in white and holding each other up as *Avô*'s coffin was lowered into the ground next to her grandmother's. It was a peaceful spot under an expansive jacaranda tree. Rich green leaves and light purple blooms provided shade for those who had come to mourn Carlos. It had been less than two days since Carlos had passed away, and as per both tradition and law, he was being laid to rest.

She felt her mother's body shake violently as each sob erupted from her small frame, and Alessandra closed her arm around Lorena more firmly in response. She thought of Betina, who hadn't been able to make it back in time. Her sister's words of deep regret filled her mind, blocking out the wails and moans of her older relatives, who believed this moment was the one in which to express the utmost grief. No need to hide it or hold back. There was nothing private about this, only sorrow that would be shared in this one moment. But for Alessandra, funerals had always felt uncomfortable. She preferred to hold back a little, and tried to remember one beautiful thing about her grandfather each time she felt sad.

She looked across the grave at her aunt Daniela and uncle Ricardo, wishing Trey was there with her. Ricardo held her aunt up with both arms as she cried. But Alessandra's own husband was missing. He hadn't even bothered to call her back. He'd made no attempt to contact her, and the grief of that reality only served to carve out another crater in her already empty soul.

* * *

Alessandra filled the horses' water pails with a hose. She was sweaty and dirty and tears streamed down her face. How could this place—this stinky old barn—be the same place Trey had transformed into a fairy tale for their wedding? Being here hurt her as much as being in the main house or seeing the guest house. Every dream had dissolved. The life she was building had slipped through her hands, grains of sand that refused to be held.

One of the horses snorted his disgust at her self-pity. Or maybe it was sympathy. She looked into his deep brown eyes, wondering if he missed Carlos too. The horses hadn't had a good brushing in many days, but she couldn't seem to muster the energy to do it just then. It had been a week since *Avô*'s funeral and she still hadn't heard from Trey. This must be his way of making sure it was over between them, of making sure she didn't start confusing kindness for love. She had ached for him to come, then spent the days after the funeral hating him. But now she decided that maybe she should be grateful he hadn't shown up. At least she was very clear on where he stood. Any ambiguity about their marriage was long gone, which meant she could move on. She picked up a brush, choosing to push on with hard work. If she kept herself busy, maybe she'd survive the pain.

"Here, let me help you." Her mother stood in the doorway to the barn. It was the first time she'd stepped foot in there since she'd come back for the funeral.

They worked quietly for a few minutes before Lorena spoke up. "Have you heard from your husband yet?"

Alessandra shook her head.

"I'm sorry. I had hoped he would be different than Otavio, but it looks like he was just better at fooling everyone."

"I don't want to talk about it." Alessandra's voice was devoid of feeling.

"Don't worry, I'm not going to say I told you so."

"You just did."

Lorena sighed. "Listen, I'm here if you need to talk, okay? I know what you're going through. At least you don't have two little mouths to feed."

Alessandra's head snapped back. "You know, when you say that it makes me think you wish he had taken us with him so you wouldn't have been burdened. I lost the little one I had to love when my husband left and I would give *anything* to have him back. I have *nothing*! How is that better?"

Lorena stopped brushing and gave her a sad look. "Of course. I'm sorry, my dear girl. You know that I never would have wanted your father to take you from me. I was just trying to find something positive to say, but it was wrong. I forget sometimes how much you loved Tomas." She stepped over to Alessandra and gave her a hug, letting her cry on her shoulder for a long time. Lorena rubbed a hand over her back. "It's okay. You cry today and get it out. Tomorrow you wake up and get on with your life."

Pulling away, Alessandra wiped her face with the backs of her hands and picked up the brush again. They worked in silence until the job was finished.

"I should go start supper," Lorena said, making her way toward the door. Turning back, she gave Alessa a weary look. "I'm selling the farm. Junior Rocha called this morning. He's sending a realtor here to evaluate the property. He promised he'll offer the market value."

Alessandra's mouth hung open, and her body felt like it might collapse under the weight of this last blow. A sob started in her chest.

"I know this disappoints you, but I can't keep it. I'm sorry. It's too much work for me. We are lucky to get the offer, otherwise it might have taken years to find a buyer for a property this size."

Alessandra's bottom lip quivered as she stared at her mother. The thought of losing their home was a knife to her heart. "How could you? *Vô* would weep to know the family is losing the farm."

"For the first time in my life, Alessa, I'm living my own dream. The thought of tying myself to this place until I die is unbearable for me. I know you wish things could stay the same, but life moves forward whether we like it or not."

Alessandra put the brush down and walked out of the barn into the warmth of the low winter sun. She staggered through the rows of orange trees to the far end of the property, at times weeping and at times stoic. Finally reaching the last of the trees, she sat on a wooden bench her grandfather had built years ago. He put it there so he would have a nice spot to rest when his work was done.

She could picture him here in the shade, wiping the sweat off his brow with a rag. He always had a smile for her, no matter how tired he was. They had sat right on this spot and shared countless oranges. He would tell her stories about Lorena as a girl or about his own child-hood here on the farm. Or sometimes he would listen to her stories about fairies, and as she got older, about someone at school who had hurt her feelings or left her out. He always had a hug and a few quiet words of encouragement for her. She thought of him the day he had died and how he'd said she was too special to leave behind. A spite-ful laugh escaped her throat at the memory. She was easy to leave. First her own father, then Trey and now her mother would leave her behind as well, taking away the only home she'd known.

Alessandra was engulfed by her sorrow, by the deep sense of profound loss from which she couldn't see her way out. She'd lost her little boy, her husband, her grandfather and now her home. If only Betina were here to cry with her, they could hold each other and hold hands as they climbed out of the chasm together. She cried until there was nothing left in her but a numb, hollow ghost of who she'd been on her wedding day. If only she could have frozen time on that perfect day and lived there forever, even if it meant the rain would never stop. If only.

The sun disappeared and the moon took its place without her noticing. She finally rose to her feet, realizing she would have to make her way back to the house in the pitch dark. The air had grown cool and she shivered in her T-shirt and jeans, which clung to her from the dampness of the day's sweat. As she fumbled through the trees, the world seemed scary now in a way it never had before. Faint beams of moonlight cast sinister shadows through the treetops, as though the trees wanted to chase her away. She quickened her pace with her hands outstretched in front of her. She could barely make out her fingertips as she moved toward home. The home she was about to lose, the place that had grounded her, the place her family had gathered to celebrate and grieve. They had come here, to this home, to share meals and drinks and laughter and life itself. It had been a beacon for her entire life, to return to where love resided. But it would be taken from her, just as love had been, leaving her empty.

* * *

"There you are. I was about to go looking for you." Lorena sat at the kitchen table, her plate empty except for the remnants of her dinner. "I put your supper in the fridge. Sit and I'll heat it for you."

Alessandra shook her head, grabbed a glass from the cupboard, filled it with ice and too much rum and then, instead of sitting at the table to eat, she went to the bathroom, quietly closing the door. Stripping off her clothes, she turned on the hot water and stood shivering beside the tub as she choked back the liquor, ignoring the burning in her throat. It would warm her and distance her from her sorrow nicely. Sinking into the heat of the tub a few minutes later, she stared at the faucet, watching as it let go of one drop at a time, each landing with a comforting rhythm into the water. She started to succumb to the pleasantly numb feeling spreading through her body. She lay there until the water was no longer warm, then wrapped her hair in a towel and managed to pull on her bathrobe before making her way to bed. Tugging the covers over her head, she closed her eyes and gave in to her exhaustion.

Tomorrow she would start again.

FORTY-FOUR

Christchurch, New Zealand

"Olá?"

"I am looking for Alessandra." Sandra, the nurse, spoke into the phone. She paused for a second. "Alessandra, *por favor*. It's about her husband, Trey." Sandra looked confused as she listened to whatever was happening on the other end of the phone. She covered the receiver. "I don't understand her but she sounds angry."

When the sound of the woman's voice stopped, she tried again. "Alessandra, *por favor*. Trey's been in an accident." Putting the phone down, she gave him an apologetic look. "She hung up."

Another nurse hurried up to the counter where they stood and told Sandra she was needed elsewhere.

"Try to rest. We'll call again later."

Damn it. This was going to be much harder than he had thought. He wondered if it was Lorena who'd answered. If it was, he was surprised she was home. Whoever it was knew enough about their situation to be angry with him. That must mean Alessandra had started telling people they were through.

Trey watched as Sandra rushed down the hall, then he made his way slowly back to his room, careful not to look in any mirrors. The sight of his bruised and swollen face was not one he welcomed. He had incisions on either side of his face where the wires were attached to his jaw. His mind quickly shifted back to Alessandra. He needed to get to her as soon as he could, to see if she would be willing to give him another chance. But it was a long road before he could do that. It would still be several weeks until his body healed. He couldn't very well show up at her door with his jaw wired shut. In his estimation, he'd be much easier to turn away in his current state. She might think he was only there for her to make him soup and nurse him back to health. He needed to go back to her strong and whole.

Bebedouro, Brazil

"So, are you going to get your thirty silver pieces?" Alessandra asked her mother, her eyes dead.

"Don't be so dramatic," Lorena snapped.

The realtor had just spent a few hours on the property, walking to each end with Lorena and carefully making notes as he measured and examined each room in the house.

"*Avô* meant for this farm to stay in our family, but you don't care. You're ripping our home out from under us! Betina won't even have a chance to say goodbye!" Alessandra's voice was pure anguish.

Lorena shook her head. "You are so young and foolish. You have no idea how quickly life passes or what I gave up for my family. I wish this wasn't the only way, but it is. I'll give you each some of the money so you can get your own places. Believe me, it will be better in the end than trying to pour money into this old house. Someday you'll thank me."

"I will *never* thank you for this. And I will never take the money."

"Enough!" Lorena barked. "I don't expect you to understand but I *do* expect you to respect my decision. When you are older, you'll understand. Until then, keep your mouth shut." She turned on her heel and stalked away from her daughter, her gait stiff.

Colorado Springs, Colorado
Three Weeks Later

Trey sat in the examining room at the doctor's office, struggling to get his shirt back on. His arm was still in a sling, but he had finally had the braces and wire removed from his jaw. His ribs hurt, but not as much as what was inside them. He was relieved to be home with Tomas and grateful to have the care of his parents as he made his painful recovery, but neither stopped him from aching to be with Alessandra every minute of every day.

* * *

Trey found Dustin waiting in the driver's seat of his truck. Trey spoke a few words when he got in. Moving his mouth again felt strange. Freeing but tender.

"You okay, ugly?" Dustin asked.

"Yup. Much better." His words were clear for the first time in weeks.

"You look a little less like RoboCop without that contraption on your face."

"Thanks."

"That wasn't a compliment. You think they'd put it back on?"

* * *

That night, Trey stared at the phone for a long time before trying her number. He waited as the phone rang, then he heard Lorena's voice.

"*Olá?*"

"Lorena, it's Trey. I need to speak with Alessandra."

"No."

"Lorena, please. I lost my cellphone and I can't find her work number on the Internet. This is the only number I have."

"No."

"Please, Lorena. I need to speak with her."

"No. You moved on without her and now she is doing the same."

"What is that supposed to mean?" His nostrils flared and he tightened his jaw, only to have pain pierce the entire bottom half of his face.

"It means she is out on a date with a real man and it's none of your business."

"I don't believe you. She wouldn't do that."

"Why shouldn't she? You should have rushed back here as soon as my father died! But you didn't. You don't want to be married to Alessandra and you're proving that every day."

"What? Carlos . . .." Trey felt like he'd been punched in the gut.

"Are you going to pretend you didn't know?"

"I didn't. I swear. Why didn't she call me?"

"She did. She left messages and texted you but you ignored her. How could you do that? I was right about you all along! You just used my daughter to help you get your son out of Brazil! I told her you would leave her and that's exactly what you did!"

"Lorena, please listen to me. I've been in a hospital in New Zealand. I got hurt at an event and when they put me in the ambulance, my cellphone got lost somehow. I tried to get a nurse to call the house for me because I had my jaw wired shut. Don't you remember that? You hung up on her. I'm sure it was you. I know you hate me, Lorena, but I love your daughter. I need to talk to her."

"Don't bother. She has sent you the divorce papers. It's over."

His protest died in his mouth as the phone was slammed down in his ear. He squeezed his eyes shut tightly and let his head flop into his hand. Carlos was dead. And Alessandra had been grieving alone, believing he didn't care about her. Tears escaped his eyes at the thought of the pain she was going through and the pain he'd caused. If only he hadn't been so stubborn, hadn't believed that bull riding was the only way to get ahead. He should have been there. He should have held her in his arms while she cried and held her up at the funeral and paid his respects to the sweet old man who had become family to both him and Tomas. Carlos had opened his life to them, shared his home and his patience and his kindness. He'd smoothed the waters for Trey and given him work. And Trey had abandoned them to go pursue his risky, lofty dream.

Lorena's words tore through his heart. Alessandra had already sent the divorce papers. It was over. Could she really be on a date so soon? It somehow didn't seem possible, but maybe she had been hurt enough by him to decide to move on as quickly as possible. A sob escaped his throat as he sat alone at the kitchen table. He let the tears flow down his cheeks, not caring if he was discovered by his parents. Tears for Carlos, for Alessandra and for his son, whom he'd taken from the one person who'd ever given him a stable life. Tears for himself at the thought of losing Alessandra. He couldn't do this without her. He didn't want to.

Straightening up, he dialed the number to the farmhouse again. He would make Lorena hear him and make her understand. Then he would find the next flight to Brazil and get his wife back.

No answer. He tried again and again but Lorena was refusing to pick up. She wouldn't be giving him his second chance. He would have to make it himself.

FORTY-FIVE

"Just how the hell are you going to travel all the way to Brazil with a three-year-old and a broken arm?" Dustin asked, sitting in front of his laptop.

"Don't worry about that. I'll manage just fine." Trey pointed with his good hand. "Please just find me a flight. It'll take me all night to type with one hand."

"You'll manage? You can't even use a computer to *book* the flight."

"Aw, forget it. Get out of the chair. I'll just do it myself."

"You're nuts. You're going to miss your follow-up appointments with the doctor."

"I'm about to lose my wife, Dustin. Do you think I give a shit about my arm?" Trey spat out. "I'll cut the cast off myself in a couple of weeks."

Dustin lifted his palms toward Trey in defeat. "Fine, man. I'm just trying to look out for you."

Trey stared down at the computer and began searching for flights, with his brother looking over his shoulder as he worked.

* * *

"Hank, I need you to help me find a phone number for Miguel and Bruno Santos. There must be a contact list at the International Bull Riders Association office in Brazil, right? I need to get a hold of them right away."

"I'll see what I can do. Everything okay, Trey?" Hank asked.

"Not even close. I need to get a message to my wife immediately. I'm pretty sure she's ready to divorce me." Trey's voice cracked.

"Oh man, I'm sorry to hear that. I'll get the numbers and anything else you need. Don't worry."

Trey stood at the kitchen counter, watching out the window as Tomas played in the yard with his mom while he waited for Hank to call back. Fern was sitting on the bottom step of the back deck, blowing bubbles while Tomas ran and chased them. Trey's heart ached at the thought of how Tomas had clung to him when he returned, not letting Trey out of his sight for the first three days he was back. Losing Gabriela and being taken from Alessandra had taken its toll on the little boy, and he hated himself for adding to his scars. Tomas had started throwing tantrums, screaming when Trey left, even for a doctor's appointment. He couldn't fall asleep unless his dad was sitting with him, holding his hand. He didn't want to go to the ranch with his grandparents unless Trey came too. Although Tomas had no way of articulating it, his wounds were fresh, his pain was real and his need for constancy was more important than anything. Trey sighed, knowing that his bull-riding career was done. He had to quit for his son's sake as much as for the sake of his marriage.

The phone rang, interrupting his thoughts. It was Hank. If he had the number, Trey could make this work.

* * *

"Miguel? It's Trey."

"Oh, hello, asshole. What do you want?"

"I'm sure you hate me but I need you to listen for a minute so I can explain what happened. And I need your help."

FORTY-SIX

Bebedouro, Brazil

Alessandra stood in her childhood bedroom, now emptied of everything that had made it hers. Sunlight, filtered by filmy curtains, danced on the wood floor. She stared at the pattern as it moved. The room was as hollow as she was. Leaning against the door frame, she let the tears flow. She'd spent the past week packing away her life and that of her grandfather. Now her body ached, a physical manifestation of her heart and soul. Her mother had to go back to work three days earlier, forcing Alessandra to finish the heartbreaking work alone. Everything was gone, and she would have to find a way to pick herself up and move on.

Her cellphone rang. "Hi, Cyssah."

"Hi, roommate. How are you?"

"Sad," she whispered.

"I know. I bought two bottles of wine. When you get here later, we can get very tipsy while we unpack your things. I thought tomorrow we could hit a nightclub, see if we can find a couple of hotties."

"I'll say yes to the wine, but I don't know if I'll be up to going out tomorrow."

"The best way to get over him is to sample what else is out there."

"I thought time was the best way to heal a wounded heart."

"No, you heard that wrong. It's sexy guys."

Alessandra managed a noise that she hoped sounded like laughter. "I'll be by in a couple of hours. The new owner should be here any minute."

"Okay. You sure someone else couldn't go through the house with them?"

"It has to be me. They are buying the animals too, so I want to make sure they know how to take care of them properly."

"But how are you going to get through all of that without crying?"

"The job has to get done, even if I cry while doing it. If they're uncomfortable, I can't help it. I should go. I hear a car." She looked out the window and saw a cab coming down the driveway. "You won't believe this. They've taken a cab. I wonder if they're going to expect me to drive them back into town after."

"That's weird."

"Yeah. I'll call you when I can."

"Good luck."

Alessandra hung up, then smoothed down her hair, curiosity temporarily edging out sorrow. It was a welcome feeling, something other than sadness. It gave her hope that there would be many other feelings again in her life soon. She knew they would come in bits and pieces for a while: random moments of calm or even happiness surrounded by pain. For now she had to trust that, little by little, the good moments would last longer and come more often, until she was alright again.

A knock at the door had her wiping her damp cheeks, setting her shoulders back and striding across the living room. She would be businesslike and matter-of-fact and just get this over with. *I'll pretend I'm acting as a representative of the property owner, an advocate for the animals. That should work.*

Drawing a deep breath, she fixed a smile onto her face and opened the door.

And there he stood. With a tentative look on his face, his eyes shining with emotion. Alessandra stared at him, her brain firing rapidly as she took in the fact that he was really there. His arm was in a sling and his face looked different. It wasn't just the yellow bruises along his jaw or the little scars on his cheeks—his cheekbones were more pronounced and he looked too thin. Something about seeing him like this melted her heart. Trey was here, and as she looked into his eyes, she felt it. Those were the eyes she had fallen in love with. And the look they were giving her right now said everything. Alessandra's mouth dropped open, her heart racing with possibility. He had come back to her.

Instantly, her legs were bombarded by an enthusiastic hug from Tomas. "Lessa! We camed back!" Tomas shouted to her.

Shock, along with the impact from his little body, almost knocked her over, but Trey caught her arm with one hand and steadied her. She reached down to Tomas, running her fingers through his hair. "Is this real? Are you really here?" she whispered.

Trey nodded. "We're here and I'm hoping you'll let us stay."

Tears streamed down her face. Love, relief, hope, regret and fear all hit her at once. She picked up Tomas and held him close, feeling his little head burrow into her neck. She kissed his head over and over until he pulled back and smiled at her.

His face fell a little as he looked at her. He reached up his little fingers and wiped her cheeks. "Why are you sad?"

"I'm not at all sad. I'm so happy to see you that I'm crying. Grown-ups are funny that way sometimes." She hugged him close, planting more kisses on his chubby cheeks. "Oh, I can't believe you're here! You got so big, *rapazinho*!"

Tomas grinned at her. "Yup. I eat my veggies." He caught sight of the old barn cat stalking through the tall grass and wiggled out of Alessa's arms to catch her. "*Gato*! Here, *gato*!"

It was just the two of them now, face to face, with so much to say but no idea of where to start. Alessandra looked up at Trey and crossed her arms, closing herself off from him.

Trey's eyebrows gathered in and his entire face looked pained. When he spoke, his voice was thick with emotion. "I'm sorry. I'm so sorry about Carlos, and I'm sorry I wasn't here. I should have been here for you." Tears sprang to his eyes but he didn't seem embarrassed by them.

"Yes, you should have. I was so sure you would come, but you didn't," she whispered. "Nothing has ever made me feel so alone."

Trey took a step forward but didn't reach for her yet. "I'm sorry. I've never regretted anything more in my life. I swear to you, I didn't get your messages. I ended up in the hospital and I lost my damn phone. I didn't know about Carlos until last week. Since then, I've tried calling the house dozens of times. I should have memorized your cellphone number. If I had known about Carlos, if I could have been here, I promise I would have come." He raised his hand up to her face, gently wiping away her tears with his thumb. "But there's no excuse. I should have known. It's all my fault. I let things get so bad until we were left with next to nothing between us. If I hadn't done that, you would have known I was injured and I would have found out about Carlos."

Alessandra closed her eyes, feeling the touch of his fingertips on her skin, but then something he had said sprang to mind, bringing out the lawyer in her. "How did you know I left messages? If you never got them, how did you know about them?"

"Your mom told me. She told me about Carlos and about how hurt you were that I hadn't contacted you. I tried to explain, but I think as far as she was concerned, it was too late. She's been ignoring my calls since then. And did you know that it's impossible to find your work number on the Internet if you can't read Portuguese?"

"No, I didn't know any of this. Why wouldn't she tell me? She just let me think the worst of you, even though she knew how upset I was."

"I think she was just trying to protect you. I honestly can't blame her after how I acted."

"So you really didn't know about *Avô*?"

"I promise. I would have come, Alessandra. If I had known, I would have rushed straight here so I could be with you. It kills me that I missed being there for you, to hold you while you cried and to help you get through that. I know what Carlos meant to you. He meant a lot to me too." Trey wrapped his arm around her back and pressed his lips to her forehead. "I'm so sorry that I let us drift so far apart from each other." He leaned back to look at her.

Alessandra closed her eyes for a second, knowing she had a lot to account for as well. "I'm sorry too, Trey. You weren't alone in letting us drift apart. I could have gone with you, at least to meet up with you on this last trip for a few days. I should have but . . . I don't know. Recently I realized that I didn't trust you enough to leave what was familiar for the sake of our marriage. It was too scary for me." Pointing around her, she said, "*This* I know. *This* place, this life. But life with you, I don't know what will happen next, and I couldn't handle it. The life of a bull rider's wife is not at all predictable."

"No, it certainly isn't. Good thing you're not a bull rider's wife anymore."

"I'm not?"

Trey shook his head. "Nope. You're a retired bull rider's wife. Do you think you could handle that?"

"I think so." She nodded quickly. "Yes, I think I would love that."

Alessandra could feel herself softening as he held her and his words sunk in. Her anger dissolved, leaving concern for him in its place. She looked up at him. "What happened to you?"

"Oh, turns out bull riding is a little dangerous," Trey answered, with a hint of a playful grin.

Alessandra's mouth curved up in a smile, but she tried to look serious again and shook her head. "That doesn't sound right to me. I've been told it's safer than air travel."

"Whoever told you that was an idiot."

Now she let herself laugh a little. "I'd say he was misinformed."

Trey tilted his head and lowered his mouth a bit closer to hers. "That's a very kind take on it. You must really like that guy to be so generous in your description."

Alessandra shrugged. "A little, maybe."

"Well, if he'd known what was good for him, he would never have left his wife in Brazil and his son in Colorado to chase some crazy dream. He would have stayed right here, where the perfect life with the perfect girl had been all along."

"Yes, he should have."

"Am I too late?"

"You made it just in time." She reached up on her tiptoes and touched her lips to his, finally letting herself give in to her love for him.

His kiss was exactly how she knew it would be. It was soft and passionate and perfect. Their mouths moved in unison, reigniting everything that was them, together. The longing and love and desire. They stayed like that for a long, sweet moment before Alessandra pulled back.

Her face fell as she remembered they had no home to go to.

"I just realized we're going to have to find somewhere to live. The farm has been sold. The new owners are coming today to take over."

He gave her a broad smile. "I know."

"How do you . . . ?" Her heart pounded in her chest. No, she couldn't hope for that.

"I bought it. I hope you don't mind me making that type of decision without speaking to you first. It was a time-sensitive deal so I had to act quickly, but I promise I won't do anything like that again."

Alessandra threw her arms around his neck, kissing him hard on the mouth. Just like that, in one quick moment, everything in her life had been restored to perfection. She had her husband, her son and now, her home back.

*   *   *

That night, as they stood next to the mattress on the floor that was to be their temporary bed, Alessandra gave Trey a questioning look. She'd just finished putting fresh sheets and pillows on the mattress, with Trey trying to help with one arm. "I have to know. Why the hell didn't you tell my cousins not to let me pack up and move everything out of here? That was a lot of work."

"I'm sorry about that. I didn't know. I asked them to tell the realtor I wanted to buy all the furniture and leave everything as is. I think the message somehow got miscommunicated."

She rolled her eyes. "You can't count on those two morons for anything."

Trey chuckled. "They tried. You have to give them credit for that."

"Well, I guess it lets us make a fresh start. It'll be much easier to paint the entire house without any furniture."

Trey gave her a look of dread. "Those morons," he said, earning a laugh from her.

He pulled her to him and smiled at her. "God, I missed your laugh. And I can't even begin to tell you how much I missed your beautiful face." He kissed her on the lips. "And the rest of your body." Letting his lips glide over her neck, he drank in the scent of her. "And your mind." His hand travelled down her spine to her bottom, which he gave a light squeeze. "Oh yeah, I missed your beautiful mind."

Alessandra burst out laughing for a moment before running her hands down his chest. "I missed you too." She let one finger trail down to his boxer briefs, pulling at the waistband. "Especially certain parts of you."

She tugged them off, leaving him standing naked in front of her. Her fingertips ran along the scar on his side. It was still an angry red. "Are you okay? Is there any part of you I need to be careful with?"

"No. I'm all healed up except for my arm. Well, and there are probably some things I shouldn't do with my jaw for a few more weeks, but as soon as I can, you can bet I'll be testing it out."

"Sure, I'll be very happy to help you test out your jaw," she said, trying not to laugh. "But are you sure you don't need your sling?"

"I'm sure the doctor would approve of me leaving it off for this." He gave her a lingering kiss that he hoped would dissolve any other worried questions on her tongue.

"I'll be gentle," she whispered.

"Thanks. There might be a few things I need help with."

"Like this?" she asked, pulling her nightie over her head.

Trey let out an appreciative sigh. "Yup, just like that."

His eyes gazed at her nude form, his longing for her now an undeniable force as he drank in her curves. He was about to feel those curves pressed up against him, and his cock throbbed with anticipation. Reaching out his hand, he traced his finger carefully over her collarbones, then down her side, seeing her shiver with delight. His lips found hers and he watched as she closed her eyes and listened as she moaned that little moan that said she was all his. He wanted so badly to take her right then, but knowing how long it had been, he needed to make sure she was ready to savour this moment of starting their life over. Her lips parted and he let his tongue search for hers. Soon they were melding together again as though no time had passed, as though neither of them had been hurt. He pressed his body against hers, feeling the silk of her skin and her hands exploring him. They moved together in small, slow steps as though dancing to a song only they could hear.

Trey brushed the hair off her neck, then planted kisses from the nape of her neck to her ear, stopping to nibble on her earlobe. "I hope you're not too tired, because I intend to kiss every sexy inch of your body."

"I'll manage," she said in a sultry tone.

"Mmm, Mrs. Johnson, how is it that just the sound of your voice makes me hard as a rock?"

"Then I better keep talking."

"Please do." He lowered his mouth over her right breast, teasing her firm nipple with his tongue before letting his lips plunge over it. Moving to her left breast, he let his teeth graze over her pink bud, feeling it tighten as he closed his lips over it. Lowering himself onto his knees, he ran his lips down her sides and across her tummy to each of her hips. He would take his time getting to know her again.

Parting her legs with his hand, he angled his face in between her thighs, his fingers gliding along her sex, which was already wet and ready for him. He ran his tongue where his fingers had been, tasting her sweet, ripe essence. Reaching for her hands, he tugged her gently to join him on the floor.

The look she gave him from under her heavy eyelids was pure

seduction. She dropped to her knees in front of him, her mouth finding his in a heartbeat. They gripped at each other's bodies with a greedy lust now. They were together again and this time nothing would tear them apart. The thrill of this truth was unlike any adrenalin rush Trey had ever had. He was back with his wife, touching her, and he didn't ever want to stop. He pulled her on top of him so that she straddled him now as he lay on the floor. Alessandra rocked her hips over his hard length before she took him in her hand and angled her body over his. She lowered herself slowly over him and he felt every beautiful inch of their joining. She was so tight, he wanted to explode right then. And watching her as she rode him in long drags was the sexiest thing he'd ever seen. "You're perfect," he whispered as her mouth hovered over his.

Their tongues found each other again, mirroring what their bodies were doing and drawing them both deeper into a world of their own. He gripped her hip with one hand and moved her over himself quicker now. Harder. The momentum picked up to an unstoppable force. The rhythm of their breath matched, bringing them to that final moment of perfect unison as they both came undone.

They held each other there, kissing and moving together slowly as they recovered. Even though they were fully sated after so many months apart, it would never be enough.

"I love you so much," she said finally, as she rested her head against his chest.

"I love you too. You're mine."

Early the next morning, they were finally ready to sleep, having made love again and again. "Are you sure you want to live in Brazil? Won't you miss your home and your family?"

"That's what airplanes are for. I'll miss them, but that seems like a small sacrifice to be with you. There's nowhere that is more a home to me than where you are. Besides, I fell in love with this place the first time I saw it, and I can't imagine a better corner of the world to raise our children."

"Children?"

"You don't want more kids?" he asked, suddenly looking concerned.

"I do, but maybe let's just give it a while, okay?"

"Whenever you're ready."

EPILOGUE

Bora Bora
Five Years Later

"I can't believe we finally made it." Alessandra smiled over her shoulder at Trey as she let the warm, crystal-clear water lap over her toes.

"Me neither. Sorry it took me so long to give you a proper honeymoon."

"Don't be. You've given me a perfect life. Besides, this was worth the wait."

"I agree," he answered, wrapping his arms around her waist and kissing her neck. "Should we call and check on the kids?"

Alessandra leaned back against him. "Not just yet. Betina and Dustin have it all under control, I'm sure. They'll be fine."

"You sure? Three kids plus the farm for eight days is a lot to handle, and I honestly don't know how much help my brother is going to be to her."

"Are you going to spend the whole time worrying or are you going to give me all that wild honeymoon sex you've been promising me for five years?" She reached up behind her to touch his face with her fingertips.

"What kids?" he murmured in her ear.

Gliding his hands over her body, he pressed himself into her back. Alessandra could feel his erection. "Much better. Shall we go back to our cabin?"

"I say we'd better. If we do what I have in mind right here on the beach, we're going to end up back home a lot sooner than I want."

Alessandra turned to face him, running her hands over his muscular arms and kissing him hard on the mouth. The thrill of his body against hers hadn't lessened with time. Instead it had grown more intense with each passing day. Lingering kisses ignited their passion for each other as they stood in the sand, water rolling gently over their ankles, their bodies pressed together. "That bikini might be the best thing you've ever worn."

"Glad you like it. You don't look so bad yourself."

"Come on, let's go get you out of it," he murmured.

"Okay."

Trey smiled. "I love Bora Bora."

They walked hand in hand through the water, then up the stairs to their cabin. When they reached the door, Trey picked Alessandra up in his arms and carried her through. "Right foot first. I remembered."

"I knew you'd remember how important the little things are."

"Only when it comes to you." He set her on the bed gently. "You know how beautiful you are, right?"

"When you're looking at me, I do."

"Then I'll have to keep my eyes on you forever."

SECRET SCENES GIVEAWAY!

Breaking Hearts

ANNOUNCING THE "I WANT MORE TREY" GIVEAWAY

Need *MORE* Trey? Here's your chance!

I have put together a booklet including two steamy scenes that didn't end up in the novel. What happens when Alessandra finds Trey alone in the barn? What happens after he carries her into their over-the-water bungalow in Bora Bora? Anyone who posts an honest review of the book will get a copy of the booklet—for free, of course! Here's how to get it:

1. Post your review of *Breaking Hearts* on Amazon, Goodreads, Google play, iBooks and/or Kobo.

2. Go to www.mjsummersbooks.wordpress.com/the-books/books/breaking-hearts/ to get your booklet!

Happy reading, everyone!

—MJ

ALSO BY MJ SUMMERS . . .

Break in Two

Book 1 of the Full Hearts Series
Romantic. Witty. Sexy as hell.

A story as satisfying as the perfect man—long and thick, with all the right moves at just the right pace . . .

Thirty-one-year-old Claire Hatley is running from Seattle, having just discovered that her live-in boyfriend has traded her in for a twenty-two-year-old hostess. Devastated and alone, Claire must make a fresh start. She answers an ad to be the chef at a guest ranch just outside Colorado Springs and finds herself face to face with Cole Mitchell, quite possibly the hottest man to ever ride a horse. Common sense tells them to stay away from each other, but their attraction is not to be denied. Cole gives Claire a glimpse of what love should be, but just as she starts to trust him, the past comes back to tear them apart.

Join Claire and Cole as they embark on the stormy love affair of a lifetime.

(Oh, and for those of you with husbands or boyfriends, please tell them MJ says, "You're welcome.")

Don't Let Go

A Full Hearts Series Novella
A sweet and sexy short read

Readers fell in love with Ben and Alicia's picture-perfect marriage in *Break in Two*, but for these two, the road to a happy ending wasn't always smooth.

Alicia Williams has been in love with Ben Mitchell since he picked her up out of the mud in elementary school. But baseball-obsessed Ben has dreams to make it to the majors and see the world, and those dreams don't include the girl next door, no matter how perfect she is. Ben is forced to choose, and he leaves Alicia behind—but dreams can change and regrets can grow. When Ben returns back home to the ranch in Colorado Springs, trying to rediscover the man he was meant to be, will the girl he can't get off his mind still be waiting?

Join Ben and Alicia in *Don't Let Go* as they fall in love and discover that sometimes life's greatest adventure is the one you find at home.

(Best read after *Break in Two* and before *Breaking Love*)

Breaking Love

Book 2 in the Full Hearts Series
Seductive. Heartwarming. Passionate.

Luc Chevalier is a satisfied man—or so he thinks. His businesses are thriving, and he has all the excitement, money and beautiful women any man could want. He dines at the best restaurants and stays at the most luxurious hotels as he makes his way around the globe. So why does he suddenly find himself so restless?

Megan Sullivan is a single mom with a rather ordinary life. She is comfortable with things just the way they are. She has a six-year-old son, Elliott, a cozy house in Boulder, Colorado, and a photography business to put food on the table. Her ex lives hours away in Florida, providing enough space for him to feed his drug addiction without exposing Elliott to his father's illness. Megan is on her own and she intends to keep it that way.

Megan is convinced by her best friend to take a trip to Paris for a few days. Little does she know she is about to be thrust into the arms of Luc Chevalier, the sexiest man to ever set foot on the Eiffel Tower. They agree to one night together and no more. In those few short hours, he manages to draw out the passionate woman that Megan has carefully hidden away for years. Once she has a taste of what she's been missing, she finds it almost impossible to go back to her life as it was.

Will two people who don't believe in happily-ever-after manage to put aside their doubts and find their forever?

Join Luc as he discovers that everything he never wanted is the only thing he will ever need.

Breaking Clear

Book 3 in the Full Hearts Series
Clever. Steamy. Inspiring.

Harper Young is a talented, feisty art director at *Style* magazine. Sitting at her desk one Tuesday morning, she answers a call that will forever change her life. Her father has had an accident and needs Harper to leave Manhattan and come home to Boulder, Colorado, to care for him. Given an ultimatum by her heartless boss, Harper chooses family, leaving her career behind. She drives across the country to find that the only man who has ever made her heart ache with desire will be her new neighbour.

Evan Donovan is a contractor who's been dealt a rough hand when it comes to love. His wife, Lisa, left him just as the recession forced him to shut down his contracting company. Now, after three years of rebuilding, he is finally getting back on his feet again. When Harper drops back into his life, he does his best to keep things on a "just friends" level. Her older brother, Evan's best friend, won't take kindly to Evan dating Harper.

Proving that old flames are easily relit, Harper and Evan quickly find themselves in each other's arms. But will Harper's career call her back to New York when her father has recovered? Will a man whose heart has been snapped in pieces learn to trust again?

Lose yourself in Harper and Evan's romantic journey as they fight for their forever.

About the Author

MJ Summers currently resides in Canada, not far from the Rocky Mountains, with her husband, their three young children and their goofy dog. When she's not writing romance novels, she loves reading (obviously), snuggling up on the couch with her family for movie night (which would not be complete without lots of popcorn and milkshakes), hiking, Zumba, yoga (to make up for the milkshakes), swimming and camping (with lots of gooey s'mores and hard cider). She also loves shutting down restaurants once a month with her girlfriends. Well, not literally shutting them down, like calling the health inspector or something. More like just staying until they turn the lights off.

MJ is a member of the Romance Writers of America, as well as the International Women's Writing Guild.

MJ would love to hear from you! She does her best to respond to all inquiries and emails personally. If you would like her to attend a book club meeting via Skype, please contact her to book a date.

Website: www.mjsummersbooks.com

Email: mjsummersbooks@gmail.com

Facebook: www.facebook.com/MJSummersAuthorPage

Twitter: twitter.com/MJSummersBooks

Google+: plus.google.com/+MJSummers

Goodreads: tinyurl.com/MJSummers-Goodreads